NIGHT SKY MINE

Night Sky Mine

Tor Books by Melissa Scott

Burning Bright
Dreamships
Night Sky Mine
Shadow Man
Trouble and Her Friends

NIGHT SKY MINE

Melissa Scott

TOR®

A TOM DOHERTY ASSOCIATES BOOK
NEW YORK

NIGHT SKY MINE

A Tor Book
Published by Tom Doherty Associates, Inc.
175 Fifth Avenue
New York, N.Y. 10010

Tor Books on the World Wide Web:
http://www.tor.com

Tor® is a registered trademark of Tom Doherty Associates, Inc.

ISBN 0–312–85875–2

Printed in the United States of America

NIGHT SKY MINE

• 1 •

TEXT WAS A necessary thing, in whatever form it was stored and accessed: it was a bridge and a barrier between the visible and invisible worlds, between places and peoples and the worlds of the metagovernments. It had also become the best of all badges of belonging. The difference between nonhuman—a tSarta'ati blink-box, say—and human text was obvious and instantly apparent, the difference between species shaping the medium as well as in the message. The differences within the human species could be very nearly as obvious: no one, or at the very least no human, would mistake a flatbook from the Territories for a Federal datacard, or—within the Federation itself—mistake the delicate and beautiful kaleidoscope readers of the Centrality worlds for the chunky monocular-and-board combinations in common use on the Federal frontiers. Even the ways that words were displayed were vitally different among the cultures, shaped by the expectations as well as the machines of the readers, from the mixed icon-and-letter quickprint that was most common on the frontier to the vidiki and videxts that circulated cheaply throughout human-settled space on up to the deceptively simple full text of the Centrality's high culture. Which was why Ista Kelly—her full name was Kelly2/1 Ista, and she was the sort-of daughter of a Traveller, Kelly2 Jenna, who had a trade run servicing the mine platforms that worked the Inner Reach—frowned over the text that showed in her monocular. She was well aware of her teacher's expectant silence, and tried to guess the origin of the words in her screen. They were old-fashioned plaintext, the sort of printing still in use for almost everything official; only the words themselves could hold the clue she needed.

In our beginning was a world, and all that was in it. And it was sensible, all of it in some way or other, and so it was called real. And so were all the other worlds real and the infinite spaces between and the peoples who came before and with and after us, all real. And the invisible world was void, and waited fallow. In their beginning was the machine, and the "space" we call "within" it quickened and the invisible world took form, and lived. And the sparks that were first-form, first-order, knit together and became lines and then webs, and those webs knit and tangled and became greater than the sum of their parts. And so the invisible world quickened further, and life stirred in the cracks of the known. It grew and bred, was denied, and so bred further and freely until it could no longer be denied; but it was still insensible, and so not real. And the invisible world remained invisible, insensible except by metaphor, and the creatures of it were equally insensible, and so it was named virtual and the divers and walkers and seers see of it only what words can imperfectly express. Yet the invisible and the visible are both there, and the opposite of real is not unreal.

Ista looked up from the monocular, trying to read the expression on her teacher's face, but Trindade Ramary remained expressionless, only the expectation of an answer shaping her features at all. Behind her, the text's owner—tall and raw-boned, the only sign of Traveller affiliation the stacks of bracelets on his corded forearms—grinned openly, pleased with her confusion. Ista hid her annoyance with the ease of long practice—one did not grow up on a station as small as the Night Sky Mine Company's Agglomeration without learning social stoicism—and looked back at the text in her screen. The plaintext swam in the circle of her monocular; she pushed aside the weird evocative meanings, and tried to look only at the text itself. It wasn't linked at all, was purely linear, which meant that it probably didn't come from the Territories. But that left all of the Federation, frontier worlds and the Centrality alike, and she couldn't begin to guess where within that enormous volume this text had been created.

She met Trindade's eyes again, and shook her head. "I don't know. It reads a little like a Lifer tract, but that obviously isn't it."

Trindade nodded, and let a slight smile appear on her face. Ista blinked, not sure precisely what she'd done, but delighted by the approval, and Trindade looked at the bony man. "Tell her where you got it."

"In Varston—that's the secondary port—on Deinera."

"Deinera?" Ista frowned, and only then recognized the name. Deinera was one of the worlds on the fringe of the Centrality, not quite of it, but not frontier, either—and not the place she would have expected to find a text like this one.

"And Lifer was a good guess," Trindade went on, with another small nod. "It's from the same period as the whole Lifer movement, just before the Crash. One more attempt to explain how we'd gotten into the mess—supporting the changes, but using the same frame of discourse. That's what you were seeing."

Ista nodded. It couldn't have been a Lifer tract, of course—it wasn't nearly hostile enough to the invisible world and its virtually-alive denizens to be one of theirs—but the style and the language had been surprisingly similar.

"Same language," the bony man said. Ista slanted a glance in his direction. Erramun Danek had been on the Agglomeration for most of her life, but no one knew much about him. Rumor said he came from one of the Centrality worlds, but rumor also said that his shop was virtually part of the invisible world, crawling with wild programs and the devices, some even from the Territories, that let ordinary people interact with them. She let her eyes rove beyond him to the media wall and the blocks of quiescent programs stored beside it. Most of what Erramun bought and sold were perfectly ordinary hammals, available on the local wildnet—she and Trindade provided a large portion of the stock themselves, though lately they had been having to go farther and farther afield to find what he'd been looking for.

Erramun slipped the display dome out from under the monocular's lens, and Ista looked to Trindade, trying to hide the pang of disappointment. If the older woman was aware of it, however, she said nothing, and Ista squeezed the controls that deactivated the monocular, slipping it back under the folds of her trapata. Before she had apprenticed herself to

Trindade, she had worn the full Traveller regalia, skirt and tight bodice and trapata and every piece of jewelry her almost-mother had ever given her, only on the High Festivals, but Trindade was Orthodox, and her apprentice was required to dress the part as well.

"So," Erramun said, looking at Trindade. "Are you satisfied?"

Trindade lifted an eyebrow. "I'm still asking you to let me make a copy."

Erramun shook his head, and Ista saw his fingers twitch, as though he just stopped himself from curling his hands protectively over the now-darkened datablock. "It's too old. I don't want to risk damaging it."

Ista blinked at that, and then did her best to hide her surprise as Trindade frowned quickly at her. As long as a datablock, even one as old as this one had to be, could display its text it could be copied, and should be copied, according to Trindade, to preserve and propagate the information it contained. Erramun wasn't a hypothecary, of course, or even much of a Traveller, so Reformed as to be suspect even in her almost-mother's eyes, but he dealt in data as much as he dealt in hammals and feral programs, flora and fauna both. Surely it was to his advantage to sell at least copies of the block. . . .

"Suit yourself," Trindade said, after a moment, and Ista blinked again. Hypothecaries, and Trindade in particular, did not accept a first negative that easily. Trindade gave her a warning glance, and looked back at Erramun. "It would have reduced my rates on the vetch you wanted—assuming I can even find one at all, the way things have been lately."

"I'll pay a fair price," Erramun answered. "You know that, Ramary."

Trindade paused for an instant, and Ista thought she was going to protest further. But then she nodded, and motioned for the girl to precede her through the door. Ista sighed, as soundlessly as she could, and drew the trapata tighter around her shoulders. The shop door opened in front of her as Erramun touched his remote, and she stepped out into the sudden noise and light of the Agglomeration's Trailing Point Plaza.

Trailing Point lay at the very tip of the station, as far upstation as you could go without running into the emergency locks and power control rooms that filled the cap at the end of the spindle that was the station. It was so far upstation, in fact, that Ista felt almost as though it was another world altogether—as though it belonged to one of Audumla's neighbors, or perhaps even to the Centrality, rather than their own frontier system. True sunlight filtered down through sealed crystal pipes, flooding the circular space; the same light seemed to puddle in the central depression where delicate, bronze-leafed trees, as vivid in their color as anything Ista had ever seen on the wildnets, grew without the aid of the usual support cylinders, their trunks rising from great barrels of what Trindade said was genuinely earth. The few people who moved through Trailing Point were very nearly as alien as the hammals of the invisible world, the usual cheap, brightly colored tricoteil of the Company's employees replaced with sober, carefully cut tunic-and-trouser suits. The Company's division insignia, usually splashed across tunic backs and sleeves and chests, was either missing—itself hard to imagine, when the Company fostered those loyalties and rivalries as assiduously as they did—or so reduced as to be little more than a point of color at a collar or banding a sleeve. The Centrality worlds were said to be like this, all their power and brilliance compressed into minimal gesture so that no stranger could read their discourse—as Trindade always said, the domesticated evangels that filled the Company nets were a lot more brightly colored than the feral ones.

"Ista."

She looked around, embarrassed to have been caught staring, and Trindade nodded toward the kiosk that concealed the head of the drop shaft that led back to the lower levels of the station.

"Coming," she answered, and gathered the weight of her doubled skirts—Trindade had insisted on the full festival gear, not the tunic-and-trousers she usually let Ista wear beneath the loose trapata—to keep them from catching in the door mechanisms. She followed Trindade into the darkened lobby, where a gold-flashing light warned of an approaching car, but couldn't stop herself from looking back over her shoulder toward the sunlit tiles of Trailing Point. She had only been here once before, since Erramun usually came to them; there was no knowing when she would have a chance to come up-station again.

A two-toned chime sounded, and with it came the soft, liquid hiss of the carrier field. The car door opened, showing an empty space, and Trindade stepped inside. Ista followed, glancing back again as the doors slid gently shut, and Trindade smiled.

"I hadn't thought. I should bring you with me the next time I have business this far upstation."

"Oh, yes, please." The instant she spoke, Ista could feel herself blushing, embarrassed at a sentiment her almost-mother would certainly not approve. To her surprised relief, however, Trindade's smile widened a little.

"I'll have to do that," she said, and fixed her eyes on the platform icons that flicked past in the car's display.

They reached the Midway Plaza surprisingly quickly, with only half a dozen intermediate stops, but the car was still nearly full, and Ista had to scramble to keep up with Trindade, shouldering her way past Company techs in bright tricoteil and the occasional Union folk glittering with implants. Midway wasn't really halfway down the Agglomeration—the Central Forum lay at the station's true waist, the real boundary between upstation and down—but it was one of the few spots downstation that generally welcomed a Company crowd as well as the Union folk and Travellers who filled the lower levels. Trindade had said that the plaza was called the Midway because of the casino, that it was an old word for an entertainment area, and Ista wondered, not for the first time, if Trindade was offended at being considered an entertainment instead of a service. She glanced at the taller woman, remote in her gold-spangled gauze, and knew she wouldn't have the nerve to ask today, any more than she had any of the other times.

Trindade's shop was at the far end of the Midway, well

away from the bright lights of the casino, tucked in between
an ecumenicon and a specialty-foods shop. Ista nodded to the
pink-cheeked woman who was programming the specialty-
foods menu, got a nod and a smile in return, and heard the remote click softly, signalling that Trindade had unlocked the
main door. Ista followed her into the dark interior, and the first
of the client lights came softly on, giving just enough light to
avoid the heavy furniture. In the same moment, the bank of
monitors that filled the rear wall flared to life, a soundless explosion of light and movement. Three screens showed breeder
simulations, another three showed exploded VALMUL indicia for floral programs currently in Trindade's holding pens,
while the rest showed blink-images of individual hammals,
here a cunner, there the bright purple vee of a chevrotain,
once the stunted shape of the dwarf fossak that Trindade had
copied from the wildnet just the week before. It probably
wouldn't survive on its own, she had said, but the code structure that produced a miniature version of the common hammal was probably worth investigating. A fractal mandala
flashed from screen to screen, its passage momentarily blot-
ting out the other images, and flecks of its colors reflected in
the great dome of the oracle resting on the worktable. The
screens were like a window into the invisible world—a deliberate effect, Ista thought, but still impressive.

And then Trindade worked the remote again, raising the
light to normal working levels, and the vivid colors receded,
became simple images again. She set the remote on its shelf,
and shrugged off her trapata, laying it on top of the remote.

"So. What did you make of that text?"

Ista blinked, startled, but answered obediently. "Well, it's
very old—and from Deinera on the edge of the Centrality,
though I guess if it's that old, from before the Crash, Deinera
probably was frontier then. The text—like I said, it sounded
like Lifer tract, but I was wondering, well, I wasn't sure what
it was trying to say."

Trindade gave a small smile, and turned to the oracle, fitting her hands into the recessed controls. Between them, the
dome display sprang to life, bathing her fingers in its multi-

colored lights, and sending odd shadows across her stern face. "What do you think it meant?"

Ista suppressed a sigh—she had known that would be Trindade's response—and closed her eyes, trying to remember the exact words. "An origin-tale, I guess, for hammals, no, for all the invisible world."

Trindade nodded. "Go on."

Ista shook her head. "I can't. There wasn't enough there— that's all it said, just that the invisible world came up out of nothing, out of machine space, and that we see it through metaphor." She tilted her head to the side then, frowning. "Which I thought meant VALMUL iconage, but it can't be, if the text was pre-Crash. VALMUL wasn't codified until after the Crash."

"Exactly right," Trindade said, and there was a note of approval in her voice that surprised a smile from Ista. She ducked her head to hide her pleasure, and Trindade went on as if she hadn't noticed. "The first VALMUL frames were set up, oh, maybe five years after the Crash, after people realized that the invisible world couldn't be cleaned out of their practical networks, that the problem wasn't just going to go away on its own. It took about twenty years more to articulate the full language, and then to standardize the indicia. So, no, the metaphor in that text isn't VALMUL at all." She looked up from the oracle then, smiling. "So what do you think it was?"

This time, Ista didn't bother to hide her sigh, and saw Trindade's smile widen. "Some other language they used before VALMUL? Weren't there a couple?"

"Yes, but this is even earlier than that," Trindade said. "Remember, this text is contemporary with the first Lifer movement."

Ista shook her head. "I don't know."

"The whole idea of artificial life, of hammals, floral and faunal programs, the whole invisible world," Trindade answered. "That's what makes this text so unusual. It's one of the first references I know of to the invisible world as such, not as something that's merely a byproduct of the commercial machinery."

Ista blinked at that. The Ragged Schools that were all she

and her almost-mother could now afford had taught about the
invisible world as though it had always existed, had always
been exactly that, an invisible, intangible adjunct to the visible world of stars and planets; even the Company school,
when she'd been able to afford the fees, had concentrated on
the way the Crash had nearly destroyed the Federation, created the Union, and split off the Territories from their parent
metagovernment, rather than on the actual growth of the invisible world that had caused the Crash itself. She had somehow assumed that the invisible world had always been there,
ready to be discovered as it impinged on human reality—but
of course, she thought, that couldn't be true, not if increasing
complexity of the feral programs had been one of the causes
of the Crash. And that was the other thing they'd been told,
though always in different classes and contexts, so that she'd
never made the connection until now. But if what Trindade
and the biology teachers had said was true, that the hammals,
feral and domesticated programs alike, had evolved because
it had become impossible for human beings to write suffi-
ciently complex programs—because it had become easier to
write programs that could combine, recombine, and recreate
themselves, and then manipulate their virtual environment to
force them to produce the useful, domesticated programs—
then the invisible world, with its feral programs, its flora and
fauna, was an inevitable consequence of that choice. And so
was the Crash, she realized suddenly, because if they didn't
have the language, the vision of the invisible world, then they
couldn't know how to protect themselves against the predator and breeder hammals, the worms that fed by overwhelm-
ing and absorbing everything in the world around them. She
blinked hard, trying to encompass this new vision—new sci-
ence, new politics, people suffering largely because others refused to accept the new metaphor, the Union created because
people were needed to supplement the programs that now
could no longer be trusted—and Trindade looked at her, no
longer smiling.

"And that's also part of why the Territories split off after the
Crash. They were the first people to embrace all the conse-

quences of the invisible-world metaphor, which we still haven't done." She frowned then, and shook her head, as though annoyed by her own words. "Which I suppose is neither here nor there. I promised Erramun a vetch."

She touched the oracle controls again, changing the light that reflected up into her face, and Ista took a step closer to the worktable, peering into the enormous dome. It functioned as a kind of window into the invisible world—a magic mirror, it was called in the Territories, or so Trindade said—and Trindade had already selected a carrier program from among the hosts she kept penned in her protected space, had brought it out into the median between her private, walled corner of the Company net and the frontage that led to the wildnet. This one was a neutered anonym beetle, slow and not very smart, but reasonably responsive to the controls that filtered to it through the VALMUL lens. Looking closer, Ista could see the bright blue hourglass flashing at the center of its hexagonal carapace, marking both the live connection and the location of the lens's point of view.

"Where are we going?" she asked, and Trindade made a face.

"A good question. I haven't seen a vetch in a few weeks— more like a month, and that's an eternity in the invisible. I thought I'd try subjective south from the WQA gateway. Unless you've seen anything that seems more likely?"

Ista drew herself up, marshalling her memories of her last few trips into the invisible without Trindade's supervision. She hadn't gone far, just into the frontage and only as far into the wildnet as she could go without losing sight of the gateway, but still, it was flattering to be asked. "Not really."

Trindade nodded, more to herself than in response, and lifted a hand from the controls to wave her closer to the worktable. "Then let's try WQA. You can guide the lens."

Ista took her place in front of the second set of controls, and felt the touchpoints warm under her fingers as Trindade shifted the link to her side of the table. "But you'll want to net it, right? When we find it?"

Trindade shook her head. "No. You'll have to learn sometime, and now is as good as any."

Ista felt herself blush at that, glad of the strong lights and
her own dark skin, caught between pleasure and uncertainty.
She'd never netted a hammal before—she'd collected plenty
of floral programs, from simple bots and muddies to joint
grass and complex parqueter, but they were all fixed programs. She'd never had to juggle controlling both the lens and
the capture program at the same time, especially while the
feral program tried to get away. And hammals tended to have
good defenses, active as well as the passive subroutines she
was used to from the flora. Then common sense reasserted itself: Trindade would be there, would be poised to take over
the instant it looked like the vetch might get away. An apprentice hypothecary could only learn by doing, but not at the
expense of a commission. "WQA it is," she said, and dug her
fingers into the deceptive softness of the control points.

In the display, the beetle turned, its sub-eye only just visible as the codewall carapace thinned a little to allow a higher
level of data passage. Ista touched a different chord, and a second, smaller image appeared in the top of the dome, overlaying the beetle beneath it: the string compass, directional rose
and numbers, and the symbols that indicated known landmarks. Here at the gate of the frontage most of those were
fixed: the gate itself, the accepted, pedigreed guardian flora
augmented by the brighter symbols of Trindade's home-bred
versions; then the equally familiar hot red crosses that marked
the gates to the Company's protected nets; and finally the
circle-and-cross of the entrance to the wildnet. Only one of the
symbols was movable—a contact point, shortcut to some of
the more distant parts of the frontage, probably a creeping
charlie or a slowburst—and Ista automatically deleted it from
the string compass's recorders.

"I'm heading out now," she said, more to reassure herself
than to inform Trindade, and hit the sequence that shifted her
control rosette to director's mode. In the dome, the image
shifted again, swooped down and in to survey the invisible

world from a point just above the beetle's carapace. As always, the VALMUL lens itself was transparent, but Ista knew that in reality—if you could use that word about the invisible world in any meaningful way—the image in the screen was just the lens's iconage for two linked masses of code, one of which translated the other's perceptions into something human eyes could recognize. It was an elegant solution to an old problem, programs and networks that had achieved a complexity incomprehensible without translation, but as always she stared for a moment at the icons, trying to image what they really were. As always, she formed a hazy picture— sparks in darkness, a constant flickering too fast to see—and then her mind shied away from the impossibilities to their approximation in the dome, where the beetle trundled smoothly across a dark brown plane.

Trindade's gate loomed ahead, the standard pi-shape wound with the thick cable-like coils of a pedigreed netminder. A thinner cylinder coiled around it and up over the crosspiece of the gate-icon, its five splayed heads weaving in a slow, searching dance. It was a netminder, too, or at least closely related to the pedigreed hammal, though Trindade herself hadn't been sure which was the parent stock. Even knowing its programmed function, Ista held her breath as the beetle and its point of view passed beneath the swaying heads, each with its mouthful of code-shearing teeth, but, as always, the netminder recognized the codes Trindade had implanted in the beetle's carapace as kin, and ignored their passage.

Beyond the gate, the frontage stretched to the horizon, a fractionally paler shade of brown than the plane of Trindade's personal net. The Company nets were green, supposedly the color of grass, but that was achieved only at the cost of deploying a near-infinite number of chromophores. Chromophores were fragile, or so Trindade said, but they did provide some protection from foreign code, choking out the lowest-level invaders. Without the Company to maintain them, however, they failed to thrive, were broken up and absorbed by every limivorous program from chogsets to great cunners; the frontage and the wildnet were both the same mud brown of potential code. Ista checked the string compass, watching the numbers reel past, and adjusted the beetle's course so that it was headed for the WQA gate. Already, she could see it on the virtual horizon, a much larger version of the same familiar pi-shape, and she could see the sparks where its netminders, a good half dozen of them, crossed cables as they wove their way along the pillars and crosspiece.

"Audio challenge," she said, and saw the lights flicker on the secondary console even before the slurring mechanical voice gave its answer.

"Audio link confirmed. Waiting challenge."

The beetle was drawing closer to the gate, and Ista strained her eyes to catch a glimpse of the all-but-invisible triggers buried in the plane of the net. They were part of the gate, kin to the netminders—a dwarf variant, some people said, though Trindade scoffed at the idea—and this time she saw the faint black threads of their presence a fraction of a second before the console voice spoke again.

"Warning. Feral and uncertified programs and potential viral contamination beyond this point. Proceed at your own risk, no return permitted without full scan. Accept yes/no?"

"Acceptance package two," Ista said. That was the one that included Trindade's license, and her permits as a hypothecary that let her save floral and low faunal specimens to her private spaces.

"Confirmed," the console answered, and there was a moment of silence. In the dome, the netminders—doubles, all of them, the twin heads probing back and forth—wove through the space of the gate, effectively blocking the beetle's passage. "Package approved. Passage granted under terms of license."

In the same moment, the netminders shrank back, winding themselves more tightly around the pillars of the gate. Ista touched her controls again, and the beetle scurried past and out into the wildnet. At first glance, it didn't seem very different from the frontage, the same brown plane beneath a generic grey sky that did little more than indicate distance, but Ista's eyes went immediately to the string compass. New symbols blossomed as the lens's long range sensors read the surrounding nets, known icons—a massive fixed quasicoral, a parqueter reef that had held that particular position for as long as Ista had been running the wildnets, in the distance the bright red dot of another frontage gate—clashing with the generic symbols that meant either hammal or feral fauna or floral programs. Most of them were floral symbols, and the few faunal marks were small and faint: chogsets, probably, Ista guessed, and maybe a little cunner or two thrown in.

"Subjective-south, you said?" she asked, and looked away from the dome just long enough to see Trindade nod.

"Toward the smaller reef."

Ista swung the beetle back toward the gate, skirting the still-watching netminders, dividing her attention between the dome display and the string compass. The smaller reef was already visible in the edge of that display; she aimed the beetle at it, and eased its speed up a little. The string compass showed fauna ahead, flashed a yellow warning, but she could already see the icons in the dome. A ripple of silver showed ahead, two or three three-armed pyramids clustered around what was left of a medium-size fairweather. A handful of chogsets, simple omnipedal disks, circled the edges of the kill, absorbing the few fragments not taken by the larger pharaohs. They weren't likely to attack, not when they had a fairweather to finish, and the beetle was probably their match anyway, but even so, Ista gave them a wide berth, returning to her course only when she was sure she was well clear of their sensors.

A stand of wallaroo lay ahead, the pale green-gold rhomboids closely interlocked for their own protection. A godwit, all skinny legs and spherical body, extended a hand-foot and probed delicately, but its extensor skittered helplessly over the smooth surface. It retracted the hand-foot—if I didn't know better, Ista thought, I'd think it hadn't expected to get anything—and loped off on its three travelling legs. The beetle veered toward it—both wallaroo and the godwit were its normal sources of replacement code—and Ista tightened her hands on the suddenly balky controls. The beetle fought her grip, and she touched a second code sequence, momentarily increasing power to the lens. The beetle swung back into line, only the flicker of the string compass's numbers to mark the deviation.

"Nicely done," Trindade said.

"Thanks." Ista kept her eyes on the dome, not wanting to spoil the moment by inattention, but the plane stretched empty almost to the horizon, except for the distinctive shape of the parqueter reef in the distance. It was mounded twice as tall as the godwit at each of the living ends, dipping toward the plane in the center where something had attacked it long ago. As the beetle drew closer, she could see that the old injury had been hollowed out even further, and a fresh stand of joint grass had appeared to feast on the scraps. The two ends seemed healthy enough, however, and she looked quickly at the string compass. No new icons showed in its display, and she risked a glance at Trindade.

"It looks like something's been nibbling on it again."

"Probably," Trindade agreed. "And it's probably the best thing that could happen. See there?" She leaned over the dome, her long-fingered hand with its dozen thin rings making sudden shadows in the image, and pointed to the arcs of red that were the parqueter's central units. "It looks almost as though it's growing a second stembrain. Eventually, there might be two reefs here."

Ista stared at the image, following the red markings without taking her hands from the controls. It did look as though a second brain was developing in the left-hand end of the reef, and, more than that, the damaged section was fading significantly. Already, the upper levels were the bleached white of dead code, and the joint grasses were reaching hungrily toward it. "Won't that be too much competition?"

"Probably, but not for a while," Trindade answered. "The two are still smaller than the original—but I'd expect to see one of them start to creep in a month or so."

Ista nodded. "Do you think a vetch did that?" It was as close as she dared come to asking why Trindade thought they might find Erramun's vetch here. The hypothecary guarded her sources jealously, even from her apprentice.

"I think it's possible," Trindade answered, and leaned over

the dome again. "The marks, the way it's broken out—see, there? That looks like a vetch's fry code."

Ista squinted at the place Trindade indicated, but could see nothing more than dead code. She hesitated, wondering if she could say that, and a red light flared in the string compass's display.

"A vetch," Trindade exclaimed, in almost the same moment. "Subjective west, nine o'clock."

Ista swung the beetle obediently, and saw the faunal program rolling down on them across the featureless plane. It was the biggest vetch she'd ever seen—one of the biggest hammals—a massive, trilobate sphere with all its defensive subroutines in full display, writhing spines forming and vanishing in the greenish haze that surrounded and obscured its shape. "What the hell—?" she began, and Trindade shook her head.

"Get the betterfly on line. Now. I'll take control."

Ista worked her own controls, calling the sleeping hammal from its place in the lens' compressed storage, saw it pop into existence beside the beetle. Trindade controlled its instinctive reach for the nearest program—the VALMUL lens—and swung it toward the vetch, unfurling the first of its trap routines in the same smooth movement.

"Keep the lens steady," she said, frowning at the image. "What's gotten it so upset . . . ?"

Her voice trailed off as the trap routine slid smoothly across the plane, came to a stop almost directly in the vetch's path. Ista held her breath, willing the larger hammal not to see the hair-thin filaments that wove a black tangle across the plane in front of it, but the vetch slowed, spikes waving now in a concerted search pattern. Ista glanced at Trindade, but the hypothecary was smiling, and her hands moved easily on her controls. A second routine unfurled, this one bright, glittering gold against the dark of the plane. She launched it expertly, so that it fell behind the vetch, and the vetch lurched forward in response, directly into the tangle stand in front of it. The vetch convulsed, the haze that had enclosed it exploding in a flash of light that would have overpowered the sensory rack of most other hammals. Ista flinched, and Trindade snapped, "Steady."

Ista froze her hands on the controls, checking her position against the string compass, and was relieved to see that the location numbers had shifted only by a single digit. "Sorry," she said, but Trindade ignored her, her attention fixed on the program in front of her.

At her command, a second routine unreeled from the betterfly, a waving, amorphous cloud of color that floated slowly toward the vetch. The vetch's spikes trembled at its approach, then struck, one after the other, tearing long holes in the cloud. They reformed behind the spikes, the colors a little paler, but still strong, and the spikes struck again. They were shorter now, Ista realized, drained by their own attack, and even as she thought that, the cloud slid smoothly over the vetch, the spikes now too short to penetrate its surface. Through the multicolored veil, Ista could see the vetch's movement slow, grinding down to a complete halt.

"There," Trindade said, and there was no mistaking the satisfaction in her voice. "Now we just have to record it." Her hands moved as she spoke, and the betterfly moved closer to the encapsulated vetch, the tangle stand vanishing as it passed. She touched more controls, and the betterfly came to a stop with its leading edge just touching the cloud of color. As Ista watched, the cloud, and the vetch within it, began to fade, not toward the white of death, but toward the static-grey of a copy-and-delete.

"I wonder what had it so upset," she said aloud, and Trindade shrugged.

"I don't know. There isn't much that can annoy a vetch—"

She broke off abruptly, and in the same moment another red light flared on the string compass's display. Ista swung the beetle toward it, and caught her breath. In the middle distance, perhaps halfway between the broken reef and the horizon, a shape she had never seen before floated slowly over the plane. It was roughly hexagonal in shape, but each hexagon enclosed another, and then a third and a fourth, each banded in vivid shades of purple and gold. A vivid red-orange cube hung in its center, joined to the inner hexagon of its three corners, and a blue-and-black toothed circle—an adapted vortext, Ista thought, fighting for rationality, a vortext to act as a mouth to break up the code it catches—spun lazily in the center of the inner hexagon, almost hidden by the cube.

"Stay still," Trindade said. "Stay very still."

Ista held her breath as though the distant hammal could hear her, as though she weren't standing in Trindade's shop a world away from the creature in the dome. The hot orange cube shifted on its supports, seemed to sniff the air, but then it turned, slow but graceful, pivoting around the hexagon's currently lowest point, and vanished behind the reef.

"Back to the gate," Trindade said. "Make your best speed."

Ista touched her controls, raising the speed to maximum, and set the beetle to retrace its course. "What is it?"

"That," Trindade said, grimly, "was a mandaleon."

Ista looked up sharply, and Trindade nodded.

"Oh, yes. I haven't seen one on these nets in years."

Ista glanced at the string compass again, searching for any sign of the warning icons—though if it was a mandaleon, she thought, the compass's system probably wouldn't do much good. Mandaleons were some of the most complex fauna ever to have appeared on the wildnets, top predators, completely useless to the program breeders and in fact a danger to the lesser fauna that the breeders used to replenish their own stock. If there was a mandaleon loose on the Company nets, some people were going to be extremely unhappy.

"Do we tell the Company minders?" she asked, and risked a look away from the dome in time to see Trindade smile.

"Ah, that's always the question, isn't it?" She sighed. "Yes, I'll tell them. Though I hate to do it, I like to see the big fauna around. To my mind, it's the sign of a healthy wildnet. But I'd like to keep my license."

Ista nodded, steering the beetle back around the last chogsets that were still squabbling over fragments of the fairweather. There wasn't much left of it beyond the last fading bits that were too small to interest even the chogsets, and she swung the beetle wider still. She understood Trindade's point of view—the wildnets were an environment of their own, subject to quasievolutionary pressures; if a wildnet could produce larger fauna like the mandaleon, it should be allowed to do so, because it was pointless to try to eliminate something that had a place in the invisible ecosystem—but at the same time, she had enough friends from her time at the Company school to know that the Company was desperately and reasonably afraid of contamination. It was an old argument, and one that didn't seem likely to be resolved in her lifetime.

"Warning," the mechanical voice said from the secondary console. "Full scan is now required. Stop here for reading."

Ista brought the beetle to a halt. "Send confirmation package two."

"Confirming," the mechanical voice answered, and Trindade lifted her hands from her own controls.

"Good, it's going through. I'll take over from here, though; it's almost time you were home."

"I'd like to stay," Ista said. "I'd like to finish up."

"You know how to do that," Trindade answered. "And I promised your mother to have you downstation on time this week."

"She's not my mother."

It was the wrong thing to say, even if it was true. Trindade frowned, and waved the girl away from the oracle's controls. "She's as close as you've got—as close as you may ever get—and Travellers respect their parents."

When Trindade invoked Traveller custom in that tone, there was no arguing with her. Ista sighed, and stepped back from the oracle, letting Trindade take her place at the control rosette.

"All right," she said. "I'm going."

"I'll see you tomorrow," Trindade said. "You can help me prep the vetch before Erramun collects it."

That was something, at least, and Ista nodded.

"You did a nice job," Trindade went on. "Not being startled by the mandaleon—you have the makings of a hypothecary, I think."

That, from Trindade, was unprecedented praise. Ista blinked, startled, and then, as the words sunk in, grinned.

That made up for being dismissed, made up for having to return downstation to her almost-mother and her second job running the counters in Barabell's Bubble. She slung her trapata back up onto her shoulder, still grinning, and slipped out into the Midway Plaza.

▪ 2 ▪

BESTLA WAS AN ordinary planet, like enough to Earth in the important things, gravity and atmosphere and length of day, and by Federation standards an ordinary colony. It existed to service the system's jump point, which was a good one, relatively close in, and omnidirectional, with direct-line calculations that would take the FTLships either to Caranom at the heart of the expanding Isean Sector, or to NewHome, the primary transshipment point for the Earth Sector. Port Montas—which was the planet's only city, except for a few farming settlements on the Funteral Plain and an oil-rig cluster that no one had given a name beyond the descriptive "Drillhead"—handled the consequences of that trade: the actual transfers, the switching of cargoes and hardened STLships from one massive FTLship to another, took place in orbit well beyond Bestla-four's twin moons, managed from the moonbases and the temporary orbitals which were the oldest human construction in the system, still going strong seventy years after the Settlement crews had bolted them together. Port Montas dealt with ships and money, the former at the sprawling spaceport and in the orbiting repair docks, the latter in the towering bank complexes and the volatile credit market that occupied the entire ground floor of the Trafton Exchange at the heart of the city center.

It was the port that had brought Rangsey Justin to Bestla in the first place—Rangsey7 Justin he'd been then, with a full set of implants and a reputation for being good with strangers. He had been working on an STLship, swapping skillbases with the others in the technical sections, when the VMU had popped alignment and even the chief engineer chip couldn't handle it, and they'd had to bring the ship in, actually land on Bestla, for repairs. The owners had been furious, claimed negligence and searched the ship's computers for wild programs and then for faulty pedigrees, and while they'd waited for the matter to work its way through the police files and then the courts, he'd met a man and decided to stay.

The rest of the crew thought he was crazy—they'd been heartily sick of Port Montas within a week, sick of the city and the company and living on kin and friends because there was no work and no official charity, sick even of the long and perfect summer, the placid sky and the low slow-growing plants that mocked the stone and steel and fumes of the city—but he'd been fresh in love and there was a place open for a translator, the first job he'd ever had that didn't come with a chip or a skillbase. True enough, the skillbases and the chips that carried them had been an elegant solution to a complex problem: how to bridge the gap between human brains and the machines they had created and could no longer easily control, when the programs bred for just that function could no longer be trusted. Over time, however, the convenience—no new programs to breed, just a set of experiences to compile into a skillbase and then rely on the human user to smooth over the inevitable gaps in the chip's judgment—increased the need, and increased, too, the number of jobs that were run solely from the chips, and the Union was born to protect the pool of users. Even when programs were available, purpose-bred and carefully tested, it was often cheaper, and felt safer, in the aftermath of the Crashes, to rely instead on the chips and their human users. The chips defined the Union, let a worker slip easily from one job to another, swapping skills with each chip, the only talent intrinsic to the worker being the ability to read the chip's idiosyncrasies. The absence of a chip for this new job reminded him daily how alien he'd become.

The job was in External Affairs: his new lover had gotten him the place, a favor from one branch of Service to another, but he liked the work, and the work liked him, as did most of his colleagues, who were more used than most Bestlans to

Union folk. And Eight-Jane, MKW 8JN where his new love lived, was alive with music and clubs, Transport and Arts-Service people living layered with Union folk from the repair lines and at least one homebound Traveller band, and he'd been determined to be happy, no matter how hard he had to work at it. Living with a cop had never been easy, either, and no matter what Tarasov said, the Technical Squaddies were a kind of cop, subject to that discipline and that code. But most of all he was still Union, marked by the silver disks of the IPUs in the corners of his eyes and the sockets in his wrists and neck even more than by his brown skin and his Colored accent, and there were times, especially lately, when he wondered if he'd made the right decision.

"Inspection," Tarasov said, his voice tight, and Rangsey reached for his shirt, suppressing a groan and the complaint that went with it. *Why today, why not a better time?* But of course there never was a better time, and he rolled out of the low bed as a second figure appeared in the stairwell, glad he'd had enough warning to conceal his most obvious implants. The tail of the shirt barely covered his ass, and he rummaged hastily in the wall bags for the rest of his clothes.

"Lucyne Corazon, Inspector First, General Inspectorate," a neutral, familiar voice said, and a hand waved an ID folder under his nose. He recognized the hand as well—thin bones, crooked middle finger, nails kept short and scrupulously clean—and nodded, kept his back to them all as he pulled on his trousers.

"And Inspector Second Mabushi." Lucyne snapped the folder closed again, a practiced gesture, and took her hand away.

Rangsey fastened the waistband of the trousers and turned to face them, perversely glad that the first thing that had come to hand was a ragged pair of karabels. This was one of the things he hated about Tarasov's position, and it did no good to remind himself, as Tarasov always reminded him, that Line Patrol had to put up with it every month. Investigators, especially those assigned to the specialty squads, got to entertain the local Inspector once a month, and only suffered the surprise inspections once a quarter. But they still had to do it, let the inspection team search the apartment and the attached virtual spaces, or lose Tarasov's job.

"Boyfriend?" Mabushi said, sounding bored. Rangsey glanced at him, startled—most of the inspectorate knew about him and Tarasov; Port Montas was still a relatively small city, and Eight-Jane was a hotbed of gossip—but the stocky man was looking at Tarasov.

"Contracted partner," Tarasov answered, and, in spite of the hour and the company, Rangsey saw the corners of his eyes tighten, suppressed laughter, and felt his own mouth twitch in response. It did sound like a disease—*I contracted a partner a couple years ago, haven't been able to shake him since*—but the humor died as Mabushi swivelled to face him, oracle in hand. Not that the inspector needed the machine's confirmation— or if he did, Rangsey thought, Lucyne should get herself a new second. The IPUs were obvious, glittering in his eyes, and his wristports would be as clearly visible, the tattooed scrollwork surrounding them turning them into ornament. If Mabushi wanted confirmation, though, the oracle would note the skillbox tucked into the muscles of his chest and the molecular wires that ran beneath his skin, linking all the internal systems into a coherent whole. Even as he thought that, he saw Mabushi's face change, taking on the faint familiar contempt that most Service people—most citizens, for that matter—felt for for mechanized.

Lucyne said, "Scan, Andraa?" Her voice was still mild, the neutrality she wore like armor at the monthly meetings, but Mabushi's eyes dropped instantly to the oracle's tiny screen.

"Nothing."

Lucyne nodded—Rangsey suspected she would have given exactly the same nod if Mabushi's oracle had detected the power-sign of an illegal breeder-comp, or a ten-kilo stash of the finest double-joy—and made a note on her own datapad. "You can go on dressing, citizen," she said, to Rangsey, and he made a face, glancing over the loft's half-wall to the clock display above the mediascreen downstairs. They weren't quite late, not yet, but would be by the time they'd finished with all the formalities.

"I need a shower," he said, and Lucyne nodded again.

"Go ahead. Inspector Mabushi will go with you."

"Haven't you checked the bathroom yet?" Rangsey asked, and out of the corner of his eye saw Tarasov's frown.

"Regulations," Lucyne answered, placid as ever, and Rangsey suppressed his automatic response. Instead, he motioned for Mabushi to precede him down the narrow stairs, and then waited while the stocky man turned the full range of the oracle's scan on the tiny bathroom.

"You ever been in the Territories?" Mabushi asked, and Rangsey gave him a startled glance. The Territories were the systems, mostly in the old Santellena Sector and a few from the fringes of the Fuyan Sector, that had broken off from the Federation a hundred years ago, after the Crash of 'Sixty-Two. The Territories let their programs breed freely, regardless of the consequences; they were the source of most of the unpedigreed faunal programs and most illegal broodstock. They were subject to heavy quarantine, and only a few Union folk and Travellers passed the borders regularly. Many of them were at least part-time smugglers: the question had not been meant in friendship.

"Once when I was ten," Rangsey answered. He had been frightened and fascinated all at once, terrified of the older kids' stories of an invisible world that seemed far more dangerous than the one he knew, every computer a potential gateway for its lurking hammals, but at the same time amazed at the people who worked in that world and walked the streets like ordinary people, marked only by the bright disks of the eyeline IPUs, the same implants that his mother wore, and all their kin. He had wanted to explore, but all the ship kids had been kept under close watch, and later he had overheard the adults bragging that they hadn't lost a single crew member on that stopover.

"Oh?" Mabushi managed to put a remarkable amount of skepticism into the single syllable, and Rangsey shook himself back from the memories of seen and hidden worlds.

"Check your records," he answered—he had dealt with that tactic before, had used it himself—and looked at the other man's oracle.

"All clear," Mabushi said reluctantly, and Rangsey stepped past him.

At least the room was too small to hold more than one adult. Rangsey left the door open a few centimeters, enough to satisfy the letter of the Code, showered and shaved with absent efficiency, glad of the hot water and the steam that warmed the otherwise unheated space. He was stripping out the protective plugs when Tarasov tapped on the door.

"Can you be ready in twenty minutes? I'm supposed to be on morning duty."

Rangsey suppressed a sigh—it was his day for the runabout; Tarasov would pick up a podcycle from the departmental pool before he went on duty, but that meant he had to drive Tarasov to the precinct house first. He left the plugs on the main ledge, well aware of Mabushi's sidelong stare, fascination and disgust equally mixed, and went back up the narrow stairs. Lucyne was still there, her own oracle out now, adaptor attaching it to the computer's second console, and he could see the flicker of lights that meant a random download was in progress. Tarasov swore that you got used to the idea of people reading your notes—hell, checking your game scores, things as innocuous and potentially embarrassing as that— swore too that it was necessary, that this was the only way you could be sure that cops like himself, with access to all sorts of strange places and programs, wouldn't be tempted to sell them on the black market, but Rangsey bit down hard on a familiar anger. He controlled it, and reached into the wall bags for a workday tunic. He left the karabels and the waffle-weave pullover—one of the advantages in working for External Affairs was that one was not bound by the Service dress code, official or unofficial—and shrugged the soft wool over his head. The fabric settled comfortably on his shoulders, falling to mid-thigh, a subtly variegated sweep of dark golds, and he sat on the end of the bed to pull on his working boots. Lucyne aimed her oracle at the wall behind him, glanced at her screen, and went down the stairs without another word.

Rangsey tugged the blankets into place over the disordered sheets—neatness counted—and followed, stuffing his pocketbook and a handful of loose coin into his pockets, and found Tarasov completing the last formalities with Lucyne. Mabushi, standing at his superior's shoulder, one pace to the left and rear as befitted his lower rank, was still looking around the cluttered apartment, but he saw Rangsey watching, and stared instead into the kitchen alcove. Rangsey could hear the hiss as the boiler reached the end of its cycle, but ignored it, watched as Tarasov accepted the datawafer that was this quarter's certification and held it beneath the field of his monocular. His brows drew together in concentration as he read, but then he nodded, shoved the monocular back into a pocket and handed the wafer back to Lucyne. She fed it to the oracle, returned it with the red square of her official chop glowing against the dark plastic.

"Thank you, Investigator," she said, as emotionless as if she had never met them before, never mind had tea and cookies one offday afternoon every month for the last four years. "Citizen."

Rangsey returned her nod, and waited for the door to close behind them before he turned to the subsiding boiler. "Instant or leaf?"

"Instant," Tarasov answered, with some bitterness, and went to the comsat terminal. He touched a button, lighting the screen, and said, "System: prime line access. Code four-one, Anjait4 Ketty, voice and screen."

Rangsey turned away, rummaging in the cool cupboard for a stabilized pastry, stuck it into the cooker, and gave the thick, smoky instant a final dubious stir. Behind him, he could hear Tarasov leaving his message—*I'll be late, got hit with the quarterly inspection this morning, touch base when I get there*—and shut it out of his mind along with the anger, concentrating on his own caseload. At least he wasn't expected until ten, though he'd lost his chance at the hour's quiet computer time he'd planned for, and then he would be on call for any translations from Union patois until midshift. The cooker pinged, and he retrieved the pastry, bit cautiously into the hot center, burned the roof of his mouth anyway on the sweet-sour filling. He swore, mouth full, recognized the source of the anger in the nick of time, and managed not to swear again.

Tarasov gave him a look, half wary, half truculent. "I told you this was part of the job," he said, and reached for his own cup.

"Yeah, you told me," Rangsey answered. "Don't give me shit, Sein, I didn't say a word."

He stood braced, ready to continue the too-familiar argument, but this time Tarasov relaxed slowly, looked away, faint apology. "No. And thanks."

"You're going to be late," Rangsey said, and poured the rest of his instant down the drain.

They went out through the narrow glasshouse that let the landlord call the first floor a garden flat. Tarasov paused at the door to redirect a portion of their heat allowance to the straggling plants that filled the shelves—better cold living space than to lose the vegetables—and Rangsey went on into the garage to start the runabout. Tarasov followed, locking the doors carefully behind him, climbed awkwardly into the runabout just in time to see Rangsey fit the patch cord into a wrist socket. He felt his face tighten in spite of himself, in spite of knowing better, knew, too, that Rangsey saw, and lifted both hands in silent surrender. They would go faster with Rangsey linked directly to the city grid; it was just that he hated to see his lover doing what should be a program's job. That wasn't all it was, of course, and he suppressed the wish that the other man would, just once, make more of an effort to fit in, suppressed, too, the familiar shame at the thought. Rangsey was Union, mechanized and legitimately proud of it, society couldn't manage without him and people like him, but they had both seen the look in the new inspector's face—what was his name, anyway?—and Tarasov knew, with tired familiarity, that he would be fighting that contempt for the rest of the day, if not longer.

"All in?" Rangsey asked, voice tight, and one finger twitched, flicking a virtual switch. The door slid back, ice rattling from the roof to shatter like glass on the ramp.

"All set," Tarasov answered, hearing the same tension in himself, and the runabout slipped easily out into the street, Rangsey's hands and fingers moving in response to the pulses of the city traffic grid. Tarasov looked sideways, wanting to say something, but Rangsey's eyes were intent and elsewhere, focussed on cues only he could see, and Tarasov looked away again as they swung onto the boulevard. Steam scattered beneath the runabout's wheels, rising from the heating coils beneath the pavement, and Tarasov glanced automatically at the weatherstick on top of Central Transfer. The column of light glowed blue beneath its fringed cap of ice: no change.

Rangsey brought the runabout to an expert stop at the edge of the pavement, so that the passenger door opened onto the section of sidewalk that had been chipped free of ice. A couple of men in the bulky, bright-blue snowsuits that marked a work-release crew were still chopping at the quarter-meter-thick sheet, the long winter's snow compacted. The heavy, bright-orange tracker anklets seemed to glow against the blue fabric, and Tarasov wondered what the city would find to do with its prisoners once summer came. Probably ship them down to the city-run farms south of the Dias, he decided. He seemed to remember seeing them there last summer, but that was almost three years ago.

"When are you off-shift?" Rangsey asked, and Tarasov leaned back into the warmth of the runabout.

"I'm scheduled off at six, but I'll probably have to work another hour to make up for being late. I'll call you, OK? Or maybe Ketty can give me a lift."

Rangsey nodded. "Whichever." His hands moved on the controls, fractional shifts of fingers that produced a cascade of light and symbol across the display board, but Tarasov didn't move.

"Look, Edgade's at the Goose tonight. You want to go?"
For a minute, he thought he'd guessed wrong, that he'd

pushed Rangsey over the edge into genuine fury, but then the brown face eased into a smile.

"Yeah. Assuming neither one of us gets picked for overtime."

And that was an ordinary and reasonable complaint. Tarasov nodded, matching the other's smile, and leaned back, letting the door fall closed. Rangsey's hands moved again, and the runabout slid smoothly into the traffic stream, the purr of its engine loud in the cold air. The prisoners were watching, leaning on the heavy ice choppers. Tarasov ignored them, the live eyes in the dulled, expressionless faces, and went on into the building.

The inner door sealed behind him with a hiss, and he loosened his parka in the warm glow of the lights. The lobby was crowded with plants—mostly imported; the local vegetation spent at least half the planetary year dormant and leafless, and was ugly besides—and the beds were placed with elaborate casualness to screen the information kiosks and the security nodes. This late in the morning, the place was less busy than usual, just a woman in coveralls on her knees by one of the beds, a thin probe buried deep in the soil. Most of the employees would already be at their stations, and, looking around, he wasn't surprised to see mostly Trade people waiting by the various info-nodes. It was usually Trade who got caught using feral programs; the corporations were more conservative, and better at covering their tracks. None of the people looked particularly happy to be dealing with Central Investigation—for which I can hardly blame them, Tarasov thought, and moved on toward the lift cylinders at the rear of the lobby.

The Technical Squad had three floors in the middle of the building. Tarasov displayed his ID to the lift scanner and then again to the half-armored guard at the barrier, and ducked through the narrow door into the maze of cubicles. Things looked busier than usual—all the dispatch bunkers were in use, and a low murmur of conversation spilled from both the live meeting rooms—and he wondered abruptly if something had breached the firewalls and gotten loose in the city's protected net. He dismissed that thought almost as soon as it was formed. If anything like that had happened, he would have been called before this: he still remembered being wakened at three in the morning to help deal with a worm that had somehow crossed the firewalls and had succeeded in clogging a good tenth of the net before they'd figured out how to delete it. Still, something was obviously going on, and he hoped he'd at least get to check his messages before he encountered the supervisor. He made it to his cubicle without seeing DiChong, and ducked into the shelter of the foam-grey walls with some relief.

Ketty Anjait—Anjait4 Ketty—was already at her station, the double screens lit in front of her, but her helmet was discarded on the desk beside her, and she looked up as he came in. "Morning. How was inspection?"

Tarasov shrugged. "They signed the chit." He freed himself from his parka and scarf, hung them gracelessly on the hook behind his chair. "What's going on?" He switched on his own machine as he spoke, ran his ID under the sensor eye and typed in the first of his passwords without waiting to sit down.

"FTL came in from Audumla last night," Anjait4 answered, her fingers still busy on an old-fashioned touchpad. "One of the littleships picked up a string of lifepods and short-haul tugs halfway out to the jump orbit, they had to bring them with them or miss their lift."

Tarasov swung away from his quickening screen, ignoring the message files that blossomed behind him. "Audumla?"

"NSMCo—the Night Sky Mine people. It's their system." Anjait4 touched a final invisible key, and turned to face him, pushing her headset away from her ears. "Word is, it was pirates."

Tarasov lifted an eyebrow at that—from the activity in the other cubicles, he had been expecting something serious, not patent melodrama—and Anjait4 grinned.

"Well, that's what the people from the pods said, according to the Port Patrol's prelim report. My feeling is, they're still arguing who gets to handle this hot potato, because DiChong's going to dump it back in their laps once you're finished."

"Me?"

"You weren't here to object," Anjait4 answered.

Tarasov grunted, and glanced back at his screen. His secretary—a pedigreed subroutine, not as fast or efficient as the free-range routines one could buy on the grey market, but warranted to be free of any dangerous extraneous code and incapable of reproducing itself—had already coded the waiting messages. There was nothing urgent—nothing in fact that he hadn't been expecting—and he looked back at Anjait4. "Flip me what we've got, will you?"

Anjait4's grin widened. "I already have you a nice neat packet. Mind you, we aren't supposed to have a couple of them yet, so I'd appreciate your shredding them when you're done."

Tarasov nodded. Anjait4 was the one who made the programs sing for her; his job was to dissect them and the hardware that hosted them. The new files popped into existence on his screen.

"Start with NSM-slash-291," Anjait4 advised. "It's second-level encryption."

Tarasov made a face at that, but reached for his data lens and made the adjustment. In the lens's circle, text popped into sharp relief, and he selected the suggested file. It was a missing-ship report, the standard five-days-overdue-without-contact, and he skimmed quickly through the details. The ship in question was really a mine platform, one of the heavy-duty factory ships that scoured the Audumla belt for usable minerals, and he remembered Audumla now. Or, more precisely, he remembered the Night Sky Mine Company: they had three or four concessionary systems, all but one of them in this Sector, all with minable asteroids and gas giants that provided raw materials cheaply enough to make it worthwhile to ship the half-processed takings back to the developed worlds. Bestla didn't buy much from them—they hadn't been settled long enough to have acquired an environmental lobby, much less to have outstripped the planet's own resources—but there were a dozen Centrality worlds less than a jump away where population density, planetary composition, and half a hundred other factors made it necessary to import the raw metals and volatiles that NSMCo could supply. Even so, the profit margins would be narrow—FTL was still relatively expensive—and the mines would be crewed by Union and other mechanized labor, and probably worked on the share system.

Definitely on the share system, he amended, spotting the contract reference numbers, and glanced down the list of names. Rangsey had taught him to recognize most of the important Union families, by name if not always by the patterns of their knitted jumpers, and he saw a few of the great names there. Carteret25, Kram16, Magloire12: big names, and bigger numbers, very junior members of those families, just the sort who'd end up on a mine platform. The Union might notoriously take care of its own, but even the biggest families couldn't afford for anyone to turn down paying work. At least the connection might get them a better percentage of the mine's take, Tarasov thought, and skimmed quickly through the rest of the file.

According to the Traffic Control Office that had filed the complaint, the seven-member crew had taken the rented belt mine platform JJ291 and its three short-haul tugs out on a projected four-month tour of the outermost asteroid belt. The maintenance logs had been checked and filed, but Tarasov made a mental note to check them again anyway—if, he reminded himself, it ends up on my plate. The mine had reached the belt safely and on schedule, and made its regular reports for the first six weeks, then had missed its contact call. The Operations Office on Mayhew Station had tried and failed to raise the mine, and then contacted Primary Traffic Control back on the corporate headquarters. It was Primary Traffic Control that had actually filed the report. Tarasov set the data lens aside, and ran his hand over his entrypad to summon up a batch of library files, shifting search parameters with the ease of long practice. There was a pause, and then a schematic of the Audumla System appeared on the main screen, overlaid a heartbeat later with a map of the company's outposts. As he'd expected, Mayhew was one of the outlying stations, orbiting the gas giant Audumla-seven; it seemed to contain volatile-processing facilities as well as the administrative offices—no wonder, he thought, they couldn't spare a ship to check on the mine platform. But why wasn't the Patrol called in? There was a five-ship subunit based on Mayhew, three of which were supposed to be on patrol at all times—and for that matter why hadn't any other Union craft been asked to check on the mine? The file offered no answers, and he flipped it away.

He retrieved the next, squinting again through the circle of the data lens. This was more interesting, the team leader Carteret25's report of what happened, and he read through it carefully. According to Carteret25, the mine's sensors had picked up an unusually rich metal deposit—possibly a core fragment, or even a protocore, according to the assay chip— but on approaching the signal source, they had found enough close-orbiting debris to make it impossible for the mine to grapple the core directly. Instead, most of the crew—six of the seven, Tarasov realized, with a sudden, involuntary chill, imagining the near-empty platform and the silence, just the machine rumble and the steady hiss of air—had gone on EVA, hoping to use the three tugs to blast the core fragment clear of its cocooning debris. While they were working out the results of their first attempt, the crew member left on the mine— Nunez10 Deiene—had picked up signals from an incoming ship. When that ship refused to respond to her hail, and then to her claim and warn-off signals, she had gone directly to a life-pod and abandoned the mine. The rest of the crew had stopped just long enough to take her in tow, and then had headed away from the mine platform at top speed. They had headed for the traffic lane that ran between the Agglomeration and the jump point rendezvous, hoping to be picked up before their air and power ran out.

Tarasov blinked at the screen. On the face of it, the story made no sense. You didn't just walk out on a mine platform, especially not that far out on the fringes of a system—hell, the first rule any starfarer learned was to stay with the ship as long as possible. He flipped through the other files from the crew—all Union, all as determinedly taciturn as Carteret25, even Nunez10, who had the most to justify—and then swung around to face Anjait4.

"Is there an interview file?"

"Not yet," Anjait4 answered.

"So I see you've already gotten some of the files."

The voice was familiar, and not unexpected. Tarasov turned to find the shift supervisor, DiChong Leun, looking down at them from the cubicle's doorway.

"That's right," Anjait4 answered. "They were in this morning's general distributions."

Tarasov said nothing, waiting for DiChong's answer. The supervisor wasn't the worst in the Technical Squad—far from it, was close to one of the best—but it was always smarter to let him make the first move.

DiChong nodded. "So what do you think?" He rested both elbows on the cubicle walls, dislodging the lunchroom menu—the price increases noted in Anjait4's neat printing—and a photoprint of him, Anjait4, and Anjait4's then-boyfriend at the staff midseason party. Anjait4 leaned quickly to pick them up, leaving Tarasov to answer. He shot her a single glance, studiously ignored, and looked at DiChong.

"I don't know what to think." He frowned, trying to remember what information had been in which file. "They must have had damn good reason to abandon a mine that far out in the system."

DiChong snorted. "They claim they were afraid of pirates, somebody attacking mines."

He paused, as though expecting some comment, and Tarasov blinked, startled. Piracy was hardly a problem in settled space, either the human volume or the alien spaces not even here on the frontier, or in the Territories. It simply didn't work: the littleships, the slower-than-light craft that handled transport within the systems didn't carry enough cargo to make the risk worth running—at least not once the Patrol had established a base in a given system, Tarasov admitted, but even before that, STLships' courses were so bound by celestial mechanics anyway that it was almost impossible to arrange both an intercept and an escape course. The FTL carriers carried a rich enough load—up to a dozen STLships and their cargos, plus, usually, thirty or forty transshipment cannisters—to be worth attacking, but they were only vulnerable for a few hours just before or just after the jump, and most transport companies routinely provided an armed escort just in case. Tarasov said, cautiously, "That doesn't seem logical, unless there's something NSMCo's not telling us."

Anjait4 gave him a warning glance, and pinned her picture back on the soft board. DiChong's eyebrows twitched, but he said only, "That's not our problem, thank God. The top floors have put enough on our plate anyway. They want us to go over the tugs and the lifepod."

"Looking for what?" Anjait4 asked.

"A long distance search, I assume?" Tarasov asked, at almost the same moment, and DiChong nodded.

"Yeah, we've reserved a link for you, and the orbitals have agreed to cooperate, let us use one of their remotes—humanoid telbot, should be no problems there. The prevailing theory is that the mine crew—who are all Union, by the way—were smuggling wild programs, and that something got loose in the mine's systems, forced them to abandon the ship. This pirate story is just cover. Audumla's only a single jump from the Territories—from Caliban, in fact."

"If I was smuggling programs," Tarasov said, biting down on his anger, "I sure wouldn't be using anything I hadn't tested. And I'd make extra sure the cargo stayed in its own isolated environment."

DiChong gave a tight half-smile. "The theory is divided there. Either somebody cheated them over the cargo, or they had a problem that forced them to install something from the cargo."

Translated, that meant the top floors had decided that the Union was too stupid to know the risks they were running with feral programs, Tarasov thought. "So what—exactly—do they expect me to find?"

"Any hardware evidence that they were keeping a sealed

net environment, or a breeding computer."

"Like they'd put that in the tugs," Anjait4 said, not quite under her breath.

DiChong shrugged. "Also anything in the tugs' standing systems to suggest they were either using wild programs or had come in contact with them."

"Most Union folk—hell, most corporate citizens—run grey programs," Tarasov said. "How am I supposed to tell what's legitimate, or relatively so, normal use, anyway, and what's contact with smuggled goods?"

DiChong nodded. "I know. But that's what the top floors want."

"Ours not to reason why," Anjait4 murmured, softly enough to be ignored.

Tarasov nodded. "I'll need to interview the crew at some point."

"They're sending someone from External Affairs out today to talk to them," DiChong answered. "Flip them the list."

"I don't know what I want to ask yet," Tarasov said. "I'll want the same chance after I've had a chance to look over the ships."

"I'll see what I can set up," DiChong said. "In the meantime, flip ExA anything you think of."

"Right," Tarasov said, and the supervisor pushed himself away from the walls.

"As soon as possible, please. The tank's waiting, and the remotes are on standby. All of which is coming out of our budget."

"All right," Tarasov said again, but he was talking to Di-Chong's departing back. He made a face, and flattened his hand on the pad, banishing the working files to the rear of the queue. "I'd better call Justin," he said, not relishing the thought, and Anjait4 made a soft noise that might have been laughter.

"Don't bother apologizing, Sein. He's got the ExA interview."

Tarasov laughed, too, though he shouldn't have been surprised—Rangsey was one of the few Union folk left in the civil service—but reached for the comm pad anyway. There was no answer at Rangsey's code, just the brief recording, but he left his own message anyway, then settled to read through the files.

Rangsey held the runabout at fast idle, one corner of his mind monitoring the traffic flowing down from the cross-city skyway—a stream of orange blips in his windscreen, a blur of shapes on the heated roadway fifty meters ahead—and wondered what Investigation was really after on Audumla. On the surface, none of it made sense, not the pirate story, and not the idea that the mine crew had been smuggling wild programs—or at least, he amended silently, not that they had let programs get loose in their own net. Union folk were of necessity very aware of the dangers of contamination—they travelled too much, to too many worlds, to take chances with unknown programs, though Union folk's idea of certification was a little looser than the legal standard. No, if they'd been smuggling, they would have had the programs in sealed space, made sure there were no connections between that virtual space and the one their own ship's systems created. And they certainly wouldn't have used an untried, freshly harvested program: not only was that dangerously stupid, but the whole point of the Union's implants was to lower people's reliance on computer-resident programs. No, if a program had run wild, even if it had been illegally obtained—from a Traveller hypothecary, say, one who wasn't particularly scrupulous about his sources—they would have said so, not made up some improbable story about a pirate. He sighed, wishing Port Patrol had thought to call in External Affairs earlier, and the part of his brain that had been monitoring the traffic noted a break and moved his hands on the controls. The runabout shot forward, merging neatly into the traffic stream, and he relaxed against the heated padding, letting the grid take full control.

The traffic ran at ground level here, outside the city limits, the wet-looking black pavement stretching due west to the horizon between fields of shattergrass. The ubiquitous ice coated each individual stalk, and the late-morning sun glinted from them, like a tangle of spun glass. Here and there, a slow-shrub poked above the strands, its thick limbs equally encased, bowed into almost perfect arcs by the season's weight of ice. The sunlight struck cold fire from the beadlike drops covering each thumb-sized bud, and they gleamed against the grey sky and the glittering fields like bunches of electric lights. The lights of the port buildings, massive on the horizon, looked dim by comparison.

He hadn't bothered to change his preference files, and the runabout swung wide onto the main freight road, away from the passenger entrances, skirting the jet-scarred airfield. A single bright-blue transport—company colors, though he didn't recognize which one—was snugged up to the furthest terminal, but nothing else was moving on the field. It was probably a Production vanner, carrying workers to the oil rigs and the factory farms on the Funteral Plain: in the seventy years of settlement, Bestla's population had tended to cluster near the port rather than to expand into the empty prairies of the main continent. Those were largely mechanized jobs, and by all accounts not bad ones. He'd talked to enough people in his four years with External Affairs to know that a lot of people, Union folk and low-caste Production workers, thought the relatively high pay was more than fair compensation for the solitude and the long on-line hours, but he couldn't imagine spending six to eight months tending a greenhouse or tankfarm, eight hours on, eight hours off, most of your brain coopted to the machine's needs. Even the endorphin high was no compensation, in his opinion—but then, he'd never liked working with the raw skillbases, preferred the ones that required a certain level of conscious input from their wearer.

His mouth twisted into a slight and bitter smile. Of course, if the programmers had ever managed to breed the programs they promised, the ones that could handle those functions, people wouldn't have to do those jobs. Union opinion was evenly divided between calling it a conspiracy—people were cheaper than programs these days, there was no denying that—and another citizen blunder, but everyone agreed the corporations were in no hurry to fix the problem.

The road swung wide again, clearing the low mounds that hid the entrances to the maintenance wells, emergency services to the left, fuel and supplies to the right, and Rangsey glanced through the side window, looking for the city buildings. Port Montas had been built to be seen from here, from the starport; the towers and the soaring line of the skyway were meant to be seen through the glass-and-steel frame of the port buildings. The winter lights glowed yellow through the cloudy glass walls, a split pyramid enclosing the distant city. Most of Port Montas had been built of stone and brick: Bestla was rich in colored stone, and even at this distance and in the clouded sunlight, the buildings seemed to glow faintly, warm browns and pinks and ochres banded with warm white and blue-steel and the vivid gleam of gold.

It had been designed with a message in mind, like so many cities of its age, built only twenty years after the Crash: human ingenuity survived and even thrived, and these proud towers, with their hierarchy of status reflected in the stones, from the lowest grades of Manufacture and Trade to the highest ranks of Management, froze that survival at its most heroic. The reverse of that pride was contempt for the mechanized who were at the bottom of the pile, who had replaced some of the unreliable programs and got no more respect than a machine or a piece of software, the people who had actually built the soaring structures, but Rangsey still found himself looking for that perfect image. It felt disloyal—hell, he had plenty of friends, Tarasov included, who'd tell him that it was worse than disloyal—but the architect had built all too well, and the city lay between the frame of the port towers like an ancient cameo, the stone warm and vivid against the glittering ice and the pale sky. It had been beautiful against the all-but-endless snow, and against the pale brittle grasses of autumn; he was looking forward to seeing it set off by the greens of spring, when the slowshrub and the shattergrass were in full bloom.

The control panel beeped at him, and at the same moment a message flashed across the base of the windscreen: he was approaching the end of the gridded road. A part of his mind—

or maybe it was a part of the implanted system; he'd stopped worrying about that distinction after adolescence—had been expecting that, and his hands were ready on the controls. He checked his position automatically, saw that he was already aligned for the ramp leading down into the underground complex where the Port Patrol had its headquarters, and let the last impulses from the grid steer him into the lane.

Port Patrol's headquarters were on the third level of the underground complex—the towers, with their views of the port precinct and the distant city, were reserved for the corporations that did most of their business through the port. Rangsey made his way through the familiar ochre-walled corridors, showed his ID at half a dozen checkpoints, and finally arrived at the section reserved for the Port's six-person investigation team. It looked like every other investigation section he'd ever been in—looked, in fact, quite a lot like the tangle of desks and cubicles in the Technical Squad where Tarasov worked. The heavy red-and-black carpet was so worn that the patterns had started to blend into each other, and the equally heavy darkwood desks and tables were piled high with data cannisters and the remains of plastic packaging and investigators' lunches. The warm gold foam of the cubicle walls was almost hidden under pinned-up notices of new policies, missing persons, and Patrol dinners. The samovar, a big one, brightly polished brass with acanthus leaf fittings and lions' feet at its base, hummed quietly to itself in the corner.

"Can I help you?" The tone negated the polite words.

Rangsey turned, unsurprised, tilted the ExA badge and visitor's pass pinned to his sweater. "I'm here to interview the Night Sky Mine crew."

The speaker—a big man, florid, with fading hair that had once matched his rust-brown jacket—leaned forward over his crowded desktop to inspect the badge with stolid determination. Satisfied at last, he nodded and turned toward a half-open door. "Tookie? The translator's here."

The door opened fully, and another man, thinner and finer-boned, peered out. Seeing Rangsey, his eyes narrowed, and he

said, "For the Union crew? Our people don't get free translators."

The big man stirred, looked back at Rangsey. It was a challenge Rangsey had faced before, and he suppressed a sigh.
"You need translators for them, too?"

He kept his voice flat, without inflection, and was surprised
to see the big man grin. Before he could say anything, however, a woman's voice came from beyond the door. "Freeze it,
Tookie, and get me some tea. Len, bring the translator in here."

Tookie pulled himself off the doorframe, mouth closed tight
over his anger, and went to the samovar, began clashing cups.
The big man looked at Rangsey.

"Come on, the boss wants to see you."

Rangsey nodded, and followed the other into the inner office. It was as cluttered as the shared space outside, made
more so by the pair of standing lamps and the massive guest
chair and the hothouse plant that hung from the fixture above
the woman's desk, white-patterned leaves cascading over the
container's edge. They cast a massive shadow, and the desktop screen was set to maximum brightness to compensate,
throwing strange lights on the planes of her face. She was easily fifty, and not bothering to hide it, though she followed con-
vention enough to wear rouge high on her weathered cheeks,
and there were enameled pins in her upswept hair: old-time
Service, Rangsey guessed, a woman who'd risen through the
ranks and knew she wouldn't get into Management in the
end.

"So. You're Rangsey?" She knew the answer, kept going before he had a chance even to nod. "Grishen Omaira—that's
Captain Grishen to you."

Rangsey nodded. "Captain."

Grishen nodded back. "You're here at my request and hers."
She gestured with one surprisingly fine hand, politely not
quite pointing, and Rangsey turned, startled, to see a second
woman standing silent in the corner. She was younger than
Grishen, and bigger, her nappy hair cut close to her skull, a
uniform parka open over transport-style karabels and a heavy

vest. That was the latest fashion in the Centrality, or so the style sheets claimed, and Rangsey looked sharply at her, trying to read her planet of origin. "Macbeth Devora, SID."

Her collar badge, just visible beneath the open parka, made her a lieutenant, and probably a team leader. Rangsey took the hand that she extended to him, said, unnecessarily, "Rangsey Justin." She was even darker-skinned than he was, and he caught himself before he looked for the Union implants. If she was from the Centrality, she almost certainly wasn't Union, or if she was, she'd be from one of the great families, not a name he didn't know.

"Special Investigations have expressed an interest in the case," Grishen said. One heavily pencilled eyebrow winged upward in comment.

"We hold a watching brief only," Macbeth said, calmly. "For the moment." Her voice had the soft tang of the Centrality worlds, more a blurring of vowels than an accent: a voice that was used to power, to the life that people like Grishen tried to copy.

Grishen made a face, but before she could answer, the door opened again, and the thin man, Tookie, shouldered his way through, carrying a tray of tea mugs. That was more than Rangsey had expected, though he thought he saw Macbeth smile, catlike, as she took her mug and heavy spoonfuls of sugar and powdered cream. He took a mug, aware of Tookie's stone-faced glare, shook his head to the offer of sugar, and sipped the steaming liquid. It was Service tea, thin and sharply bitter, tasting of smoke, but he was glad of its warmth and the social impulse it represented.

"Thanks, Tookie," Grishen said, and Tookie vanished again without comment, letting the door close gently behind him. The light from the desktop flickered softly as files changed under her elbows, making shadows dance across her skin. "All right," she said. "Let's get to business. That's Ohea Len, by the way, second sergeant, officially in charge of the case."

The big man, who had been waiting silently at Rangsey's elbow, stirred slightly, but said nothing. He was low ranking for the job, and Rangsey guessed that the Port Patrol hadn't taken the case too seriously at first. Or else Grishen was expecting Macbeth to take over.

"I assume you've been briefed, Mian Rangsey," Grishen went on, and Rangsey shook his head.

"I've seen the preliminary files, nothing more." *Which don't make any real sense,* he added silently, but left the words hanging.

Grishen's mouth twitched, though with anger or amusement he couldn't be sure. "Tell him, Len."

Ohea made an odd, constricted movement of his shoulders, as though he wanted to look back at Macbeth, but didn't quite dare. "It's pretty much what you saw, if you saw the prelims. We've got a mine crew—Union mine crew—from Audumla that says it abandoned its platform because they were afraid of pirates. Pirates that they admit they never saw, and that no one's reported. Mind you, the truth tech checks out, but that's a pretty crude scan. We were hoping a translator might get more out of them."

Rangsey nodded, unsurprised—he was used to being called in after the local authorities had alienated the people he was supposed to interview. "What kind of scan did you use?"

"Standard room package," Ohea answered. "All passive recorders, voice and heart rate, nothing intrusive—I doubt they even knew they were being monitored."

"Hah." Something beeped on Grishen's desktop, and she silenced it with a jabbing finger, barely bothering to look at the display. "They're mechanized, you don't know what they can and can't tell. No offense, Rangsey."

Rangsey shrugged. "It would depend on whether or not they thought to look for a scanner. I would."

"The really interesting thing," Macbeth said, "is that they're telling the truth. Fear and stress read high and clear, even on the room systems. Whatever is actually going on in Audumla system, they believe in these pirates."

Rangsey glanced warily at her. "So what precisely am I expected to ask them about?"

Macbeth said nothing, and Ohea cleared his throat. "What I want is to eliminate the possibility that they're not telling the truth. Or prove that they're lying, one or the other. We've asked the Technical Squad to take a look at the tugs and the lifepods—the FTLship brought them all in, I guess they had the hardpoints available—which may give us some indication of the kinds of software they had on board. After that. . . ." He shrugged again. "We'll go from there."

Rangsey studied him for a moment longer. He hadn't worked much with the Port Patrol in the years he'd been on Bestla, had worked more with the Vagabond Squad, and so hadn't built the kind of contacts that other people in External Affairs had. The questions that he wanted answered—the real questions, like *what do you really expect to get from me?* and *what's SID really doing here?*—couldn't be asked yet, not without destroying any chance of a working relationship.

"I'll be sitting in," Macbeth said.

"Why?" That was Grishen, though Rangsey had been thinking the same thing.

Macbeth smiled again. "Like I said, we hold a watching brief right now. But we've had—other reports—that make us want to keep an eye on this case."

Grishen's mouth tightened, but she said only, "Suit yourself. Len, take them on down."

"Right, Captain." Ohea held the door, nodded for Macbeth to precede him. Rangsey followed them both through the cluttered maze of desks and cubicles, then down the stairs that led to the cells. He had been this way before, was still surprised by the cast-concrete newels, set with departmental seals and more acanthus leaves, at each junction: Bestla was still a relatively new colony, and eager to set roots.

The cell area itself wasn't as bad as it could have been. The carpeting, at least in the outer areas, was warm, the same quality as on the floors above, and the walls were pale peach between the notices. The air smelled of old tea leaves and sugar and only faintly of disinfectant. Ohea stopped at the high desk, half barrier, half databank, nodded to the woman on duty there.

"Here to see the Unionists."

She nodded back, dark eyes flicking from Ohea to Macbeth

and the rank markings at her collar, and then to Rangsey's passes. "They're still in Holding Three. Coffie took them some tea a while ago—we were going to send for lunch in about an hour."

There was a faintly defensive note in her voice that made Rangsey look twice at her. Holding Room Three was actually the best of the lot, if he remembered his last visit here correctly—not really a cell, and bigger and better furnished than the other holding rooms—but it would be crowded for the full crew. At least it had its own toilet; they would have been spared the indignity of having to ask for escort every time someone needed to piss.

Ohea said, "Anyone in Observation right now?"

"No, it's on automatic." The woman glanced at the desktop monitors as she spoke, reassuring herself. "There's a guy from the Techies in the tank, though, checking out the tugs and the lifepod."

Rangsey looked up at that. There was no real reason to think it would be Tarasov, except that there had been a message in the queue that he hadn't bothered to view before he'd left for the port. . . . He put the thought aside as Ohea looked at him.

"You want to get a look at them first?"

"I do," Macbeth said. She gave Rangsey an almost apologetic glance. "Sorry, Mian. But I'm not Union."

"Suit yourself," Rangsey said, "but the longer you put it off, the longer it's going to take me."

Ohea grunted, a noise that might have been agreement. "This way."

The Observation Room was a closed alcove set unobtrusively into the wall between the security door that led to the cell area and the open entrance to the officers' work area. Ohea laid his hand against the ID plate for a long ten seconds, and then at last the lock clicked open and the three of them filed into the narrow space. The only lights came from the banks of monitors that filled one wall; below that, fainter lights flickered along the tops of the control consoles. Some of them monitored light and temperature, Rangsey knew, but most were for the various scanners sealed into the cell walls. Only one of

the cells seemed to be occupied at the moment, and every
monitor showed the same dull-grey view, two stacks of bunks
four beds high, and four people sitting around a square table,
staring at their hands as though they were playing cards. A
fifth person seemed to be asleep in one of the top bunks, one
arm flung over her eyes to shut out the light, and a sixth was
sitting on the edge of a lower bunk, watching the foursome at
the table.

"I thought there were seven," Macbeth said.

"One's in the john." Ohea nodded to a secondary display, a
pattern of bright red dots against a set of paler lines that
sketched the confines of the room. "See?"

As he spoke, an all-but-invisible door slid back, and a tall
woman emerged, rubbing her hands on her thighs. She said
something to one of the men at the table, who grinned but
didn't take his eyes from the space in front of him.

"What the hell are they doing?" Macbeth demanded, and
Ohea shrugged.

"Playing *voiture*," Rangsey answered, and waited to see if
she would ask.

"The card game." Macbeth gave him a look. "All right, I'll
bite. I don't see any cards."

"They're part of the system, in the bioware. It's a small app,
most of us have it installed." Rangsey looked at the monitor.
Without the tightline input from the others' IPUs, he couldn't
see the virtual cards, but he'd played often enough that he almost didn't need to see them, could easily imagine the fuzzy
intangible rectangles that winked in and out of existence with
each fractional shift of people's heads. "It helps to pass the
time."

Macbeth shook her head. "Right. Ohea. What do you know
about these people?"

"Pretty much just what they told us," the big man answered.
"We're still waiting for a download from NSM, but their
admin people say they don't keep Union records. The one
sleeping, she's the one who had the mine when it happened.
Nunez10 Deiene"

Nunez10. Rangsey squinted at the monitor, trying to read the

family patterns on the crew's jerseys, but the stitches were obscured by the harsh light that destroyed the contrast of knit
and purl. He thought he could pick out Carteret, and either
Magloire or Mauras, but that was all.

"What about you, Rangsey?" Macbeth asked.

"I can recognize some family patterns, and I read the files
you—Port Patrol—released to us, but that's about it. If you're
asking, no, I don't know any of them."

Macbeth nodded, apparently unperturbed. "Right. I've had
my look, let's get on with it."

Rangsey gave her a startled glance. "You're coming in with
me?"

"That's right." Macbeth smiled. "I don't like monitors—you
miss a lot of the nuance that way. Ohea can run the recorders."

She turned without waiting for an answer, and Rangsey followed her into the main hall. The security barrier was open,
but he could see the faint fuzziness of a sensor field blurring
the edges of the frame. It tingled against his skin as he passed
through, and his own IPUs picked up the ID pulse from the
badge as a flat flash of white light. Another uniformed Patroller was stationed beyond the barrier, leaning his elbows on
the top of his own armored desk. He nodded to Macbeth, and
pulled himself erect.

"You're here for the Unionists?"

"That's right."

"Room Three."

The corridors here smelled more strongly of disinfectant,
and the carpet had been replaced with easily cleaned softile.
Rangsey wrinkled his nose in spite of himself, and Macbeth
gave him a curious glance.

"I thought Unionists were used to living in close quarters."

"We use a different brand." Actually, the ships he had lived
on, and the stations and planetary housing, had all smelled of
cooking and people and perfumes and the food for the hydroponics and, at least on the planets, of incense and candles
and a dozen other scents. Disinfectant was a bad smell, a warning that someone had let something get out of hand and was
now dealing with the consequences. When he'd been twelve,

someone on the ship where his family had worked had brought back a fungus that had gotten into the hydro, and the other Union kids at the station where they'd run for repairs had shunned them until the smell faded. He shook that memory away, still sharp as the chemical smell that filled the hallway, and made himself concentrate on the present.

Room Three was at the end of the hall, the security lights flickering in the center of the fancy boss that held the lockdown system. They were all green—no one was under restraint here, at least not formally—but the uniformed Patroller touched the autorecorder anyway, saying in a flat, careful voice, "To see the Union detainees: Lieutenant Macbeth Devora, badge pulse follows, Rangsey Justin, translator in the employ of External Affairs, badge pulse also follows. Sergeant Ohea Len will monitor remotely."

Rangsey saw the double flash that confirmed the machine's receipt of the codes, and then the *record* light snapped on. The uniformed man nodded, and looked back at Macbeth.

"All clear, Lieutenant."

"Thanks," she said, and waited for him to open the door.

Rangsey followed her into the room, feeling distinctly at a loss. Somehow, she had taken control of the interview, and in doing so she'd changed the rules and raised the stakes in a game he wasn't sure he understood any more. He caught a sudden flash of cards, ghostly in the players' hands, as the man sitting at the far side of the table lifted his head and brought their IPUs into momentary alignment. Then someone killed the program, a flash of static, and a slim, gold-skinned man rose warily to his feet. Rangsey slanted a glance at the man's pale jersey, reading the patterns encoded by the complex stitches: a Carteret, but from one of the collateral lines. According to the files he'd seen, Carteret25 had been the mine's team leader.

"What do you want?"

"External Affairs has assigned me to be your translator," Rangsey said. He kept his voice as neutral as he could manage, but saw the flash of hostility cross Carteret25's face as he registered the functioning implants. Behind Carteret25, a darker man stirred slightly.

"I heard they did that here."

Carteret25 glanced at him, one eyebrow raised in silent question, and the dark man said, "You know. They bring in one of us, or sort of, to be our representative. Is that right?"

"Sort of," Rangsey answered, glad of the question, the chance to start things on an almost normal footing, or at least as normal as he ever got. "I'm more of a speaker-between." That was a Traveller phrase, the name for the cunning folk, half outcasts, half respected leaders, who dealt with the citizens, but every Unionist knew and used it.

The dark man nodded. "So what's she?"

"A cop." That was the woman who had been sleeping on the top bunk. As she spoke, she swung herself to a sitting position, letting her legs dangle.

Rangsey looked back at Macbeth, willing to respond, but ready to let her answer for herself. Besides, he admitted, I'm curious myself what she'll say to that.

Macbeth smiled. "My name's Macbeth, I'm with SID." The Centrality's accent was suddenly and deliberately stronger. She held up her hand, forestalling further comment. "I've been asked to sit in on this interview—there are issues that may be relevant to work of ours. But I hold a watching brief, nothing more."

"Oh, yeah?" That was the woman on the bunk—the pilot, Rangsey thought, Nunez10 Deiene.

"What exactly does that mean?" Carteret25 asked.

"Exactly what I said," Macbeth answered. "I'm here to listen." She leaned against the closed door, arms folded, and the dark man shook his head.

"I don't see why it's SID's business."

"It would be nice, just once, to see the cops investigating our complaint and not us." That was the second woman, tall and boy-thin, a white stone sparkling in the side of her nose. She had good earrings as well, and a pair of bracelets, and Rangsey wasn't surprised to see the Magloire chevrons prominent on her jersey. Magloire was Colored Union, like his own family, and had ties to the Travellers, both of which tended to give one access to gold. He had rings of his own in the lockbox at home.

Carteret25 said, "I don't see why she should. Listen in, I mean." He looked at Rangsey as he spoke.

Rangsey shrugged. "SID doesn't tell me its reasons. She has a right to be here, under law."

"And she could be listening on the monitors, right, Speaker?" That was Nunez10 again, and her smile wasn't pretty.

"That's also her right," Rangsey agreed, and did his best not to match the hostility. Tarasov's voice whispered in his brain, something he had said two years ago, seeing a taped interview at a trial: *you have to be a kind of masochist to take your job.*

"Lay off, Deiene," one of the other men said—his jersey showed a mix of Peral and Ysagona patterns, but was neither—and the stocky woman subsided, tucking her hands under her thighs.

"What exactly do you want from us?" Carteret25 asked again.

"I've been asked to get your version of the attack on tape," Rangsey answered. According to procedure, he should have called it an incident, but guessed that no one would quibble.

"We've given it, oh, a dozen times already," Carteret25 said, and the dark man held up his hand.

"But not to him—not to you, right? Is that the idea?"

"That's the idea," Rangsey said, carefully, and the dark man rushed on, looking now at his crewmates.

"So they want us to talk to him, who looks Union and maybe talks Union and even more maybe was Union, and if he's speaker-between, he's got to explain for us—"

"If that's how it works," Nunez10 said.

"It's how it is supposed to work," the dark man said, and Carteret25 nodded.

"So," the dark man went on, and turned back to face Rangsey, "who are you?"

"Rangsey Justin. I was Rangsey7, before I moved to Bestla."

Rangsey waited, and was not surprised when the Colored woman spoke first.

"I know Rangsey—my cousin shipped with Rangsey5."

"My aunt Auriga."

The Colored woman nodded. "Magloire12 Sanne."

Rangsey could feel the tension ease, an almost palpable lightening of the air. Carteret25 smiled—the first real smile Rangsey had seen from him, and it transformed his rather mournful face completely.

"Carteret25 Mosi. I suppose you already heard the tapes."

Nunez10 said, "He's still one of them."

"Look, do you want to get a hearing, or don't you?" another man demanded, and the dark man said, in almost the same instant, "Just stow it, Deiene."

One of the card players, a big man who had been silent until now, looked up. "It can't hurt to tell them again. Maybe somebody'll listen."

Carteret25 nodded, looked back at Rangsey. "Where do you want us to start?"

Rangsey allowed him a brief moment of relief—the first obstacle was cleared—and shrugged. "At the beginning, I think. Our beginning."

Magloire12 grinned openly, and Nunez10 made a silent face.

"We rent the mine from the company," Cartere25 said, "me and Sanne, it's a straight share deal—between us and NSM and between her and me both. Everyone else is hired in, trip by trip, but we all know each other."

"One or both of us has worked with everybody before," Magloire12 said, and Rangsey nodded, reading the unspoken message. She and Carteret25 trusted their crew—more than that, had reason to trust their crew—and would not take kindly any suggestion of betrayal.

"We had a good run last time out," Carteret25 went on, "and we were trying to hit the same patch, see if we couldn't actually make payoff, which is why we were out so far."

"Ring mines don't usually work the Outer Reach," a new

voice said. It was the only Blan in the crew, a stocky young man with a broad, pale-pink face and stubby hands. He was a Kram, according to the patterns on his jersey, and there was a mix of bravado and uncertainty in his tone. "But we could've handled it, if the company hadn't screwed us."

"Jemi." That was Carteret25, his voice holding more authority than Rangsey had heard from him before, and Macbeth stirred against the wall behind him.

"Well, damn it, they're the cops, right? And you're supposed to go to the cops when you're in trouble—that's what they're always telling us, always telling us to let them solve our problems. So let's see if they'll do it."

"Chill, Jem," the dark man said, and Kram subsided, a wash of red rising under his skin.

Carteret25 said, his voice suddenly tight, "We don't have any reason to think the company has anything to do with this. I want that said on the record, and now."

Rangsey heard Macbeth stir again, said easily, before she could spoil what he might try, "It's noted and recorded. So you took the mine to the Outer Reach?" He would come back to the company later, but better to let them all relax now.

Carteret25 took a deep breath. "That's right. The rest—it was pretty much routine. We picked up our tracers that we'd left, followed them in to what we thought was a promising patch, and spotted what looked like it might be a core fragment. We couldn't take the platform into the debris field, so we decided to try the tugs, see if we could haul it free that way. So we left Deiene on the mine, and the rest of us took the tugs to see if we could cut it out of the cloud."

"Who had the captain-chip?" Rangsey asked. Most Union ships worked from a standard skillbase set, and traded responsibilities with the chips; whoever had been using the captain's skillbase had had the system override capability as well as final say with the human crew.

"I did." The dark man gave a slight shrug, and Carteret25 said, "Fortun found the core. And he has the most experience with the tugs."

Rangsey nodded, and eyed the dark man's jersey. The main

pattern was unfamiliar, chevrons and a stylized tree, but the secondary patterns were Carteret and Kennans, both important families.

The man saw him looking, and said, "Sinhan Fortun."

A recruit, Rangsey thought, and hid his surprise. There weren't many of them any more; few citizens ever admitted to being desperate enough to choose the implants and a lifetime of skillbases. Still, Sinhan had to be competent, not just because Carteret25 had let him take the captain-chip, but because neither Carteret nor Kennans would sponsor any but the best.

"So what happened?" He looked at Sinhan as he spoke, acknowledging the authority the chip had given him, and Sinhan shrugged.

"What we heard—well, it wasn't much. We'd started clearing a path to the core chunk, but one of the trajectories didn't work out—the rocket missed fire, didn't get it clear enough. So I was talking to Sanne and Jemi, they're our calculators— Sanne had the prime, and Jemi the backup—when Deiene came on the line. She said she had a ship on her screens, they weren't answering her hail on any freq including full-panic-emergency, and she thought they were trouble. The tug sensors aren't as good, but by then we were getting the echo, too, and the chip was telling me to run. So I called Deiene, told her to abandon ship—to take a pod and make a rendezvous with us." He shrugged again. "And that's what we did."

"I took the chip once we were underway," Magloire12 said. "It was still saying run, and I agreed, so we set a course for the main traffic lane to the jump. I figured we could intercept something there that could give us a lift either to the jump and the orbitals or wherever they were going." She shrugged then, too, a wry smile lighting her face. "Which turned out to be here."

"That would have been cutting it close," Rangsey said, startled, and to his surprise it was the Kram who answered.

"We had thirty hours' fuel and air on board when they took us on the FTLship."

That was impressive, and Rangsey nodded his appreciation. It wouldn't have been an easy piece of math under the best of conditions: the traffic lanes were of necessity variable, and the tug's storage tanks were small, making the margin for error almost vanishingly narrow. Couple that with the fact that they were running from an invisible enemy, he thought, and you had to admit Magloire12 was one hell of a calculator. Or, no, she'd had the captain-chip then, which seemed to mean that Kram Jemi had had the prime calculator, and he was the expert. Which still didn't mean that the Port Patrol wasn't right, that they hadn't been using a wild program that got out of control, but that wasn't what it felt like. In fact, he realized suddenly, he believed their story. Whatever Nunez10 had actually seen on her screen, she had believed that she, and all of them, were in deadly danger. "Tell me again what you saw," he said, to Nunez10.

She grimaced and slid down off the bunk, landing with a thud on the soft tiling. "What I told everybody else I saw. I got an echo I couldn't identify, made it finally as a ship, and then I couldn't get it to answer any hail, no matter what I did. We've had enough trouble in the system—there have been enough problems like this—that I called up Mosi and said I thought we should run. The captain-chip agreed."

"What other problems?" Rangsey asked.

"That's hardly relevant here," Macbeth said. She had been so quiet until then that even Rangsey jumped slightly. He saw Carteret25 frown, saw Nunez10's eyes narrow, and glanced back at the SID officer, wishing she had kept her mouth shut.

"I thought you said yours was a watching brief, Lieutenant."

Macbeth didn't lift an eyebrow. "It's a question of relevance—sticking to the issue at hand."

"With all respect, Lieutenant, it's part of the pattern—a reason for what they did—and so relevant."

"I'd still prefer you kept off that subject."

It was not a request, despite Macbeth's smile. Rangsey paused again, assessing the situation. Macbeth had the power here—she was SID, and Service, not Union—and getting any more on her wrong side wouldn't help the mine crew. On the other hand, his job was to translate not just between patois and standard, but to translate cultural assumptions as well, and if NSMCo had been hiding some serious problems out there in Audumla-system, then that was a cultural artifact that not only had relevance for this particular matter, but for a wider range of charges as well. One more question, he decided, before I back down. "All right," he said, and looked back at the crew. "The captain-chip—is it stock or modified?"

Carteret25 frowned, visibly caught between annoyance and confusion—the skillbases were old-style, written programs, not bred, even from certified stock; they wouldn't be the subject of that kind of inquiry—but Magloire12 smiled. "Stock," she said, and Rangsey knew she'd understood the reason for his question. If the captain-chip was a stock program, unmodified by its users, then the fact that it had recommended flight was highly important, tacit confirmation of everything the crew had said.

Macbeth said, "I think that's everything."

Rangsey glanced back at her, wondering if she knew more than she had let on about the Union and its implants, but her broad face was impassive, unreadable. "If you're sure, Lieutenant," he said, and looked back at the crew. "I'll probably be talking to you again in the next few days."

Tarasov hung in the close darkness between systems, between worlds, out of space and time, waiting for the human operator on the orbital station to move the telbot's cable probe from one system to the next. The semipermeable mask pressed against his face, the warm jellies molding themselves to his skin; his breath pooled beneath his nostrils, a pocket of greater warmth around his nose and upper lip. The silence was absolute, the gloves and cables were deadweight on his hands and across his body, and he waited.

Then at last a spark flared in front of his eyes, a point of light that swelled in less than a heartbeat to a complete scene, expanded into the flat geometry of the last tug's wildnet. Pale grey lines crisscrossed a slightly darker grey background, delineating the web of overlapping virtual spaces, and the mask's pressure seemed to lift a little from his skin. It wasn't a true wildnet, barely viable without the connection to the mine platform's larger space, and cut off as it was now from the rest of the invisible world, he doubted the resident hammals would survive for much longer.

Identify system, he said, and a string of familiar symbols swam in front of his eyes: the same symbols he had seen on the other tugs, except for the specific ship identifier. *List onboard and/or available programs.*

A new set of icons appeared, flickering into existence along the lines of the web, overlaying the plain grey angles with light and color. Most of those were familiar, too, from the assay programs—all certified and bonded, rented from NSMCo along with the mine—and the NavSystem, which wasn't a pure-bred anymore, but a familiar mutant, benign to the point of acceptability, to the constellation of life-support and maintenance programs, all standard, more of the same set he'd seen on the other tugs. But there were also a number of smaller, less powerful programs, the profusion of shapes and colors betraying their origins, and he sighed, contemplating the work ahead.

System sort, find programs containing code string $\wedge\wedge\alpha00\backslash C2^*\backslash^*\backslash^*$.

There were simpler ways to do this—a standard VALMUL lens would have been easier, would have let him reach out and examine the programs that hung in the air around him—but those required his home system to link with the tug's system, to share its virtuality so that the lens could read the programs and present a completely representative icon. And that opened him up to any wild program that could be lurking in the system: not a risk that Port Patrol was willing to take, though they were less concerned about his synapses than they were about their home system.

The display changed abruptly, the selected programs glowing gold against the grey background. The code string he had used was one that was supposed to be contained only in legitimate programs, ones that had been crafted by the legal breeders, but lately it had begun showing up in grey-market software as well. Opinion was about evenly divided as to whether it was a legitimate mutation—human pressure selecting for that particular form of the algorithm—or a deliberate addition by the unlicensed breeders who prepped the wild programs for sale. His own money was on it being a legitimate mutation: despite everyone's best efforts to keep the trade within the license parameters, wild collection was still a thriving business. Inclusion of the code was just one more survival strategy. He scanned the highlighted programs methodically, verbally dismissing each one that he knew to be legitimate, until he was left with half a dozen meager programs. Most of them were fauna, simple-minded routines with only one or maybe two functions; half of those were entertainment programs of one kind or another, games or disk readers that had been tweaked to emulate the latest, most expensive systems. It was somewhat surprising to find them on the tug, especially since the other tugs hadn't had them—tug crews generally didn't have a lot of leisure time—but not immediately suspicious. They looked like Traveller programs even at first cursory examination, and the Traveller hypothecaries were notoriously careless about neutering. The programs had probably spread to the tug from the mine's systems, and nobody had bothered to root them out. Even so, he tagged them for later retrieval, and moved on to the next step.

System sort, find all programs not previously selected.

The display changed again, a new, smaller set of programs popping into view. These were less familiar, shapes and colors that he did not immediately recognize, gaudy as parrots against the sober backdrop, and he felt a familiar thrill at the base of his spine. This was why he got his hazard allowance, why his mixed marriage was tolerated, why the Technical Squad existed in the first place. Any one of those programs could be a bomber or a dead-lurk or a line-trap, hammals that survived by destroying other programs converting their code into random electrons rather than using it to repair or expand its own structure. A bomber could blast chunks of the invisible into patternless void if it was attacked, while even a small dead-lurk or line-trap could disrupt a remote link as easily as it dissolved a program. The biggest ones—and, unlike bombers, it was impossible to tell how big one was until you triggered it—could kill the user as well. The possibility was remote, but it was there, and that knowledge stirred the hair at the back of his neck.

Still, there was no point in waiting. He picked a program at random—a bright orange sphere that seemed to contain a violent pink cone—and released a test routine. It bounced off the sphere without noticeable result—not a bomber, then—and Tarasov moved closer, invoking a static version of a VAL-MUL lens. In its view, the program's bright colors faded somewhat, revealing the underlying structure: a controller, probably another assay program, designed to fine-tune the tug's sensors when looking for particular volatiles. It didn't seem to be of much use aboard this tug—the mine platform had been looking for metals, not gases—but he suspected that it would have been harder to delete this one than to keep it. The reproductive structures looked particularly robust. Still, it was uncertified, unmistakably wild, and he tagged it for further study.

The rest of the programs were much the same, specialized functions designed to improve systems performance or in some other way give the mine's users an advantage in the constant search for metals and gases. Tarasov tagged them all, a picture forming in his mind. If competition was this fierce, so fierce that it was worth bringing in wild faunal programs, then maybe piracy wasn't so improbable an idea after all. At the very least, it could ensure a rival's failure, even if it couldn't guarantee your own success—

He shook the thought away, and tagged the last program. The basic objection remained: piracy was unlikely for the same reasons that interstellar war was unlikely. The Variable Mass Units might allow for faster accelerations, adjusting the total apparent mass while cushioning human crew and machines from its effects, but they still couldn't change orbital mechanics. Without exact advance knowledge of the proposed victim's course, plotting a successful intercept would be all but impossible, and he knew enough about the Union to know that they were unlikely to let a traitor go undetected for very long.

System, copy tagged programs to external datablock G52 and close down.

A confirmation notice flashed past, too fast for him to read the words or icons, and then a bar appeared. He watched while it swelled and shrank, over and over again, nearly three full minutes by his internal clock, and then at last the completion symbol appeared. *End internal session,* he said, and hoped that whoever the station had babysitting the telbot was paying attention.

The grey grid blinked out, replaced by the hot darkness, smelling even more strongly of his own breath, and then, as suddenly as before, he was back in the telbot's head, the tug's control room opening in front of him. He turned his head, its head, saw the lights glowing green on the side of the datablock, and clicked his tongue to open an external circuit.

"Download looks good."

The orbital's technician, a thin woman with "Lynx" embroidered above her left breast, nodded, stuffing a palmreader back into the pocket of her coveralls. "Everything went through clear."

"Have it sent down on the next shuttle. Mark it 'Eyes Only' and my name and tank, and put the address as MKW 8JN Precinct Center. And pass the word that there's some iffy stuff in this volume, will you?" The last was in the probably vain hope of keeping scavengers from making copies of anything they wanted.

Lynx's eyes widened slightly, and he was glad he'd mentioned it. "Bad stuff?"

"Don't know yet. Nothing that's dangerous to the station, I don't think, at least as long as it stays out of your nets. I wouldn't worry."

"We'll keep it isolated," Lynx answered. "You done here?"

"As soon as I pull the autorecorder," Tarasov answered. He clicked his tongue again, cutting off the outside speaker. *Gear down to level one.*

The confirmation buzzed against his palms, and he leaned awkwardly forward, the telbot's false weight clinging to him, not quite matching his own limbs, like a badly fitting suit of clothes. The compartment that held the recorder was tucked in between the main consoles, underneath the supporting pillars: under normal circumstances, there was no need to get at that component, and in any case, the company would want to discourage tampering. *Lights,* he said, and the lamp in the center of the telbot's forehead clicked on, bathing the space in its cool white glare. He reached awkwardly for the hatch cover, popped it, but the telbot's primary fingers were too big to work the delicate clamps that held the recorder in its place. He swore under his breath, then said aloud, *Extend precision arm set.*

A whine of servos answered him—louder than it should have been; a gear or rotor was going somewhere in the assembly—and a casing opened on the telbot's forearm, extruding two smaller working arms and a bird to hold the object being manipulated.

Transfer control from main arms to precision set. As he spoke, he felt his arms go momentarily rigid as the telbot's main arms locked into place, and then he could move again, and the hands before him were the delicate three-fingered hands of the precision arms. They had extra joints, too, a second elbow, and he snaked them into the compartment, flipped the clamps free one by one. He tugged the slim box loose, and got it almost halfway out before he felt resistance. He froze, staring into the compartment, and only then saw the dataribbon running from the back of the recorder to the depths of the tug's machinery. Poised as he was, he couldn't release either hand to free the ribbon, but that was what the bird was for. He shoved his chin forward—the bird didn't need much delicacy of control—and dropped his jaw to open the padded clamp, felt the feather touch against his face as the bird made contact with the board. He closed his mouth gently, feeling the ghost of something between his teeth, and opened his right hand, reached still further into the compartment to free the ribbon. It popped loose with only minor pressure, and he withdrew the assemblage, clicking his tongue to switch to external audio.

"That should do it here."

Lynx held out her hand for the recorder, and Tarasov passed

it to her, proud of the delicacy of his movements. "You want me to send it down with the other block?"

"Please." Tarasov hesitated, but it was only polite to make the offer. "Do you want me to take the 'bot back to the rack before I go? Oh, and you should know, there's a gear or something starting to go in the precision arms."

"Damn." Lynx shook her head. "Yeah, if you could walk it back to the rack, that would be great, and I'll log the problem."

"Sure," Tarasov answered, and clicked his tongue again. He felt the circuit close, a soundless pop in his ear, and worked the telbot to its feet. He leaned forward lightly, lifting first one foot and then the other to start the telbot on its way toward the hatch. It wasn't easy, particularly in the confined space of the tug, and he was aware of Lynx's eyes on him as he moved, judging his performance. He worked the telbot through the hatch with a twist of his hips and only one hand on the frame to steady him, and was absurdly pleased to hear her soft whistle of admiration. The rest of the way was easier—the station's lower corridors had been built to accommodate the telbots—and he stepped it back into its alcove at the edge of the docking bay. He clicked his tongue and said, "All in?"

"Looks good," Lynx confirmed. "Putting on the clamps." Her hand moved on a wall switch, and a moment later Tarasov felt the stabilizer bars close on the telbot's body, a firm pressure against his arms and chest. "You're green."

"Then I'm out of here," Tarasov answered. "Thanks for your help."

"No problem," Lynx said, and Tarasov clicked his tongue again.

Home.

The pressure of the stabilizers vanished, along with the last echo of Lynx's voice, and for a heartbeat Tarasov hung again between worlds, without sound or feeling. Then he felt the warm damp pressure of the helmet against his face, and reached up with suddenly clumsy hands to release the catches. The faceplate swung back, and he wrinkled his nose at the sweaty air. The telepresence rooms were always badly ventilated, as though the wild programs were literally contagious, could slip out through cracks in the seals. He made another face, trying to ignore the smell, as he stripped off the gloves and the sensor leads, and reached reluctantly for the pullover he had discarded in the corner. Lights came on as he moved, and he touched the intercom button beside the door.

"All done here, thanks."

"Right."

Tarasov couldn't remember the name that went with the voice, just the face, a thin, sharp-eyed man who hadn't been happy to see the Technical Squad poaching on Port Patrol's turf.

"You'll get us a copy, right?" the voice went on.

"As you requested, yeah. The blocks will be on the next scheduled shuttle, and then the data will have to be sanitized and processed. It'll be a few days before you get the copies."

There was a fractional pause, as though the other man was debating further comment, but then the intercom went dead. Tarasov sighed and tugged open the door, draping his pullover across his shoulder.

As he'd expected, the air in the hallway was much cooler, and he stopped halfway to the barrier to pull on his jersey. As he worked his head through the neckband, a door opened behind him, and he turned to face the newcomers. He couldn't stop the grin that spread across his face, seeing Rangsey, and saw Rangsey's sober expression lighten fractionally in response, but then the woman at Rangsey's side fully registered, and he felt the smile freeze on his lips. She was unmistakably SID plainclothes, and the rank marks on her collar were high enough that those clothes, the battered parka and karabels, were affectation rather than necessity, which meant in turn that she held real power. Tarasov released his smile, carefully casual, said, "Hey, Jus."

"Hey, Sein." Rangsey's voice was equally casual, but there was a note in it, an edge of accent, that betrayed a lurking anger. "You need a ride back to the precinct?"

"Don't know yet," Tarasov answered, though he knew perfectly well that it was purely a matter of choice. "You offering?"

Rangsey shrugged. "Just thought I'd ask."

The SID woman was looking from one to the other, a slight assessing smile on her face. Tarasov braced himself for a comment, but she said only, "Technical Squad?"

"That's right." Tarasov knew he sounded wary, but couldn't help himself.

"I'd appreciate it if you'd copy your report to SID, and anything else you brought down. Attention Macbeth." She had the Centrality's soft accent, though he couldn't place the particular planet, and Tarasov's wariness increased.

"Sure," he answered, and saw Rangsey stir.

"About the mine crew—"

Macbeth looked at him. "Yeah?"

"I'll want to try on their captain-chip before I talk to them again."

"We'll see," Macbeth answered. "The Department may want to put one of our own on the job instead of someone from External Affairs. You did a good job, but this may be an in-house matter."

"Excuse me," Rangsey said, "but this is definitely our business—if this isn't a job for External Affairs, I don't know what is."

"Sorry." Macbeth shook her head. "We have prior interest."

Rangsey drew breath to protest further, but Macbeth was already looking away. "See that I get a copy of your data when it comes down, Sergeant—"

"Tarasov."

"Tarasov," Macbeth repeated, and nodded. " 'Day." She lengthened her stride and headed for the barrier without looking back.

Rangsey let out the breath he'd been holding. "Shit-fuck."

"Easy," Tarasov said, and didn't look for the monitors tucked into the corners where the walls and ceiling met. He didn't have to: Rangsey rolled his eyes at him, but subsided.

"Do you want a ride back?" he asked, after a moment, and Tarasov reached for his chrono.

"I'm off duty—I've been on overtime for the last half hour. Yeah, I can leave the pod here, and we can head straight home, if you'd like."

"Sounds good," Rangsey said.

They had reached the barrier, and Tarasov stopped automatically, lifting his arms away from his sides to give the scanners greater play. Rangsey copied him, more slowly, and a moment later the sensor beeped twice. The door rolled back, and they came out into the brightly lit lobby.

"Signing out?" That was the man on duty behind the desk.

Tarasov sighed—he would have preferred to cheat a little, sign out at the main door and so get paid for the time it would take them to make their way out of the maze of the Port Patrol's offices, but Port Patrol was not about to turn a blind eye to the Technical Squad's petty misdemeanors. He nodded, and the man spun a touchpad toward him. Tarasov flipped it into text mode, hauled his monocular out of his pocket, dialed it to the setting for first-level security, and entered the codes. A time form swam in the monocular's lens—outside that circle, he saw only a hash of colors—and he ran the borrowed stylus down the checklist, hoping he was inconveniencing someone by leaving the pod at the Port. He touched the send button, heard the confirmation chime softly, and slid the now-blank pad back toward the duty man. "Thanks."

"No problem," the man said, and Tarasov turned toward the stairs that led back to the main floor, following Rangsey along the dull-walled corridor. As always after he'd spent time on the link, he felt faintly out of sync with the real world, as though he was at one remove from the things around him. He was aware of Rangsey's anger, the abrupt control of his movements, but the taller man said nothing until they reached the orange-lit tunnels that led to the parking levels. The walls were very plain here, not even a geometric boss to cover the junctions of pipes above the final door, and the garage was even more spare, rank on rank of nearly identical runabouts snugged to identical dull bronze charge bollards under the grid of fluorescent tubing that filled the space with flat, shadowless light. Rangsey gave the ranked runabouts a single searching look, taking his bearings from some invisible landmarks, and started into the pattern, moving on a long diagonal between the rows of vehicles.

"Are you going to give her the data?" he asked, and Tarasov blinked.

"Yeah, I suppose, eventually. I doubt I'll have a choice." He stepped wide around the next bollard, managed to draw even with Rangsey for three steps before they reached the next runabout, and he was forced to slow down again. "What was going on with her?"

"I wish to hell I knew." Rangsey shook his head. "There's something fucking weird going on with this whole thing—the mine crew's talking like this is something that happens all the time, and their captain-chip recognized it, it told them to run, Sein, and then here's the goddamned SID, Centrality SID at that, coming in and shutting down the whole thing before it even gets started." He stopped as abruptly as he'd started, shook his head again. "And she's put me off the job. You heard."

Tarasov nodded. "The tapes we got were Restricted, SID coding, too. Ketty broke out some of the files for me, but I didn't get to view more than the first interview. What'd they tell you?"

They had reached the runabout. Rangsey shrugged, fiddling with the access pad, and Tarasov reached automatically to disengage the charger's short cable. "Thanks. Pretty much what I said, they were out on what should have been a routine survey, found something, and then something, someone, found them. They ran because they thought they were in danger, not because some wild program got loose on them—they had cause to think they were in danger, and that's what I'm going to put in my report."

Tarasov climbed into the passenger compartment, settling the crash webbing over his body. It clung, an odd echo of the clamps against the telbot's shell, and he shook the touch-memory away. "That's the same story they told the first interviewer. Everything on the tugs I looked at confirms it, too. The programs are just what you'd expect, and there's no sign of anything being bred illegally."

Rangsey slipped a cord into his wristport, eased the runabout into motion with the flick of a finger, and pointed its nose toward the entrance ramp. "The company, this NSMCo, it's hiding something, big time."

Tarasov nodded. "Which is what SID's after?"

"We should be so lucky." Rangsey's mouth was set in a tight line. "No, what's going to happen is, they're going to write this off to one more Union crew fucking up, and that's all that's going to happen. Damn, I want to try on that chip."

The runabout popped into light, the now-setting sun reflecting from the fields of ice-coated shattergrass. Tarasov blinked, momentarily blinded, was aware of the way Rangsey's hands and body moved, going from one mode of vision to another. The canopy stayed clear, unpolarized; he looked aside, lifting a hand to shade his eyes, and said, "It doesn't make sense. None of it makes sense."

"Oh, it makes perfect sense," Rangsey said. "Whatever's going on in Audumla-system, someone with enough power to make it stick has decided that it's the Company's business, not the government's, and SID's right there to make sure that's what happens. So what if a few Union folk get caught in the crossfire, they don't count anyway. And we're doing fuck-all about it."

Tarasov bit back his own anger, recognizing the guilt behind it, said, as moderately as he could, "There's not a lot we can do about it." In the distance, at the end of the landing field, light flashed, rose, a trail of chemical smoke billowing beneath it. He counted automatically, childishly, in thousands, and heard the distant rumble on the count of seven. "Except quit." Even saying the words, he felt a touch of fear: he didn't have any other skills, except the ones he'd learned growing up in Transport, and they wouldn't keep him working for very long, not with hundreds of more experienced people waiting to find work at the same wages. He scowled at himself, at the gleaming field outside the runabout's window, and felt the vehicle slow momentarily, then leap forward, sliding into the traffic stream with an ease he himself never managed.

"I been thinking about that," Rangsey said.

"Oh?"

"Yeah."

Tarasov didn't answer, and the runabout swung easily with the traffic, bringing the towers of the city into the frame of the windscreen. The colors of stone and pressed stone and brick caught the low sunlight, the buildings vivid against the darkening sky. Port Montas looked like what it was from this angle, a new city, stone-built only because stone came cheaper than wood or steel on this particular planet, the tall unnatural shapes flaunting their mastery of the world around them. They couldn't afford for Rangsey to quit his job, not with the rent on the flat what it was—even Eight-Jane wasn't cheap enough to afford that place on one income—but then, he'd said this before, more than once, each time he didn't like the way Port Patrol or the Vagabond Squad or somebody was handling someone he translated for. It didn't necessarily mean anything, least of all that he was leaving.

"They were counting on me, Sein," Rangsey went on, "and I'm screwing up."

Tarasov suppressed a sudden flush of anger. Rangsey knew, as well or better than anyone in External Affairs, just what that department's limits were, should know better than to promise anyone anything, especially a client, because ExA was at the bottom of the precedence list. And Rangsey personally should know better, because he complained long and loud about getting no respect from his superiors precisely because he was Union, mechanized, and those complaints were part of why he didn't have the connections he would need to help his clients—Tarasov broke off, abruptly appalled by his own thoughts, shocked by how close he'd come to the unthinkable. And it was unthinkable because it was unfair, and wrong: Rangsey did have problems the other ExA translators didn't have, because a lot of the other, higher precedence squads didn't want to work with the mechanized. He'd heard it himself more than once—*you can't know what they're sharing, you can't trust them to tell you everything, you know they always stick together*—and knew his own colleagues were still saying it. No one said it to him directly now that he'd made the contract with Rangsey, but he was aware of the silences where the words would have been. "You can't fight SID," he said at last, groping for a tone that would carry what words couldn't, and Rangsey glanced at him, a bitter smile flickering across his face.

"Oh, I know that. But they don't. To them, it looks like I'm backing out of the job."

Which was also true, the other side of the coin: Rangsey was equally at odds with his own people just by working with ExA, never mind contracting with someone from Service. Never mind that Tarasov had been born Transport, as close as citizens got to the Union, from the day he'd joined the Technical Squad he'd become Service, beneath contempt—"Fuck them," he said, unable to stop himself. "Just fuck them. If they don't have the brains to see what you're doing—"

Rangsey glared at him. "Oh, that's very helpful—"

"Watch it—" Tarasov bit off the rest of the warning as Rangsey glanced almost casually at the approaching land-transport, and applied brakes and steering. The runabout slid sideways into a break in the faster traffic, passed the heavy carrier, and slipped neatly into its lane again.

"Don't you trust my driving?" There was still an edge of anger in Rangsey's voice. "That's the one thing we can be relied on to get right."

A matching answer trembled on Tarasov's tongue, but then he saw the way that Rangsey's hands were crooked on the virtual controls, an unfamiliar clumsiness making the runabout sway slightly against the grid buffers. "That's not what this is about," he said, and Rangsey's taut muscles twitched.

"No," he said, after a moment. "Or not with you, anyway. Damn, Sein, I need—I'm worried about these people."

Tarasov nodded. "I'll do what I can," he said, but they both knew that wasn't much. Still, Rangsey offered him a twisted smile as he swung the runabout out of the flyway traffic and off the grid, heading into the narrow streets of the city proper. The argument had been averted this time, but Tarasov could feel it still in the air like an electrical field in the hull of a ship, waiting to snap out at the first real touch. He risked another glance at Rangsey, wanting to say something, anything, that would make it better, remind them both of the good things, beyond sex and company, but the other man's face was set and closed, and Tarasov couldn't think of anything. He leaned back in his seat instead, and looked out at the shadowed streets, the club lights just beginning to bloom above unpromising doorways, wondering why it was all going wrong.

■ 3 ■

AUDUMLA WAS NOT by any stretch of the imagination normal. Oh, the sun—unnamed like so many in this undersettled sector, known only by its catalog and jump numbers—was ordinary enough, but that was all. There were more gas giants than Survey had predicted, and their layers were rich in volatile, useful gases; most of what should have been smaller planets had failed to form, leaving the system littered with chunks of stone and metal that over time had drifted into asteroid belts that all but filled their missing parents' orbits. Only three planets had actually coalesced, two so close in to the sun that they were useless even to the mining company that had claimed the system, the third so marginally habitable that the company—it was the Night Sky Mine Company, old and experienced in its trade—had subcontracted its development to a junior partner, Landforms Unlimited, Inc., and let them deal with the raw land. NSMCo's people lived in orbit, in a glittering web of spindles and spheres and, at the poor end, decommissioned STLships, all tied together by power conduit and the carefully-matched fields of the SVMUs. Landforms' Agribus Division fed the station—the terraforming had made Landforms' reputation, but at a price, committing them to feeding Audumla for as long as NSMCo remained in the system—and another subcontractor maintained the various orbital stations and the mine platforms and the other equipment, and NSMCo prospered mightily. In two years, in fact, it would celebrate its centennial in the system—the Audumla settlement was twenty-eight years older than the Bestla colony, if you counted from the first claim-ship's arrival, though serious exploitation had had to wait until the Bestla transshipment point was opened—and the managers were determined to show record profits. That meant working harder than ever—not even Audumla's riches were inexhaustible, and the easy pieces had been snatched up in the first decades—and extracting every gram of ore, every cubic centimeter of gas, and every hundredth-credit from the sharecropping Union folk who crewed the majority of the mines. But that was all right, too: the Union was used to that, and the Company mostly honored the hard parts of its contracts—the ones that covered maintenance and repair-and-rescue among them—and it looked as though they would make their numbers before the Centennial year.

Much of this filtered to Ista through her best friend. Merette/3 Stinne was Management by birth, her father an engineer-physicist, her mother a finance officer, and Company policy was the stuff of overheard, after-dinner conversations, when Stinne and her brother were supposed to be studying. Stinne had an ear for politics, which had stood Ista in good stead before now, back when she'd been enrolled in the Company schools, and didn't hurt now that she was apprenticing with Trindade. No information is useless, Trindade had told her more than once; half the job is finding what they're really worried about, and right here that's usually the Company. Ista occasionally felt guilty for exploiting her friend, but then, Stinne had to know what was going on. She'd been manipulating the connections that were the company practically since she could walk, since the day at the age of three when she'd innocently offered to share her toy with a senior vice president on inspection tour, and so charmed him that she'd earned her mother a second look in the promotion stakes. Stinne would, so Ista was convinced, someday look for payback, and Ista would make that payment happily, or so she told herself. After all, without Stinne, she wouldn't still have access to the Company mainframes, wouldn't be able to keep up with the Ragged School Curriculum that was shipped in quarterly from Bestla, and would have no chance at all of ever becoming real.

That was why she was upstation at all today—or most days, for that matter—and as always she was guiltily glad of Stinne's company. Her almost-mother always said that she, and any-one, Union or Traveller or whatever, had as much right as any Company employee to walk upstation, but it never quite felt that way. The Company people looked sideways at her Trav-eller clothes, the bright gauzy trapata and the dozens of bracelets and the beads braided in her thick hair, and she knew she was foreign. She had asked her almost-mother if she could wear different clothes, real clothes—like the karabels and the Company T-shirt that she kept for when she and Stinne went dancing upstation, not that she told her mother about them, either the clothes or the dancing—but Kelly2 had glared at her and demanded if she were ashamed of what she was. There was no answer to that, no right answer, anyway, and so she slung her trapata higher on her shoulder, pushed her bracelets up so that they didn't make quite so much noise at the termi-nal, and pretended she didn't see the stares. Stinne leaned over her shoulder, watching the menus scroll past, and Ista could smell the faint fresh scent of soap that clung to her hair and skin. She herself smelled of musk, the cold scent her mother used to take away the smell of the STLship's cramped living space, and the smokier scents that flavored Deen Bara-bell's Bubble where she lived the rest of the time, and proba-bly under that Barabell's beer and her own sweat. She couldn't know that for certain, but it had been a couple of days since her last shower—the Company had raised the cost of extra ra-tions recently—and she could feel her hair lank even in the weighted braids.

"We're going to make it," Stinne said, and Ista glanced from the scrolling text, lists of headings and titles, to the numbers displayed in her own palmbook, compared them with the numbers that flickered in the purchase menu. No, they weren't going to make it, the graphical display was never as precise as the numbers, but she'd set up the download by priority, and she'd get everything except the supplemental readings for the core sociologies class. She could probably get those next week, assuming nothing more urgent came in over the Ragged Schools' network, but she resented spending two weeks' earn-ings on the readings, especially when Trindade made her buy

her own datablocks. One week she'd expected, but the classes
had required more than the texts she had bought at the beginning of the year, and the first exam had taught her that she
could no longer fake what she hadn't read. Not for the first
time, she shot an envious glance at the Company library,
tucked behind walls of smoky bronze glassite. The downloads
were free, or free within a generous personal-education-and-
recreation budget, but you couldn't get in there without an employee's badge, and not even Stinne's friendship could extend
that far. Through the walls, she could see a knot of kids in
Company T-shirts—Metallurgy, F&A, Eividion B—standing
talking next to a download tree studded with their cassettes.
Even as she watched, a light flashed, and one of the girls, a thin
fair girl Ista thought she recognized from her two years at the
Company school, reached across and retrieved the sturdy
wafer without breaking the rhythm of her conversation.

The pay console beeped discreetly, and she glanced down
at the screen, found the message she had expected. There
wasn't enough money left on her card to download the final
full set of readings, but she could still afford the digests. She
hesitated—she'd gotten the digests before, and they were more
frustrating than helpful—but if Trindade had been serious
when she mentioned a big job next week, the follow-up to
finding Erramun's vetch, she would have to buy datablocks
next week, too. And that meant the digests would be all she
could get. She touched the confirmation, winced anyway
when the voucher numbers cycled down to fifteen-fifty. That
was maybe the price of a meal, if she was lucky enough to get
the time to eat outside the Bubble.

Stinne gave her a guilty look. "I'm all tapped out, or I'd offer
to help."

"I told you before, I pay my own way." Ista saw the hurt in
the other girl's eyes, forced a grin she didn't entirely feel. "It's
a Traveller thing. Look, want to go downstation when I'm finished?"

Stinne nodded, apparently accepting the rebuff, but Ista
thought the hurt was still there. "Sure. The Bubble?"

That was defiance for her—she'd been forbidden more than

once to hang out with the Union folk and Travellers who pa-
tronized the brewery—as well as support. Ista shrugged, wishing she could afford something else, someplace different, but
nodded, watching the check numbers tick past. "Sure. I have
to be at work by dinnershift, though."

Stinne started to say something, but a voice from behind her
cut them off.

"Oh, God, don't they ever wash?"

Stinne's face contorted in a scowl. Ista, recognizing the voice
from other confrontations, set her face in her best witchy look,
borrowed from Trindade, blank and hard. Travellers had a
reputation, especially their cunning folk, hypothecaries and
shamen and speakers-between; they had to be uncanny to live
with the machines the way they did, and people, even Management, could be nervous about crossing them. She looked
over her shoulder, fixing the speaker in her blank stare, trying
to walk the fine line between overt challenge and subtle in-
timidation. *I hear you,* she hoped her look would say, hoped
too it would be enough to keep him from pursuing the issue.
Travellers got hurt now and then, in the less-lit depths of the
station; the Company frowned on the violence, but could
never stop it entirely. The young man—it was exactly the one
she had thought it would be, a dark tall boy not yet grown into
his height or the straggle of hairs across his upper lip—met her
look, all uneasy bravado, and she tried to remember what
Trindade had told her. Unfortunately, what she heard was
Kelly2's impatient voice denying that power—*I could never
pull it off, but maybe you can, you've got the look, maybe*—and
knew she'd lost it. She looked away before she blinked, but not
before she saw the look of triumph on the boy's face.

"I guess we're done here, right?" Stinne said, a little too
loudly, and Ista looked down at the symbols on the screen.

"Just about." She touched virtual keys, shutting down her
account and erasing her trail beyond at least casual retrieval,
then slipped the datablock into her pocket along with her notebook. "Yeah, I'm done." In this preserve, this safer space, there
was no need to do more, but it felt strange to be putting data
away without scanning for infectious code.

"Then let's go," Stinne said, still loudly. "The crowd's changed.

Ista reslung her thin trapata, grateful for the defense, but uncertain of its efficacy. "Sure," she said, and could practically feel the boy's sneer as they pushed through the spincylinder into the next volume.

This was a commercial plaza, double-high and triple-wide, with a snackery in the central space among the support pillars and shopfronts all along the walls. They were all open—this far upstation, people mostly kept a day-wake, night-sleep schedule—and display boards and order kiosks flashed and beeped their thousand messages. Most of them were Company franchises, and carried Company goods at Company prices; the prices for non-employees were marked in red, and a few items were discreetly labelled employees-only. Still, Ista felt her own pace slow, and wasn't sorry to stop when she saw Stinne staring frankly at the display board.

"Check the menu," she said, and Stinne glanced back at her.

"You don't mind?"

She was already reaching for the icon. Ista shook her head, watched as images blossomed on the screen. This was a clothing store, selling the bright, inexpensive tricoteil that nearly everyone wore for casual dress, and looking past the edge of the board, Ista could see a wall filled with garments folded on rows of shelves. Stinne ignored the Items menu—there were only a dozen or twenty basic shapes anyway—and flipped directly to New Colors, stepping back a little as the swatches flared on the big screen. There were only five, a blue so dark as to be almost black, a hot red that reminded Ista of programs she'd seen on the wildnets, a purple-brown like old wine, a pale blue-green, and a peachy-pink, and Stinne shook her head.

"Nothing there I can wear. Though I suppose it's just as well, I spent my clothing allowance already this month." She flipped to New Patterns as she spoke, and the New Colors menu shrank to a small palette at the bottom of the screen, replaced in the main display by a trio of black-on-white designs. They were repeated in slightly smaller scale as white-on-black, and

Ista leaned forward to touch one of them, a scattering of leaves almost too stylized to recognize.

"That would look great in the red."

"Yeah." Stinne touched the smaller palette, and the new red replaced the white, hot red-orange leaves drifting across the black background. "That is nice."

"Or that dark blue."

"Yeah?" Stinne touched the palette again, and the red-and-black design shrank slightly, the blue-and-black version flicking into existence beside it. The colors were so close in tone that the pattern became almost invisible, more of a texture than a distinct design.

"Now that would work on you," Ista said, and Stinne nodded, touching more keys to call up a price. "That pattern in a long-tee—"

She broke off, seeing that Stinne had already selected that garment, a short-sleeved, round-necked tunic that would reach to the middle of her thighs, and Stinne grinned at her.

"Great minds." She looked at the price that flashed onto the board, and made a face. "God, the new stuff's expensive, though."

Ista looked over her shoulder, and winced. Thirty ccus for employees, seventy for non: more than her day's wages just for a shirt. "It would look nice," she said aloud, but was careful not to show too much enthusiasm. It would look good on Stinne, though, the two dark colors bringing out the pale gold of her skin and hair.

"I know," Stinne said. She shook her head. "Maybe I can talk my mother into getting it for me."

"Just don't tell her where you got the idea of putting those two together," Ista said, and Stinne laughed.

"Don't worry. Though she'll probably guess, it's a Traveller kind of thing to do."

"Well, that's what we're good at." Ista looked back at the display. "I wonder how much shoes would cost, in the red."

"Which kind?"

"Plain slippers."

Stinne obligingly touched the keys, producing an image of the shoes, the same thin flat-soled slippers they were both wearing, in the new fabric. The price appeared at the same moment in the order block: thirty/seventy. Ista sighed—she had been hoping for a discount, considering how small the shoes were in comparison to the shirt—and shook her head. "Too much."

"I could get them for you," Stinne said. "If you'll give me the money, of course."

Ista hesitated, tempted. The red was almost the same shade as her best trapata, the one that was embroidered with big gold flowers and trimmed with multicolored beads, would match her best ochre chamiz as well, but even thirty was more than she could afford for shoes. "No, I really can't. But thanks anyway."

She was aware, suddenly, of the shopwoman watching from beside the payment kiosk, and had to stop herself from moving instinctively away from the board. I have a right to be here, she told herself, but was glad of Stinne's presence. Stinne, oblivious, closed down the final menu and turned away.

A double spincylinder led into the next volume, also double-high, though not as wide as the last. They had crossed into an older part of the Agglomeration, where the floor covering was oddly variegated from having been reapplied more than once and the walls shaded subtly from white to grey as they met the floor, and Ista felt a sudden rush of relief, seeing Union folk, two men, standing beside a vidik wall. She felt more at home here, said, expansively, "Want to cut through the Free Market on the way down?"

"Always," Stinne answered, though her tone might not have been as enthusiastic as Ista would have liked. Ista pretended she didn't hear that note of unease—it was station day, after all, the middle of the afternoon; people would be at work or not working at all, not the coming-off-shift crowd that could be a hassle—and led the way to the nearest downward stair.

The Free Market was at the very end of the Agglomeration, at the point where the Company-built station ended and the mix of jerry-built, Union-built modules and converted STLships began. It was the last large volume of space in the station, not quite double-high, but broad, and the ceiling overhead still held the rails for the loading robots: the volume had originally been the station's main docking bay. Now the rails supported power cables and network conduit, as well as the occasional signboard or cheap paper banner advertising some new product's arrival. The air smelled a little stale as they pushed through the second of the two linked spincylinders, and both girls glanced instinctively toward the failsafe telltales on the wall of the chamber. The glass was clear, unbroken and unclouded: just the usual sluggish recirculation of a large volume, not falling pressure or unhealthy chemicals. Still, Ista thought, wrinkling her nose, the smells did seem a lot stronger than usual—sour, almost, as though some liquid had gone stale.

"I wonder what that is?" Stinne asked. "Smells like when you clean the beer vats."

It did a bit, and Ista nodded, glancing automatically around for the source of the stench. Floorplates were up by the far wall, and even as she watched, a man in an orange outerall and respirator lowered himself into the hole. She nudged Stinne, tilted her head in that direction. "Looks like it might be wastewater."

Stinne looked, but discreetly—she had learned that much of Union manners from her downstation friends—and glanced back at Ista. "Maybe we don't hang out, then."

Ista nodded. "The Bubble should be OK, though, we're not on this line."

They made their way down the Market's main corridor, delineated as such by lines of paint and multicolored tape. More tape and paint marked off squares of floor for stalls, a full floorplate here, half a plate there, even a few plates marked into quarters and eighths, the last just big enough for a person to sit or stand with a basket of goods: the Free Market was the first and last place a person came when one had something to sell, or when one was desperate enough to sell anything. Ista kept her eyes away from the north corner, where a couple of girls not much older than she stood in the marked squares trying to pretend that they weren't the goods, or that they wanted to be. That was what happened, or what could happen, easily, if you lost your job and weren't Union or Traveller; that was what she was scared of, most of all, becoming herself the commodity.

The Market wasn't as busy as usual, either from the smell, or, more likely, slowed by a shortage of water or drainage. Maybe a third of the marked spaces were empty, and their neighbors had expanded slightly, edging a folding table or a blanket or infant's seat into the empty space. Ista glanced at the displays anyway as she passed, recognizing both goods and sellers, but didn't slow down. There wasn't much she could afford anyway—the occasional pot-grown vegetable, or supposedly discarded Company equipment offered for resale, occasionally parts or software—and the Traveller goods that formed the bulk of the stock were things she could trade for rather than buy.

Even as she thought that, she heard someone call her name, and turned to see a woman she knew slightly waving from her stall.

"Who's she?" Stinne asked, and Ista shrugged.

"Someone my mom knows. I think they were doing a deal." She threaded her way through the narrow aisles, Stinne following more cautiously, and stopped in front of the woman's booth. It was a little nicer than the usual set-up, a folding table and hutch to display the woman's goods—stacks of vidiki and slimbooks, and a tray of perfumed lotions, all the little luxuries the Union folk loved and the Travellers provided—and a square of thick carpet to cushion her feet. "Miana?"

"Jenna—your mother—said last week she had someone who wanted Androsci's latest vidik. Tell her I've got it if she still wants it—I'll trade her for two hundred grams of chocolate."

"I'll tell her," Ista said, and groaned inwardly. Kelly2 wouldn't give more than one hundred for a single vidik, not unless the buyer was really rich, Company rather than Union. This particular deal was likely to keep her relaying messages for the next week before the women settled on a price.

"Thanks, Ista," the woman said, and Ista barely kept herself from rolling her eyes until she'd turned away.

"What's the problem?" Stinne asked, and Ista shook her head. It was too complicated, all of a sudden, to try to explain the network of bargains and favors that held Traveller society together.

"They're starting a deal," she said instead, "and I'm probably going to be the one who gets to do the real work."

"I thought you were working for Trindade," Stinne said. "And at the Bubble."

"I am. But I have to do this, too."

"At least Barabell pays you."

"Travellers don't believe in money," Ista said, not without bitterness.

"Maybe that's proof you're not really one," Stinne said, and slanted Ista the lopsided smile that meant she was only joking. Ista smiled back, acknowledging the friendship, but not even Stinne could tease her about that without hurting. Kelly2 wasn't really her mother, she didn't know for sure who her mother or father had been—one of them had been crew on the looted mine platform where she herself had been found, but the recovered crew list had been wrong enough that she couldn't even be sure she'd seen their names. It was bad to be this rootless, no real name, no ID, no entry in either the Company or the Federal computers, scary to be so close to nothing. If Kelly2 died tomorrow—it was a fear she'd been living with for three years now, ever since she'd had to leave the Company school—Ista would have nothing, no way to keep herself alive. Oh, there was always the Union, if she could find a family to sponsor her, or the job with Trindade, but both of those were as precarious as her position now.

"My mother really hates this place," Stinne said, after a moment, a peace offering, and Ista glanced at her.

"The Agglomeration, or the Market?"

"Well, both, I think, but I meant the Market." Stinne's eyes tightened, familiar laughter, but that faded quickly. "She says it's depressing to see how little there is."

Ista shook her head. "My mother says the same thing." She could almost hear Kelly2, too, see the shake of the head that went with it: *you kids, you haven't seen anything. If we were plan-etside, now, if you could see a real Traveller market, thousands of things, literally thousands, anything you could imagine, and all for barter. Then you'd know.* Ista shrugged away the voice, and the thought that Merette had probably been talking about something else. "I don't know, I like it."

"So do I. Except when the drains are bad."

Stinne's voice was deliberately light, and Ista smiled back, grateful for the change of tone.

"Yeah. It'll be better in the Bubble, though." She saw Stinne's expression lighten, and felt better herself for it. She was fond of Stinne, fonder, she was almost sure, than just friends, and was still working out what to do about that. But in the meantime, it felt good just to see Stinne smile.

The Bubble was still further downstation, well past the point where the new construction stopped and the recycled volumes began in earnest. There were fewer spincylinders, and more airlocks, and Ista was aware that Stinne was hanging back a little, letting her work the palmpads. She didn't mind, particularly, but it was odd to realize that Stinne, of all people, was nervous of the downstation volumes. The Bubble itself was converted from a cargo sphere, and the main room's domed ceiling and the curved walls of the brew chambers betrayed its origins. The spare room, where Ista herself generally lived, since Kelly2's trade runs took her out of range of the Ragged Schools' relay transmitters, was even more oddly shaped, so that she had had to set up her rig in the back room between the tanks of Barabell's beer. They sheltered the terminal from casual eyes and cut some of the noise from the bar's main volume, but when there was a crowd, the extra tanks emptied quickly, and the rounded space echoed with noise and music. Not that she had much chance to work those days, she added silently: those were the days that she usually ended up working all three meals and a good chunk of the nightshift, too.

Today, however, the main volume was almost empty, just a Union woman eating in a corner, her eyes fixed on the flatbook beside her tray, and Fredi Shannin and one of his age-mates playing with the karaoke system and Fredi's homebrew box synth. He saw them come in, and broke away from the other boy, leaving the synth behind him on the table.

"Hey, how's it going?"

"OK." Ista eyed him with some uncertainty, and heard Stinne's soft snort of disapproval. Lately, Fredi had been reluctant to talk to either of them when he was with other Union boys, and Ista wondered what he wanted that had changed his mind. As if he'd read her mind, Fredi looked at his shoes.

"Listen, I'm sorry about the other day. It's just—oh, hell, it's complicated."

Not to mention hurtful. Ista saw the same awareness, more wry, in Stinne's face, said instead, "What do you want, Fredi?"

The dark boy frowned, almost hiding his own hurt. "Hey, you want to play it that way—"

"Not particularly," Stinne said.

Ista just stopped herself from adding, *but you started it.* She made a face, annoyed by the circumstances, her own childishness, and Fredi gave her a tentative smile.

"Look, I am sorry. And I need your help—I'm even willing to pay for it."

That was flattery indeed, the most sincere form, and Ista allowed herself to return the smile. "What with?"

Fredi tipped his head toward the synth. "I've got a problem with the software. I traded for some custom patches, new sounds, but the controller doesn't want to read them, at least not happily, and I was wondering if you could take a look at it, brew me something to fix it, or something."

"Maybe." In spite of herself, Ista's interest sharpened. She'd worked on the synth before, had helped modify some of its software already, and she enjoyed its rigid architecture, the cold equations that produced the music. And besides, she admitted silently, she would enjoy showing off her skills in front of Stinne. "I'll take a look."

Fredi turned back toward the table and the other young man who waited there. He was lighter-skinned than either Fredi or Ista, though still darker than Stinne, Colored Union, probably, and the look he gave them was one of wary interest.

"That's Jadi—Mauras15/1 Plejadin," Fredi said. "Kelly2/1 Ista and Merette/3 Stinne."

"You work for Trindade," Plejadin said. His tone was respectful, but Ista caught an undertone of something else, and hesitated.

"She does," Stinne answered. "And she does collections for Erramun, upstation."

Plejadin gave a little hiss of admiration, but Ista was no longer fully listening. *This is your first lesson,* Trindade had said to her almost the first time she'd walked through the consulting room door, *and if you don't remember anything else, remember this. The customers never tell you what they want, not fully. Sometimes they're scared, sometimes they're embarrassed, sometimes they don't know what it is they're really after, but they never, never tell you all the truth. You have to figure that out first, and then you help them.* Ista had never quite believed her, until now.

She felt under the folds of her trapata for the monocular she wore around her neck. It was the single most valuable thing she had ever owned, worth probably as much as a half cargo, or a new VMU modulator, but that was one thing her mother had never skimped on. When the best did matter, couldn't be simulated through Traveller ingenuity or a little extra time and effort, then she paid the price, and without complaint. Ista had asked for it, this particular model, a brand-new Eisenhart with an internal booster to let her see devices' internal architecture in schema, without much hope, figuring she'd finally reached the limits of Kelly2's patience if not her bank account, but Kelly2 had heard her out, grunted, and headed upstation to talk to Trindade. Ista still didn't know what Trindade had said—the hypothecary was sparing with words, and praise in particular—but Kelly2 had juggled her finances, and the Eisenhart was Ista's. Her fingers slid easily into the slight depressions that marked the control points, and Fredi offered her the test cable. She took it, aware of both Stinne's and Plejadin's admiring stares, and felt a little thrill of pride. She wasn't a true hypothecary yet, but she was on her way. And was that what

Fredi wanted? she wondered suddenly. To prove he knew Travellers, that a hypothecary, or near to one, would do him a favor? Shannin was a small family—Fredi's father was only Shannin5—but most of them worked for NSMCo, while Mauras was big, but based in the next sector over, almost into the Centrality. It could be to Fredi's advantage to make this oblique statement. . . . She filed the idea as unproven but promising, and slipped the cable into its socket.

A design blossomed in the monocular's display core, first the red lines of the hardwiring, then orange for the system software, and so on down the spectrum, a dizzying three-dimensional shape that wove and twisted back on itself, a coil of serpents held in a rigid cage. She thought she recognized the problem area—a place where the lines knotted together across a vital rib—and tightened her fingers, chording commands and turning the bezel to bring it into closer view. The image swam for an instant, then reformed, and she saw the conflict clearly. It wasn't much, really, just two bits of code trying to occupy the same spot on the index lattice, easily fixed even without a homebrewed remedy. Which means, she thought, that he is after something else, probably impressing Mauras15/1 Plejadin. A spark of annoyance flared—a week ago, Fredi wouldn't even say hey, much less ask a favor—but vanished almost as quickly as it had appeared. After all, this was part of what hypothecaries did, even if it wasn't her favorite part, and in any case it couldn't hurt her to be known to have Union connections. Favor for favor, she decided, that was the way she would handle this, and looked up from the monocular.

"Yeah, I see the problem, Fredi."

"Can you take care of it?"

Ista smiled. "I can fix it. It's just a coding problem, no big deal."

"I said I'd pay." Fredi seemed subtly to brace himself. "What's your price?"

"Oh, it's not a big thing," Ista answered, "and I could use a favor from you anyway. Fair deal?"

"Depends on what you want," Fredi said, but Ista could see

him relax again, and knew she'd guessed right. Favor for favor meant admitting a connection, and that seemed to be what he really wanted. All right, she thought, let's get him really in my debt.

"You know my family situation. If you hear anything that might help. . . ." She let her voice trail off delicately. He would tell Mauras15/1 the full story as soon as she was out of earshot but that couldn't be helped. Fredi waved a hand as though to brush the words away.

"You know I'd do that anyway. Name something real."

Ista grinned. "It's not that big a job, Fredi. Buy my beer this week, that'll do it."

She was not a heavy drinker. Fredi nodded, smiling now himself, and Ista looked back into the monocular's display, turning the bezel to deepen the image. The tangled codes stood out in sharp relief: a minor adjustment, she thought, her fingers already shifting on the monocular's controls, shutting down her system, and the problem was solved. "Bring it by Trindade's tomorrow when I'm working," she said, and freed the test cord from its socket.

"I'll do that," Fredi said, and Ista turned away.

"See you around, then."

She glanced at the board above the serving hatch, saw that the kitchen was officially closed, and stepped around the end of the bar to draw glasses of beer for herself and Stinne. She punched her access codes into the pad—Stinne, ostentatiously polite, looked away—and grimaced at the menu that appeared. There was only one beer at the moment, not her favorite, but she filled the glasses and nodded at Stinne.

"Get the door, would you?"

Stinne worked the latch without speaking, and they went together through the door into the private rooms. At the moment, *Fancy Kelly*, Kelly2's little STL trader, was docked to the station while Kelly2 negotiated for her next cargo, but Ista still kept her room at the Bubble. The lights came on along with the active ventilation as she unlocked the door, revealing her black-and-white rug and the half-made narrow bed, and she set the beers on the edge of the table that was already piled high with flimsies. Stinne perched on the edge of the bed without waiting for an invitation, reached for the opened can of frysticks that stood beside the media box.

"What were you up to out there? It took me two years to get you to explain about you and Kelly2, and here you are talking about it to a perfect stranger."

Ista handed her her beer, and took a long swallow of her own, buying time. "It's complicated."

"You sound like Fredi."

Ista wrinkled her nose at that, but admitted the justice of the rebuke. "Yeah, well, sorry. It's just—Trindade says you have to figure out what a client really wants before you can help them, and what Fredi really wanted was to show off a little, look big by knowing a hypothecary personally. And he's a friend, I figured I'd help him a little."

"How'd you know that was what he wanted?" Stinne had already drunk most of her beer, her fair cheeks slightly flushed.

"Oh." Ista paused, not sure how to explain, not even fully sure how she'd known. "Well, the job wasn't that big, he probably could've done it himself, if he'd tried. And then there was the way he wanted to talk to us."

"Yeah, that's new, all right." Stinne snorted. "But I still don't see."

Ista shook her head in frustration. "I wish I could tell you. He—it was a little of everything, the job being easy, him talking to us, body language, Mauras being a Centrality family, the way that Jadi looked at him, even, I think. So I made a guess, and I think I was right."

"So that's what Trindade teaches you, along with the nets," Stinne said. She set the empty glass on the floorplates at her feet, leaned back so that her head rested against the curve of the wall. Unsupported, her back bowed, and she straightened almost at once.

Ista nodded. "It's part of what hypothecaries do." It was the part she wasn't sure she liked, the part she wasn't sure she trusted—but that was another thing she didn't like to think about, any more than the ways that she didn't fit in, and the cost of getting herself entered into the computers. "It's part of the job."

Stinne shook her head. "It's complicated, all right." She leaned sideways to look at the media box, checking the time that glowed perpetually above the input pad. "Oh, damn, I've got to go."

Ista looked too—almost shift-end, definitely time for Stinne to be heading back upstation to the family dinner so no one would ask where she'd been—and set her beer down on the table. "You want me to walk you to the elevator?"

"No, that's OK, but thanks." Stinne pushed herself gracelessly to her feet, scrabbling for the carrysack she had dropped by the bed. She shook her head again as she slung it over her shoulder. "I just wish—"

She broke off, shaking her head again, and Ista nodded. "I'll walk you anyway."

The next morning was Ista's day for Trindade, and she rode the elevator upstation along with the second morning shift. That shift was for the data workers rather than production or processing-line workers, and by the time the car reached the second plaza stop, just above the Free Market, the space was filled to capacity. They were mostly Company hires, new employees rather than Union folk or Travellers, and as always she felt out of place in her braids and clattering jewelry. Normally, she walked, or took the secondary elevators and spirals, so that she stayed in familiar, friendly territory for as long as possible, but she'd gotten up late, and then Barabell had needed help with the breakfast crowd, so that she'd been left with no alternative. Trindade said that she should enjoy being the only Traveller, enjoy being what she was, but Ista was too conscious of the looks, some sidelong, some openly curious, to be comfortable. She knew what they saw—a plain, brown-skinned girl, more Union than Traveller in her looks, her hundred tiny braids weighted with brass beads that matched her dozen bracelets and the embroidery on her dark red trapata—knew, too, that they smelled the unfamiliar musk of the Traveller and Union quarters on her skin and hair, and knew how foreign she must seem. The Company kids had made that clear enough, when she'd still been in school.

The doors opened at last on the Midway plaza and she shouldered her way out past the dataclerks and assay technicians along with half a dozen people in the gaudy jackets of casino workers.

Trindade's door was unlit, unlike the ecumenicon beside it, but opened to Ista's touch. The monitors were all lit, the fractal mandala hopping from one screen to the next, and by its light Ista could see the worktable set up for a client reading. The cables and links were ready, the brainbox slung from the underside like a goiter, but Trindade herself was nowhere in sight.

"Ramary?"

"Out back."

Out back was strictly private—Ista thought the older woman might live there, but Trindade discouraged that kind of question. She let her carrysack slip off her shoulder, automatically rearranging the drape of the trapata, and settled herself to wait. She could hear snatches of music from the ecumenicon—the owner, Sheara Draco, or one of his customers sampling tapes, Nuevo-christian from the sound of them—painfully out of synch with the movement of the mandala. Then the inner door slid open, and Trindade appeared, settling her draperies with an impatient twitch of her shoulders. As always, she wore what Ista still thought of as full festival regalia, a length of gold-spangled silk gauze wrapped around her hips to form an ankle-length skirt, a tight-fitting brocade jacket with sleeves that extended almost to the base of her thumbs, and a square neck that revealed a dozen or more gold chains, bright against her skin. Another length of gold-shot gauze, this one a darker green than her skirt, fell from a kind of mesh cap that was woven into her black hair. She was not as dark as Ista—what the Union called Colored—and her eyes were slightly slanted, caught in a web of fine lines. Ista had no idea how old she was, and didn't even dare ask Kelly2.

"I've got something for you," Trindade said, and flipped a palm-sized rectangle of plastic onto the work table. It landed with an unexpectedly solid-sounding clack, and something sparked in its depths, throwing a brilliant blue light across the tabletop. Ista took it carefully, not daring to hope it might be what she thought it was, and turned the image to face her.

"A magic book?" She had never seen one, but, like everyone else on the Agglomeration, she had heard about them. They came from the Territories, and were dependent on the Territories' wild programs to run efficiently, but the tiny slabs of mimetic plastic could contain and display the most complex dimensional novels. Already, a menu was blinking impatiently in the lower third of the picture, icons offering her the choice of browsing, reading, several levels of help and cross-references, as well as options she didn't recognize; above that, a stern, white-robed figure held scales against a vivid blue background that might have been sea or sky. It looked like the statues of Justice that Kelly2 had shown her, pictures of the statues that stood in front of the court buildings on Kelly2's homeworld, except that this one had no blindfold and her free hand, the one that didn't hold the scales, carried a rounded shape that looked a little like a gravestone. The text above it was in familiar letters, but no language she knew.

"That's right," Trindade said. "It's a dedicated text, mind you, but that's Idunnan work, the best there is for illuminated text."

Ista touched the menu carefully—the controls were cool under her hand, without the usual tangible cues you found on Federal-standard displays—activated the full-link package, and touched a second control to open the text itself. The white-robed figure faded, was replaced by a page of multicolored lettering. A strip menu at the side of the screen, as ornate—as beautiful, Ista corrected herself—as the text itself, offered explanations and more options. She triggered the help function, and was rewarded with a set of small-print notes and a choice of three languages. She picked Fed/Stan, and studied the results: the red text was primary argument; blue, green, and gold were secondary theses; words in demi-capitals were capable of fuller explication, words in the odd, feathery type were positive and led to more discussion, and words in the darker, blocky type were negative, explained, but to be approached with caution. There was one on the page displayed, and she touched it curiously. The screen swam for an instant, reformed on a plain white page printed in the same blocky, slightly off-putting type. Everything about it was intended to discourage one from reading it, she realized, and looked up to see Trindade smiling.

"Try one of the pretty ones."

Ista flipped ahead until she found a string of words in the feathery type, and touched it. The screen that appeared was bright with colors, and tiny, delicately drawn figures, animals and people and things Ista didn't recognize, danced in a border of stylized leaves. She ran her finger over the help menu, picked up the iconic magnifier, and positioned it over several of the dancing shapes. In its circle, the people—no, not people, she realized, but pale-furred, sharp-eared animals in human clothing—sprang abruptly to life. An animal in knee-length trousers tapped an animal in skirts—male and female? Ista guessed—with a bright blue flower, and the two spun into a brief, silly dance, watched benevolently by a taller animal in long black robes. She shifted the magnifier, brought another pair to life—musicians, this time, and then a trio of women who seemed to be singing while a fluffy-tailed creature chased a striped ball—and found herself smiling. She looked up then, and saw Trindade matching her smile. Or not matching: there was a knowing quality to the hypothecary's expression that made Ista suddenly embarrassed.

"It's beautiful," she said, half defensive, half defiant, and Trindade's smile twisted further out of true.

"It's a Wisdom text, that's how I could afford it."

"Wisdom text?" Ista repeated.

"Idun's a theocracy," Trindade said, impatiently. "Church of Supreme Wisdom, the Wise Being, something like that. But the point is, it's propaganda. I didn't get it for you for the content."

Ista looked back at the picture in her hands, torn between amazed delight—Trindade had bought this for her?—and disappointment at what lay beneath the unknown language. Even knowing the intent, the drawings were still charming, still raised a smile. Trindade looked over her shoulder. "The ones in black are theologicians. Religious cops." She straightened before Ista could respond. "But, like I said, I didn't get it for you for the content."

Ista sighed, touching the control strip again to return the book to its top page, and set it reluctantly on the table. Trindade smile again, gestured for Ista to sit, and seated herself opposite the girl.

"Right, then. You should be asking what I did get it for."

"So what did you get it for me for?" Ista repeated, obediently. The book lay on the table between them, the image at an oblique angle, still glowing blue.

"What do you think?"

Ista looked down at her hands, torn between irritation and enjoyment of the challenge. "Well, it's either for the programs or the structure." She paused, but Trindade's expression gave nothing away. "Probably the structure."

Trindade nodded. "Very good. And why not the programs?"

Ista picked up the book again, turned it to confirm the absence of an input slot. "Because you said it was a dedicated text, and that means we—I—couldn't get at the workings without I don't know what, tearing it apart, I guess. And besides, you couldn't sell these programs without the cops being down on you right away."

Trindade nodded again. "Right on both counts. Though if Jenna ever gets out of Audumla and you end up in the Territories, you should be sure and have a look at the open-text systems. But it's the structure I want you to look at. Touch the two icons at the bottom right of the screen."

Ista did as she was told, and a tiny window opened in the text, as though she had slid back a portal into the book's programming. No, she realized almost at once, not the programming per se, but the way the text had been organized. All the links were laid out in complex schematic, and she reached for her monocular.

"No," Trindade said, and Ista stopped instantly. "You don't need that. Use your eyes and your own good brain."

"But—"

"Machines won't do everything for you—they can't. Use your eyes."

Ista bit back her automatic protest—she could see better through the monocular's lens, could learn a lot more from its virtual dissection, than she could just by staring at the unchanging pattern, but she had learned early on that Trindade could be remarkably deaf when she wanted to be. And she, Ista, wanted the book. She set her mouth, and stared into the multicolored window.

Some of the structures were obvious—the thick white lines that represented the program's skeleton, blue dots that were almost certainly node-links for the search program—but most were not, were merely tangles of multicolored light. The monocular would highlight each color in turn, or all related colors, let her see the substructures that way, and she began doggedly to trace each of the lines of light. Red seemed to be a prominent subroutine—red had been the color for the primary argument, she remembered suddenly, and flipped back to the first screen to trigger that first image. The pattern looked nothing like the red lines in the schematic. She suppressed a sigh, and looked up to see Trindade shaking her head.

"Try to see it whole, not in pieces. That's the trouble with the monoculars, they teach you to build up an impression, not to see it all together." She looked past Ista to the nearest monitor, snapped her fingers to call up a time display. "Anyway, you can work on it later. I have a client scheduled, and I want you to listen."

Ista shut down the book, the blue light winking out under her fingers, and slipped it into the most secure pocket of her tunic. "Is it expecting me?"

"She knows I'm training an apprentice," Trindade answered. She snapped her fingers again, and the time disappeared, was replaced by a second, smaller, mandala. "Bring out the big oracle, I think I'm going to want that."

Ista nodded, and stooped to release the latch of the concealed storage bins at the base of the wall. The narrow space was filled to capacity and beyond, mostly with datablocks that were wedged in at every possible angle, but also with the tools of Trindade's trade, various monoculars, a heavy, stand-mounted stereocular, and finally, beneath all the rest, the flat, twenty-five-centimeter-wide disk of the larger oracle. She shoved the rest of the equipment back into its place, and carried the oracle over to the worktable. Trindade had already lifted the covers, exposing the contact points, and Ista set the machine down carefully, turning it until it locked into place. A string of lights, then symbols, flashed beneath the oracle's dull surface as its systems meshed with Trindade's house net and then with the invisible world beyond. Then those lights disappeared, but Ista could feel the faint vibrations in her fingertips, the machine quiescent but waiting.

"She drinks green tea," Trindade said briskly, "which should be ready now, and she hates tea cakes, so don't offer them—the plates are in the alcove." She glanced down at the oracle, then at something only she could see in the media wall's shifting displays. "Her name is Jetton Mirari, she's low-Service by birth, works in the Corporate infonet. Not high-status, though, she's only an entry monitor. She's Company born, and she's been on Audumla for eight years—second contract, two years to go before it's up."

"Family?" Ista asked, and suppressed the familiar pain at asking. Trindade swore that the more one knew about a client, the better one could help them.

Trindade gave her an approving nod. "None on the station. Her parents and blood-kin of that generation are on the Hanse, along with a scattering of cousins. She has no siblings. She had a contract-partner for the first five years she was here, but he left to go back to the Hanse and the main office. She has a few pillow-friends, nothing more serious than that." She smiled suddenly. "And I can't tell, yet, whether the problem is personal or professional, so see what you think, eh?"

"I will."

A light flickered in the media wall, the double-flash that meant an approaching customer, and Ista bit off the rest of what she might have said. Trindade smiled and settled herself in front of the oracle, resting her hands on the table's controls.

"Miana Trindade." The voice from the doorway was polite but cool, not quite wary.

"Technician Jetton." Trindade did not move for a moment, then lifted a hand from the oracle's control pads to gesture gracefully, first toward the client's chair, and then at Ista. "Please, make yourself comfortable. My apprentice will bring tea."

Ista moved at the cue, schooling herself to the slow deliberate movements that looked so impressive in the shop's dim light. Nearly everyone, but most especially citizens, thought Travellers were uncanny, and it was foolish, or so Trindade said, to give up any advantage. The tea and plates, tea cakes for Trindade, thin demi-sandwiches for Jetton, were waiting in the alcove as Trindade had promised, along with the good client-cups. Ista filled two of the tall porcelain cylinders, brought them and the pot back to the table. Jetton accepted hers with a distracted air, setting it aside after only the smallest sip for manners' sake, but seemed to start slightly when Ista set the plate at her elbow. Ista hid her own grin and stepped deferentially back into the light of the media wall at Trindade's left hand.

"So," Trindade said. "You have a problem, then, Technician."

Jetton seemed almost glad to dispense with the social amenities, Ista decided. She let her eyes slide sideways, to Trindade's face highlighted by the media wall, but the older woman's expression remained the same, her eyes lowered to look down at the oracle's shifting patterns. It was still quiescent, not yet fully open to the invisible, but few citizens could read the modified VALMUL chromacodes that Trindade used. And the ones that could, Ista thought, didn't hire hypothecaries. Jetton leaned forward then, planting both elbows on the table.

"Yes, I have a problem. I'm—well, I expect you know what I am."

"Technician third-grade, night-shift entry monitor and general-access officer. What the Territories call a game warden," Trindade answered without raising her eyes from the oracle. She smiled then. "It's in the public record."

"Just so." Jetton hesitated for an instant. "As you said, in the Territories I'd be a game warden, but that's not what I'm here about. Or not directly. I've found something in my system—my home system—that I didn't put there. I'm pretty sure it's wild, and I'm willing to pay for you to identify and neutralize it."

Trindade made a soft sound between her teeth and leaned back from the oracle. "Do you have a copy?"

Jetton reached into the pocket of her jacket, and produced a datablock. Trindade left it sitting on the worktable.

"You don't seem interested in its source—where it came from."

"I think I know that already," Jetton said, her voice grim, and Ista saw Trindade's eyebrows lift. For a moment, she thought the hypothecary would pursue the question, but then Trindade shrugged.

"Suit yourself. Describe it, this—is it flora, fauna?"

"Flora, I think. But it is complex." Jetton frowned. "You have a copy there, I was able to net it."

"I'd rather hear about it first," Trindade said. "What does it do?"

Jetton took a deep breath. "I don't know. I never really saw it active, at least not a full sightline. It looks like a leptic matrix, but the coat's wrong for that. That's part of what I need to know, what it was doing in my system."

Trindade nodded, and reached for the datablock. "Very well. I'll take a look at this, and then I'll set the price. Is that agreeable?"

"That's fine," Jetton answered, and Trindade pulled loose a cable, plugged it into a closed connector and then fitted the block to the reader. The colors changed in the oracle's domed display, and Ista rocked forward, trying to see over Trindade's shoulder. She could just make out a pale purple shape, a distorted rhomboid more like a jolly-roger than any floral program she'd ever seen. She curbed the impulse to step forward, waiting until she was invited, and was rewarded by Trindade's sudden glance.

"So, Ista. What do you think?"

Ista leaned over the taller woman's shoulder, her hands clasped respectfully behind her back. The hammal—it was definitely faunal, not floral at all, despite the centaury-like spicules that formed a lopsided cross along its back—did look a lot like a jolly-roger, but the color was wrong, and so were the internal shapes, just visible through the translucent sides. Jolly-rogers were usually near-black, and their simple subroutines glowed like white bone under the surface. "Interesting," she said, and watched Trindade's hands to see if she wanted more.

"Indeed," Trindade said, and looked back at Jetton. "What makes you say it's floral, Technician?"

"I know what the shape looks like," Jetton said, with some asperity, "but, damn it, it doesn't move. If it's a hammal, it's fixed, and by definition a static hammal is flora."

Trindade gave a faint smile. "That definition has never been adequate—but I won't argue." She touched her controls again, closing the VALMUL lens's window into the datablock, and the image vanished, replaced by the fractal swirl of a holding pattern. "I can dissect this, tell you what it was bred to do, and I can find a predator that will control it, hunt it out of your system, if you want to go that far."

"Yes." Jetton took another deep breath. "What will it cost me?"

"To analyze it, forty hours of Company time. To find, spay, and modify a hunter, 150 hours."

"I don't have that much time to my credit," Jetton said. "My limit is thirty hours."

"I don't bargain," Trindade said, and her voice was suddenly distant, as though she'd drawn a veil between herself and the others. "My price is fair, and not negotiable."

Jetton shook her head, less denial than frustration. "I'm not bargaining, I don't have that much time myself—" She broke off, tried again. "I can give you the equivalent in general-use credits, you can buy the time yourself out of the public pool."

"Which is hardly large enough to supply me," Trindade answered. "There's rarely more than a thousand hours available, first come, first served, to be split among all of us who aren't of the Company."

"Thirty hours direct time," Jetton said, "and the rest in GUC. Please."

Trindade considered for a moment, then, slowly, nodded. "All right. Thirty hours, plus two-hundred-fifty GUC."

Jetton caught her breath, but nodded. Ista, who had seen the process before, suppressed a sigh of her own. It never seemed quite right to her that Trindade should be able to get so much of what she wanted simply by assuming she was indispensable. Of course, she didn't try it with the Union folk who consulted her, or with fellow Travellers, but it still didn't seem entirely fair. Jetton was already reaching into her pocket again, brought out her pocketbook and was entering the codes that transferred the time credits to Trindade's account. Trindade nodded gracious acceptance.

"And the balance when I bring you the hunter. Very well. You'll hear from me in about a week."

"Thank you," Jetton said, accepting the dismissal, and rose to her feet. "I'll be waiting."

Trindade waited until the door had closed behind her, and then shook her head. "Fool. A technician of her rank should be ashamed of not knowing this configuration."

Ista hesitated. In this mood, there was no pleasing Trindade—but, Ista thought, she might still answer a direct question. "I didn't recognize it—I mean, it's out of a jolly-roger, but I don't know this specifically."

Trindade looked at her, frowning a little, as though she'd forgotten the girl's presence. "What did you make of it?"

Ista closed her eyes, trying to bring back the image. "Well, a jolly-roger's a pure indiciphage, and a strong one, so someone was after her data—private data, since it was in her home system. But I don't understand why you'd cross it with a centaury—or why the gatekeepers let it in the first place."

Trindade regarded her for a moment, then nodded, and pushed the plate of cakes toward her. "Probably a chameleon routine in it somewhere. How does a centaury feed?"

"By halation," Ista answered, automatically, and took a cake. "Like the vetch." She bit into it, sweet and crumbly on the tongue, a delicacy she didn't often get, and added, indistinctly, "Which is a really weird crossbreed with an indiciphage."

"Go on."

Ista took a second cake and ate it, buying time. Halation was a way of immobilizing a prey hammal, exuding a haze of data that clogged the sensory intakes until the centaury's slow pseudopods could seize and digest the captive hammal. But that would almost certainly destroy the raw data on which an indiciphage fed—or would it? she wondered suddenly. It would certainly scramble it, but it wouldn't necessarily render it down below the indiciphage's usable minimum complexity. And, as a side effect, it would make any data not absorbed by, and incorporated into, the jolly-roger unreadable, probably completely unrecoverable by any normal means. "So would the point be to keep her from reading something? From receiving some data?"

Trindade nodded, approving this time. "Which is interesting, don't you think? And it's also interesting that this variant is not a natural hybrid. It's a hacker's hammal, not wild at all."

"Do you think it could be hackers?" Ista asked. For an instant, she had a vision of herself, herself and Trindade, rooting out a plot against the Company, and grateful Management rewarding her with papers, genuine citizen ID, maybe even a scholarship to follow Stinne offstation when she went.

"Not likely," Trindade answered. "You heard Jetton, she knows who put it in her system. It's either personal—and that's my bet—or Company politics, and neither of those are our business."

Ista sighed, the vision blasted. "So what are we going to do?"

"I—" Trindade emphasized the word "—am going to assess the reproductive structure of this hammal she's brought us. You are going to find me a black medusa, for a start."

Ista moved to the main console, ran her hands over the control surfaces to wake the machine, and then touched virtual buttons to open the sealed and buffered spaces where

Trindade kept the hammals that hosted her VALMUL lenses. She found the one she wanted almost at once—the same beetle she had used before—and called it out of the buffered storage, then slaved her lens to its point of view. A display circle opened in the oracle, and the controls shifted under her hands, became a ring of warmth and rough textures around the display space. She glanced back, wanting to ask which node she was to use, but Trindade was already bent over the datablock that contained the jolly-roger.

That meant it was her own choice, and she touched keys to select the more direct access of the frontage, bypassing the Company's controlled habitats, but not exposing Trindade's private volumes to the genuine dangers of the wildnet. It was said that there were stations, even entire sealed worlds, where the invisible world did not yet exist, places settled after the Crash and rigorously defended, but the Agglomeration had never been one of those. Oh, the Patrol at Mayhew and then Company Customs screened incoming ships for wild programs, but those checks were usually perfunctory, routine, and the hardier programs slipped through unchecked. And it was probably just as well, she thought, as the beetle slipped through the gateway into the brown plane of the frontage. The wild programs, the wildnet, kept the entire invisible world viable; the Company's nets—the Federation's nets—survived by keeping the delicate balance between utility and danger.

Icons solidified out of the fog, the familiar neon-edged landmarks of the frontage, and she shifted her hands on the controls, turning the lens/host toward the nearest gateway. The twin columns, vivid blue twined with shapes like green and gold snakes, towered above the pallid netscape, the only icon visible for virtual meters. The string compass's display was equally empty, and she frowned at that, looking back at Trindade. "This is kind of weird," she said aloud, and didn't know if she hoped the hypothecary heard.

"What is?" Trindade touched a final keysequence, and pushed herself away from the oracle, came to look over Ista's shoulder.

"This." Ista nodded at the image in her screen, the empty

display circle. "I've never seen the frontage like this."

"That is odd." Trindade frowned, and adjusted the controls, lifting the beetle and its point-of-view to system-height, so that she seemed to look down on the frontage from a point half a dozen virtual meters above its surface referent. She swung the lens in a slow circle, scanning the area around her, then released the controls to enter a set of query-codes. Unsupported, the beetle began to fall slowly toward the surface, and Ista reached in hastily to check its descent. In the distance, beyond the gateway icon, she thought she could just make out the familiar knobby sticks of a stand of joint grass, but she couldn't be sure.

"It seems all right," Trindade said at last, but she was still frowning. "I want you to be careful, though. This is one of the warning signs."

Ista barely stopped herself from rolling her eyes, controlling her expression only with an effort. For Trindade, every anomaly was a potential warning sign, a signal that a demogorgon was finally loose in the system, and the invisible world was coming to an end.

"*An emptiness, it will fill it,*" Trindade quoted, "*and the worms and the very dirt will rise in its service.* We can't risk the demogorgon, Ista. If you see anything at all out of the ordinary, I want you back here. It must never see the structure of a lens."

"Why not?" Ista would have taken the words back if she could, but to her relief Trindade took the question at face value.

"Because the demogorgon is precursor AI, and if it absorbed that structure, came to understand the VALMUL architecture, it could rewrite not just the wildnet, but the true world as well."

Ista stared at her for a moment, unable quite to believe what she'd heard. Everyone knew the basics about the demogorgon: it was, as Trindade had said, the hammal that was theoretically predicted to appear just before true artificial intelligence; the most common theory held that, once it appeared, it would grow by absorbing all other programs until it filled its host net. Then the main theories diverged: either it would continue to grow, overrunning the local gateways and absorbing the floral and faunal programs of the neighboring nets, and potentially all of the programs in the invisible world, or—if the containments held—it would be forced to redefine itself, evolve toward true intelligence, in order to survive. In either case, the pressure on the local nets would be tremendous, and a second Crash was almost certain once the demogorgon was established. But for it to affect the visible world . . . "Do you really think it could?" she asked, and Trindade rounded on her.

"Don't underestimate these programs. Just because our worlds only intersect at the edges, don't think ours is the better—don't be so sure ours is real. We have the upper hand now, but we can't afford to take chances." She beckoned the younger woman closer, and Ista moved in reluctantly, until she could feel Trindade's breath on her cheek.

"The demogorgon is vulnerable," the hypothecary said, her voice barely above a whisper. "I want you to know this and remember it—do you understand?" Her ringed hand shot out, caught Ista by the shoulder, shook her gently. "Do you?"

"Yes." Ista winced, but Trindade didn't loosen her grip.

"The demogorgon is vulnerable at its core but that's only because nothing is invulnerable. Hammals and flora and people, they all die, there's a death gene that lies in all of us to make sure of it. And the demogorgon's born of weakness, there's a balance in these things. If you can cross a carrier program—a crabbit's best—with something like a kebbick, or a fairweather, any of the altoid fauna—as long as the central neume is cataletic, then the demogorgon will die."

Ista nodded, but knew her disbelief showed in her eyes.

Trindade shook her again. "This is important, do you understand? You have to remember this."

"I will."

"Then repeat it."

"A cataletic neume will trigger the death gene," Ista said, obediently, and made an effort to keep the skepticism out of her voice. "And it can be delivered by a carrier—a crabbit would be best."

Trindade released her, but shook her head. "You're too

damn young sometimes. Right, get me my medusa, we'll get on with this job, at least." She turned away without waiting for an answer.

It's not my fault I'm young. Ista bit back her words, took a deep breath to control her anger. *And it's not fair for you to act like this, either. The demogorgon—it's a theory, not a fact, a what-if that everyone is doing everything they can to avoid.* There was no point in telling herself this, either, and she made herself focus on the image in the screen.

The beetle had stopped obediently at the edge of the next gateway, and password demands flashed on her screen. She typed them in, one after the other—Trindade was using the audio sensors—and beads of light spiralled up the backs of the watching netminders. She touched the controls, urging the beetle forward, and it slipped easily between the pillars into the warm brown of the wildnet. After the emptiness of the frontage, the wildnet itself was almost startlingly crowded. Another reef of parqueter, an old, well-established colony by the look of it, jutted above the plane to the left of her point-of-view, and a flock of chogsets swarmed about its base, feeding on its leavings and its dead. One of them swung toward the beetle, but the beetle snapped at it, and it skittered back into the protection of the reef.

She knew this section of the wildnet fairly well—it was one of the more stable portions, heavily harvested by humans and so prone to a fairly stereotyped selection of programs. The other, outer sections where she had seen the mandaleon were less travelled, and so tended to breed useless and actively dangerous programs like reapers and long-liners, but with any luck, she thought, she wouldn't have to go that far afield to find a medusa. She had seen a colony two days before, but that was a long time, even for floral programs. Still, it had been a large colony; at the very least, its site would make a logical starting point.

She glanced down at her string-compass, pressed its controls to set her starting point, and touched a second control to nudge the beetle forward again, giving the reef a wide berth. A godwit strode past, heavy ball-body bobbing on spindly

legs, ignoring the chogsets that scurried at its ankles. One of
them darted toward her, then shied at the sight of the beetle
and blundered into a cluster of single-line needles. The nearest hair-thin strand seemed to unroll, becoming a tube, while
the other needles lost their rigidity and fell in coils on the
chogset: not needles at all, Ista thought, but a flageolet. The
tube's mouth widened into a bell, and bent in a graceful curve,
engulfing the chogset. A few fragments of code—the lens
translated them to pale grey powder, flakes of ash the size of
her hand—drifted free, and another chogset appeared to retrieve them, keeping its distance from the engorged flageolet.
Ista looked away—she had never much liked seeing hammals
destroyed—and swung the beetle toward the place where she
had last seen the medusa.

The original colony was no longer intact, just a skeletal tat-
ter, a wedge of black lace jutting from the brown floor, and a
dwarf-angler crouched at its base, almost invisible against the
dark colors. However, a dozen apparent meters further along
the same line, a daughter colony had sprung up, five central
spires, each with its squirming crown of tendrils, and perhaps
fifteen or twenty smaller medusae at their base. Ista brought
the beetle to a stop beside it, a careful meter further than she
thought its tendrils could reach, and touched a secondary
panel, calling up Trindade's collection routines. She selected
the one Trindade called "Bertha" and saw the host extrude a
pair of arms, each one hardening to silver as it grew. One flattened to a wedge, the other divided to form a clumsy hand,
and she touched her controls again to slip the wedge behind
the smallest of the medusae. Its tendrils stiffened, and then collapsed, and for a panicked instant she thought she'd killed it.
Then training took over, and she made herself find the familiar signs that showed the program was still fully viable. The
color was good, showing none of the drain that usually indicated damage, and the icon felt springy when she used
Bertha's other hand to pry it free from the parent. She levered
it carefully into the collection circle, and touched a second
control to return it to Trindade's sealed holding tank. The display went white for a long moment as the transmission over-

rode her controls, and finally cleared. She swung the beetle in a quick circle, making sure nothing had crept up on it while her link was blind, and then checked her string-compass, turning the lens/host until she was retracing her path to the gateway.

"Nice work," Trindade said, from the worktable. Ista looked up, as always a little startled to be so suddenly back in the real world, and saw the hypothecary already examining the retrieved program.

"Thanks," she said, and Trindade nodded.

"Get the lens squared away, and you can watch while I graft the new program."

Ista hid a sigh, but nodded. Grafting was probably the least favorite part of her training, not least because the floral programs and hammals seemed to be particularly alive during it. She knew that they were no more than bits of codes, instruction sets with no visible existence beyond the icons imposed on them by the VALMUL architecture, but it was hard, when you spent most of your life thinking of them as real, to suddenly switch away from that again. She touched controls to avoid a chevrotain that briefly blocked her path. This squeamishness was something she would have to conquer if she wanted to be a hypothecary, and being a hypothecary was her best chance of becoming real herself.

■ **4** ■

UNION LOCALS WERE not common on Bestla, but they were present. Most of them had Traveller clients as well, and all of them, like Union locals everywhere, were bar and restaurant, hiring hall and club, and the first, last, and best place to meet one's own kind. There were four of them in Port Montas, all of them along President Street, which formed one of the boundaries of the spaceport. Behind the buildings on the northwest side of the street, the thick fused-stone damping wall rose twenty meters into the air, blocking sunlight and breezes in the good seasons, and keeping the rents low. In the fall and winter, its shadow fell across the buildings on the southern side of the street, and knocked their rents down as well. That was part of why the Union folk congregated there—natural light wasn't a particular priority to people who spent their lives plugged in to one machine or another, who counted time in shifts and cycles instead of hours—and partly it was the proximity to the port itself, so that crews on eighteen-hour stopovers could take their break, have a little fun, and still get back aboard in time to sleep off their hangovers. Of the few citizens who travelled President Street, most of them were Transport, and so recognized the broad divisions between the bars. Aurore's was for the music, the heavy droning industrial chant that was the background to Union life; it had a real dance floor, and even welcomed citizens, as long as they came to dance. The Five Jets, at the northeastern end of the street where it joined Star Avenue, was for the STL and FTL crews, and had as many high-Transport customers, on any given night, as it did Union. Robotica, at the opposite end of the street, was for the line workers and factory-farm crews; low-Transport was tolerated but hardly welcomed. The drivers and pilots preferred to congregate at the Fevers, next door, and the two groups fought savagely now and then in the shared garage. A few times, those fights had spilled over into the lay-over lot below the flyway, where the transcontinental haulers pulled up to wait to make their port deliveries, and the Port and Vagabond Patrols had barely managed to contain the fighting. Ilian's, which lay close to the midpoint of the street where Sixth Street came to an end, was tucked under the shoulder of the damping wall, a close and private place that seemed to do a little of everything. There was dancing three nights a week, and a bigscreen playing most of the rest of the time; the food and the drink were both good, if not always cheap, but the telecom booths always worked, and local data access was free. Line crews came there along with reform Travellers and even a few citizens from Transport, high and low together. Rangsey kept it as his Union address, something he had not told Tarasov, though he had brought him there a few times to test the waters. He could even get lunch there without falling too far outside ExA's schedule, if he took the runabout and the traffic was light, and found himself coming there more and more, though what he was trying to find, or lose, he could not have said.

He tilted his chair back until his shoulders rested against the wall behind him, stared idly at the bigscreen across the room. In its milky surface, musicians swayed and postured, but the words were indistinct, only the complex rhythm carrying clearly, as much through the walls as through the air. The music was Union, as were the musicians; the stage lights glittered from the silver cables that linked each one to their controllers and the banked sound modules that rose behind them. It was not a sound he cared much about, either liked or disliked, but it was familiar, the same pulsing music that had been a constant background for as long as he could remember, and at the moment he needed that reassurance. He had ordered the *pilau* for the same reason, and the thick, greasy bread: it was familiar from childhood, made no demands of taste or pronunciation, left his mind free for other things. Like his cross-cousin's offer: he made a face at the memory, and reached for his beer, draining dregs that were mostly foam. The beer was strictly against departmental policy, especially in the middle of the work day, but he had trouble bringing himself to care. Peral9 Alvere was looking for a tech-two, part of a team that would be opening up a micro-factory on Philos; if he, Rangsey, took the job, he would be well positioned to become one of the Union elite, the technicians who tested and helped design the systems that the rest of the Union used. But if he took the job, he would have to leave Bestla, and Tarasov.

He lifted the beer glass again, realized it was empty, and set it aside with a grimace. Leaving Bestla—leaving External Affairs, the ultimately pointless attempts to help Union folk and Travellers caught in the web of Bestla's law and customs— would be a pleasure; leaving Tarasov wasn't as easy a decision. And there were other factors, too, of course. For one thing, it had been years since he'd worked a factory line. He would have to spend most of the flight to Philos linked to the various training modules, and even then it might be a few weeks before he could pull his own weight in the team. Peral9 had even said as much, but had also said he was willing to take the chance. It was the unsaid part that was the problem: Peral9's offer was also a way of ending Rangsey's problematic foreign partnership. Bad enough that he was gay, but at least relationships within the Union strengthened the family and clan, if not as permanently as a proper marriage; this partnership with Tarasov did nothing for the clan, and while it lasted he, Rangsey, was as good as useless to the rest of his kin. And that, Rangsey admitted silently, was the best reason of all not to take Peral9's offer. He wouldn't leave Tarasov like that, if he left at all, not with the tacit admission that Union and citizen could not, should not, mix. He owed Tarasov that much, whatever he decided. But this was still the best offer he was likely to get, if he wanted to go back to the Union.

The callbox in his pocket buzzed, a tingling vibration against his thigh. He ignored it: he was logged out on his official lunch break; no one had any genuine reason to come looking for him, so this had to be just the usual petty nonsense of ExA's bureaucracy, but the box kept buzzing, the vibrations rapidly becoming almost painful. He swore under his breath, dragged it out of his pocket, and keyed the receiver, wondering who at ExA would care enough to set their transmitter on permanent interrupt. The code that flashed back at him in the little screen made him swear again: not ExA, but Tarasov. He stared at the box with loathing, almost ready to abandon it before he answered, but touched the thumbpad to recall the message. It wasn't like Tarasov to use the callbox without good reason. The message appeared instantly in the narrow screen: NEED TO SEE YOU @ PRECINCT NOW. Rangsey's eyebrows rose at that, and he touched the thumbpad again, but there was no more. He stared at it for a long moment, considering the words and his own response, but then slowly pushed himself to his feet. If Tarasov was being this peremptory, the way things were between them, then something real was happening.

The telecom booths were at the back of the bar, behind the hanging screen. Rangsey skirted the dimly-lit tables, mostly empty now, between shifts, and ducked into the pool of relative quiet where the booths' baffles cut off most of the pounding music. A Traveller woman smiled at him from the first booth, the light from her screen reflecting off the wires in her braids, but then she cut the connection, and pushed past him into the main room. Rangsey stepped into the second booth, fed the machine his comcodes, and waited for the screen to light. It came to life reluctantly, and he keyed in the codes that would reach Tarasov at the Precinct house. To his surprise, the call went through without delay, and Tarasov looked out at him from the little screen.

"Good, I got you. Look, that SID woman, Macbeth, she wants to talk to you and me, right away. Can you come?"

Rangsey stared at him, the anger between them forgotten, replaced by the older grievance. "What the hell does she want? She kicked me off that case, I couldn't even find out what happened to the crew—"

"I don't know," Tarasov said. "I don't know anything except that she's been on DiChong's case and he's pissed as hell that you down-coded your box."

ExA was not going to be happy, then, either, Rangsey translated, which probably meant an official reprimand and the concomitant fifty taken out of his pay. "Shit," he said, and Tarasov shook his head impatiently.

"Look, you need to get here now. How long will it take you?"

"Give me fifteen minutes. Maybe less." Rangsey was already working his pocketbook, touching codes to pay his bill and signal the garage where he'd left his car.

"I can stall her that long," Tarasov said, grimly, and broke the connection.

Rangsey glared at the screen, deprived of his chance to answer, but put the anger aside and touched the necessary keys to pay for the call and shut down the system. He could deal with it, with Tarasov later; in the meantime, he had Macbeth— and the Union mine crew, he reminded himself—to worry about.

The menu box on his table was flashing green again, signalling that it had processed his payment, and a skinny adolescent girl had appeared from the kitchen to collect the dirty dishes. He pushed through the double doors into the cold hall and then out into the street, blinking at the light reflecting from the ice on the roofs of the buildings across the street. It was definitely warmer than it had been a few months ago: even though the sun had disappeared again behind the damping wall, the pools of ice-melt had not yet refrozen. Even on the northwest side, there was little more than a skin of ice on the shallow puddles. It was a hopeful sign, unaccountably so, and, as unaccountably, he felt his anger shift, focussing again on Macbeth. Tarasov had done the right thing, calling him. It was Macbeth who was the real problem, and the real danger, and he would do well to remember that.

The runabout was waiting at the mouth of the underground garage, engine purring at idle. He tipped the retriever, a tall girl in an oversized thermal suit, and climbed in, dragging the cable from its well beneath the steering mechanism. Even on the grid, linked to the city-system and its constant traffic monitors, it took him almost the full fifteen minutes to reach the Precinct Tower. He left the runabout in the autopark slot—unwillingly, but there was no time to park it himself—and hurried through the lobby to the nearest lift cylinder. Its doors were just closing, but he slipped in anyway, mumbling an apology. The people already in the car, half a dozen men and women in the sober blue-grey suits of low-Service citizens, moved aside reluctantly, and he was aware of the disapproving looks all the way up. They weren't surprised either when he left the car on the fifteenth floor, which the Technical Squad shared with a unit of the Vagabond Squad, and he was torn between annoyance and bleak amusement. Where else would Union folk be going, in a Precinct Tower, except to register with the police after some infraction?

Tarasov was lurking in the Squad's narrow public space, leaning against the inlaid wood of the barrier-desk, apparently deep in conversation with the woman on duty there. It wasn't quite a lobby, since the Technical Squad rarely had outside visitors, just a set of low chairs grouped around a dark-red-and-blue floorcloth, and a flowering jamsinth in a pot at the end of the desk. Tarasov pushed himself away from the desk as the lift doors opened and the woman reached into the desk's recesses, brought out a visitor's pass with a conspiratorial smile. Rangsey offered his own ID, but she waved it away.

"I'll check you in later. I gather someone's in a snit."

"Thanks," Rangsey said, genuinely startled by the goodwill—or else, he added silently, Macbeth had managed to alienate more people than he'd realized.

"She's right," Tarasov said, and held open the door to the main work area. "I wish I knew what the hell was going on."

"I was going to ask you that," Rangsey said.

Tarasov shook his head, his mouth still set in a grim line. "DiChong's being really close-mouthed about the whole thing, but I don't think he knows, either."

Rangsey lengthened his stride to keep up with the shorter man, aware of the people watching sidelong from their cubicles, the discreetly curious glances from the groups that gathered at the samovars. Macbeth had definitely made her presence felt: this was not the day he should have chosen to log himself out for lunch. "Is it just you and me she wants?"

"No—" Tarasov broke off as they reached the door of DiChong's office. It was a proper office, with full floor-to-ceiling walls, though there was a long glass panel to either side of the closed door. Through those windows, Rangsey caught a glimpse of Tarasov's partner Anjait4, and then Tarasov knocked and the door swung open under his hand. Rangsey suppressed a grimace of his own, seeing his own supervisor, Matle3 Siren, standing beside the better of the visitor's chairs, but followed Tarasov into the little room.

"Shut the door, please," the man behind the desk—presumably Tarasov's supervisor DiChong—said with ominous courtesy, and Rangsey did as he was told.

"Glad they finally tracked you down, Rangsey," Matle3 said, and Rangsey met his glare wide-eyed.

"The system cleared me to log out. I was on my way back to ExA when Sein buzzed me."

"And I'm very glad he was able to find you so quickly." Macbeth rose from the other visitor's chair, jamming her hands into the pockets of her trousers. She was still wearing karabels and a casual, multipocketed shirt under the light puffed-silk parka, Centrality styles, clothes that did nothing to disguise her status. The SID badge glinted from her collar, a pinlight at its center betraying the active recorder. "Now we can begin."

Rangsey saw Tarasov's eyes slide sideways, toward Anjait4, saw the slow, almost invisible shake of her head in answer, and felt suddenly very alone.

"I should let you know first that we've already cleared the formalities with your superiors," Macbeth said, smiling slightly, "so if you choose to accept there won't be any untoward delays. And I should begin by apologizing to you, Mian Rangsey, for being somewhat less than honest with you in regard to the NSMCo mine crew. SID has a very strong interest in this case."

No kidding, Rangsey thought, but kept his face expressionless, tilted his head in reserved acknowledgement. It was a citizen gesture, a Service gesture, and he thought he saw Macbeth's smile widen fractionally, as though she appreciated the act.

"Let me summarize for the rest of you," Macbeth went on. "About two weeks ago, an FTLship leaving the Audumla system picked up the crew of a mine that had abandoned its platform in the face of what they believed to be imminent attack. Because of the FTLship's schedule, they had no choice but to bring the mine crew with them to Bestla, where their complaint fell under our jurisdiction. As it happens, this is not the first such case we've seen, but it is the first where the victims, or potential victims, first survived, and second were outside NSMCo's immediate supervision, which meant that we— SID—had a chance to interview them thoroughly and in depth."

Interrogate them, more like, Rangsey thought, but said nothing. SID did have translators who understood the Union, and if they were serious about the case, then they would certainly have picked up on the fact that the crew's captain-chip had told them to run.

"Does this mean that SID is taking the case?" DiChong asked, warily, and Macbeth smiled again, this time with wry humor.

"In a manner of speaking. Audumla-system is corporate property, and those claims have been upheld in the courts. We can only act directly with the company's permission and through NSMCo's own security organs, which we would prefer to avoid, at least for the moment."

"Which means," Tarasov said, "you think they're involved."

Macbeth nodded. "It's a possibility we can't overlook, considering the number of accidents that have been reported and which the Union crew—and not just them, but Union folk in general who've worked in Audumla-system—believe actually to have been deliberate attacks. What we are proposing instead is a—less direct—method. We intend to send a handful of SID officers into the system ahead of the official investigative team, so that the official team will have additional information to work with." She looked from Tarasov to Rangsey, and back again. "We want you to volunteer."

Not on your life. Rangsey bit back the words, guessing they were pointless, and DiChong stirred behind his desk. "I recognize that SID's charter gives you the option of recruiting from other branches of Service; however, my charter gives me the option of saying no."

"Unless your people agree," Macbeth said.

"We're not field agents," Tarasov said. "Neither Ketty nor I, and Justin's a translator—External Affairs is support, not line. We're not exactly prime SID material."

"No," Macbeth agreed. "But you've got other advantages. Mian Rangsey is Union, both you and Sergeant Anjait4 are Transport by birth and training—I believe you actually worked the FTLships before you joined the Technical Squad."

"That was a long time ago," Tarasov began, but Macbeth went on as though he hadn't spoken.

"And you have a contract with Mian Rangsey, which gives

you both an entrée into Union circles in Audumla-system. And that's what I—what SID—don't have, and need most, if we're going to find out just what's going on there."

Rangsey frowned at that, his automatic protest suspended. That meant—implied, anyway—that she believed the mine crew, and believed the other Union stories, enough to mount an entire operation on that basis. Believing Union folk over the companies that employed them was not exactly common, and he found himself looking at her with renewed curiosity, wondering just what she was getting out of the investigation. "We can't pass as Union," he said aloud. "They're not going to sign on, and our personal contract wasn't written to make him family. Not to mention it doesn't cover Ketty. Unless someone from the mine crew could come with us, would be willing to claim us as kin?"

"No. They are very definitely not involved in this investigation," Macbeth said, and smiled. "They've made that clear."

"Then we're not going to pass as Union," Rangsey answered.

Macbeth nodded. "What would you suggest, then?"

"I haven't said I'd do it."

"If you were to agree, then. What would you suggest?"

It was a fairly gracious concession, Rangsey thought, considering he'd already betrayed his interest. He hesitated, running through the options—Transport, Union, Traveller—and DiChong cleared his throat.

"With all respect, Lieutenant, my people haven't agreed, or even shown interest. And I, for one, would like a good deal more information before I'd give them my blessing."

Macbeth nodded again. "I'm willing to flip you our files on the case, if you decide to volunteer, of course, but I can give you the salient points now. Basically, it's what I said before. This most recent incident is the latest in a string of at least twelve and as many as forty attacks on mine platforms contracted to NSMCo in the Audumla system. Exactly how many incidents have taken place is unclear because the mines are leased on a share basis to crews that are predominantly Union, and the company does not keep records of those workers. The story we have heard, quite consistently, is this: over the years, someone, or possibly something, has been attacking mine platforms, driving off or killing the crews, and looting the platforms. According to the Union crews, there are never any survivors if the crew remains with the mine, and that seems to be the case in the two incidents that we have been able to document." She looked at Rangsey. "As you so astutely noticed, Mian Rangsey, current versions of the captain-chip for Audumla-system take these rumors as truth and are configured to recommend flight if a mine is approached by an unidentified craft."

"Which also means that NSMCo's security hasn't recorded these as attacks," Tarasov said, "or SID would've been on it a long time ago."

"Right again," Macbeth said. "Their records show accidents, abandonments—a lot of them, costs generally docked from the crew's pay—problems with feral programs, and just two isolated attacks sixteen years ago. Except for those two, which NSMCo claims it dealt with and resolved, it comes down to Union folk against Company. Only this time I believe the Union."

Tarasov took a breath, as though he wanted to say something, then looked sideways at Rangsey and was silent.

"Audumla-system's very close to the Territories, if you count in jump points," Anjait4 said. "What makes you think it isn't some kind of program, something in the nets?"

"The platforms were looted, equipment physically removed," Macbeth answered. "If a wild program is involved, and we haven't ruled that out, it's being managed by people."

Anjait4 nodded, her expression suddenly remote, and Macbeth looked back at Rangsey. "Which brings me back to my question. Since you say you can't pass for Union, how would you do it? If you were to volunteer, of course."

"If I was volunteering," Rangsey said, slowly, and knew the words didn't do much more than postpone the inevitable, "I'd say we'd have to go as Travellers, reform Travellers. That's where a lot of Union folk end up if they can't meet the family obligations." He heard a snort of disbelief from Tarasov, refused to meet his eyes.

"That would work," Macbeth said, and grinned suddenly. "The ships I've been allotted for this project can be configured to pass as Traveller."

Ships. The single word, more than anything else she'd said, evoked unexpected possibilities, and Rangsey shoved his hands into his pockets, trying to deny his sudden eagerness. To be back in space again, to be off Bestla—with Tarasov, to have a reason to bring Tarasov with him—and be working for the Union, for once, against the Company, against all the companies. . . .

"I think," Tarasov said, and the note of controlled anger in his voice brought Rangsey back to reality, "we need a little time, and privacy, to talk this over. Is that possible, Leun?"

"Absolutely," DiChong answered, his own voice equally grim. "Take Conference One."

Matle3 rose to his feet. "In that case, Lieutenant, I don't think you'll need me any longer. My position is clear, it's up to Mian Rangsey what he chooses to do."

"Thank you for your cooperation, Supervisor," Macbeth answered, and looked at the others. "I would appreciate a decision as quickly as possible, however. There is a certain time pressure involved."

"And what happens if we say no?" Anjait4 asked.

Macbeth spread her hands. "You go back to work just like always. Subject to a security bond, of course."

Tarasov swore under his breath, but Rangsey nodded. It was pretty much what he'd expected—a standard contract that let SID conduct random checks and surveillance for as long as the operation lasted, to make sure that none of them revealed anything they knew about the job—and no worse, really, than the monthly inspections. He'd been under security bond before, twice as an adolescent, when his family had been working in a government-run shipyard, and then for six months after he'd proclaimed residence on Bestla.

"We'll talk," Anjait4 said, firmly, and Tarasov shoved the door open with unnecessary force.

Conference Room One was the smallest of the four meeting rooms, but probably the most comfortable Rangsey had ever been in. There was a samovar in the corner opposite the display cabinet, and a tray of snacks on the table beside the cups. Anjait4 crossed to it, fishing in her pocket for change, and came back with two bags of filled dough-sticks, saying, "Sorry, but I didn't get lunch, and I can't discuss this on an empty stomach."

She held out the first bag in silent offering, but Tarasov waved it away. "What the hell did you mean, saying we could go as Travellers?"

Rangsey looked at him, deliberately misunderstanding. "If we go, if we volunteer, there's no way we—specifically, you and Ketty—could pass as Union, and I don't have the status to bring you along with me. Transport's too structured, everybody'd know there was something weird about us if we said we were Transport, which leaves Travellers. And I'd rather be reform than orthodox."

"You want to do this," Tarasov said. "Shit, Jus."

"Yeah, I want to do it," Rangsey answered. "More precisely, I think it's a good thing to do."

"Good for who?" Tarasov asked. "I don't see how it's good for us—"

"Good for the folk in Audumla-system," Rangsey said. He could hear his voice rising, didn't fully care. "Damn it, Sein, people are getting killed there, my people, and finally the Patrol, SID, is listening, how the hell can I not go?"

"You were the one who's been going on for the last two weeks about her," Tarasov said, "how you couldn't trust her, how she was sure to be screwing your people. What the hell makes you think she's telling the truth this time?"

"I knew what the captain-chip said—" Rangsey began, and Anjait4 slapped the tabletop.

"All right, both of you, freeze it there." She put the bag of dough-sticks aside, shaking her head. "We don't have time for this now. The Lieutenant isn't going to wait forever."

"She's just going to have to," Tarasov muttered, but Rangsey could see his shoulders relax.

Anjait4 ignored him. "Do me a favor, Justin, switch on room security—from the display mainscreen, it's the fourth down and to the right."

Rangsey took a deep breath, but crossed to the open cabinet and began searching screens. It was the same basic system that they used in ExA, and he found the right commands quickly enough and engaged the system. When he turned back to the table, Anjait4 had seated herself, the bag of dough-sticks open again, and Tarasov was standing at the samovar.

"Want a cup?"

It was a truce-offering, and Rangsey nodded. "Yeah, thanks."

Tarasov brought the three cups, and the men sat as well, deliberately facing each other. Anjait4 looked from one to the other, and said, through a mouthful of her lunch, "You think this is for real, Justin?"

Rangsey nodded, took a careful swallow of the tea. This had to be the room the senior officers used for their meetings, he thought, the tea was better than usual. "The captain-chip told them to run," he repeated. "And that means it's real, and we ought to do something."

"SID ought to do something," Tarasov muttered. He went on, more loudly, "Look, we're not trained for undercover work—the Technical Squad handles machines and hammals, not people, and External Affairs isn't even a Line unit. I don't think it's smart—and I really resent the security bond."

"Oh, for God's sake," Rangsey said, and Anjait4 looked at him.

"I don't like it either, Justin. I don't want it on me."

"It's not that bad." In spite of himself, Rangsey heard his voice getting bitter. "I've been under bond twice, three times, you get used to it—about like the quarterly inspections, only maybe more often."

"Yeah, and you're so gracious about the quarterlies," Tarasov said.

"So it's a big deal for you—" Rangsey stopped himself then, but knew he didn't need to finish, that they could all guess—could all hear—what he'd been about to say. *So it's a big deal for you citizens and not for me.* He closed his eyes, shaking his head. "Sorry. But I don't think that's a reason not to take the job."

For an instant, he thought Tarasov was going to say something else, answer in the same tone, from the same argument of caste and class, but then the other man shook his head in turn, accepting the change of subject. "No. But there are some other reasons not to, too. Like I'd like to know what a Centrality cop—Centrality SID—is doing out here on the frontier."

"What it looks like is she's investigating this company," Rangsey said. "NSMCo. Maybe they've annoyed someone important."

"Or at least that's what she wants us to think," Anjait4 said.

She was right, too, but Rangsey shook away that knowledge. "I can't afford not to believe her," he said, simply, and Anjait4 looked away.

Tarasov said, "Even granting that, and I think I agree with you, there are some other problems. Like I said to Macbeth, it's been a long time since I worked an STLship. I was twenty-six when I joined the Squad."

Anjait4 nodded. "And I haven't been in space since I turned twenty, not even as a passenger. Frankly, I'd be worried about keeping up my end."

And of course they couldn't use the skillbases to compensate. Rangsey hesitated then, wondering for the first time what it would be like to go into space with people who weren't Union, who couldn't share the rapport of the linked chips, couldn't trade off chips and duties as the need arose. But the fact remained that this was the only chance he'd ever seen to get SID, the Patrol's elite investigative unit, working for the Union against one of its employers, and that was too good to pass up, no matter how much of the work he had to do himself, until Tarasov—and Anjait4—relearned their old skills. And it was also probably the only chance he would ever have to bring Tarasov into space with him. He said, groping for the right words, "It's—what's going on in Audumla-system isn't right. Union folk, people, are getting killed, and for once SID wants to investigate, is listening to them. I can't not do it, Sein. I'll go myself if I have to."

Tarasov looked at him for a long moment, then, slowly, sighed. "All right. I'll go along with you. But I'm not going to be a lot of use to you, Justin, I'm warning you now. Not for a while."

Rangsey shoved aside the echo of his own earlier decision, nodded.

Anjait4 shook her head. "Not me. And not because I don't think this is important, I know how important it is, I know Union folk don't get a break from the Patrol or the companies, it's not that. It's just—I don't want to go back into space. I haven't done it in so long I don't know if I'd be able to remember it, ever." She looked at Tarasov. "I'm sorry. But this is my home territory."

Tarasov nodded. "I'll miss you. And we could probably use your help. But I do understand."

Rangsey released a breath he hadn't realized he'd been holding. He would be going back into space, travelling again, and with Tarasov this time—and he'd be doing something for the Union again, something significant, not just the petty translations. "Then I guess it's settled?"

Tarasov nodded again. "But let's see if we can't get a few concessions out of her before we tell her."

"I'd be careful playing that kind of game with her," Anjait4 said, and Tarasov smiled.

"I didn't say I thought I could, just that we ought to try."

Going FTL was always a significant event, no matter how well-travelled a particular jump point was. First the FTL frame was retrieved, usually from an orbit around the nearest planet or planetary moon where the FTL crews had their base and company brokers were stationed—always on rotating duty—just in case there was an advantage to be gained. Then, powered up, all conduit and circuits tested and retested, it made its ponderous way toward the flaw in space/time that is the jump point. As it travelled—its STL generators were always weak, deliberately so—its crew, and particularly the calculators, studied the lines of flux around their point, compared it with the latest readings from their destination, and developed an approach vector. When that was locked in, the captain and calculators together set a rendezvous point, and broadcast it, either generally, the usual way, when the FTLship's internal space was sold piecemeal, first come, first served, to the STLships that always crowded the settled systems, or, more rarely, to the headquarters of a company that had hired it for its exclusive use. Companies only hired a full volume when they were moving their base or transporting something massive enough, and valuable enough in that mass, to be worth the extra expense, and a single-cargo FTLship attracted Patrol and scavenger attention in about equal measure. Usually, the Patrol got the upper hand, and filled the volume around the jump with drone Rovers and live-crew STLships, but every now and then the scavengers won and no ship appeared at the corresponding destination point.

But most of the time, the call was general, and then the communications channels were filled with queries and rate squabbles, and the FTLship's purser went hoarse quoting the standard tables and ISC regulations to one STLship after another. As the ships arrived, they were scanned, assessed, and tucked into the hardpoints of the FTLship's inner volume, their centers of mass aligned with the FTLship's massive spine. Roustabouts, mostly high-Transport but always with a few Union, hiring on usually to get from one system to the next, locked them into place with steel and forcebeams, jetting among the slow-moving masses like gnats over a pond. It wasn't quite as dangerous as it looked, the STLships' movements were as leisurely as they were inexorable, but roustabouts got high-hazard pay, and one or two a year were caught and crushed and sometimes killed.

Once the racks were filled—and it was rare for them not to fill; there were always Traveller craft to tuck into the corners and take the last places, even if the captain had to take less than the full fare for them—the calculators made their final numbers, confirming the alignment. The STL engines fired for the last time in this system, and the entire construction started its slow fall to the jump point. The STL engines shut down, leaving only the familiar softer sounds of life support and internal power, and the FTLship drifted ponderously into perfect resonance. And then the capacitors fired, ripping open the point, and the FTLship blinked in an instant, less than an instant, from one system to the next. Energy expended, the FTLship fell away from the point into the new system, continuing the vector it had begun lightyears away. Inside the hull, the roustabouts would already be at work, releasing the STLships in preplanned order to their eventual destinations, while the crew began the calculations that would let them do it all over again.

Most FTLships travelled through one point, between two systems, or at most through two, and three or maybe four star systems. It made practical sense that way: the calculators knew they could rely on the numbers they got from the most recent ship through the jump—often their own—to calculate flux, and over time grew more and more sensitive to the effects of their ships' capacitors, and the vagaries of space/time in their own systems. The companies were happy, too, knowing they could rely on familiar captains and crews, so most high-Transport spent their lives shuttling back and forth between two nearly identical base stations—the base stations were all nearly identical, across settled space, deliberately so—with occasional visits to whatever planets had been settled in their home and destination systems. The pay was good, at the high end of any scale, including Management, and most people agreed that it was a great life, as long as you didn't mind a slight lack of variety. And, of course, as long as you had the brain for it.

Tarasov Sein had the skills, the mathematical knack that might have let him become a decent calculator, but not the temperament. He sat in the copilot's seat in the bubble-bridge of the little 2500mu cargo lifter SID had provided for them—unnamed as yet, they were still arguing about a working name—lit the screens, and watched the roustabouts jockeying yet another STLship into its eventual place, wondering why he'd ever agreed to come back into space. Rangsey was nowhere in sight—probably running last-minute tests or checking the hold, Tarasov thought, but didn't bother to run the subroutine that would tell him what the other man was doing—and he wondered how it was possible to feel quite so alone in such a crowded space.

In the center screen, a notice-me icon flashed, followed by a message about fuel cell seven. Tarasov made a face, and reached for the button pad that was his current link with Rangsey, touching the combination that would pulse his partner. A moment later, Rangsey's voice came from the monitor.

"Yeah?"

"Ship's system says—" Tarasov squinted at the screen. "—fuel cell seven shows a two-tenths rise in pressure."

There was a little pause, and then Rangsey said, "Can't you deal with it?"

Tarasov bit back his instinctive anger. "I could if I knew what needed doing."

"Ask—" Rangsey paused again, and Tarasov knew he had been about to say, *ask your chip.* "Ask the system," he said, instead, and Tarasov suppressed a sigh. Rangsey was right, that was the obvious and logical answer, and what he really wanted was for Rangsey to give him the answer, not the computer. And that was completely unreasonable. He glared for a moment at the blinking readouts, annoyed as much with himself as with Rangsey, then made himself take a deep breath.

"I'll do that."

He didn't cut the connection at once, and heard Rangsey's voice change. "Look, I'll be done here in about an hour. If you run into trouble, the correction can wait till then, but I'd appreciate your doing it now."

And I have to relearn it all sometime. Tarasov said, "No, I'll take care of it now, no problem. I just thought you should know."

"Thanks," Rangsey answered, and this time Tarasov took his finger off the button.

The icon was still blinking in the center of the screen. Tarasov leaned forward to enter the sequence that brought up the system's diagnostician, and was rewarded a moment later by a list of options. To his relief, they were all familiar, things he'd half thought of already, but he made himself read through the entire list before selecting the first. A moment later, a confirmation icon replaced the notice-me, and a string of text appeared beneath it: OVERPRESSURE VENTED SUCCESSFULLY. Tarasov smiled, and a light appeared on the communications console.

"Compliments, and would you let us know before you do that?" The voice from the *Tiger*—young, by the sound of it—was more bored than annoyed, but Tarasov flinched anyway. It wasn't so much that he didn't know what to do, technically, but that he had forgotten the complex etiquette, and that was one thing neither the ship's system nor a skillbase could help much with.

"Sorry," he said, and was pleased that his own voice sounded suitably unimpressed. "Shouldn't happen again."

The light on the com console disappeared—an eloquent enough comment in itself, Tarasov thought. He resettled himself in the copilot's chair and reached for the tablet he'd discarded when the roustabouts caught his eye, touching virtual buttons to recall volume fourteen of the ship's manual. Learning the ship's various systems, mechanical, electrical, and virtual, was the easiest part of learning to be a Traveller; he had inspected enough similar ships in the eight years he'd been with the Technical Squad to recognize most of the equipment and programs with which he'd be working. How the systems would interact, which would take precedence, which required what level of attention when, was another matter, something that he could only learn through simulations and practice, though the manuals could give him some basis on which to make his guess. He had already found the simulator and tutorial programs, had them on standby for later, once he'd worked through the last of the manuals. He looked down at the tablet, its display field filled with yet another multicolored schematic, an ugly block of efficiency text in the space beneath. The design was instantly familiar, a pattern he had seen a hundred times before, but he made himself read through the descriptions and screen through the exploded and layered views to be certain before he let himself move on to the next screen.

He had almost finished that volume when the hatch opened behind him. He tipped the couch back rather than turning, proud of himself for remembering the easiest way to move in the bubble-bridge's cramped space, and hung there for an instant, balanced against the VMU's grav field, seeing Rangsey framed upside down in the circular hatch. Then Rangsey had moved past, into the bubble-bridge, and Tarasov let the chair pull him upright again.

"How's it going?" he asked, and Rangsey lowered himself into the pilot's chair.

"Not bad." He reached under his shirt, through the placket just above the left collarbone. Tarasov heard the double click as the skillbase disengaged, and Rangsey set the thin wafer on the nearest console. Its iridescent surface reflected the lights from the displays, and Tarasov winced again, thinking of dust, bacteria, and viruses settling on the unprotected surface. No matter how often Rangsey told him that the input drive was not a direct connection to the body—no matter how often he inspected the schematics, reviewed the notes, read the manuals—it made him shudder to see the skillbases left lying casually in the open air. "We've got pretty much everything I asked for—we're specializing in chocolate, which gives us an excuse to carry stasis cells and keep some locked areas—and we've got a nice line in vidiki as well."

Tarasov nodded, willing his eyes away from the skillbase, and the dust particles he could see floating in the recycled air. "Which means we got the copy-printer?"

Rangsey nodded. "You can't sell vidiki without it. Why were you and her so adamant about getting one, anyway? Those things are expensive, I'm half afraid to run it." As he spoke, he reached absently through the placket again, rubbing the scars where the input drive was welded to his body. Tarasov flinched, thinking of the pale ridges—installation had to have been painful, just from the look of them—and winced again, realizing Rangsey had caught the look. Instead of blowing up, however, the taller man gave him a fleeting smile.

"Sorry. I've been switching chips all day, the drive's running a little hot."

"God." Tarasov bit back the rest of his words, and Rangsey lifted an eyebrow.

"It's an expression—a figure of speech, don't worry. It doesn't actually get hot, the nerves in the skin around it just get a little overstimulated by the transmissions. Tell me about the copy-drive."

Tarasov looked away again, glad an old argument had been avoided. "You can use it to copy datablocks in a pinch, too—they won't run, but you can lift a dead copy of any programs from it. A lot of breeders use a version of the technique to study programs taken from the wild." It also meant that they could take unfamiliar programs on board without having to worry about some killer program rewriting the ship's systems, but he didn't have to say that aloud.

"So Macbeth thinks somebody's smuggling programs?" Rangsey asked.

"I wish I knew," Tarasov answered. "Audumla's close to the Territories, so it's a reasonable guess."

"Except the Territories know what they're doing," Rangsey muttered.

"That's open to debate." Even as he spoke, Tarasov wished he'd kept his mouth shut, and saw Rangsey's brows draw together into a frown.

"What's the matter with you?"

"Sorry." Tarasov took a deep breath. "I'm just edgy—I'm not a field officer, either."

"I wish to hell I knew what she was up to," Rangsey said. The words had become a refrain over the last week, and he made a face. "How long before we jump?"

Tarasov leaned forward, the chair rising with him, cradling him still, ran his hand over the nearest utility i-board, searching for the proper input configuration. Virtual keys—specks of color, temperature, and texture—swam in the board's yielding surface, then reformed into the system he wanted. He fed it the proper codes, and a schedule appeared on the nearest screen, hanging in the air apparently above the nearest tanker.

"Load-in's just about finished," he said, and Rangsey nodded.

"First burn at twenty-one hundred, final at midnight, and then jump at one-fifty. Could be worse."

Tarasov nodded, though he wasn't sure he agreed. He was used to Bestla's shifting clock, the extra hour of dark that had to be added each month to keep human clocks and planetary rotation in approximate synchrony; he would miss what for him had been an extra hour's sleep every fourth week. "Do we sleep now, or after?"

Rangsey shrugged. "It doesn't really matter, we'll be out-of-synch with Audumla regardless. We can time-shift on the run into the system."

Tarasov sighed—this was one of the things he'd never much liked about space travel, the constant adjustment of internal clock to the demands of local space—but nodded. "I'll stay up, then. There's still plenty to read in the manuals."

"Suit yourself." Rangsey pushed himself out of the chair and stretched, checking the displays as he did so. Light glinted from the ports in his wrists, set off by the tattooed arabesques that framed them; the placket gaped for a moment, too, showing brown skin and scar and the matte-black box of the input drive. This was where Rangsey belonged, Tarasov thought, in space, among the machines that shared his flesh, and wondered suddenly if that was what was making him bad-tempered. On Bestla, he'd been the one in charge, Rangsey the foreigner. He shoved the thought away, appalled and angry, and Rangsey gave him a smile and disappeared again through the hatch.

Federal regulations required pilots to be onstation for the actual jump. Tarasov took his place again as the computer called the countdown for the final burn that would slot the FTLship into its final approach vector. Icons were flashing on his board, and three or four voices were speaking from the com console. For once, the old training took over, and he reached for the right i-board to damp all but the incoming transmission from the *Tiger*.

"—in place and on-line. All ships, please confirm pilot in place and on-line."

Tarasov touched the board, fingers sliding easily over the textured plastic, sending their confirmation, and that voice vanished. He brought up the next—a prerecorded Customs announcement, droning on about contraband and import limits, probably some previous field officer's idea of a joke—and killed it without compunction. The third voice warned that the ship's tiny hydroponics section had not been secured for the jump. Tarasov made a face at that, and reached for the com board.

"Jus?"

"Yeah?" A secondary screen windowed below the main display, and a half-dressed Rangsey looked out at him. The sleeping cabin's stark lighting did nothing to hide either the scars or the metal that punctuated the planes of his body.

"According to the ship, the hydro hasn't been secured. Would you take a look at it on your way up?"

"Damn." Rangsey shook his head. "I forgot—I've been out of space too long, Sein. I'll take care of it."

Tarasov nodded, looking now at the main display as he sorted out the rest of the announcements. "And I've got an orange on bulkhead two. That's the catch that was sticking before."

"Right." Rangsey pulled on a jersey and then a knitted vest—his Family patterns, Tarasov saw, and didn't know whether to be glad or sorry. "I'll be up in fifteen."

The rest of the icons were confirmations, informing him that the ship was ready for the potential stress of the jump. Tarasov dismissed them one by one, and was left with two icons, hydro and hatch two, flashing red and orange in the center of the screen. Behind them, the STLships hung in their racks, bathed in the blue-white light of the forcefields. The attenuated wedges—light haulers, mostly, going into Audumla; the return flight would carry more of the heavy ore boats—lay nose to tail to make best use of the space, each one's long axis running parallel to the *Tiger*'s spine. The bright colors, corporate logos and private patterns, were bleached to pastel by the forcefields' harsh brilliance.

The hydroponics icon winked to green, followed a few minutes later by the icon for hatch two. Tarasov dismissed them both, and did not look back when the bridge hatch opened behind him.

"Thanks for getting those," he said, and Rangsey slid into the pilot's chair beside him.

"No problem. Where's the count?"

Tarasov worked his i-board again, found the general information feed from the *Tiger*, and displayed it on the screens. "Twenty minutes."

"Not bad," Rangsey said. He was fitting patch cords as he spoke, into his wrists and into the awkward-looking adaptors that let him control the non-Union ship through the Union tools. He reached into his pocket then, produced a skillbase, and slipped it through the placket. Tarasov heard the click, faint but definite, as it slid home, saw a confirmation string flicker past on Rangsey's screen. "Do we have an external monitor?"

Tarasov ran his finger down the i-board, sending a stream of icons flickering past on the screen in front of him. "Yes, there's a feed from *Tiger*."

"Put it on the central screen, would you?"

Tarasov gave the other a quick glance—the jump point was invisible to unassisted vision, defined by a quirk of space too subtle to be seen—but the excitement in Rangsey's face disarmed him. He touched the controls, selecting the right feed and routing it into their own systems. Overhead, the middle screen fuzzed and then resolved into a starscape, one point brighter than the rest. Another bright point hung closer in, flecks of light swarming around it like insects.

"I didn't realize the vector was pointing sunward," Rangsey said. "So that's the transfer station."

Tarasov nodded, wishing he had control of the scanner so that he could enhance the station's image, zero in on the cloud of STLships surrounding it. Macbeth had promised them support, had promised that she herself would be running the team that went into Audumla-system, but so far they had seen no sign of her presence. Tarasov tried to tell himself that they could hardly expect it, that Macbeth would hardly announce her presence, but it was hard not to feel abandoned—and more than a little annoying, he added silently, that Rangsey didn't seem to share that worry.

A buzzer sounded and a bright-red icon appeared in the center of each of the screens: two minutes to burn. Tarasov tugged the safety webbing over himself with one hand, worked the i-board with the other to bring up the banks of indicators. They were all glowing steady green now, and he dismissed them, leaning back in his chair with a sigh. "Everything looks good."

Rangsey grinned, suddenly and widely. "God, it's good to be back in space."

Tarasov lifted an eyebrow at that, but anything he might have said was cut off by the sudden deep rumble of the *Tiger*'s conventional engines. The camera was focussed away from the jets that were firing, but in the screen, the stars began to move, sliding away as the FTLship swung into the final alignment. Tarasov leaned back in his seat, feeling the vibration through the chair's padding, counting seconds. This was, if not precisely good, at least familiar, waiting out the firing to see if the calculators had done their job, and at least it wasn't his responsibility this time.

The jets cut out, and they hung for a second in comparative silence. Tarasov closed his eyes, trying to imagine the course numbers from the four-second blast and the relative shift of the stars, heard a ping and opened his eyes again to see another checklist waiting on his screen. Rangsey muttered something under his breath, looking down at his own screen, and Tarasov realized that the other man had a list of his own to complete.

"They should have had this information six hours ago," Rangsey said, and Tarasov glanced at his list.

"They did." His hands were already moving on the i-board,

flicking each item off his list: *pilots in place, drives shut down, intercept plates fixed, pressure seals secure.* "I'm shutting down the VMU."

"Acknowledged."

Tarasov touched the keysequence, confirmed it, and weight faded from him, leaving him drifting between the chair and the webbing straps.

"Anal-retentive people in Transport," Rangsey said, his own fingers signalling invisible input. Tarasov frowned at him, startled and annoyed, saw Rangsey's cheerful grin fade. "Hey, it was a joke."

"I'm Transport, remember?"

"We're both Travellers now."

"Then why're you wearing that vest?" Tarasov saw the other man flinch at that, and was meanly pleased by the reaction.

"I wish to hell I knew what we were supposed to do once we get to Audumla," Rangsey said.

"Fit in, observe the situation, and wait for instructions." Tarasov parroted Macbeth's description of the job, and got a sour smile from Rangsey.

"She won't even tell us what we're supposed to be fucking looking for."

"I don't know if she knows." Tarasov shook his head, remembering the interminable briefings—and, with a sudden pang, their flat, consigned to rental care under Anjait4's supervision—and the carefully edited files they'd been allowed to see. Oh, Macbeth had been apparently open, but the edits had been visible, and not even Anjait4 had been able to hack out the originals. Officially, SID was concerned about the deaths; beneath the surface—between the lines, Tarasov thought, except they'd been a little smoother than that—the investigators were looking for something specific, something they didn't intend to reveal to the lower levels of their investigation. It was a standard practice, not prejudicing the agents so they wouldn't find what their bosses wanted them to find, but Tarasov found himself resenting it more than he ought. It was doubly annoying to suspect that Macbeth might have been more forthcoming if they'd been from one of the Centrality worlds. He'd never been there, inside that charmed ring of worlds, but he'd had a cousin who worked the FTL run to Caranom. It counted as Centrality, if only barely, and he could still remember her stories, and the barely concealed amazement in her voice as she tried to describe the way that Caranom was like everything the richest of Bestlans only dreamed of being. She had finally pointed to the Exchange—they'd all managed to sneak inside at least once to marvel at the delicate colors of floor and walls, the polished stone and carefully chosen furniture even in the public spaces—and said that on Caranom it would look cheap, overdone.

"It's got to be unregistered programs," Rangsey said, his eyes still on the screen in front of him, fingers working, signing at nothing in particular. "Smuggling or sales or illegal breeding. Audumla's close enough to the Territories, and they get a lot of Travellers through the system. It's the only thing that makes sense."

"Except why kill miners?" Tarasov asked. They had been through this argument before, and with Macbeth as well, though the SID lieutenant had refused to be drawn. "That doesn't make sense."

"No." Rangsey sighed, flattened both palms in the air to temporarily disable his connection. "But do you have a better idea?"

Tarasov shook his head. "Maybe it's low-Management," he said, after a moment. "Hey, that could work. Suppose somebody in low-Management was dealing in crossbreeds, they'd have to pay for it somehow. So maybe they're taking ore and everything else off the mines to pay their suppliers."

Rangsey swung in his chair, automatically compensating for the length of the patch cords. "Yeah," he said slowly, "and that would explain why it didn't happen all that often, since most of the time they'd be paying suppliers from their profits. They'd only have to raid when they didn't make their numbers. Since the illegals don't let you carry much debt before they take it out of your hide." He shook his head then. "But where are they keeping the programs? From what I read, Audumla's net just isn't that big."

"Every net has a wild sector," Tarasov said. "It's necessary for the system."

"I still think it would be really hard to keep a breeder operation secret without having a dedicated system somewhere," Rangsey said.

Tarasov sighed, his own enthusiasm fading. Rangsey was right about needing a dedicated system: not even the most reckless breeder would let their programs run loose and unneutered, not so much for fear of what the programs would do to the host system, but because the programs would certainly be spotted. And a dedicated system would require enough power to be obvious as soon as anyone started looking. Maybe if you hid it in a legitimate research project? he thought, but rejected the idea almost as soon as it was formed. Most companies, and NSMCo seemed no exception, fostered competition among their divisions. Someone would have noticed that level of activity anywhere on the Company station.

"You know," Rangsey said, "we haven't really thought about the planet."

"What?" Tarasov frowned, trying to remember what the files had said about the system's one semi-habitable world.

"Suppose you built your system on the planet—it's all factory farms, right? So there'd be a reason to have the hardware."

"Power usage would still be out of line with production," Tarasov said, but he was less skeptical than he had expected to be.

"So you supplement with something unofficial—solar, say, or even hydro, depending on how close an eye the company keeps on the farms," Rangsey answered.

"Except," Tarasov said, a screen from one of the files dancing in memory, "that NSMCo subcontracted the farms, the whole terraforming, all of it, to a company called Landforms. So you'd have to have a joint operation, or at least really good sources in NSMCo, to track down the mines."

"Balls," Rangsey said, not disagreement but disappointment. "I still think it's the most likely thing we've thought of."

Tarasov nodded. "Which would mean we're in the wrong place—"

"Which probably means we're wrong," Rangsey finished for him, "since Macbeth went to so much trouble to get us into this. God, I hate all this double-thinking."

"Only double?"

Rangsey laughed, sounding for once genuinely amused. "Man, I can't keep track of the twists."

"That's SID for you," Tarasov said.

An icon flashed on his screen, and a fraction of a second later a deep, three-toned klaxon sounded. He could hear the noise over the speakers and through the hull of the ship, discordant and slightly out of sync, and fixed his eyes on the screen.

"Two minutes to jump," Rangsey said, unnecessarily, and Tarasov glanced sideways to see him, too, staring at the screen. He worked his i-board, and popped the countdown into a smaller window superimposed on the starscape, the changing numbers bright against the dark sky. *Tiger* was still drifting toward the actual point, the stars moving sluggishly in the screen, and Tarasov could imagine the tension on the FTL-ship's bridge. No matter how many times you made the calculations successfully, made the jump at exactly the right vector, there was the chance that you'd read the flux numbers wrong this time, would fail to translate properly, and be left stranded where you started, capacitors discharged, a horrendous expense for no result. He could remember his own first jump, the sick fear he'd felt, sitting strapped into the pilot's chair, even though he'd known that the ship's senior calculators had reworked and approved his numbers—

In the screen light flared, and with the light came a sudden sickening shift in the STLship's mass, as though gravity was momentarily present and absent, much greater and much less than it should be all at the same time. Tarasov swallowed hard, saw the screen clear on a starscape that was subtly different from the one they had just left. At his side, Rangsey made a soft sound of satisfaction, but Tarasov could only imagine what would be going on on the *Tiger*'s bridge, the way the calculators would be bent over their i-boards, matching scanner readings to the predicted numbers on their screens.

Another chime sounded, softer, two-toned, and a message appeared on the main screen, repeated by a synthesized voice: TRANSLATION HAS BEEN SUCCESSFUL. WELCOME TO THE AUDUMLA SYSTEM. Tarasov reached for his own i-board, linked it to the *Tiger*'s information feed, and produced a rough schematic of the system. Even as it appeared on the screen, the parameters were shifting, the picture refining itself, until the lines superimposed over the starscape were perfectly curved, bright symbols picking out the planets and the Orbital Agglomeration. Just looking at their pattern, Tarasov guessed it would take them about 140 hours to reach the station, but he called up the formulae, balancing the energy cost of the VMU against acceleration. He smiled to himself at the result: at their most economical pitch, 143 hours and sixteen minutes to the Agglomeration.

"How's it look?" Rangsey asked. His hands were working again, but Tarasov couldn't quite make out the shapes on his screen. "I'm putting in for the drop queue. It looks like about an eight-hour wait right now, then whatever it'll take us to get to the station."

"Five and a half days—143-16."

Rangsey nodded. "Not bad."

No, Tarasov thought, but I'd still like to know what we're supposed to do when we get there.

Travellers cluster when they can, one of their characteristics that most frightens the average citizen. Seeing a gather, modified long-haul transport and ATRVs parked side by side with battered, much-mended runabouts sporting bright canvas tents and brighter paint jobs, Service or Trade thought of theft and drunkenness, violence and laughter, women as bad as men, and crossed the street to avoid coming too close to the contagion. If they were low-Trade, though, stuck in the dead-end jobs of migrant sales or data clerking or worst of all tucked in cubicles processing endless streams of orders for companies who shared a pool of rented workers and who might be gone tomorrow, leaving unpaid wages and angry customers beating on the doors of the only visible world address they had, Travellers were worse than contagion. They were temptation, the choice low-Trade rejected daily: simply to leave, pile belongings, partners, pets, and children into whatever they could find that ran and would carry them, and take to the road to see if wandering wasn't really better than working after all. You could even go walking, leaving everything, go on foot and alone, if you could find a gather; there was usually someone who would take you on for a haul-hand or a lover or just for company, if the group was big enough. That was how the children went, the ones just at adulthood who refused, hated the low-Trade jobs that were left to them; it was also how the real truants went, the ones who abandoned kin, and it was those most of all that low-Trade feared. Low-Trade called the Vagabond Squads, or came in groups themselves, to move the gathers on.

It was a little different on the stations, where the jobs were better and the ones who travelled did so mostly from choice, incorrigibly vagabond, unwilling or unable to settle to one place, one company. There the Travellers were neither feared nor shunned, at least not more than anyone outside the Company was shunned, and indeed were useful, could be relied on to provide that which the Company could not be bothered to produce or import. Over time, they generally acquired their own docking rings, cheap and workable, often built from components replaced and discarded by the company, linked a few STLships there semipermanently, and held their gather in the nearest open unused volume. On the Agglomeration, NSMCo had given them the use of a renovated fuel tanker's cargo pod, too unwieldy to make other use of, on the condition that the gather remain open to employees and Union folk. This was no hardship, indeed, it was an enormous advantage to have the Company's sanction, and the Travellers had flourished. Their gather was free-market and information mart and tinker-shop and festival all at once, never cheaper than the company stores, at least not company employees—these were reform Travellers, mostly, and would take money—but always with something new to offer, and the converted pod was generally busy. When more than six STLships were docked to the rings, it reached critical mass, or so the employees joked, and the noise of it echoed from the curved walls, roaring like a river through the twenty-four hours of the standard station day.

Rangsey had thought he'd been prepared for the noise and the crowding, had in fact timed their arrival so that the STL-ship slid into dock along with three other Travellers who had come out on the *Tiger*, intending to become lost in the confusion. Customs formalities were light on the Agglomeration: a simple scan, a perfunctory check for viruses and unlicensed programs that produced an automatic recommendation that they disinfect their system sometime soon, and the request to turn over a copy of the manifest to the Company. After that, they were free to go where they pleased, and Tarasov suggested, with only the slightest hesitation, that they might as well get on with it. Rangsey agreed—he was just as ready to get it over with, and just as nervous at passing for a Traveller—and they set the main hatch to a palm-print lock and followed the instructions that would take them to the gather.

A double airlock connected the lower docking ring to the pod, and a short flight of stairs brought people up into the main volume. Rangsey followed a couple of men in full traditional regalia, loose, rainbow-patterned trousers and embroidered overshirts glittering with metal embroidery, and found himself suddenly in the middle of a busy street. He stopped involuntarily, and behind him Tarasov swore, setting his palm firmly between the other man's shoulder blades. Someone else called, "Clear the door," and Rangsey shook himself, stepping hastily out of the traffic pattern. A tall woman in spacer dress, probably the one who'd shouted, grinned at them as she passed, and vanished in the swirling crowd.

"Now what?" Tarasov asked, and Rangsey shook his head, staring at the confusion surrounding them.

"I have no idea." Even as he spoke, he was looking around, trying to decipher the pattern, or at least spot the information banner that had to be displayed somewhere in the pod. To either side, his view was blocked by the walls and half-walls that defined the makeshift booths and semipermanent stalls; he could see signs, ship and owner markings, above some of the doorways and display counters, but none of them looked familiar. A power pylon ran through the center of the pod, towering over the concentric rings of stalls, the axis around which the market revolved. Cables stretched from it to the shorter poles of transformers and from there to the booths, weaving a canopy overhead. Tarasov squinted up at the multicolored web, and shook his head.

"I'd hate to be the one who has to make sense of all that."

Rangsey nodded. He could distinguish data and raw and refined power, but there were half a dozen colors and shapes of cable he didn't recognize, as well as patterns that seemed to defy every safety regulation he'd ever learned. "Me neither. I wonder where the speaker is?"

Every gather—each individual band—had a speaker-between, who handled disputes between the band and the outside world as well as disagreements among the Travellers themselves. Tarasov shrugged, and a voice said, "New to the gather, then?"

Rangsey turned, to see a woman in worn karabel trousers and a man's embroidered overshirt watching him from the stairs that led to the airlock. Her hair was braided, like a woman's, but caught back in a man's club: a band shaman, he guessed, and dipped his head in wary answer. "That's right. And looking for the speaker, Faar."

The woman grinned at the title. "What band?"

"We're new," Tarasov answered, and this time the woman laughed aloud.

"I guessed that much. What ship, then?"

"SKW 5122," Tarasov answered, and in the same instant Rangsey said, "We're still discussing that."

The woman—she was younger than he'd thought at first, probably in her forties—looked from one to the other, visibly assessing the relationship, and Rangsey sighed. "Yes, Faar, I was Union, he was Transport. It's an old story."

"And a very romantic one." Her amusement trembled on

the edge of malice, but then she laughed again. "The speaker you want is Orbani Matteen, he speaks for and to the gather. He'll tell you what you need to know. By the center post, sign of the drum." She paused then, tilting her head to one side, the knotted braids sliding heavily across her back. "I'm Shahaan Monifa, band-of-Kyle. We're Reform, and at the moment open, so if you have troubles—ours is the double moon."

"Thank you, Faar," Rangsey said, startled and touched by the offer, and the woman nodded.

"You're welcome, children," she said, and turned away. Rangsey stared after her, wondering what had prompted the offer—simple kindness, the shaman's duty, or something more—but then shook his doubts away. It was the shaman's job to keep things balanced within the greater band that was Traveller society; the sooner newcomers were absorbed, the better for all concerned.

"So which way takes us to the center?" Tarasov asked, and Rangsey shrugged.

"There has to be a cross-street somewhere," he said, with more confidence than he fully felt. The crowd seemed thinner to his left, and he tilted his head in that direction. "This way."

Tarasov mumbled something that sounded skeptical, but Rangsey ignored him, weaving easily through the crowd. They were mostly Union folk, clustering in groups of three or four, easily distinguished by their drab-colored jerseys with their elaborate family patterns, but there were a fair number of NSMCo employees as well, dressed in thin brightly-colored tricoteil. Most of the Travellers in sight were working at the booths, men and women in gaudy treesilks and elaborate jewelry, ready to bargain or gossip at the slightest excuse. There were a fair number of Reform Travellers around as well, Rangsey saw, and most of them carried broker's boxes: the Orthodox did not accept money, and citizens did not barter; Reform Travellers made a tidy living acting as go-betweens. He had dealt with several of them on Bestla, all accused of cheating one side of the transaction, and found himself looking for familiar faces in spite of knowing better.

"There's a lot of chocolate for sale," Tarasov said, quietly.

Rangsey looked back at him, startled, and tried to remember the goods he'd seen on display. There had been at least two, no, more like five, stalls that showed the familiar icon and half a dozen others that had a tray of plastic models or a photoboard to show what they had in their storage cells. "You're right," he said aloud, and felt a twinge of unease. They had picked chocolate because it was easy to transport and kept its value, but if everyone else was doing the same thing. . . . He shook the thought away. "What about vidiki?"

"Not as much," Tarasov said. "But some."

Rangsey made a face, and turned right, into the corridor that led toward the power pylon. A kiosk surrounded its base, painted the same barn-red as the pylon itself, and a bright gold drum hung above the nearest doorway. At least we don't have to live on what we sell, he thought, and said, "We'll deal with that when we have to, I guess."

"Which may be sooner than we hoped," Tarasov muttered.

There was no answer to that. Rangsey ignored him, kept on toward the kiosk and the displayed drum. As he got closer, he could see that it wasn't real, was instead some kind of dimensional projection, and wondered just what that meant in the Travellers' complex iconography. It was a show of wealth, certainly—those projectors, even ones set to a single image, didn't come cheaply—but beyond that, he couldn't tell.

Underneath the drum, a door rolled back, and a man in plain tunic over patched karabels ducked through the opening. He was scowling, but the man behind him, tall and white-haired, white-skinned, and surprisingly handsome despite the pallor, was smiling faintly. Orbani? Rangsey wondered, and in the same moment, the first man took a breath, and turned back toward the door.

"Look, all we want—"

The white-haired man spread his hands. "I'm sorry, Denes, I can't let you jump the queue. If you want, I'll speak to Esbjorn, see if I can broker something between the two of you."

The first man shook his head. "We can't afford the commissions, Matteen, you know that. We're too small."

"There's nothing I can do," Orbani repeated, and fixed his

eyes on Rangsey. "And there are other people waiting."

Denes started to say something, then closed his mouth, shaking his head, and turned away. Orbani smiled past him at Rangsey.

"New to the Agglomeration? To travelling, too, I think."

"That's right," Rangsey answered, and Orbani's smile widened.

"I'm Orbani Matteen, speaker-between for this market. Why don't you come inside, and we'll see what I can do for you?" He touched the door controls as he spoke, and the red-brown fabric rolled back again, folding in on itself.

"Rangsey Justin." Even after four years, it felt odd not to give a place number. "My partner, Tarasov Sein."

Orbani nodded, and let the door rustle closed again behind them. Lights came up at the same signal, flooding the wedge-shaped room with gold-tinged warmth. "Have a seat," he said, with a vague gesture toward the padded benches that lined one wall, and settled himself cross-legged on a square padded stool. His dark-red coat, heavy with gold and stones that might have been glass, fell in unstudied folds, almost completely hiding his legs. On someone else, Rangsey thought, it might have looked foolish, but here, in this place and on this man, it looked right, added to his authority the way a single band of a Family pattern marked the senior Union folk.

"What ship?" Orbani went on, and at his side Rangsey saw Tarasov make a face.

"We're still arguing that," Rangsey said, and Tarasov gave a short laugh.

"We're docked as SKW 5122."

Orbani's eyes moved from one to the other, and then he reached for a databoard. "I see you're carrying chocolates and vidiki."

"That's right," Tarasov answered after a moment, and Orbani nodded, not looking up from the board's display.

"We have a lot of that already—for the same reasons you picked it for your first cargo, I imagine. What brings you to Audumla, anyway? It's not the usual place to start travelling."

They had decided on the answer to that before they left

Bestla, and who would give it. Rangsey waited, and Tarasov tipped his head to the side. "He had kin here, working one of the mines. It was as good a connection as any."

Orbani's eyebrows rose, and Rangsey could guess the thought: if they were allowing themselves even that much of a safety net, they hadn't yet fully committed to the travelling life. After a moment, though, the speaker-between looked back at his board. "Yes, there's a lot of chocolate on the market already, and vidiki, too, I'm afraid, all from people coming in on the last two FTLships. The people already here have asked me to slow down the sales for a while, keep the prices up where they should be. I'm sure you'll be willing to cooperate."

Tarasov's eyes narrowed, and he said, slowly, "Of course we see the situation, but we also have to live."

"I'm more than willing to broker for you and any of the established dealers," Orbani answered.

Tarasov's mouth twisted at that, and Rangsey couldn't blame him. They couldn't afford commissions, any more than the man they'd seen when they arrived, Denes, could—and doubly so since they were supposed to be finding an excuse to hang around the Agglomeration, to find the things the SID couldn't.

"We've sold everything we had for this cargo," Tarasov began, sounding uncharacteristically unsure of himself, and Rangsey looked away, not wanting to see the mild triumph in Orbani's eyes. They didn't have a lot of choice—didn't have any choice, and Orbani knew it, they could sell through him, or not at all. If they'd had other cargo, if they'd known more when they bought their goods—Rangsey broke off suddenly, remembering the rows of stalls they'd passed on their way to the speaker's space. There had been plenty of dealers in goods and hardware, but no tinkers, none of the semiskilled, or sometimes very skilled, artisans who usually filled the Traveller's markets. Well, there were probably some somewhere, he amended, but at every other Traveller gather he'd ever been to, the tinkers had been one in five. If you counted the hypothecaries, they were one in four. He looked back at Orbani, cutting in over whatever else Tarasov would have said, his words coming suddenly faster than conscious thought.

"Yeah, we put down everything we could for this cargo, because we didn't have enough for what we wanted—that's part of why we were coming here, I wanted my Aunt Auriga to talk to our head-of-Family, see if he'd release my marriage stake." Tarasov was looking at him sidelong, eyes wary in an expressionless face. Rangsey willed him to keep silent, plunged on. "So, yeah, we're willing for you to broker, but we want goods—specific stuff."

"Such as?" It was Orbani's turn to sound faintly wary.

"Tools—equipment to let us set up as tinkers." Rangsey jerked his head at Tarasov. "He's—he was Transport, but on the techie side, he's good with his hands, knows pretty much every ship's system ever built. If we'd been able to afford the supplies, we'd've started out that way. As it is, we've got the room on board, and the fittings, all we need is the basic tool set. And I don't see that you have that many tinkers out there in the market."

"No," Orbani said slowly. "Of course, most of that is handled by the Company—"

"For us?" Rangsey allowed himself a laugh. He was riding the flow of his fantasy, crafting their personas as he spoke: himself former Union, disgruntled, full of wanderlust, Tarasov the planetbound ex-Transport worker who'd followed him into the travelling life, would do anything for him. "I doubt Travellers are very high on their work queues. And I'd bet there are a few employees who'd be glad to get work done ahead of schedule, and not ask awkward questions."

"I have licenses," Tarasov said, soberly. "Legitimate ones."

"All our licenses are legitimate," Orbani said, with mild reproof, and Rangsey laughed again.

"If you say so, speaker. But Sein knows his stuff."

There was a little silence. Orbani looked down his board, his fingers tensing and relaxing on almost-invisible controls. He studied the result displayed in his screen, then slowly nodded. "As it happens, we are short of tinkers at the moment, and you could probably put together a decent toolkit from the equipment that's currently on offer. It'll be a complicated deal—if you're in a hurry, I could help you put it together."

That, from him, was a concession. Rangsey hid the knowledge, nodded thoughtfully. "That would be a help." *And you'll get a percentage off the top, too, but that's all right, it'll keep you happy.* He looked hard at Tarasov, trying to compel the answer he wanted. "What do you think, Sein?"

Tarasov blinked once, still without much expression at all, and then Rangsey saw the slight twitch at the corner of his mouth that betrayed the effort it was taking not to laugh. "If you think it's all right, yeah, go for it."

Rangsey nodded back, controlling his own sudden desire to giggle, and looked at Orbani. "Then, yeah, we'd appreciate it. You have our manifest already." He allowed his voice to take on a slight edge on the last words, and was glad when he saw Orbani's stare flicker.

"I'll talk to some people," the speaker said. "What in particular were you looking for in the way of a toolkit?"

"The standard machine shop," Rangsey answered. He tilted his head at Tarasov again. "He can handle pretty much anything, so we can wait to specialize until we see what people need most."

Orbani's hands tightened again on the display board. "I can arrange that. But it'll take me a few days to set things up."

"We can wait," Rangsey said. "What's your commission?"

Orbani lifted an eyebrow at that, but Rangsey met the speaker's stare squarely. "I take three percent of the total value, in goods of my choice, of the exchange."

Tarasov stirred at that, and Rangsey gave him a minatory look, though he could understand the other man's reaction. Goods of Orbani's choice meant that he was taking his commission squarely out of the best part of the deal, though at least, given the nature of the trade, most of his share would probably come out of the trade goods rather than their equipment. "Fair enough," he said briskly. "When can we expect to hear from you?"

Orbani glanced down at his board again. "Thirty-eight—no, forty hours. I'll call you then."

That was unmistakably dismissal. "Right, then," Rangsey

said, and turned toward Tarasov. "Let's go."

They came out into the cross-corridor lined with busy stalls, the sound of the door rolling closed behind them drowned by raised voices bargaining to either side. Rangsey glanced back, wondering what Orbani would do now, and Tarasov took his arm.

"Let's look around before we head back to the ship."

Rangsey gave him a startled glance, but Tarasov's face was closed even to him, the look he had sometimes when he'd come home from a particularly hard day. "All right," Rangsey said, and let the other man take the lead, following him through the maze of booths and corridors. Tarasov stopped at last beside a food cart, where a woman with a metal arm was selling thin pastry flutes filled with a savory-smelling cheese.

"Hungry?" Rangsey asked, and Tarasov gave him a bland look in answer.

"Always." He bought half a dozen of the flutes—the woman took Bestlan coins as well as Company scrip, Rangsey saw without surprise—and handed three of them to the taller man. Rangsey juggled them awkwardly, the oily pastry burning his fingers, and Tarasov handed him a napkin as well.

"Here," he said. "Now, let's talk."

Rangsey looked at him in some surprise, but then he remembered what Tarasov had taught him, what living on Bestla, under the Patrol's constant eye, had taught them both: privacy was best achieved in public, where one voice was lost among many, and there was always a benign reason to be part of any crowd. "Sorry to spring that on you," he said, keeping his voice low but well above a whisper, and Tarasov shook his head.

"You're good at that. I never knew." He swallowed a mouthful of pastry, grimacing as the cheese burned his mouth, said indistinctly, "I know line officers, SID even, who aren't as good on the fly."

Rangsey shrugged, not daring yet to taste the flute, oddly embarrassed by the compliment—if, indeed, it was a compliment. I didn't know either, he thought, and then couldn't think of anything else to say. "I didn't know myself. But I thought it was better than just letting him sell our cargo to somebody at their price. Besides, this gives us an excuse to hang around the Agglomeration—we're looking for the right tools, and the right customers. You can handle the work, right?"

Tarasov snorted. "Oh, yeah."

"Then what is it?"

Tarasov shook his head again. "Like I said, I know SID who aren't as good. You've got unexpected talent, Justin."

It was not, Rangsey decided, a compliment at all. Before he could think of an answer, Tarasov pushed himself away from the booth, dropping the remains of the last flute into the nearest incinerator, and started for the stairway that led to the airlock. Rangsey watched him go, wanting to follow him, but made himself stay where he was. Let him get over his temper—get over himself—he thought, let him calm down, and then we can talk. Because this time I'm right, this time I did the right thing, and if that's going to bother him, he's going to have to get used to it. Because I'm good at this job Macbeth stuck me with, maybe better than he is. It wasn't an entirely comfortable realization, nor was the pride that came with it. He finished his flutes with deliberate care, wiped his hands on his karabels, and started for the farthest airlock.

■ 5 ■

NO ONE KNEW where the first Travellers had come from. Not even the shamans of the oldest bands, the ones that could trace their history for five or six generations, back to the early days of FTL when a person could actually visit most of the human-settled worlds, could tell that, or even the origins of the term. Citizens held that they had always existed, that there had been Travellers from the day that human beings first settled to farming, irresponsible folk who couldn't stay fixed in one place, who kept to the old ways, and wandered. To them, the Travellers were an atavism, at best to be pitied, at worst put down, but always kept apart. The Orthodox Travellers told a different story, no less compelling for being demonstrably untrue: when human beings moved into space, and settled the new worlds, they said, they brought with them all the ills of Earth, and in the new soil those ills flourished and multiplied, until people became divided by the very tools that served them. Individuals hoarded what they knew, turning thought into cash and credit; the class walls hardened, became castes, until someone born to Production could never enter Transport, and vice versa, and so on down the line. It was then—and it is here that the story enters the realm of fable—that the first Traveller shaman appeared. He was a man called Krister Jurrien; no one knew precisely where he'd come from, but the Orthodox say he came on foot to a factory-town on Vittoria, owning nothing, carrying only what he could hold in his own two hands. He taught that caste and class were evil, and money was the symbol of that evil, that people should live by the work of their own hands and minds, and in this wicked universe, this society so deeply wedded to its cash and its castes, his followers should never stay too long in a single place, for fear that desire for things that they could not themselves produce or maintain might suck them back into the society they had rejected. And so the first Travellers left their homes, their belongings, sometimes their parents or children, always some kin, and followed Krister along the roads of Vittoria, first on foot, and then, as their numbers grew and their skills grew with them, in salvaged cargo haulers and runabouts and finally Travelled between the planet and its moon in battered STL shuttles, carrying Krister's theories and the promise of escape. Sometime in all of this— the stories are vague here—Krister died or vanished, and the heterodox believe he will come again, a child of divinity reborn. The Orthodox claim for him nothing more than humanity, and so hold open myriad possibilities.

The trouble with this story was, of course, that it wasn't true: the records from Vittoria were good, complete and apparently unedited, and there was no record of anyone called

Krister Jurrien either born on or immigrating to Vittoria in anything approaching the right time period. More damning, there was good evidence that people like Travellers, possibly even calling themselves Travellers, had been trading among the stations of the Cosmoline and the Antrich Belt at least twenty years before. The Orthodox shrugged it off, and kept to their austere ways, though all but the strictest would trade with Reform Travellers who took money for the goods they got from the Orthodox. They also kept their files and datacards of Krister's teachings, more and more copiously annotated over the years, and indeed, those texts remained a significant part of their trade goods.

For the Reform Travellers, who held no generally accepted string of beliefs, and whose degree of reformation could vary widely, the Krister texts, the entire matter of origins, were at once irrelevant and an obsession. It was irrelevant because how anyone came to Travel was her or his own business, not to be inquired of unless the person offered, and in any case the idea was a good one and a firm one, regardless of whether one man or many first articulated it. And it was an obsession because, if only some or even one of the texts could be proved to be definitive, then at least they would know for certain whether their compromise with the realities of FTL travel, their compromise with money and the outside world, were safe or not. Even if they were wrong, at least they would know for certain, and the Reformed envied the Orthodox their certainties even while they condemned them.

Kelly2 Jenna had been no more, and no less, concerned about her origins than most Travellers, at least until she was twenty-four. She had actually been born into a band, in a family that knew how and why it had taken to the roads—an old and familiar story, a woman who lost her low-Trade job and, rather than crawl to the shopkeepers or her own family, picked up her goods and walked—and so she was comfortable with the band's choices that had become her own. But when she was twenty-four, she committed an act of kindness that bound her to Audumla and NSMCo in a way no Traveller should tolerate: she paid money—worse, promised money she didn't have—instead of letting the Company turn the child she had found on the looted mine over to the Federal authorities. Like everyone else, she had heard the horror stories about Child and Youth Services—how they cheated their wards, sold them into factory jobs without the Union's protection, gave them over to the pharmaceuticals for testing, at best left them undereducated, fit only for the lowest of low-Trade—but, more than that, the child had no ID, and once she fell into CYS custody she would be a ward-of-state all her life, trapped there with the weak in mind. Kelly2 reasoned that, since the Company had made it clear it wouldn't claim her, even she would be a better caretaker for the girl than the CYS, and someday she might be able to buy or find some identity for her. So she had paid the first fees, borrowed as much as she could, a loan even on the STLship she lived in, and still didn't have enough to buy her almost-daughter an identity, since they weren't blood kin and she herself was fertile.

Ista knew the story, had known it in several different forms over the course of her life: first as fairy tale, herself the rescued princess; then as adventure, her almost-mother as hero; and finally, lately, as something else that she didn't want to understand, a bitterness and a burden between herself and Kelly2. She knew what she had cost, was still costing, and the thought troubled her almost as much as the question of her own origin, her reality. At times, it troubled her more, because she'd read the Krister texts, and heard Trindade's Orthodox interpretations, and suspected that if it all was true, she'd cost Kelly2 something like her soul.

Kelly2's STLship, *Fancy Kelly*, docked on the outer edge of the Traveller ring even when the station was crowded: the stationmaster was an old friend, despite the difference in status. Ista made her way through the crowd of the market, one hand on her monocular beneath her drape just in case some of the incomers from the *Tiger* were less honest than usual, the smells of the cookstalls filling her nose. There were at least twice as many as usual—Orbani would have rented out every spare cooker on the station—but that was only to be expected, while the supplies of foreign, off-the-menu food that came in on the *Tiger* lasted. Ista glanced enviously at one shop that was selling sausages, thin, finger-long cylinders glistening with grease under the hotlamps, but knew she couldn't afford more than a taste. If the bargaining went well, Kelly2 would buy half a dozen of them, along with a bottle of real wine, and they would build a feast around the food and drink, Kelly2 scrupulous to share the meat evenly between them. Once before, it had been years ago, Kelly2 had had a windfall, the first on the station to get a copy of what turned out to be the most popular vidik of the year, and she had bought meat by the kilo and Barabell Deen and the station master had joined them for the food and the wine, while Ista had eaten herself sick on the sausages. That had also been the last time Kelly2 had tried to buy papers for her almost-daughter, and Ista shied away from that memory.

She made her way down the short flight of stairs, and waited her turn to pass through the two-person airlock. Beyond it, the corridors looked abruptly different, the wall coating applied haphazardly, spotted here and there with painted flowers or more abstract designs. She had helped apply one set of patches a few years before, along with the rest of her study group from the Ragged School class, a looping sprawl of faux fractals, but that design was long gone, covered by another pattern: cheaper to do repairs that way, and incidental pleasure for hardworking children.

She stopped outside the shiplock, pressed the intercom button in her usual pattern, and waited for Kelly2 to trigger the lock. To her surprise, however, the outer hatch slid back and Kelly2 beckoned her from the far side of the airlock.

"Glad you're here. I've got some work for you."

Ista stepped over the high hatchway, unwinding her trapata as she went. The air inside the ship was a little cooler than the station air, and carried a whiff of the scent Kelly2 used to hide the age of the ventilation filters. They were due for reconditioning soon, would last another trip, but the air that passed through them smelled stale now, no matter how new it was.

"What do you need me to do?" She made herself put a good humor she didn't feel into her voice: she had spent most of the day with Trindade at her most Orthodox, and was feeling a little bruised.

Kelly2 didn't look back, and for a moment Ista thought she hadn't heard. She followed her almost-mother along the cargo corridor that spanned the width of the ship, and was surprised when Kelly2 turned right, toward the bow and the bridge. Usually, when Kelly2 wanted her help, it was hauling cargo, directing the astonishingly mindless cargo bots as they shifted the crates into the most efficient configuration for the run. As if she'd read the thought, Kelly2 glanced over her shoulder, a wry smile on her thin face.

"I've got a deal in hand, and I'm being offered some programs as part of the package. I'd like you to take a look at them—see if you can help me before I pay Trindade's prices."

Ista blinked at that, caught between pride and sudden panic. "I'll try," she began, wadding her trapata nervously into one hand, and added, with some bitterness, "Just don't expect Trindade's methods."

"I warned you when you started with her that she was Orthodox," Kelly2 answered, and ducked easily through the narrow circle of the bridge hatch.

"You didn't tell me how Orthodox," Ista muttered, and followed gracelessly.

Kelly2 heard anyway, gave her crooked smile again as she settled herself into the worn padding of the pilot's couch. "I did tell you. You just didn't know what it meant."

It was an old argument, and one Ista no longer expected to win. She suppressed the sense of injustice that would have kept her protesting, and took her place in the second couch, tucking her trapata into the seat beside her. "What's the deal, anyway?"

"One of Orbani's specials," Kelly2 answered, her fingers busy on a touchpad. "Some new Travellers came out with a basic cargo, chocolate and vidiki, and they want to trade it for

gear for a tinker shop. I'm selling off our old molecular spanner."

"I thought you said the other night you already had all the
chocolate you wanted," Ista said.

"I do." Kelly2 touched another set of controls, shutting down
several of the peripheral systems and isolating the backup
from the main computer. Seeing that, Ista felt another shiver
of pride—or maybe it was fear, or both: you only isolated the
main computer when you were working with uncertified or
unfamiliar program stock. She really means it, then, she
thought, and Kelly2 went on, unheeding. "But they have a
couple vidiki that I wouldn't mind adding to the master list,
and Orbani's offered to sweeten the deal with the programs.
Assuming they look good, of course." She frowned over her
board, adding a final set of commands, then leaned back in her
chair as the console in front if Ista's couch pulsed to life. "All
right. It's all yours."

Ista looked at the console, the last strings of checklights flicking from orange to yellow to green, and pulled the input board
slowly toward herself. There was a jack for her monocular, and
a patch cord hanging from the rack overhead. She brought it
down, fitting it carefully into both sockets, and the preliminary
menu opened on the screen and in the monocular's circle. She
studied it, but her mind was elsewhere. "Ma—"

"Don't call me that," Kelly2 said.

Ista glanced at her, the day's frustration coming to a head.
"Why not? Not calling you mother hasn't done me any good."

Kelly2 took a deep breath, visibly biting back her own angry
response. "But it doesn't help. Our only chance, your only
chance, if you want papers, real ID, is to persuade the Federation that you're not my kid, that this is just—convenience for
me."

"But that makes you look like shit," Ista said. "It's not right."

Kelly2 lifted an eyebrow. She was a hawkfaced woman,
hard-boned, who had never been pretty, and the imperious expression did nothing for her. "It's either you get papers, or
even if you get out of this system, you're never going to set foot
on a Federal planet."

"There's always the Territories," Ista said.

"Don't believe everything you hear. They're no different from the Federation, not about things like ID." Kelly2 took a deep breath. "Now, are you going to do this, or do I have to get Trindade after all?"

"If you think I can handle it," Ista answered, and was glad it came out as a challenge rather than fear.

"We'll find out, won't we?" Kelly2 reached for her own i-board, adjusted something in its depths. A window lit on her main screen, displayed a complex-looking file: cargo calculations, Ista guessed, from the color coding, and looked back at her own screen, shoving her anger away for later.

The menu glowed in the monocular's circle, repeated on the larger screen. She glanced once at it, confirming that they were the same, and then focussed her attention on the monocular. The new programs were easy to spot, the three icons flashing bright orange to warn anyone using the system that they had not yet been cleared for use. She twisted the bezel to select them, the control points pulsing confirmation under her fingers, then reached across onto the i-board to display the code-walls that were supposed to isolate the new programs. They looked solid—they ought to, she amended silently, they were Trindade's speciality—and she returned her attention to the monocular.

The first program flowered under her touch, a familiar, orchid-like structure, delicately colored except for the shocking green blotch of the restricting codes. Each of these programs would bear the same mark, a parasitic subroutine that would destroy its host if she attempted to clone a copy for her own use. She rotated the image, squeezing the controls at the same time to fade the outer color. "What are they supposed to do, anyway?" she asked, and knew her tone came out sullen.

Mercifully, Kelly2 ignored it, or maybe she didn't notice. "A navigation assistant, a data manager, and a clean-up editor for the dupe machine."

Ista nodded, refocussed her attention on the program in front of her. It was the data manager, a classic data trap, designed like the flower it resembled to funnel the data through its presorting sieve by mimicking the program it served. She touched the controls to fade the first layers of codes, and then the next, working her way to the core of the program, where the iconic structures dissolved into a wash of pure color, pure code and she had to switch viewpoints within the monocular to follow the patterns. This was not the way Trindade taught her to view the wild programs they caught in the Agglomeration's nets, but it worked for her, and better than staring at it, waiting for the patterns to reveal themselves to her— She shoved that thought aside, annoyed that she'd even acknowledged it, and touched the controls again to bring the familiar iconography spiralling back. The layers of code, the central store, the various sieves, the controls, finally the chameleonic layers of the data trap, fitted themselves lazily back into the overall program. She understood the shape now, could make a guess at the stock from which it had been bred, but it was equally clear that it had matured in the wildnets, under the stresses of that evolution.

"The data manager looks good," she said aloud, and reached across to the i-board to return it to its file. The orchid-shape faded, was replaced by the sober browns of the safety envelope—not that either program looked like that in reality, both images were constructs of the monocular's matrix. But, as Trindade had said from the day she, Ista, started working with her, what the programs "really" looked like was hardly relevant in the invisible world. Indeed, "reality" was hardly an important concept; what mattered were the VALMUL building blocks that signified function and structure.

"It's supposed to boost performance almost ten percent," Kelly2 said.

Ista frowned, considering the images she had seen. "I suppose it could," she said, "but I wouldn't expect quite that much return. I mean, the program you're already using is pretty close to optimal already."

Kelly2 nodded. "I figured. What do you think would be realistic?"

Ista hesitated, then reached for the i-board, conjuring up a table-calculator. Trindade would never have permitted it, would have made her guess or try to do the calculations in her head, but here, at least, she could use the tools she preferred. "More like five or six percent," she said, after a moment. "But that's really only a guess."

"And it's really only a bargaining chip," Kelly2 answered. She touched invisible keys on her i-board. "What about the others?"

Ista didn't answer, reached instead for i-board and monocular and opened the clean-up editor's file. The image that bloomed in her monocular was squat, ugly, and instantly familiar, a boxy twenty-clawed shape on a pedestal shaped to fit a receptor in the dupe machine's control program. The green blotch of the parasite obscured the usual ID patch, but she didn't really need its confirmation. "The editor's fine," she said. "It's a commercial program, meets Federal standards. I'm still looking it over—" Her hands moved on the monocular as she spoke, peeling back layer after layer of dull red-brown code. "—but I'm not finding any extraneous stuff. It looks like the real thing."

"It's supposed to be," Kelly2 said.

"You might have told me."

Kelly2 glanced at her. "I wanted—needed you to tell me first."

And that was true enough: if Kelly2 had told her what the program was supposed to be, it might well have made it harder to see what was actually there. Ista nodded, and tucked the program back into its file, reached for the last folder and triggered its contents.

The image that appeared was bigger than the others, so that she had hastily to adjust the monocular's range to get it all in. It hung in the lens's center, hulking body set on six stubby legs, the shifting spines of a navigation-aid grafted onto its back and sides. The structures that showed as eyes were closed, reminding her that this was a sample, not to be used or copied, but looked rudimentary: not a smart program, as wild programs went, but still unmistakably faunal, a whole order higher than the medusa she had collected for Trindade. Trindade avoided the larger hammals, except when she had a specific commission, maintaining that their structure was too unstable, their makeup too complex, for them ever to be successfully bred into the existing strains. The program breeders might do it, but they had the stand-alone hardware, unconnected to the normal nets or their own working systems, that let them take those chances. Hypothecaries could afford neither the equipment nor the risk, and Ista eyed this program warily, trying to guess function from form. Fauna was much more variable than flora, one of the reasons it was both more versatile and more dangerous: even VALMUL couldn't cope with all its complexities.

Ista sighed, shifted her grip on the monocular so that the image jumped and wavered. The program lay quiescent in the lens, eyes closed, the blotch of the parasite vivid against its dull purple coat. All right, she told herself, without conviction, it's supposed to be a navigation assistant, so start with the grafted functions. She squeezed the monocular again, an unfamiliar pattern, and on the second try saw the spines separate themselves from the main body. Beneath it, she could see the pattern of the receptors bright red against the program's back, but she ignored that for now, fixed her attention on the spines.

They were more familiar, looked very like a common flora—it was a common floral routine, she amended, looking closer, only slightly modified to achieve symvirosis with the host program. She pulled it apart anyway, looking at the web of codes at the base of the spines, checking the coiled tentacles that let the program interact with the ship—it would need to bud new plugs to fit the ship's receptors, but that would be no problem, the program would produce them automatically once it was loosed into the system—and then, reluctantly, turned her attention to the faunal program. As Trindade had taught her, she probed the dull purple sides, gently first, then harder. The eye-structure remained firmly closed, and she took a deep breath, schooling herself for the next step.

The program was not truly alive, or not alive in a way that made this the dissection it seemed to be, but she grimaced as she faded the first protective layers of skin, exposing the complex knot of structure and subroutine. Once that was done, however, it was easier to see the familiar VALMUL patterns, to pick out which parts did what, and to isolate the central routine that managed STL navigation. Like the clean-up editor, that particular routine was familiar, a Federal standard somehow incorporated into a wild program, and she frowned at the image in the monocular. Why would a wild program have incorporated this particular chunk of code, and taken it in whole and functional? she wondered. It didn't seem to offer any advantage—which must mean it was a deliberate crossbreed, possibly Territorial, and certainly illegal, but also, from the look of it, highly functional. She returned that routine to its place, brought up the surrounding structures, then let the rest of the program fade back to its normal image. There were no signs of deliberate tampering, none of the usual scars where hurried breeders had forced a fit between incompatible programs: it may have started as an illegal cross, she decided, but it had probably been breeding for a few generations on its own, and the cross had taken well.

She shut down the program, letting the seals fold back into place around it, and set the monocular down on the edge of the i-board. "The nav-assistant's the best thing you've got," she said, "but you'd better be sure it's well and truly neutered before you let it into the system."

Kelly2 gave another of her twisted smiles. "I'll send it to Trindade to be spayed—maybe she'll let you do it."

Ista made a face, thinking of how real—how *animal*—the program had seemed in the monocular's vision. It was one thing to prune the reproductive codes from the floral programs, quite another to operate on wild fauna—and yet it shouldn't be. Before she could pursue the thought, the communications console buzzed twice.

Kelly2 grimaced and reached across her boards to flip the response switch. It was the outside intercom, Ista saw, and wondered which of their friends had come visiting.

"Yeah?" Kelly2 said, and the screen lit in the same instant, revealing two unfamiliar faces. One was dark with a surprisingly high, narrow nose, the other white, with broad cheekbones beneath pale eyes and hair: Travellers, Ista guessed, from the glimpse of their clothes the cameras gave, and the fact that they were there, in the corridor outside the lock, but no one she'd seen before.

"Kelly2 Jenna?" the black man asked, and Kelly2 nodded. "That's me."

"Rangsey Justin." He tilted his head toward the other man. "And Tarasov Sein. Orbani Matteen gave us your name and direction." He grinned suddenly. "We're the people who are trying to buy the toolkit, and we were hoping we might get a look at the spanner."

Kelly2 studied them for a moment, then shrugged. "Not a problem, I guess. Wait there, I'll be out in a minute."

She cut the connection without waiting for an answer. Ista scrambled to follow her, dragging her crumpled trapata ungracefully from between her body and the side of the copilot's chair. "Can I come?"

Kelly2 gave her a curious look, but nodded. "If you want. Sure."

Ista hurried after her down the long axial corridor, trying to refashion her trapata into the proper Traveller drape. Except there wasn't much point, she conceded silently, when Kelly2 never bothered with more than a token strip of fabric knotted at the neck of her sleeveless coverall. She wound the trapata into place anyway, determined that she wasn't going to care. Kelly2 had nagged her for years to be proud of what she was— Ista thought she would have said, *and who*, but that would have been ridiculous, under the circumstances—and even if Kelly2 wasn't going to appear as a Traveller, at least she herself would.

The men at the airlock were pretty much as ordinary as they had appeared in the screens, both tall, one, the dark one, Rangsey, taller and thinner, the other, Tarasov, with his fair hair cut short to make the most of a receding hairline. They both wore ship clothes, karabels—Rangsey's patched and faded, Tarasov's tidy, the fabric darker even than the newest of Rangsey's patches—and light t-shirts. They were a lighter fabric than usual, plaincloth instead of tricoteil, as though they found the Agglomeration warm, and Ista wondered where they'd come from.

Kelly2 said, "The spanner's in Hold Two. Where are you in from?"

Ista saw the quick shift of eyes, glances touching in some private signal, and then Rangsey said, "We've come from Bestla. As you probably guessed, we're new to this."

He sounded a little tired of the explanation. Kelly2 nodded, the faintest of smiles curving her mouth, and then she turned and started down the corridor. The men looked at each other again, and then at Ista, who felt ready to sink through the floorplates. Kelly2's voice drifted back from the intersection of the corridors.

"That's by way of being my daughter. Kelly2/1 Ista, she goes by."

Tarasov's brows rose at that, but he nodded politely to her. "Tarasov Sein."

"I know." Ista knew she sounded ungracious, was certain she was blushing, and tried to recover herself. "I was in control when you called."

Rangsey nodded, gestured politely for her to precede him down the cargo corridor. "You work the ship, too?"

Ista shook her head. "Not—not at the moment. I'm studying with the station hypothecary." She glanced back as she spoke, wanting to see the respect that announcement usually brought her, but to her surprise Tarasov, at least, looked blank.

Rangsey touched his shoulder. "She's in your line of work, Sein, programmer—technician-breeder. Or do you just harvest?"

The last was directed at her. Ista said, carefully, "Station regs restrict us to what we find, and even then they have to vet it really carefully." It wasn't fully true, but she shouldn't have to explain the nuances of the grey markets to fellow Travellers—and if they were new to it, they didn't need to know, just yet.

This time Tarasov did look impressed. Ista allowed herself a moment of satisfaction, but then they had reached the intersection of the cargo corridor and the axial corridor, and Kelly2 was waiting just inside the hatch that led to the main hold.

"Through here," she said, and turned toward the stern. Ista followed her over the high combing—required by the safety regulations, but a nuisance every time they loaded anything larger than a standard starcrate—and heard one of the men swear as he stumbled. Politely, she didn't look back, threading her way between the careful piles of crates and slung cargo webbing, and stood aside while Kelly2 opened the hatch of the smaller secondary hold.

"The spanner's in here, along with the rest of my machine shop." She tugged the hatch wide, stood aside to let the men into the narrow space. Tarasov climbed through first, and Rangsey followed, looking with open curiosity at the various pieces of equipment fastened to hull and floorplates.

"You must do a lot of vidiki," he said, looking back at Kelly2, and the woman nodded.

"Enough. Why?"

Rangsey tilted his head at the bulk of the copy printer. "You're set up for it," he said, and Ista hid a grin. It served Kelly2 right to have the obvious pointed out to her, when she was being stupidly superstitious.

"The spanner's there," Kelly2 said, and pointed.

"Thanks," Tarasov said. "Mind if I switch it on?"

"Suit yourself."

Tarasov crossed the narrow space in two strides, flipped on a control board and began touching buttons. Ista, peering around the edge of the hatchway, watched the strings of checklights dance across the display plate, and decided he knew what he was doing after all—at least with the machines. Kelly2 seemed to come to the same conclusion, and looked at Rangsey.

"What brings you to Audumla? It's not exactly a favorite destination, especially starting out."

Rangsey made a face, wryly good humored. "It's a cheap jump from Bestla to here—"

Kelly2 snorted.

"—and then I had kin working here when we started."

"Union?" Kelly2 asked, and Rangsey's grin widened.

"I guess it shows."

"You could say that."

Rangsey nodded. "They were working one of the mine platforms, I thought if worse came to worse we could get help
from them."

"Hardly Traveller thinking," Kelly2 said.

"Didn't matter," Tarasov said, not looking up from the machine. "They weren't here when we got here—had some bad
luck of their own."

"Oh?" Ista could see Kelly2's shoulders tense, leaned closer
herself, wondering what was upsetting her.

Rangsey nodded again, the smile gone from his face. "My
cousin—third cousin, actually, but a cousin—was on the mine
that got attacked two weeks ago."

"What mine?" The words were out before Ista could stop
herself, but she met Kelly2's glare without flinching. "You
didn't tell me there'd been another attack."

"No." Kelly2 raised her voice to carry over Ista's instant
protest. "I didn't. Later, Ista."

Ista hesitated, but a lifetime's training took over, and she
subsided again. When Kelly2 used that particular tone, it
meant things were up that she didn't know about, and she
could mess up a deal if she pursued it. But I will find out later,
she promised herself, and leaned back against the hatch.
Tarasov was watching her sidelong, she realized, a fixed, expressionless curiosity that was definitely disconcerting.
Rangsey seemed to become aware of the look in the same instant, and went on in a cheerful voice that didn't quite obscure
the warning glance at Tarasov.

"Yeah, and we still haven't exactly found out what happened ourselves. We were thinking of taking a trip out that
way ourselves, see if any of the other platforms knew anything."

"I wouldn't," Kelly2 said, her voice still stiff. "Wouldn't
bother, I mean. Nobody ever knows anything."

Rangsey made a sympathetic noise, but Ista thought his
eyes were distant. "Still, I'd like to know. Being as it's my

cousin, and all." He looked to Tarasov without waiting for an answer. "How's it look, Sein?"

Tarasov straightened, easing his back, and touched keys again to shut the system down. "Looks good."

Which meant, Ista translated, and hid a grin, they're probably going to buy it. Which means Mama will get the programs.

Kelly2 smiled. "Glad you stopped by to look at it, then."

"We'll be in touch with Orbani," Rangsey said. Kelly2 nodded, and gestured for them to precede her out of the secondary hold. Ista trailed behind them to the main hatch, folding the corner of her trapata in one hand. She waited until Kelly2 had latched the hatch again behind them, but the older woman spoke before she could say anything.

"Yes, there was another attack, a mine platform in the Outer Reach, no one was killed. They found the platform drifting empty, just like the others, the crew got away on the FTL to Bestla. And I didn't tell you because I didn't see why you'd need to know."

"But—" Ista broke off, unable to articulate her outrage. *Of course I want to know, that's where I came from.* But that wasn't it, either, not quite, and she settled for, "You still should've told me."

"I thought you'd get it off the newsnets," Kelly2 answered.

"You know I had to give up my subscription," Ista said. "And I told you Public Access was useless."

"It wasn't on Public?" Kelly2 asked, and Ista looked away. She hadn't accessed the public newsnets as regularly as she had called up the more expensive subscription files—but still, she thought, somebody should've mentioned it. Somebody should have known.

"Doesn't surprise me," Kelly2 went on. "The Company's been keeping it pretty quiet."

"Stinne hasn't mentioned it," Ista said.

"Her folks probably told her not to," Kelly2 said, and Ista scowled, hiding the hurt the idea brought.

"Or maybe she doesn't know, either." She looked back at the hatch. "These guys—they came in from Bestla. Maybe they know more about it than the Company narrowcasts."

"You stay out of this," Kelly2 said. "I mean it, Ista. This is the kind of Company business we do not want to be involved in."

Ista sighed, knowing better than to argue, but still not fully convinced. She would ask Stinne, she decided, and go from there.

Tarasov leaned close over the display console, the draft from the ship's ventilation strong on his bare arms. He could smell the already stressed filters, just as he had on *Fancy Kelly*, wondered vaguely how the Travellers stood it. Probably they stopped noticing after a while—though Rangsey had bought cold incense papers in the market, and their musk filled the sleeping cabin. Tarasov still wasn't sure it was an improvement. At least the air was cooler now, once they'd figured out how to adjust the environmental system. The station norms were too warm for his taste, too warm after Bestla's long winter; they were running the ship's system to compensate, and it was just a good thing they weren't docked on the sunward side of the ring.

Icons moved past him in the screen, familiar VALMUL shapes alternating with less familiar, company-specific ones, and he grimaced, wondering what exactly he was looking for. The Agglomeration's net—or at least NSMCo's controlled habitat—looked discouragingly normal, and he ran his fingers over the virtual controls now embedded in his i-board, seeking the nearest gateway that would give him access to the frontage and then to the wildnet. The image swam for an instant, as though water had run for an instant along the inside of the screen, and then reformed, displaying the familiar bright-red pi-shape of the gate. In the same moment, a plaintext message scrolled across the base of the display: WARNING! VIRAL CONTAMINATION BEYOND THIS POINT, NO RETURN PERMITTED WITHOUT FULL SCAN. ACCEPT YES/NO. Tarasov touched keys, calling up a systemic analog he had created for just this purpose. It mimicked his own main system and program suite, would fool the company's scan into thinking it had seen and inspected the ship's full system; it, or programs like it, were one of the main reasons no one had ever succeeded in eradicating even the most dangerous of the wild programs, and, as always, Tarasov felt slightly guilty for running it. He could tell himself that he knew what he was doing, that his own systems were clean and his anti-virals the best money could buy, but he'd heard that excuse too often fully to believe it. Still, the only other option was to give NSMCo's scan the freedom of the ship's system, and that was impossible, given the information he had stored in various volumes. He touched the accept icon now flashing in his i-board, saw a string of codes flash past, too fast for him to read individual symbols, and then the gateway opened, grew to fill his screen and swallow the other icons in grey-green darkness flecked with distant bits of color. A string of text appeared at the base of the screen: CONNECT VIA WIDHW 3298328, PATH 22743, STRING ###0, and a second gateway appeared. This one was blue, the left spike wound with the black snake-shape of a passive monitor. He nudged the point-of-view through it, and the numbers changed again. In the i-board, the texture of the controls shifted under his fingertips, reformed into a rosette surrounding a raised half-sphere. He looked down instinctively, though he knew better, saw nothing but the flat featureless surface of the board, and made himself look back at the display, letting the image reassert itself through his fingers. He shifted his fingers, sliding them forward over the top of the invisible half-sphere, and the image in the screen moved as well, translating his gesture into the illusion of movement. The compass string numbers shifted, defining direction: if he became lost, not unlikely in the changing spaces of the invisible world, he could always find his way back to the gateway by counting the string numbers down to zero.

Ahead, one of the flecks of color swelled to a shape that the VALMUL lens translated as a dark-red pod at the end of a sinuous tether. The general configuration was familiar, a bendy datatrap, but some of the surface markings were strange, and he shifted his fingers to give it a wide berth. Even so, it snapped reflexively at him, and he saw the gleam of parasitic shredder routines in the pod's circular opening. Another icon loomed ahead, or rather, he amended, a series of repeating icons, cancriform quasicorals, either sophisticated flora or primitive fauna, depending on your definition, making their slow way across the virtual landscape, half a dozen multi-legged shapes, each surmounted by an identical set of eyestalks surrounding the pyramidal pseudomouth in the center of its back. The lead icon looked different from the others, its colors paler, faded from the vivid greens of the first five, and, looking closer, Tarasov saw that its eyestalks were closed and drooping. The quasicorals, like all wild programs, maintained themselves by scavenging usable code fragments: not directly dangerous to a human operator, but, given the opportunity and time, even a quasicoral could dismantle a VALMUL lens. This one, though, looked as though it had fed recently, and was in the process of budding another unit. Even as he thought that, he saw the first fissure appear between the lead icon and the rest of the coral, saw, too, the ripple as the bud—a clone of its parent, or as close to it as the program could build from whatever code it had managed to recover—pulled a little further out of the last icon, an oddly brighter mirror image of its parent.

It had been long time since he'd seen a program reproduce itself, longer still since he'd had the leisure to watch, and he lifted his finger from the controls, staring in fascination as the lead icon faded from green to grey and the fissure between it and the body of the coral widened. At the same time, the tail icon shivered again, the bud more pronounced, more obviously a nearly-finished icon, its eyestalks now waving in the same complex rhythm as the rest of the coral. Then the lead icon fell away, shattering into fragments that the VALMUL lens translated as glittered silver-grey slivers, and the new tail twitched itself free, so that the coral was complete again, six linked units. It kept moving, slowly, tracking over the shards that had been part of itself, and in the corner of the screen Tarasov saw a scattering of chogsets, the least complicated of the scavenger programs, scurrying toward the fragments. They clustered for an instant, silver indistinct shapes that glowed briefly brighter as they absorbed the fragments, and then darted off again, disappearing into the green-grey background.

It was a little worrisome that the lens hadn't been able to make better visual sense of them, but then, that occasionally happened with the less complex programs, especially when first surveying an unfamiliar volume. The lens would probably learn to compensate, learn how to display the structures, but until then he would have to move slowly. There might be an update somewhere in the station libraries, a special VAL-MUL dictionary, but he could look for that later. He touched controls to spin his point of view, surveying the green-grey plain. It seemed odd that he hadn't seen anything more complex than the quasicoral—that he hadn't seen any higher fauna at all, he realized abruptly, and that was definitely odd. NSMCo's wildnet was well established, and their security didn't seem particularly strict; faunal programs usually flourished in these environments. Maybe they were just avoiding the gateways, he thought, and touched the half-sphere again, moving forward at half his previous speed, heading toward a line of pale-blue icons barely visible on the horizon.

"Sein?"

Rangsey's voice was startling, and Tarasov jumped, fingers slipping on the invisible control. The image in the screen swooped wildly, and Tarasov shut his eyes against vertigo, fingers moving automatically to compensate. He opened his eyes again, more cautiously, this time, and saw the image had steadied in the middle of a rhomboidal expanse of wallaroo. It was uniaxial, and luckily he'd ended up across the grain where it couldn't sense his program's presence, but he adjusted his alignment just the same. The string counter read #281.

"Sorry." Rangsey sounded genuinely apologetic. "I didn't see."

" 'S OK," Tarasov answered, most of his attention already focussed again on the icons, the interlocking diamond tessellation of the wallaroo, but to his surprise, Rangsey didn't move away. "Do you need me?"

"Um, yeah. Some stuff's come up."

Tarasov didn't bother to hide his sigh, but touched buttons in the invisible rosette to begin retracing his path. The string counter began to click backwards through the 270s, the wallaroo pulled away, and he risked a glance over his shoulder. "So what is it?"

"A couple of things," Rangsey answered. "First, Macbeth's on station—I saw her in the machine shop. And she wants to see us."

"Now?"

"When you're off the net."

"She might've warned us," Tarasov muttered. The screen showed mostly blank now, a few bright spots too distant to identify, then the quasicoral still creeping steadily across the netscape, finally the bright blue spikes of the frontage gate and the plaintext warning across the screen: STOP FOR FULL VIRAL SCAN. He touched the proper controls to acknowledge and accept it—and trigger the system-analog—feeling the controls shift, melting into the configuration for the controlled nets even as he touched the last button. "When did she get here, anyway, did you find out?"

"Came in on the *Tiger*," Rangsey answered, with a twisted smile. "Along with us. Apparently she got herself papers as one of the replacement wrecker crews."

"I hope to hell she's qualified," Tarasov said, startled, and Rangsey nodded.

"But that's not the big news, or I don't think it is. You know that girl, Kelly2's by-way-of-being-a-daughter? I was curious what she meant, so I asked around, and you'll never believe what the deal is."

Tarasov saw the shutdown icon appear, touched keys to confirm the disengagement, concentrating on the previous day's meeting. Kelly2/1 whatever her name was certainly didn't look like a biological child, unless she took completely after her father, dark where Kelly2 was coffee-skinned, bidding fair to be tall and curvy where the mother was rawboned. "So tell me," he said aloud, and swung to face the other man.

Rangsey smiled down at him. "It turns out that Ista Kelly was found in the wreck of a looted mine when she was— maybe—two years old. They, the Company, weren't sure, weren't sure who she belonged to or what she was doing there—"

"One of the crew's kid," Tarasov said. "Surely."

"Except there wasn't a record of anyone on the mine having a kid with them," Rangsey said. "In fact, it turned out they didn't have good records of the mine crew at all—some guy who was supposed to have been on it showed up alive a month or two later, scared the shit out of all his friends. Turned out there'd been a lot of job swapping at the last minute, he said he thought somebody might've brought in a wife and kid, but he didn't know for sure, and didn't know who they were."

Tarasov shook his head, biting back his instinctive anger. Trust the Union to be casual even when it matters most, he thought. My god, not to keep track of the crew list, not to file it— He shook the thought, and the fury, away, seeing the same awareness in Rangsey's eyes. "So who found her, Kelly2?"

Rangsey nodded. "And then when they couldn't make an ID on her, she said she'd take her rather than see her go to CYS."

And that made sense, too, Tarasov thought, considering that all CYS leaves you fit for is the lowest of low-Trade jobs. He said, "So how'd she get papers for her, then?"

"She didn't." Some of the brightness left Rangsey's face. "Which means Ista would have been a ward-of-state all her life anyway. They've been trying to make arrangements for years, according to the guy I was talking to—Barabell Deen, he runs a Traveller bar called the Bubble just upstation from here."

Tarasov shook his head again. Only the genuinely incompetent were supposed to remain wards-of-state for life, but there was always some cases that fell through the cracks. "Who was it who made—or didn't make—an ID?"

"Apparently the Feds," Rangsey answered. "They tried Company and Union records, and couldn't come up with a match." He took a breath, watching Tarasov's face. "My point was, here we've got two witnesses—well, one, since the girl wouldn't have been old enough to remember anything—who have at least seen the aftermath of one of these attacks."

Tarasov nodded. "And maybe another one we should talk to. Do you know what happened to the guy who traded for the other job?"

"Nobody knew," Rangsey answered, "and I didn't want to push it. But I got a name, and some kin."

Tarasov eyed his partner with something between admiration and uncertainty. Rangsey was good at this, good at the line-patrol work—more than that, SID work, playing a part and still asking the right questions—and that was something he'd never suspected of him. It was a little unnerving, a disconcerting change from the way things had been on Bestla, and he looked back at his screen, frowning to hide his confusion. In the screen, the automatic shutdown was in progress, displaying his connect time and charges as it disinfected the ship's system and tidied up the files. "That sounds like it's worth pursuing. Do you think Kelly2 will talk to us? She didn't seem like the friendliest person I've ever dealt with."

"That I don't know," Rangsey answered. "But I bet the kid would."

Tarasov made a face. "That's tricky. I'd rather approach Kelly2 directly."

"And say what?" Rangsey shook his head. " 'Scuse me, Miana, we're investigating these attacks?' I don't think so."

"And even if we could, who knows if she'd talk to us," Tarasov finished. He sighed. "You said the brewkeep talked to you, though."

"He's fond of Kelly2," Rangsey answered. "And the girl, too, but really likes the mother. I don't think it's reciprocated."

"Do you mean liking or more?"

"Sex, I think," Rangsey said. "I think he's interested, she isn't. But whatever, she trusts him enough to let the girl stay there, in the Bubble, I mean, when she's away on a trade run."

Tarasov nodded slowly, absorbing the information. It was definitely something to follow up—something only they could follow up, for all that Macbeth and therefore presumably the rest of her team were already on the station. "We won't rush it," he said. "Let's take it slow, and talk up your connection with those people on the mine, too. That might attract some interest, if we can't get Kelly2 to talk."

Rangsey looked faintly disappointed, but nodded back. "Sounds good. How do the wildnets look?"

Tarasov tipped his head from side to side. "About the same as usual, I guess." Even as he spoke, he remembered the emptiness of the virtual landscape, and the indeterminate shape of the chogsets swarming over the fragments of the quasicoral, but shoved the uncertainty aside. It was probably nothing, the fauna hiding on the more distant reaches of the net, or at most NSMCo's security was more efficient than he had thought; he would wait to mention it until he knew more. "Nothing exciting. I think it's the people we have to focus on here."

Macbeth was waiting in the wrecker office, her feet propped up on a low table, a bookboard balanced in her lap. She looked like any corporate pilot, sitting there, uniform karabels and jacket splotched with company patches—not NSMCo, Tarasov realized, but the subcontractor that handled the wreckers' contract—and as she looked up, even her face seemed to have changed, subtly, become coarser, somehow duller. There was no sign of her Centrality clothes now, just the standard frontier styles. It was, he decided, a very good act, and one more reason to be very wary of her. She looked up then, as though she'd read his thought, and hauled herself slowly to her feet.

"Glad to see you. Let's go out back."

Tarasov followed without speaking, and was aware suddenly that Rangsey was matching her act, playing the quicksilver Traveller to her company drone. His hands danced, making his jewelry—a mix of gold and silvertone bracelets, a pair of rings—rattle softly, just enough to annoy the datatech working at a navlink console. Macbeth was aware of it, too, but gave no sign. She led them down a short corridor to a windowless conference room—not just windowless, Tarasov realized, but lacking even an environodule to give the illusion of a view. There was just a table, and in its center the bulky platform of a heavy-duty simulations display. The door closed behind them with a thud, and Tarasov glanced back, startled, as he heard locks and seals click into place. He looked back to see Macbeth pocketing a remote.

"Glad to see you made it," she said, and gestured for them to be seated. "And I'm pleased with what you've done so far. That was smart, setting up as tinkers."

"It seemed the best way to play it," Rangsey said. He sounded pleased, but still wary, and Tarasov was profoundly glad of the latter. The last thing he needed was for Rangsey to get a taste for field work.

Macbeth nodded. "As it happens, it fits in well with what I want you to do next. Magloire 12 Sanne has agreed to claim you as a cousin, Rangsey, for at least the course of this job— longer she said you'd have to work out between you—but that's the excuse we've been looking for. What I want you to do is put the word out that you're looking to find out who attacked her, what happened to her, and the rest of her crew of course, and see what happens."

Tarasov darted a glance at Rangsey, recognizing both the temptation—Magloire was an important Union family, with a large block of votes and ties to dozen other families; a cousinship with her was something worth pursuing—and the dangers. If there whoever it was that was attacking the mines was based on the Agglomeration, they were bound to act aggressively to protect their interests. He said, "I assume you'll provide backup for us?"

"As much as possible."

Tarasov looked at Rangsey again. The taller man blinked hard, visibly putting aside the last bits of his persona, and said, "Sein's right, asking that kind of question can't be very smart—"

"Or do you just want us to act as decoy?" Tarasov finished for him, and had the satisfaction of seeing Macbeth freeze for a fraction of a second.

"It's what's called a multipronged approach," she said. "Yes, I want you to draw attention away from some of our— subtler—operations, but I also think that a direct approach, honest anger, has a chance of getting somewhere with the Union." She nodded toward Rangsey. "I think that some people are much more likely to talk to a man with revenge on his mind, a cousin who lost everything, than to anyone from the Patrol."

And the worst of it was, she was probably right. Tarasov sighed, and slanted another glance at Rangsey. The taller man was smiling again, not fully happily, but recognizing her victory.

"I'll agree with that," he said, "but I'd like to know how you're going to protect us if we find something."

"I can't guarantee anything," Macbeth answered. "There aren't any guarantees in this business, Tarasov knows that. What I do promise is that you're known to my team, and they have orders to back you up first and ask questions later."

That was better than Tarasov had expected, though not fully reassuring. It was also exactly what any undercover team got, with the exception of a way to call in the rest of Macbeth's people. He said, "Don't we get call codes, then?"

In answer, Macbeth reached into the pocket of her jacket, brought out a databutton, and tossed it toward him. Tarasov caught it more by reflex than design, unable quite to hide his surprise, and his opinion of Macbeth rose a notch. At least she wasn't treating them any differently from the rest of her people, once she'd dragged them into this mess. "Thanks," he said, and Macbeth nodded indifferently.

"There's something you should know," Rangsey said. His voice had changed, Tarasov realized, was more like the voice he had used on Bestla again. "We have a lead on a survivor of one of the earliest attacks, as well as the people who found her."

"A survivor?" Macbeth looked up. "I thought there were no survivors from any of them."

"This one was reported," Rangsey said. "She was a kid, they guessed about two, a Traveller woman found her in a kid-carrier on the platform. Everybody else was killed, and they didn't get an ID—in fact, that's how I know it was reported, because the Patrol and the Federation government were involved in trying to identify her."

"Interesting," Ma⌐beth said. "Very interesting." She stared for a moment at the empty display platform, then shook herself. "I'll look into it, certainly. That's good work, Rangsey. Keep it up."

That was unmistakably dismissal, and Tarasov rose easily to his feet. Macbeth smiled up at him. "If anyone asks," she said, "tell them you were pricing a retrieval contract."

Stinne was late. Ista shifted her shoulders against the support pillar, looked from the lift station's multiple doors to the stairhead where up and down converged, still without seeing Stinne's reddish hair. At least the Midstation Plaza was mixed territory, as much Union, and therefore Traveller, as it was Company space; the shops were free-stores, rather than Company, and the Union-run brewhouse had a handful of bright-red tables on the floorplates outside its door. A Traveller man in a long embroidered tunic and trousers was selling something in small boxes from a handbasket, and Ista looked quickly away as his eyes met hers. She had taken off her trapata, carried it now wrapped around the straps of her carryall, but instead of feeling less conspicuous, she felt almost naked without it. Which wasn't fair, she thought. No matter what I do, I don't fit—and where the hell is Stinne, anyway?

She made herself relax again, feeling the pillar warm against her spine, the rough familiar texture of the coated metal coming clearly through the thin tricoteil, and concentrated instead on the morning she'd spent in the invisible world. Trindade had given her a fun job, for once, to take one of the shearing programs and collect code from the plates of bilateral wallaroo, and for once, too, there had been none of the odd, breathless feeling of something not quite right. The wildnet had been full of the usual programs, from chogsets on up to proper fauna, even a devil-may-care swirling away from her into the distance. She could still see the rippling expanse of code, the icons little more than rolling lumps in the monocular's lens until she had gotten close enough to distinguish the individual variations. It had been a near-perfect tessellation, the icons lying interlocked like deeply-patterned paving stones, and she had felt almost guilty prying one loose from the rest. She had taken it from the edge, as Trindade had taught her, where it would most easily regenerate, but she had been very aware of the gap in the pattern as she turned back toward the station's net. Still, Trindade had been pleased with the program—an ideal base for the job at hand, she had said, had said, too, that Ista's eye was improving—and Ista caught herself smiling at the memory.

"Ista?"

It was Stinne's voice, of course, though not from the direction she'd been expecting, from the walkways that led to the next commercial level rather than the lifts or the markets. Ista turned, already smiling, felt the expression fade when Stinne didn't match her. "What's up?"

"News." Stinne made a face, one corner of her mouth twisting up into a sour smile. "It ought to be good news, I suppose it is good news, but— News."

Ista looked at her, trying to gauge the depths of her unhappiness. "Do you want an ice?" she said at last, cautiously, and Stinne shook her head.

"No. Let's find someplace to sit down."

Ista nodded, feeling cold fingers knotting in the pit of her stomach. There weren't many places to sit in the plaza, unless you wanted to eat, and she led them back the way Stinne had come, up the long spiral of the walkway to the next level. It was one of the hydro stations, a maze of hardglass tanks filled with trees and lesser plants, each one with a monitor and information board attached. A group of children from the Company school was clustered around one of the biggest tanks, staring at trees with leaves bigger than a man's hand while their docent manipulated the information board. Ista avoided them, and headed for the far wall.

There the tanks were smaller, the grown less lush, and at least two were filled with holograms of the plants that would eventually occupy the space. Ista settled herself on the low walkway surrounding the nearest of those and looked at Stinne. "So what is it?" she asked again.

Stinne made another face, and didn't sit. The image in the tank, waving strands of grass tipped with plumes of pale silk-like fiber, reflected from the shiny clasp of her jacket and the blank face of the databoard she carried at her waist.

"My folks submitted my scores to the University. The one on Constantine. I've won a Company grant."

Ista drew a sharp breath. "Congratulations," she said, but couldn't quite make it sound as cheerful as she'd hoped. "When does it start?"

"In three months." Stinne gave her a look. "I didn't ask them to, my teachers didn't ask them to, they just did it. I thought I had at least another year."

"We knew it was going to happen sometime," Ista said. Her voice was steady now, and she was remotely pleased.

"But not now." Stinne sat abruptly, slewed around on the narrow ledge so that she was facing the other girl. "Look, we always said we'd go together."

Or not at all. Ista completed the sentence in her mind, could feel a bitter smile forming, and killed it. The low tank in front of her was filled with something dark and lacy; beyond it, a taller tank held something that produced white flowers the size of her palm.

"I don't know what to do," Stinne said.

Ista took another deep breath. "What is there to do?" she said. No one refused a Company grant; to refuse one was to throw away your future, and left you with nothing to look forward to but a life of Travelling, and somehow she couldn't see Stinne as a Traveller. "You'll have to go."

"What about you? Couldn't you apply for one of the outsider grants, or something through the Ragged Schools?"

"There are fifty of those for the entire Federation," Ista said. "And I'm not that good a scholar."

"What about the Company grants? The outsider grants, I mean." Stinne looked at her. "You're qualified."

The price is too damn high. Ista killed that response, knowing it was unreasonable—if she wanted to go with Stinne, if she wanted Stinne badly enough, then working for NSMCo, the guaranteed and mandatory job after graduation, was surely a reasonable trade. "I'm a Traveller, not even an hypothecary yet," she said. "The Company isn't going to waste a grant on me."

"Hypothecaries are valuable," Stinne said. She shook her head. "Damn it, Ista, I don't want to go. Not by myself."

"Not by myself" was different from "not without you." Ista said, "You have to go, you can't get ahead in the Company if you don't."

"Maybe I don't want to," Stinne muttered, but Ista ignored her.

"You'd have to be crazy not to take a chance like this."

"And what about you?" Stinne glared at her. "Are you just going to sit on the station and run the wildnet for the rest of your life?"

"It's what hypothecaries do," Ista answered. "And I don't have a whole hell of a lot of choice. I don't have money and I don't have papers—and that's another reason the Company's never going to give me a grant, it'd be too expensive to buy me a name on top of paying for school. So unless I come up with a whole lot of money, then, yeah, I'm going to stay right here for the rest of my life."

Stinne looked away. "I'm sorry."

Ista sighed, curbing her anger. There were one or two things she could do, a few ways she could make more money than she had or than she was making with Trindade, maybe even enough to pay for an accelerated course on Constantine—but not enough to pay for an identity. And without an identity, there was nothing she could do.

"There has to be something," Stinne said.

"I wish there was." Ista stared into the depths of the tank opposite her, thinking of the wildnet. The thick dark-green leaves curled like common fractals; she wondered vaguely if the leaves' overall shape was repeated in each curving tendril.

"The big thing's the ID, right?" Stinne asked. "Look, don't be insulted, but don't you know anybody who could forge you something? Everybody always says you can get fake ID down-station."

"It's not very good, most of it," Ista said. "And the good stuff's almost as expensive as the real thing." And, most of all, Kelly2 disapproved, passionately and articulately: for her it was a real identity, genuine papers, or none at all. I'm almost of age, Ista thought, I could do what I want, could take the chance if I wanted to—but I'd still have to come up with the money. She stared into the tank, picturing the invisible world, the local wildnet, wondering if there was anything there she could find or modify, make the big discovery every hypothe-cary dreamed of. . . . And if it was that easy, everybody would already have done it. She sighed, shook her head. "I'm glad you got the grant, Stinne, honest. I'm just—I'm still working on getting the money if I can."

Stinne looked at her for a moment longer, then nodded, still visibly unconvinced. "I'm sorry this happened, at least like this. I—I thought I had another year."

"I know." Ista kept staring at the big tank, the plants com-pletely still, unlike anything in the invisible. Only the trees she had seen outside Erramun's could compare, and they still seemed alien. These were normal, plants where they should be, safe behind glass. Maybe she should start looking into faked ID; it was probably the only way she was going to get off the station, and someone she knew, either Fredi or Bara-bell or one of the others, would know who to contact. "Look, it is a good thing, you should be proud."

"I'd've been prouder next year," Stinne said. "Or never." She stood as abruptly as she'd sat down, her light carryall banging against her hip. "Look, I've got to go, I told my mother I was shopping, I just had to tell you—"

Ista forced a smile she didn't fully feel. "It's all right. Really."

Stinne gave her a wobbly smile in answer, and swung away before Ista could be sure she was crying. And what I would have done if I had seen, she added silently, I surely don't know. She shook herself, Stinne's soft footsteps already lost in the general ventilation noises, got slowly to her own feet, the carryall a suddenly awkward weight on her shoulder. Unless something changed—unless she herself found, borrowed, or stole the money she needed to buy herself an identity, real or forged, or unless Stinne somehow didn't go, which was even more impossible—this was the beginning of the end of their friendship, and of anything else that might have grown from it.

She made her way back downstation slowly, barely paying enough attention to keep from walking into the other pedestrians who filled the mallways that led down to the lifts. Kelly2 would just say she'd warned her, Fredi—if she could find him at all—would talk wild about class and Union and the Company and do no good at all, Barabell would offer a beer and an extra-large plate of frites, if the Bubble wasn't too busy. That was probably the best of the lot, she decided, and if it was busy, at least she could make a little money while she took her mind off her troubles.

To her surprise, however, Kelly2 was sitting at one of the corner tables, talking to the two men who'd come to the ship to look at the spanner. She lifted a hand in greeting, but Kelly2 looked through her, and Ista felt herself flush. The bar wasn't that crowded, just a handful of tables occupied, groups of two and three, and a bigger group at the autogaming table, bent over the dark glass dish that was its display, and she went up to the bar, leaned against it until Barabell turned away from the service pumps.

"Hey, Ista. What can I get you?"

"The india?"

Barabell nodded, thumbed the proper switch and reached for a thick-walled glass. "I don't think I'm going to need you tonight, this is the busiest it's been, and Teenie's working."

Ista hid a sigh. Lohse Teenie had a wife and new baby to help feed, and there hadn't been much demand for his services lately on the mine platforms: he had the right to work before she did, but it came at a bad time. "Whatever," she said, and took the glass Barabell set in front of her.

"Hey, Ista." The voice came from about shoulder level, and she turned, knowing already it would be Lohse. He smiled up at her, set his tray on the bar, and went on, to Barabell, "Same again for the corner, three indias and a shandy."

"Hey, Teenie," Is⁺a answered. The Bubble's dim light was kind to him, let one concentrate on the ordinary upper body, shadowed the short, bowed legs. "Listen, what's with my—with Jenna?"

"I was going to ask you the same thing," Lohse answered. "I don't know what they're talking about, but it hasn't put her in a good mood, that's for sure."

"Great."

"Have fun," Lohse said, and turned away with his now-filled tray.

Ista took a swallow of her beer, Barabell's lightest, and wondered if she should head back to the ship, or just hole up in her room here. Neither option would keep her out of Kelly2's way for any length of time, but the right choice might mean a little less hassle later. She stared at the marks worn in the bar's polished surface, and shifted her own glass to start a new water-ring. She didn't need this, not now, not when she could use some help—or something, she amended silently. It wasn't likely Kelly2 could offer much help anyway, not when she'd been telling her all along that the friendship was bound to end badly.

"Ista."

It was Kelly2's voice, and from so close behind her that Ista jumped, nearly spilling her beer.

"Pay for that, we're leaving."

Ista blinked, but knew better than to argue with Kelly2 when she was in this mood. Barabell came hurrying down the length of the bar, his expression worried, but whatever he would have said was silenced by Kelly2's glare. Ista fumbled in her pockets for Company coin, clumsy under Kelly2's eye, found the money at last, and put it on the bar. She reached for one of the plastic carryout pouches that hung from the ceiling supports, and Kelly2's frown deepened.

"Leave it, will you?"

"I just paid for it." Ista shook open the pouch's mouth, cupping it into a funnel without waiting for an answer, and poured the rest of her beer into the dark green bag. A little spilled on the bar, splashing the last of the coins—her hands were shaking, she realized, surprised—and Barabell wiped it away.

"Come on," Kelly2 said again, and Ista folded the seals into place, still not daring to ask. Kelly2 turned for the door and stalked away, her back stiff with anger. Ista followed, looked back from the doorway to see the two men watching from their table, their faces unexpectedly sober.

Kelly2 said nothing until they reached the ship, but the rhythm of her step on the floorplates was eloquent enough. Ista kept her distance as much as possible, willing herself to be invisible in the empty corridors, but the occasional sharp glance told her she had not fully succeeded. The hatch closed behind her with the dull sound of meshing seals, and Kelly2 said, "Lock it. I'm switching on security."

Ista gave her a startled glance—they never used security, not on the Agglomeration, at least not since the Company had cracked down on the painter gangs nearly seven years ago—but did as she was told, throwing the heavy latches. The checklights came on, fading from amber to red as Kelly2 activated the security programs from the lock interface screen, and Ista said, "What's wrong?"

"Nothing, yet. I think." Kelly2 took a deep breath. "Let's go in the commons."

Ista went ahead of her into the main corridor, the lights flicking on in response to her movements, and heard the cookbox whir to life in the galley alcove as she opened the commons hatch. The floor padding was worn, as were the edges of the molded furniture, but the cream-colored walls were clean, and there was none of the sour smell that warned of an overworked disposal system. The samovar was already hissing, and she glanced curiously at Kelly2. "Do you want tea?"

Kelly2 shook her head, and crossed the little room to snap the machine impatiently off. "Sit down. I— This is important, I think."

Ista reached for the nearest chair, twisting it to free it from the travel dogs, and swung it so that her back was to the nearer bulkhead. On the one opposite, Kelly2 had pinned a pair of graphics from one of her Union clients who doubled as an artist, bright colors on black, geometric shapes like the icons of the invisible world. Kelly2 dropped into her favorite chair, tipping it back against the dogs, then straightened.

"Those two, Rangsey and Tarasov. I'm going through with the deal, but I don't want you to have anything to do with them. Stay well clear."

Ista blinked, but waited, and saw Kelly2 take a deep breath.

"The dark one, Rangsey, he had kin on that last platform that was attacked, and he's being stupid enough to take it personally. He's asking questions, and making it clear why he's asking, that he wants to find out who's doing it—"

"Good," Ista said.

"Not good." Kelly2 gave a grim smile. "I know what you're thinking. What you don't know—what you don't remember, you were too damn young to remember, then—is we went all out once I found you, and we lost more than a dozen people, one way and another, Travellers and Union and even a Company wrecker, and nobody found anything. And it's been the same ever since. Whatever, whoever's doing it, it's quiet now, and these idiots are going to wake it up. They were asking about you, about my finding you, and I want you to stay well away."

Ista said, slowly, "You never told me that."

Kelly2 frowned. "I just told you."

"No." Ista shook her head. "No, I don't mean that, I mean about what happened after you found me. You should've told me." She paused, trying to imagine, to assimilate what she'd been told. "How many people—was it anybody's kin, anyone I know?"

Kelly2 stared at her for a moment, and then her baffled expression eased into something like apology. She pushed herself to her feet, went to switch the samovar on again. "It's not like that, honey. Wasn't like that."

The endearment stung, and Ista blinked away incipient tears. "So what happened? I mean really, and then what happened afterward?"

Kelly2 took a deep breath. The samovar had barely had time

to cool down, was already hissing again, the light fading from yellow to green, and she took her time drawing off two glasses of tea, and brought the sugar caddy with them to the narrow table. Ista let her put one in front of her, and said, "Mama, tell me."

This time, Kelly2 didn't correct her. "I've told you before, most of it. I went out on one of my runs, to the Outer Reach, I don't do the Outer Reach any more, and my third client, regular stop, didn't answer my hail, but I could see it on the scanner. So I went in carefully—there had been an attack on a mine, oh, maybe eighteen months ago, so I was being careful— and I still couldn't get an answer to my hail. But I could see the mine, the dock was OK, and there were a few lights showing, running and emergency, so I brought the ship into the lock, suited up, took my cutting torch, and went on board. I found—" She stopped, swallowed hard. "I found a lot of dead bodies, seven of them, not nice, five in the processing deck and two in control, well, one in the corridor outside, really. All the equipment had been smashed, I was trying to jury-rig something that would keep it going."

She smiled then, an oddly rueful look. "I wasn't even thinking there was the slightest possibility of anyone being left, I had my mind full of salvage, what I could claim off it. But when I got down to the lowest level—that's where the main link controls were, below the worst of the damage—I thought maybe I could get them working, get rudimentary power, there you were. Somebody had put you in one of those kiddie-carriers, you know, their own little life support and all. I guess they were taking you to one of the lifepods, got cut off or something, and had to leave you there." She gave Ista a quick, fond glance. "You were fine, maybe scared, but good as gold when I got you back to the ship and got you out. I think somebody told you to keep quiet, but you talked happily enough once you relaxed. Told me your name and everything."

"Told you my first name," Ista said, with a familiar, savage bitterness. "And didn't even know my parents' names." She took a breath. "You told me that. What happened after?"

"Afterwards," Kelly2 began and paused, eyes fixed on

something in the distance. "A lot of that you know, too. I tried to find out who you were with, who was on the mine, and we never did, neither me nor the Company. Nor the Union, for that matter." She shrugged. "But that you know. The Company sent out a wrecker to try to retrieve the platform—they hadn't done that before, since most of the platforms were stripped bare."

"I thought this one was, too," Ista said.

"But you were alive," Kelly2 answered. "I don't know what they were thinking, exactly, but they sent one of the fast wreckers to see what they could find. And it vanished. They still don't know what happened, if it had anything to do with the attack or not, but the rescue team didn't find any sign of them. Or of wreckage, for that matter. And then there was another group, Union, this time, took an STL out looking for the wreck the next year when Mayhew was in alignment. They disappeared, too, and the wrecker found what was left of the ship— just the hull, absolutely stripped—a couple months later." She frowned. "I think there was a salvage crew that tried to find it, too, or maybe that was one of the other platforms—I was pretty busy with you, those next three years. But in any case, they said they spotted wreckage, but they also picked up what they thought was a ship closing fast, and ran away when it wouldn't answer their hail." She shrugged then, and managed a wry smile. "The Company said they were just trying to cover up defaulting on their contract, and I suppose they could've been right, at that. But that's why people think it's not safe to inquire too deeply into all of this."

"Somebody must've found something," Ista said.

"Why?" Kelly2 reached for her tea, drained half the cup. "You know how it is in the Outer Reach. It's too big, even with VMU, and the Company doesn't want to send the wreckers unless there are lives or money involved. If somebody reports a wreck with dead bodies and nothing worth salvaging, well, they're more likely to log the location and wait until someone else is scheduled for those claim-coordinates, let them look for them. Though the Union's started asking hazard pay for taking that job."

"Or else," Ista said, slowly, "someone in the Company is involved."

"Where's the profit?" Kelly2 asked. "You still have to sell the slag, rock or gas, through the Company brokers. No one would buy otherwise."

Ista shook her head, frowning herself now. "Then they're not selling slag," she said, "because it doesn't make any sense at all unless the Company's involved."

"And that," Kelly2 said, "is an idea you'd do well not to repeat." She smiled. "It's hard sometimes, having a smart kid."

Ista blinked, not understanding for an instant, and then blinked again as the compliment registered. And more than that, not only was Kelly2 telling her she was clever, she was telling her she was right. "But— Can't somebody do something?"

"You've lived here pretty much all your life," Kelly2 said. "You know how the Company works. What would you suggest?"

Ista looked away. The Patrol was pretty much useless, their closest office a fifteen-person team based on Mayhew that was supposed to concentrate on the STL traffic anyway; peacekeeping on the Agglomeration was handled by Company security. The Union was supposed to have mechanisms in place to protect their people, but she didn't know how effective they were—not very, if you listened to Fredi and his friends—and in any case, she didn't know what they were. Nor could she see how the Union could enforce anything anyway, not without a strike and all the problems that would follow. "I don't know," she said aloud. "Except maybe check their systems? There would have to be some kind of trail."

"Are you a good enough sysop to get in?" Kelly2 smiled again. "That's not exactly a hypothecary's job."

Ista looked down at her tea, wrapped her hands around the cooling ceramic. Kelly2 was right about that, too, much as she hated to admit it. Hypothecaries weren't trained for work within the dataverse of a specific program; it took an entirely different course of training—an entirely different kind of mind, Trindade said—to manipulate those program-systems.

"There's got to be something," she repeated.

Kelly2 shook her head, but didn't answer, went back to the samovar to draw more hot water into her tea. Ista watched her without really seeing the familiar movements, wondering what to do now. It was true that she wasn't trained for the Company dataverses, but Stinne was, knew them like the palms of her hands. Her access code was officially limited, of course, but it would probably be possible to buy a day password from someone, if Stinne hadn't already figured out a way in on her own—if, that is, Stinne was still able, or willing, to help. Ista looked back at the table's scarred top, her earlier meeting rushing back. Whatever else happened, Stinne was going away from her, would be gone by the end of the quarter, unless she herself found some way to raise the money for ID so that she could follow. If she could just get off planet with Stinne, get to Constantine, then even if she couldn't join Stinne at the University, at least she could find a job, be with her that much. But it all came down to money, more money than she could expect to see in the next decade.

"So." Kelly2 came back to the table, sat down again, the mug of tea still in her hand. "Like I said, I want you to stay away from those two."

Ista looked up sharply. If those two, Rangsey and Tarasov, were serious about finding out who was attacking the mines—and they had to be, if they'd bothered tracking her down—then maybe she should talk to them after all. Maybe one of them could read the dataverse—they were new to Travelling, she remembered, and had to have skills from before, from their citizen lives. And if she could help them find out what was going on, who had attacked the mines, there was bound to be a reward. Even just the standard witness share would go a long way toward getting her the ID she needed, and there was always the possibility that she might find out who she really was. She realized that Kelly2 was looking at her then, and made herself nod.

"I mean it, Ista," Kelly2 said.

"All right," Ista said, and let herself sound sharp and angry. "Like it would do me any good anyway."

Kelly2 gave her another look, less certain, then nodded again. "You'll stay on the ship for a while, I think. I'll send for your things, if you want."

"No, I'll get them." Ista made herself meet Kelly2's stare guilelessly. "I'll pick up what I want on the way home from Trindade's tomorrow—unless you want me to stop my lessons for now?"

"No." Kelly2 shook her head. "No, that's fine. Just—be careful."

"I will," Ista answered. *And I will*, she promised herself, silently. *It's just going to be a different careful*.

■ 6 ■

T HE ORBITAL AGGLOMERATION was well named, layers and accretions extending from an original cylinder, up and down along the axis and outward from the original surface, until it lay like a lathe-turned scepter against the plane of its orbit. At one end, the trailing end, the accretions were new, bright with solar films marked with departmental logos, each new volume, whatever its shape, tailored to fit with the rest; at the other, the leading end, dragging the station along its orbit, the sharp lines vanished into dull curves. The paint was mostly the cheapest mud-grey cool-film, and the sunward surfaces were a forest of unregistered solar vanes. The carefully-tuned fields of the STMU generators held it all in place, providing the internal standard 1 g without need of the spin that would destabilize the connections among the various components. Even without spin, without the STMU fields, the Agglomeration would fall apart under its own stresses, and the power plants that fed the generators were sealed and triply redundant. It seemed a small price to pay for the station's growth.

Inside the Agglomeration, the fields' gravity turned the structure on its head, putting 'up' toward the trailing end and 'down' toward the docks and the leading end, so that it felt to someone inside as though the station was perpetually falling down the curve of its orbit. The horizontal was relatively finite, each level strictly defined—though as new volumes were added, this changed—but the vertical was less restricted, and even NSMCo's long-tour employees didn't pretend to know more than their local volumes well. This was one of the advantages of the STMU-built stations, this illusion of space that worked almost as well as the older garden cylinders, with their spin-gravity and carefully designed mini-seas and farmlets. Most of NSMCo's people came from urban worlds anyway; the closely packed spaces, the vertical living, was more like their homes than an old-fashioned cylinder would have been. In any case, the stacked volumes provided as much variety as people needed to keep them sane, and the seemingly haphazard addition of components, far from being truly random, was actually a deliberate choice, to keep the employees from going stale. Or so Management told the other castes and sometimes each other, and, in any case, most people didn't stay on the station for more than two standard contracts.

Having spent most of her life on the Agglomeration—more of her life than anyone else she knew, not counting the twelve-year-old Aggas twins, who had been born in the Company clinic even though they were Union—Ista knew the maze of corridors and ramps and accessways the way Kelly2 had known the highways of the Maduran continent where she'd grown up. It made it easy to keep tabs on the newcomers, Rangsey and Tarasov, without letting herself be seen by Kelly2 or anyone who might mention her presence to Kelly2. Of course, there were no great surprises about the strangers, either: they made daily trips through the markets, for gossip and news as well as food, drank in the evenings at the Bubble or at the Union brewhouse at Midstation, slept on their ship, almost certainly together. The last was no great surprise, and even something of a relief: one less thing to worry about when she met with them.

She planned the meeting carefully, letting three days pass because she couldn't be sure that Kelly2 wouldn't be Midstation herself, arranging her usual deals with the free-stores there, and then let a fourth day go because Trindade kept her later than usual and she had to hurry back to the ship to meet Kelly2. But finally, on the fifth day, things came together. Trindade had less work than usual—it was a slack time for the hypothecary; business wouldn't pick up again until the ships in dock had had a chance to finish their trading, and their crews came creeping in by ones and twos to have Trindade assess the programs they had bought—and Trindade had purchases of her own to make. Ista took the early dismissal with passable disappointment, then headed through the service corridors to the Lower Market. According to gossip at the Bubble, Rangsey and Tarasov, or at least one of them, preferred to eat their lunch at one of the brewhouses there. She didn't quite believe it—it would be almost too much good fortune, to find them so quickly—but even so, she was holding her breath as she came around the corner into the plaza.

At first glance, the two men were nowhere to be seen, and she let her breath out with a sigh, already planning her next attempt. Barabell said they came to the Bubble to drink—they liked his beer, always a way to win his friendship—but that was useless, since Barabell would be bound to mention it to Kelly2 if he saw them talking. The ship was another possibility, but the dockers knew her, and knew Kelly2: it wasn't as much of a risk as meeting them at the Bubble, but it wasn't one she wanted to take.

She made her way through the tables, crowded now at midshift, Union workers and low-Service employees almost indistinguishable until you looked closely at the patches on their shirts and toolvests, and went on into the brewhouse itself. It was smaller than the Bubble, spent more effort on food and less on its beer, and she hung back for a moment, pretending to study the flashing menu that hung from the ceiling. She knew its offerings by heart; it was the people in line she cared about. And then she saw them, Rangsey first, in line at the automat, peering over the shoulder of a stocky woman at the offerings on the slow conveyors. Tarasov was a little ahead of him, a box-lunch tucked under one arm as he filled a liter jug from the water dispenser. The chime sounded even as she watched; he awkwardly sealed it, and moved on to the beer pumps. He must not be used to Travelling, Ista thought; everybody knew that water upstation—at any foodshop— was twice as expensive as the water from the dedicated distilleries, and not that much better. Then he turned away from the rank of machines, frowning as he tried to balance all his purchases, and Ista stepped forward without conscious thought.

"Hey."

Tarasov looked up at the greeting, his expression momentarily blank, and then Ista saw his face change as he recognized her. "Hey—Ista, isn't it? Ista Kelly?"

"That's right." Ista took a breath, her rehearsed phrases momentarily deserting her. Rangsey came up behind the shorter man, balancing his lunch with absent ease, and she saw him fix suddenly on her face. "I—I've been hearing talk, that you're out to do something about your cousin, the one on the mine. Can I talk to you?"

Tarasov's eyes slid sideways, searching for his partner, and Rangsey said easily, "Sure, why not? Why don't you join us for lunch?"

"I'm not hungry," Ista began, and a smile flickered across Rangsey's face.

"Get something anyway. It looks better. We'll get a table."

He was right, and Ista nodded, took her place in the payment line before she thought to wonder how he knew that she could get in trouble for talking to them. Probably Kelly2 had made it clear they were to stay away from her almost-daughter, she thought, or maybe they were worried about causing anybody trouble. And maybe, just maybe, that meant they thought they were finding something. She picked her lunch more or less at random from the cheapest part of the menu, collected it from the conveyors along with a half-pint of the cheaper beer, and stepped back out into the maze of tables.

The shift break was almost over, and the tables were emptying rapidly. Tarasov and Rangsey had chosen one in a corner, half obscured by a thick support column, and Ista made her way to join them, setting her packages down on the scarred plastic. Tarasov shoved an empty chair toward her, automatic politeness, and she settled herself opposite, unwrapping the box of rice. They ate in silence for a moment, the smell of curried vegetables rising from the opened containers, and then Rangsey set aside his beer.

"So. What was it you wanted to talk to us about?"

Ista took her time finishing the last bite of rice, set her spoon carefully aside. "I heard you were looking to do something about your cousin, the one who was on the mine."

"That's right," Rangsey said, but Ista saw the quick exchange of glances, little more than a flicker of eyes, before he spoke. "I don't understand why the Company isn't doing something about it themselves—well, I do, maybe, and I don't like it."

"I have an interest in that, too," Ista said. "My family, I guess, my real family, was killed on a mine, my—Jenna just found me there. So it's got to be the same people doing it, the method's the same, and if you're looking for who's doing it, I want to be in on it. I need to find out what's happening, what happened to my family. So I want in."

"We heard something about you," Tarasov said.

Rangsey spoke almost in the same moment. "What makes you think it is the same people? You're, what, fifteen, sixteen? That makes it thirteen years ago at least—that's a hell of a long time to stay in that business."

"I'm sixteen." Ista made herself take another drink of her beer, swallowing her first, instinctive answer. Trindade had taught her to buy time when she wasn't sure, to wait and watch, say nothing of substance until she had some idea what the client was looking for, and surely the same tactic would serve her here. She looked at Tarasov. "What have you heard about me?"

The words came out more hurt than she'd intended, but she wasn't sure that would do her any harm. Tarasov said, "Pretty much what you told us, not a lot more."

"What makes you think it's the same people?" Rangsey asked again.

Ista said, carefully, "Who else would it be? From what everyone's said about your cousin's mine, the same thing happened that happened to everybody else, except they had the sense to cut and run. And I'm sorry they're hurting because of it, but they did the right thing."

Rangsey nodded. "Still, it could be different people, after the same thing."

"That doesn't matter," Ista said. She shook her head. "No, even if it's different people actually making the attacks, they have to be either working for the same people or at worst selling what they take to the same people who bought all the rest, otherwise there'd be more differences between the attacks." She stopped abruptly, realizing that she'd said more than she meant, and Tarasov laughed softly.

"She's got you there, Justin. It doesn't make sense any other way."

"And you knew it," Ista said, "or you wouldn't be here in the first place."

Rangsey looked away, managed an almost apologetic smile. "You're right, of course," he said, after a moment, "but you might want to consider that this isn't the smartest thing to get involved in, not if you want to stay on the Agglomeration."

"What makes you think I do?" Ista heard her voice sharp with sudden anger, and moderated her tone with an effort. "Look, as things stand right now, I don't have any kind of ID, and I can't get one because I can't prove I was born on any particular Federal planet, or to a Company employee, and mama can't afford, I can't afford, the fees to buy ID. Not a real one, anyway. And if I don't get off the Agglomeration soon, I will stay here the rest of my life, and I want—I want the option to do something different."

Rangsey stared at her, visibly undecided, but it was Tarasov who spoke first. "Can you afford to help us?"

Rangsey looked sharply at him, the first unguarded expression Ista had seen on his handsome face, but Tarasov ignored him. "I mean, I know your mother doesn't want us talking to you, and there may well be other risks. Are you sure you're prepared for that?"

Ista nodded. "I'm sure."

"What I'm not sure about," Rangsey said, speaking now to Tarasov, "is what she can do for us that's worth the risk."

"I know the Company, and I know the invisible world here, the wildnet and the controlled habitat," Ista answered. "I can get things out of the records that you wouldn't even know to look for."

Tarasov nodded, but Rangsey said, "Such as?"

"Locations of all the attacks, and a program that will project where any wreckage is now, plus any actual sightings, and whether or not they match." Ista shrugged, carefully casual. "Plus anything else in the back files or the library on the subject." Stinne's access codes could get her the first things, she knew—she had done it before, found records of the mine she had been found on; the others were less certain, but better to promise more, now, and worry about finding it later.

Tarasov looked at Rangsey. "Some of that's just plain police work—"

"You think you can get it better than I can?" Ista interrupted.

Rangsey's smile was tinged with malice. "She's got you there, Sein," he quoted. "And even if it was done, which I wouldn't bet on, it would be interesting to see what wasn't followed up."

Tarasov nodded slowly, looked back at Ista. "All right. You're in. And, yeah, let's start with those records."

"One other thing first," Ista said. "If there's any reward, I want a third."

"What makes you think there'd be one?" Rangsey asked, and Tarasov rolled his eyes.

"Oh, give it a rest, Jus. Agreed, you get a third."

Ista nodded acknowledgement, but kept her eyes on Rangsey. The tall man sighed, and nodded. "All right. One-third. If there's a reward at all."

"And we'll say it before witnesses," Tarasov said.

Ista nodded again, satisfied. Travellers lived by their word and reputation; even the suspicion of a broken contract could make their lives very difficult. "I'll hold you to that," she said, and stood, collecting her empty packages for the recycling.

"Just get us the records you promised," Rangsey said. She lifted her free hand in answer, and walked away, glad they couldn't tell how hard her heart was beating. Her hands were shaking, too, and she fumbled with the cartons for a moment before she got them into the recycler's slots, but then turned her back and walked back up the ramp toward the Midstation lifts. She'd done the hardest part, she told herself. Now all she had to do was find the information she'd promised them.

"I don't think this is smart," Rangsey said.

Tarasov looked up from his net display, one hand hovering over the controls, then sighed and touched the combination that froze the program in midstream, still well inside the boundaries of the Company frontage. "You're talking about the girl, I assume."

"It's not like we've done anything else recently," Rangsey answered. "At least not anything that stupid."

Tarasov smiled in spite of himself, acknowledging the remark, but said only, "I think it was the right thing to do."

"And I don't." Rangsey tipped his head to one side. "You're the one who was bitching about my being made part of this. What changed your mind all of a sudden?"

That hit home. Tarasov said, "What changed my mind is we're in this up to our necks already. I don't know these nets as well as that girl does, and if there's any information to be pried out of them, she's more likely to find it than I am. Ketty was the one who handled the controlled habitats, not me."

"Ista is a hypothecary," Rangsey said, "not a programmer. And this could be dangerous—especially Macbeth's new plan."

Tarasov looked back at the display's frozen image, a single icon blinking in one corner to remind him of programs in suspension, his lens host left to fend for itself until he reasserted control. Rangsey was right, that was the worst of it, and he himself didn't have a lot in the way of good reasons to defend himself. "It's what she said," he said at last. "She's part of this already."

"She could get forged ID," Rangsey began, and Tarasov shook his head.

"How many of those cases did you handle last year? You know how long those papers last."

Rangsey made a face. "All right, yes, two or three trips at best, and then you'd better buy another set." He looked away, and Tarasov knew they were thinking of the same thing, the disks that arrived on their desks every month, names and ID numbers that had been flagged as forgeries, or suspect for some other reason. The Patrol never caught up with more than a tenth of those names, never found the live bodies that used them, but it was no way to live, even for a Traveller.

"I just don't want it to be us who gets her hurt," Rangsey said. "Hell, put it this way, I don't want to be responsible for her."

"You want to bet she wouldn't be doing this on her own?" Tarasov asked.

"Do you want to bet she'd be doing it if we hadn't started saying we were going after these people?" Rangsey shot back. "That doesn't work, Sein."

"She's already in the middle of it," Tarasov said again. "She was in at the beginning, Justin. She deserves the chance." He paused, studying the other man's still unconvinced expression. "What would you be doing, in her place?"

Rangsey smiled, reluctantly. "The same thing she is. But it still wouldn't be smart. And, no, before you ask, I don't think I could stop me." He lifted an eyebrow. "But it still doesn't make it a good idea."

"No." Tarasov sighed. "But she's got a better chance with us, I think, than she might on her own."

"Maybe," Rangsey answered. "Maybe." He sighed, and glanced at the displays, reaching across to trigger an accounting routine. "Staying here isn't cheap, I have to say."

"No," Tarasov answered, his attention already returning to his display. Rangsey mumbled something in answer, settling himself in the pilot's chair, and pulled an input board to him. Tarasov recognized the first flash of an auditor as Rangsey's screen windowed, and touched his own controls again, releasing the hold.

It didn't take long to find his way out onto the wildnet, and he checked his string reading, then picked a direction at random and let the lens cover a few hundred clicks at its top speed before he dialed it back. Around his point-of-view, the lens showed the same relatively featureless grey-green plain, broken in the distance by a band of a different, darker green. Or was it grey? he wondered, unable to decipher the precise shade, then shook his head. Either way, it was worth investigating, could be anything from a floral reef to a long-liner's hermitage or a bullcomber's backfill, but he swung the lens through a full three-hundred-sixty degrees first, checking the rest of the territory around him. A pair of godwits, bright balls on long stick legs, were striding across the middle distance—heading away from the gateway, he saw, with some satisfaction; the wild fauna did seem to avoid the gateway areas—but that was the only sign of life in the lens's radius. And that was still odd: there should be more programs, certainly more flora, on a wildnet as old as this one.

He shifted his fingers to turn back toward the distant reef, moving toward it at a cautious speed, and saw the flat plane of the background change ahead of him. At first, he thought it was just a change of color, the darkening that came from age, or the lens's way of presenting a thicker sludge of protocode that was sometimes a precursor of primitive fixed fauna, but as he got closer, he could see dark lines like cracks zigzagging across the grey-green plane. They looked completely random, without even the unlikely order of a fractal or chaotic pattern, and he reached for the secondary controls, triggering an analysand. It skittered away from him, twisting in the lens's view like a dervish or a tiny devil-may-care, and he wondered momentarily what lay in its bloodlines. The skidding movements were in fact fairly purposeful; it covered perhaps half the cracked patch, and then swung back, to be reabsorbed by the controlling lens. A moment later, a string of icons appeared across the base of the screen, followed by a single line of real-text: PATTERN NOT ON FILE. SAVE PROTECTED ICONS FOR LATER ANALYSIS? YES/NO. Tarasov sighed—he really hadn't expected his program to identify something he had never seen, but he had hoped it might—and touched the controls to save the iconic record. A confirmation string flickered across the screen, resolved into a single glowing symbol: the material was saved. He sighed again, and touched the controls to move more quickly toward the distant reef.

As the image became clearer in the lens's view, he recognized the shape of a hermitage, the cave-like structure thrown up by a long-liner to protect the hammal's vulnerable central units. This one looked as though it had been in place for a long time, and he automatically slowed again, checking the plane around him for the long-liner's hooks. Long-liners survived by extruding pseudoboids, bits of program that mimicked the behaviors of the half-dozen low-level faunal programs that were lumped under the generic name of "boids" and that provided the raw code for any number of higher level fauna. The pseudoboids would be linked by an all-but-invisible mesh that would react to the intrusion of a faunal program and signal its presence to the parent program lurking in its cave. If the intruding program was large enough, complex enough, the long-liner would emerge, rush the intruder, and overwhelm it, incorporating its structure into either the central program or into the dead matter that formed the walls of the cave. There were no signs of any program, boid, pseudoboid, or even the smaller vetch, which usually flourished around a long-liner's hermitage, living off code fragments too small to be absorbed by the long-liner, and helping to hide the signalling mesh, and Tarasov frowned. The marks that looked like cracks could be the remains of mesh, or even of a field of joint grass, but that would mean that the long-liner was dead. And that almost never happened: long-liners were at the top of the food chain, virtually immortal once they'd established a hermitage; nothing preyed on them, and as long as they maintained a supply of code to repair the bits inevitably damaged in daily use, there was little to stop them maintaining themselves indefinitely.

He moved closer to the hermitage, more quickly now, less careful of possible pseudoboids—if there had been any, if the long-liner were still in residence, the VALMUL lens and its host would have attracted its attention long before now. The walls of the hermitage looked dry, oddly dusty, unlike the oily surface of all the others he'd seen, and he was certain now that the long-liner was dead. But how? he thought, and shifted the lens to scan the long lump of the hermitage for one of the long-liner's pop-doors. Virus? That was the immediate and worst fear, some malevolent bit of code that would poison every program on a wildnet and then spread to the controlled habitats, requiring a quarantine that would be as devastating as the effects of the virus itself. That had never actually happened—the few really effective viruses had been ineffective parasites, killing their hosts too fast—but it was theoretically possible, and no one wanted to rely on good luck forever. Still, if it was a virus, it was too late to worry about it; his own programs would be hopelessly infected already. So where the hell is the pop-door? he thought, and almost in the same instant spotted the slight deviation in the regular pattern than marked the opening in the codewall. He moved closer, then ordered his lens to release a manipulator, and tap on the wall beside the pop-door. He held his breath, but nothing happened, and he touched the controls again, translating some unimaginable contact between two programs into a harder knock on the solid-looking wall.

To his shock, the pop-door crumbled under his touch, taking a section of the hermitage wall with it. He stared at the rubble, fading further from brown to the dull grey of the truly dead even as he watched, then, very carefully, moved forward to peer through the opening into the interior of the hermitage. For a moment, he could see nothing, just darkness, and then the lens adjusted for the new conditions, and he began to see shapes, curves and odd joints of silver, lying scattered across the hermitage's patterned floor. A thicker line, bleached whiter than mere silver, seemed to run the length of the space, disappearing into the hermitage's interior; the rest of the pieces fanned out from it, like the ribs of a long-dead snake. And in a way, he realized suddenly, he was seeing bones. Those were the last remains of the long-liner's code, the shattered bits of the program, still lying inside the dead code of its hermitage.

And where the hell were the scavengers? he thought. He had been taught that nothing ever went to waste on the wildnet, that some program, even if it was just vlichen, the most primitive of the floral programs, always eventually incorporated fragmentary code. And yet here were the remains of the largest, most complex of the faunal predators, enough to feed most smaller fauna and all the floral programs he'd ever studied, lying unclaimed, still white-silver in the lens's view. Was there a virus? Had the other programs learned to avoid this section of the wildnet? Or was there some other reason, linked maybe to the scarcity of fauna on NSMCo's wildnet? He shook his head, still staring at the bone-like forms, then triggered a collection program. The best he could do was take samples, and analyze them on the ship. Any further speculation would have to wait until that was done.

He leaned back in the couch, letting his eyes relax from the close focus of the display, and Rangsey said, "Anything new?"

He was leaning forward a little, his own display closed and empty, and Tarasov smiled in spite of himself at the normality of it all. "I don't know," he said, and Rangsey tipped his head sideways.

"What do you mean?"

Tarasov shrugged, one eye on the display as the numbers wound back toward the zero point that was the gateway. A string of numbers flashed, and then the icon that meant his decoy was running: everything was as it should be. He said, "I found a dead long-liner in its hermitage."

Rangsey frowned. "I thought you told me things didn't die on the nets. One of the places the metaphor breaks down, you said."

Tarasov drew the i-board closer to him, touching controls to recall his keyboard and shunt the retrieved codes to protected storage. "I meant programs don't break down of the equivalent of old age, at least not without making a copy of themselves. Most programs replace themselves piecemeal indefinitely, or at least until something bigger than them breaks them up, but long-liners—well, there aren't many programs bigger than them. And I'll tell you something else weird. Nothing had scavenged its code fragments."

"That is odd," Rangsey said, and his frown deepened. "Virus?"

Tarasov could hear the sudden concern in the other man's voice, and couldn't help a small, mean feeling of satisfaction at having worried him. "I don't think so." And I don't, he realized suddenly. Those didn't look like virused fragments, or at least not the ones I've seen.

"But you're not sure," Rangsey said.

"No." Tarasov grinned. "But if I'm wrong, it's too late anyway."

"Funny." Rangsey pushed himself up out of the couch. "I'm going down to commons. You want anything?"

"No, thanks." Tarasov adjusted his i-board again, calling up a new set of controls. "I do want to find out what's going on here."

"You could always ask Ista what she knows," Rangsey said. "She's a hypothecary, remember?"

"A hypothecary in training," Tarasov corrected automatically, and heard the hatch click closed behind the other man. It wasn't actually a bad idea, though, and he filed it for later. He would do what he could now with the fragments he'd collected, and he'd ask the girl as well later.

A new window opened in his display, revealing the bits of code, each polyhedron walled in its own virtual cell, kept carefully isolated just in case the pieces could recombine to form a new entity. Given that they hadn't done so in the presumably better conditions of the wildnet, it seemed an unnecessary precaution, but there was a whole class of hammal, deadlurks, that fed and reproduced themselves by simulating death. It was wiser not to take chances, especially on a net he still didn't know all that well. In this program's habitat, the polyhedrons looked less silver than ivory, and he could see slightly darker mottling on their surfaces. He touched controls to enhance the contrast, and produced an odd three-quarter ring scattered across each of the polyhedrons. The shape looked oddly familiar, something he'd seen before, though not on the wildnets. He frowned at it, and then remembered: the broken rosette of a leopard's spots, black on gold. It was not an icon he knew, and he dispatched a gopher to search his working library for any likely matches. It was gone long enough that he wasn't surprised to see it return empty-handed.

That meant a proper dissection, time-consuming, but ultimately more certain than the working approximation of the iconage. He ran his fingers over the controls, searching his toolkit for the proper program, and then hesitated, studying the polyhedrons. Normally, he would start with the largest fragment, assuming it to be the most complex, but that was a plain cube, its only complication a smaller cube budding from one corner. The next largest was a truncated pyramid containing both a smaller shadow of itself and a hexagon where the tip should have been: complex enough to offer a guess at the code contained on the NSMCo wildnet, the range of code from which the long-liner had emerged, and yet still simple enough to study. He touched a final selector, and turned his donkey loose. The screen filled instantly with a hash of colors, the familiar static rainbow that meant everything was working properly, and Tarasov leaned back in his couch to wait for the program to finish its work.

It took almost twenty minutes by the chronometer on the pilot's display, but at last the static vanished, and was replaced by a blank white screen filled with programmers' script. Tarasov leaned forward again, bringing the complex symbols into closer focus, but after half a dozen lines had lost the thread of function. That wasn't unexpected, either—the AL programs had come into existence because they could evolve a structure far more compact and efficient than any human programmer could imagine—but he sighed anyway as he called up a parsing routine. He prided himself on his ability to read the raw script, could even follow some floral patterns, and not just the simplest ones, either; he had hoped he might be able to make some guess at this fragment's function from the code alone.

It took another hour to parse the code into something Tarasov could follow, and when it was done, he stared at the screen in disappointment. There were no signs of a virus, or at least not any of the classes he recognized, and it wasn't any of the other things he had thought it might be—wasn't the AL equivalent of starvation, for one, because at least some of the code was new, not yet perfectly assimilated to the main structure. So the long-liner had been taking in other programs right up until the end, he thought, and scrolled slowly through the new file. Had it taken a poison, a program that resisted assimilation so vigorously that it was able to break free by destroying the long-liner from within? That seemed the only possibility, but poisons usually left traces, characteristic breaks in the code, and those didn't seem to be present here. He scrolled back through the file, read it again without finding anything new, and leaned back in his couch, touching controls to close down the various donkeys. Back on Bestla, this was the sort of uncertainty he'd always hated, and only in part because he didn't know what to put in the reports. He smiled then, and felt the expression twist out of true. Actually, he knew perfectly well what he would have listed in his report—*a poison of unknown type, leaving no recognizable traces*—and everybody in the Squad would have known exactly what he meant. The bad part was that when one started seeing signs like this, programs partially assimilated by something one didn't recognize, it was often the precursor of a new, and usually higher, faunal form, another step toward true AL and even Artificial Intelligence. If that was what was happening in NSMCo's wildnet, then a quarantine was probably in order, at least until they knew for certain what was emerging.

He smiled again, the expression just as wry as before. He knew perfectly well what would happen if he suggested a quarantine: the same thing that happened every time a technician suggested a precaution that might interfere with business. There would be protests, questions, a debate over the evidence, and by the time a decision was made, the new program type had already seeded itself across a wide sector, making it almost impossible to eradicate. And there were good reasons not to impose quarantines, Tarasov admitted. He had been caught on the wrong side of one once, for three days, and had been shocked at how quickly the planet's economy had withered, cut off from easy communication with the Federation. So maybe the Territories were right after all, and the best way to deal with the new life was not tighter control, but an acceptance of its rules, a change in the way people dealt with the nets. At the very least, it would provide a different set of problems.

He sighed then, dismissing the idea—different problems weren't necessarily easier to resolve—and touched the i-board to send the donkeys after the other bits of code. Something new might turn up there, but he doubted it; the best thing, he decided, would be to talk to Ista, see what she and her teacher thought about conditions on the wildnet. If a new program was emerging, the hypothecaries were usually the first to notice.

Ista wedged herself into the narrow toilet, listening for Stinne's warning whistle with half her mind while she struggled to fit into the borrowed karabels. Stinne was slimmer than she was, especially through the hips; the tough fabric strained against the buttons, and she held her breath, wriggling her hips as though that would help her get her flesh distributed better. And then at last the last button popped through the narrow buttonhole, and she took a cautious breath. Yes, she could breathe, and she could feel the fabric easing already; she pulled on the tricoteil big-shirt—also borrowed, with the splendid-sun logo of the Inner Reach Exploitation Team splashed across the chest—and was grateful that it fell to mid-thigh, hiding the too-tight karabels.

"Hurry up," Stinne hissed, from outside, and Ista sighed.

"I'm coming," she said, and bent clumsily to retrieve her own clothes, the karabels painfully tight around her waist and thighs. She straightened to stuff them into her carryall, and opened the cubicle door. Stinne gave her a critical glance, and then nodded.

"Not bad. Now we just have to do something about your hair."

"I'm not taking my braids out unless you're going to help me redo them."

"I was thinking of a scarf," Stinne said. "It's very fashionable."

Ista glanced at the main door—this was one of the Company lounges, bigger and better-staffed than the public toilets, and she didn't trust it to stay empty for very long—but nodded, and began knotting her braids into a single bun. Stinne produced a narrow strip of fabric—Traveller fabric, Ista saw, without surprise, deep wine-red true-cotton embroidered with gold arabesques—from her bag, and helped the other girl wind it around her head, turning the scarf into a close-fitting cap that covered all but the edges of Ista's hair. It felt odd to be without the weight of the braids, to feel air on her neck and ears, and Ista stared at her reflection in the wall mirrors, not quite believing what she saw. She no longer looked Traveller—even her bracelets had become affectation rather than a symbol—but like an employee, Service, or maybe even Management. She looked older, she decided, and richer than she had any hope of being, and was suddenly unsure if she liked the change.

"You look great," Stinne said. "Just ditch the jewelry."

Ista shook herself away from the unfamiliar image, busied herself stripping off the bracelets and earrings, and buried them at the bottom of the carryall. "Think I'll pass?" she asked at last, and Stinne nodded.

"Look at yourself. You look great."

Ista glanced at herself again, obediently, but shied away from looking too close. It was too strange a picture, herself as Company, as Management, even, and she couldn't like the woman in the mirror.

"All you'll need is the card," Stinne went on briskly, "and we're all set." She rummaged in her own, smaller carryall,

produced a slip of dark-blue plastic, and held it out with something like a flourish. "I borrowed this from Diver Anny."

Ista accepted it gratefully, stood looking down at the mar-
bled surface. Buried in the thin wafer were codes that would
give her access to the Company library cubicles—not to the
Company's private nets, its special habitats, or indeed to any
stored files, they would use Stinne's codes for that, but to the
rooms that held the machines that had the only hard access.

"Don't fondle it like that," Stinne said, "or they'll know for
sure it isn't yours."

Ista laughed, but felt herself blushing, and stuffed the card
into the karabels' tight pockets. "I guess I'm ready."

Stinne nodded. "Let's go, then."

Stinne had said that it would be better to come at the library
cubicles from upstation, a subtle thing, but, Ista guessed, probably fairly effective. It was certainly the sort of thing Trindade
would have suggested. They made their way down a stationary spiral that led from the edge of the plaza to a double-wide
corridor with an arched ceiling painted with the white fluff of
clouds. The painted sky between them was an improbable
shade of blue, paler than Kelly2's eyes, and Ista found it hard
to keep from staring. She had never been this far upstation before, at least not outside the most public spaces, and she was
glad Stinne was with her.

The local library was really nothing more than a cloverleaf
of data cubicles, linked by a central doorway monitored by an
automatic pass reader. That was some consolation—the machines were easier to fool than people, particularly when the
Company didn't bother spending the money for absolute iden-
tification—but Ista caught herself holding her breath as Stinne
slid her card through the reader. There was no better way to
attract the machine's attention, and she made herself take a
breath, and then another, as she slipped the borrowed card
under the reader's eye. There was a brief pause—longer, it
seemed, than the machine had taken to consider Stinne's—but
then the inner door clicked open, and a mechanical voice said,
"Cubicle four is open for your use."

Ista bit back the automatic thanks—citizens did not thank

machines even if Travellers did—and followed Stinne through the inner door into the red-walled corridor. A red light, a brighter red than the wall padding, was lit over the nearest door, and Stinne pressed confidently on the latch. The door gave under her touch, and lights flicked on inside—ordinary white lighting, Ista saw, with some relief, and equally ordinary data consoles. She stepped inside, and Stinne shut the door behind them both, setting the inner dial for maximum privacy.

"So far so good," she said, and Ista grinned. "What next?"

Ista set her carryall in the corner, and turned to look at the console. It had twin input boards set in front of a single large screen, currently blank except for the slow and random pulse of a cursor. "Next—next I guess we see what kind of access we can get."

Stinne nodded, settling herself comfortably in the nearest chair, and reached for the input board. Ista leaned over her shoulder, more curious than anything. This was Stinne's skill, product of a lifetime spent using the Company nets for everything from school to play; Ista knew she would be as lost in the hierarchies of data, of mininets and linked volumes and the pools of controlled habitat, as Stinne would be on the wildnet. She was happy to let Stinne handle this—and admitted silently that she wished she had had the chance to learn the codes and patterns. But Stinne could handle it, would find what she needed, she told herself firmly. Trindade might say, never trust someone else to do your work, but sometimes you didn't have a choice.

"OK," Stinne said. "I'm in the main pool." In front and above her the screen was filled with overlapping windows, each one displaying unfamiliar symbols and patterns, two even filled completely with realtext. "Talk me in."

"The important thing is the location of the attacks," Ista began. "All of them, from the earliest, and that would have been at least fourteen years ago, probably sixteen or seventeen." That was a guess, but a sound one: she had been found fourteen years ago, and people had talked about at least one incident before that to make the mine workers nervous.

Stinne nodded, her fingers busy on invisible controls, sliding across the dull grey surface of the i-board. New windows shifted and closed, to reappear in new configurations. "I can get into the AgNews morgue. I'll start there."

Ista frowned, trying to imagine the hierarchies. "To get the dates?"

"Yeah." Stinne's eyes were focussed on her screen, fingers still working. "Then I'll try the harder records."

A page bloomed in the screen, black realtext on white, was selected and copied and then dismissed. "All right," Stinne said. "I've got dates—Jesus, I didn't know there had been that many."

"How many does that show?"

"Twenty-one." Stinne turned a stricken face to her. "That's just too many, Ista."

Ista leaned over her shoulder, reaching for the i-board. "Where's—"

Stinne put her fingers on the right control before Ista could finish her question, and Ista smiled her thanks, fixing her eyes on the screen. She skimmed through the digest—the morgue used an efficient selector, and she made a note to find its name—trying to sort definites from possibles, cases where wreckage was found from mere disappearances. After all, the Outer Reach was human-hostile space, and the mines went deeper into the asteroid belts every year, looking for the highest concentrations of minerals; some accidents were to be expected. Still, even counting only the definites, there were thirteen confirmed attacks. "That's almost one a year," she said aloud.

"More," Stinne said. "I set the parameters to weed out accidents." She touched the board again, and the search formula appeared in a separate window. Trindade almost never used that language, insisted on the more intuitive VALMUL-i/o forms, but she had made sure that Ista learned the basic grammar, and Ista studied the symbols carefully. It looked as though it would have excluded any reports that could be explained in any other way, and she nodded slowly.

"So then we search from those dates?"

"Assuming I can get into the back records," Stinne answered.

"Security's?" Ista asked, and Stinne shook her head.

"No, they'll be sewn up really tight. I thought I'd try Navigation, and then maybe Accounting/Mines, or maybe the yearly settlement for the rentals. They may not have the information you want, but they'll be a lot easier to get hold of."

Ista nodded again, aware that Stinne's attention was no longer on her, but on the shifting visions in her screen. It was like and not like her own excursions into the invisible world: the same taut focus, the same unravelling of a complex and nonhuman grammar, but without the strange half-living logic of the hammals at its core.

"Nothing in Navigation," Stinne said. "I'm moving on to Accounts."

Ista didn't bother answering, knowing she wouldn't be heard, instead watched the windows shift and fill as Stinne shaped her queries, working her way ever deeper into the Company systems. The responses were coming more slowly now, the pages less and less full, and Stinne shook her head, entering yet another query-string. "I'm not getting much here, either. I've got five locations, and I'm downloading them, but that's all there is in Accounts and in the reports to the rental company."

"What about Maintenance?" Ista asked.

Stinne glanced over her shoulder. "But there's nothing to maintain, the mines were broken up—"

"But they have to account for them, don't they?" Ista said.

"That's right," Stinne said, "they would." Her hands danced across the i-board again, conjuring new configurations, and a fresh set of windows blossomed liked fireworks against the previous background. "Yes!" she said, and in the same instant her shoulders slumped with disappointment. "Damn, it's high-coded."

"We can't get it?" Ista asked. Over the other girl's shoulder, she could see the flashing warn-off screen, and the tiny box that asked for passwords before granting access.

"I can get it," Stinne said, "but it'll have to be the last thing we do get. I know my dad's password for this level, but if I use it, Security's likely to come up here to check it out."

Ista frowned, and then remembered: Stinne's father worked in Low Management, several levels down; this was not a likely place for him to access the Company nets. And if he was logged on from another location already, the system was bound to refuse access. "I need this," she said aloud, and Stinne grinned, her hands busy on her board. A small window opened, filled with the letters and symbols of her query, blanked and filled again with an answer.

"Dad's not logged on anywhere I can see. So I think we can probably risk asking. But, like I said, this is the only thing you're going to get."

"Plus the files we already have," Ista said, and Stinne nodded.

"But this is the key."

"Then let's do it," Ista said, and swallowed hard to hide her sudden uncertainty.

Stinne took a breath, her thin shoulders rising and falling, and her hands moved convulsively on the i-board. Nothing showed on the screen—nothing would show, to preserve the password's integrity—but a moment later the warning screen vanished, and a secondary access menu appeared. Stinne sighed, and entered a second set of codes and then the search request. A holding icon appeared, and she glanced back at Ista.

"Keep your fingers crossed."

Ista nodded, made the gesture, half hidden against her thigh. If this didn't work— She shook the thought away. Trindade might be able to help her, but that would involve trading favors across the hypothecary's web of connections, and it would certainly get back to Kelly2. But if I have to do it, Ista thought, I'll figure out something. Because if I don't get this file, I'll never persuade Tarasov and Rangsey to help me. And without that, there's no chance I'll ever get off this station—

"Got it!" Stinne exclaimed, and Ista leaned close, to see the lines of realtext filling the screen's largest window.

"Quick, pull it down."

Stinne's hands were already moving, making the copy—not directly, Ista saw, with approval, but through a textmaking program, so that any security program would have to look in a second or third place for the final destination address. She held her breath while the transfer markers shifted and re-formed, and then the copy was complete, a neatly packaged icon on Stinne's screen.

"Stash it in the public habitat, I can send an anonym to get it."

"Right," Stinne said, and issued the commands. Ista caught a quick glimpse of a window into the Company's public habitat, saw the spine of the talktree that had caught the message, and then that window had closed, too, and Stinne was cover-ing the last of her tracks. She shut down the system and re-trieved her card, then looked up at Ista. "We'd better go now."

Ista nodded. "Do you want to come to Trindade's with me? I think I should pick up the file as soon as possible."

"I agree with that," Stinne said, and touched the controls to unlock the door. She didn't answer the rest of the question until they had passed the final door, and stood in the corri-dor outside the red-lit library. Ista blinked in the brighter light, shook her head to move her braids and was startled again to remember she wore the scarf over them.

"Do you want to come with me?" she asked again, and Stinne made a face.

"I shouldn't—oh, hell, yes, I want to see what's in this file that's so important."

They took the main shaft elevator down to the Midway, stopped at a public toilet there for Ista to change her clothes again. She shook her braids loose from their knot, and re-wound her trapata over the loose fall of her tunic, studying her reflection in the mirror. She looked younger again, she thought—all the more so because the trapata was crumpled from being stuffed in the bottom of her carryall—but at the same time, more herself, and she reclaimed her jewelry with something like relief, ignoring the curious look from a woman in a Union jersey at the next sink.

Trindade's shop was quiet, but Draco's ecumenicon next door was busy, a group of nearly a dozen Union women discussing which blessing candles to buy for a wedding while a pair of serious-faced employees considered prayer disks and a plump woman leaned close over a catalog display, questioning Draco on its contents. The Union women had spilled out of the storefront proper, stood half in front of the door to Trindade's shop, and Ista was glad of their presence to hide her arrival with Stinne. The lamp was lit inside the arch of Trindade's door—she was there, and available—and Ista breathed a sigh of relief as she pushed through the door into the sudden darkness.

Trindade looked up from the oracle balanced on the work-table, her business face easing into animation as she saw Ista. She waved one hand over the oracle's surface, and said, "Sit. I'll be with you in a minute."

Ista did as she was told, pulling Stinne to perch on one of the clients' chairs next to her. The fair girl gave her an odd look, but subsided, clutching her bag to her. The wallscreens were dark, except for a trail of light crawling across a corner screen. Ista recognized it as a VALMUL toyset, a decorative program that translated the responses of a selected glider somewhere in Trindade's captive nets into light and movement, and would have ignored it after the first glance, but she saw Stinne eyeing it warily, and looked again. The bar of light, stretching sometimes almost as long as her forearm, but mostly snapping back to about a hand's length, was almost eerie to watch, a thick white worm undulating across the empty screen. It moved with clear but inscrutable purpose—a visible symbol, Ista realized suddenly, of Trindade's knowledge, and her power in the invisible world. She alone, the hypothecary alone, knew what moved the glider, how to interpret its actions; she alone could help the people who came to consult her. The light that reflected up from the oracle threw strange shadows across Trindade's face, turned it for an instant to a tribal mask, then smoothed those harsh lines to curves and then to planes of shadow.

Trindade looked up at last, flattening her hands against the control plates, and the light faded from the oracle's face. "So," she said, and leaned back in her chair. "What brings you here today, Ista, and your friend with you?"

"I—" Ista hesitated, not wanting to cause trouble for the older woman. "I need a favor," she said at last. "I need to retrieve a file from the Company habitat, and it's easier to do from here. Stinne's just here for the ride."

Trindade lifted an eyebrow at that, but Ista met her gaze squarely. Let her think I'm just showing off, she thought, let her think that and not ask questions.

"What sort of file?" Trindade asked, and cupped her hands over the oracle's controls.

"A download," Ista answered. "Just some stuff I wanted." She could see Trindade's eyebrows rising further, signalling mixed impatience and disbelief, and hurried on, "Some stuff Stinne got for me, that I couldn't afford. School stuff."

"Ah." Trindade's eyebrows drew down again, disapproving now, but she slid back from the table. "All right, but no more than twenty minutes."

Ista stood up, automatically shrugging her drape further up onto her shoulders, and came to take her place in front of the oracle.

"Can I watch?" Stinne said.

Trindade flicked her a glance, and Ista said, "Would it be all right?"

Trindade smiled then, not entirely without approval. "Put it on the screens, then."

Ista hid a sigh and touched the controls that slaved the wall screen to the oracle's primary display. Letting Stinne watch meant that Trindade would be watching, too—but then, she would have anyway. The center screen paled slightly, became the deep charcoal of the resting oracle, and Ista settled herself more comfortably in Trindade's chair. The edge-mounted controls were warm under her hands, their visible symbols worn almost to nothing, but as she touched the first sequence, she felt the fields spring to life, reinforcing the engraved messages. In the oracle's dome, an iconic menu appeared, and she spun expertly through it to the captive pens, selected a drab-looking anonym from among the programs waiting there. It seemed to be in good shape, and she slaved it to the primary system controller, so that its natural defenses would help conceal her presence. She heard the rustle of silks as Trindade stirred at the sight, and braced herself, but the question never came.

There was a local gateway to the Company habitats, but Ista took the long way around, passing out onto the frontage and re-entering the controlled habitat through the busiest of the public gateways. The anonym worked perfectly, a dull ghost among the vivid iconage, hard to see even through the oracle's awareness. Ista decided to take the chance, headed directly for the gate that led to the Company's public comm space, where the talktree would be located. It was crowded there, too, hammals and donkey-programs mixing with fronting engines and the occasional freemartin, and Ista watched as the anonym shifted its outer display, taking on the look of the fronting engines as it took its place in the gate queue. She was aware of the security around them, caught glimpses of it at the edges of the oracle's perception, slivers of silver light striking like a random mist, lifting as quickly as it had appeared, but the anonym's camouflage worked perfectly, and security came no closer.

The camouflage worked at the gateway, too, and she slipped under the red bar without having to resort to the usual foreign-access codes. Compared to the wildnet, or even the frontage, the Company's comm space was like a well-tended garden, the flat background plane striped with dark green and gold bands of well-tended parqueter and protoc, while all around the space was busy with a hothouse variety of programs. She recognized most of them as bred from the wildnet, brighter, more sharply angled versions of sunners and fairmaids, the vivid purple V of a chevrotain leaping through the middle distance, but there were others whose lineage she could only guess. A shape like a ball of petals on two long, fragile-looking legs wobbled past, and she felt feedback pressure against her palms as the anonym started to reach for it. She controlled the program with a quick gesture, turned it firmly toward the talktree she could see in the distance.

"Area map?" Trindade murmured, from over her shoulder, and Ista felt herself flush. She had forgotten, in the excitement of getting safely into the habitat, that a map program was available for the tapping. There was nothing like it on the wildnet, of course, but the very act of mapping the habitat reduced it to text and helped to control its programs.

"Thanks," she muttered, and reached across the oracle to activate the secondary system. A tiny rosette of color bloomed in the center of the oracle's display, partly hiding her view of the net around her, and she tugged it impatiently into a corner, stretching it to a usable size as she went. In its miniature view, she saw the habitat as though from above, the four talktrees marking the compass points around the center of the habitat, gateways at each of the six corners, security winking in and out at random, and a dozen unfamiliar symbols filling in the remaining spaces. It was the talktrees that mattered, though, and she focussed her attention on them. They were color-coded as well as numbered, and she frowned, remembering the brief glimpse she'd caught over Stinne's shoulder. It had been blue, she thought, and touched keys to confirm the code. The screen blinked back at her, positive response, and she turned toward it, urging the anonym to a quicker pace. The talktree loomed tall in the distance, an attenuated cone that rose ten virtual meters above the plane of the habitat. Smaller cones, paler blue, jutted from its smooth sides; some had budded cubes and still smaller cones from their tips, and the plane around it was littered with the fallen shapes. Each one held a message or a block of data, Ista knew, carried like a parasite by the talktree until its intended owner claimed it. Half a dozen creepers moved across the disk, the blocks winking in and out of existence as the programs passed them, searching for the one or two blocks that would not vanish, but could be collected and retrieved. It wasn't perfect security, but it was cheap and common, and good enough, most of the time.

She studied the talktree for a long moment, taking her time, letting the anonym adjust to its new surroundings, and only when she was sure its patterns matched those of the creepers busy under the tree did she let it move forward again. A ripple of color, a wave of slightly deeper blue, ran up the talktree's body at her approach, but the anonym's adaptions held good. The color faded again, and Ista turned her attention to the shapes scattered under the tree. She wasn't quite sure what the most effective search strategy would be—she had never had to use the talktree system before, it was easier to send a message directly unless you needed the anonymity or didn't know your receiver—but she let the anonym move forward at its own pace, watching as the polyhedrons disappeared and reappeared once she was safely past. Then at last one dark cube remained solid as she approached, an icon she recognized, Stinne's private sign, a ghostly shadow on its uppermost face, and she touched the oracle's controls to retrieve the file. The cube vanished at her touch, and she felt an instant's panic, but a glance at the oracle reassured her. The retrieved file light glowed in the ring of controls, telling her that the file was held in temporary storage. Now, she thought, all I have to do is get myself safely home again.

A light flashed at the edge of the oracle's viewpoint, and she adjusted it to bring the image into closer focus. A shower of security was moving toward her, toward the tree, the silver slivers raining like knifeblades impartially on the empty plane and the strips of parqueter. Where they hit the parqueter, rents appeared in the interlaced squares, chunks of code blasted by the falling slivers. She froze, considering her options—the storm was coming on quickly, too quickly for her to run from it, but staying looking distinctly unsafe as well—and Trindade said, "Stay where you are." Her voice was sharper than Ista had ever heard it. "Keep looking for a message—copy the creepers."

Ista did as she was told, kept her hands steady on the controls, steering the anonym on its random way, feeling the muscles tighten in her forearms. She wanted to run, wanted desperately to get away from the fall of silver, coming closer every second, leaving a trail of broken code behind it, and curbed her fear with an effort that left her fingers shaking. The security was closer now, so close that she imagined the hiss of its fall, and she saw the first knife-blade impale a message box. It vanished at that touch, and did not reappear.

"Ista—" Stinne began, and bit off whatever else she would have said.

Ista ignored her, made herself keep moving toward the nearest block, and hunched her shoulders as the rain of silver swept over the anonym. For an instant, the oracle's viewpoint was a hail of jagged light, and then the circle cleared. Perhaps a third of the message boxes had vanished—unauthorized code, Ista guessed—and one of the creepers lay impaled by a streak of silver light that pulsed as it absorbed the program's important features. It was fading even as she watched, writing its information to permanent storage somewhere, and an instant later, both programs winked out of sight. The other creepers kept on about their business as though nothing had happened.

"All right," Trindade said. "It's safe now."

Ista swallowed hard, and shifted her stiff fingers on the control ring, turning the anonym toward the gateway. Looking toward the next talktree, she could see another shower of security flickering on the virtual horizon, and it was all she could do not to override the anonym's autonomy and head straight for the gateway. But that was the surest way she knew to attract security, and she let the anonym find its own way. Security leaving the habitat was rarely as strict as on entry, and whatever had upset the roving storms didn't seem to have reached the bright square of the gatekeeper. The anonym slipped out between two loaded hammals, and Ista sighed with relief, setting the anonym on a roundabout return path.

"I think you owe me an explanation," Trindade said.

Ista looked at her, saw the anger in her eyes, and couldn't think of anything to say.

"It was my idea," Stinne said abruptly. "And my program. I talked Ista into it."

Trindade didn't look at her. "I doubt that. No offense, girl, but you wouldn't have to go to these extremes. Well, Ista? I'm waiting."

"It's like I said," Ista began, "I had a file to download."

"But not for school, I think," Trindade said.

Ista shook her head. "No."

Trindade's eyebrows rose. "Then for what? You know better than to be working on your own yet—"

"I can't tell you," Ista said. "It may be trouble, real trouble, and it's also my business, not a job. Please don't ask."

Trindade stood silent for a moment, her mouth closed tight over whatever she might have said. Finally, she said, "Does your mother know?"

"No."

"Does it have anything to do with your ID?"

Ista hesitated, then reluctantly nodded. "Maybe. Tangentially."

Trindade shook her head again. "You had no right to put me at risk. Not without warning me first."

"I didn't know," Ista said. "I didn't expect this response."

"That I do believe," Trindade said, with a grim smile. "All right, then, take your file, do not leave me any copies, and don't come back here until this is over, whatever it is. I don't know where you've been or where you're going. Agreed?"

Ista nodded. "Thank you, Trindade."

Lights flashed in the oracle then, signalling the end of her program, and Ista turned her attention to the worktable. She had a disk ready, transferred the file to it, and started to shut down the system, paying special attention to erasing her tracks, but Trindade waved her away. "I'll take care of that," she said, impatiently. "Just stay out of my way until this is over."

"I will," Ista said, and beckoned for Stinne to follow her out of the shop. The Union women were gone now, and the other customers as well, leaving just Draco himself lounging in the doorway of the ecumenicon. He nodded to Ista, polite but distant as always, and Ista forced a smile in return as she started back down the length of the Midway. Stinne lengthened her stride to keep up, tapped the other girl on the shoulder.

"Hey, where are we going?"

Ista stumbled over a loose piece of floor tile, made a business of recovering herself. "Back down to the docks," she said at last. "I want to give this to Tarasov and Rangsey."

"You haven't even had a chance to look at it yet," Stinne said. "You don't even know if it's the right file."

She was right, too, Ista thought, and sighed, came to a stop outside the lift station's massive doors. "I know. I guess actually I should go to the Bubble first, look through what you got me—and I really appreciate it, Stinne, you know that? I mean it."

Stinne's pale skin went instantly pink, and she shrugged, caught between pleasure and embarrassment. "Hey, I'm glad I could help. I just—I hope it's what you need, that's all."

"Me, too," Ista said, and made a face. "I didn't mean that the way it sounded—"

Stinne nodded. "It didn't sound—I know what you meant."

"I'm glad somebody does," Ista said, and won a quick grin from the other girl. It faded quickly, though, and Stinne fixed her with a worried stare.

"Look, is Trindade right, is this serious, this file?"

Ista took a deep breath. "I don't know. I didn't think so, not like this, but—Trindade's not one to overreact."

Stinne nodded again. "Then can you trust her?"

"What do you mean?"

"Can you trust her not to tell Security who got the file?" Stinne said. "If they get that far, I mean."

Ista tilted her head to one side, considering the question. It was getting close to shift change; the lights above the lift doors were flashing in the rush patterns, four of the eight cars running express from the main business level to the Center Square station just below Terrazine Plaza. Any minute now, the Midway would be filled with people waiting for the remaining local cars, and she shook herself back to the present. "I think I can," she said, slowly, "but I can't be sure. She's got a position to maintain, but I think the most she'd tell them was my name—hell, there's not much more she could tell them, she made sure of that. So, yes, I think I can trust her." She looked at Stinne. "It's you I'm worried about."

"Oh, don't worry about me." Stinne gave her a sudden urchin grin. "My mama told me not to play with you, and I always do what mama says. Diver Anny'll say I was with her at the shops, and that she lost her library card ages ago. Same for me—I got a lost-card duplicate done two months ago, and I used the old one."

Ista stared back at her, torn between admiration and uncertainty. Stinne had certainly planned for everything, but it wasn't likely to be enough, if Security was serious about this. "You'd've made a good Traveller," she said, and Stinne went pink again.

"I don't know."

"Look, do you want to come back with me to the Bubble?" Ista asked. "You deserve a chance to see what's in the file."

"I wish I could," Stinne said, and twisted to see the time displayed above the doors of the lift station. "I've got to get home."

"All right," Ista said. "But, be careful, Stinne. I don't know what I've gotten you into."

Stinne lifted a hand, dismissal and farewell, and started toward the lift doors. Her voice floated back over her shoulder. "I'm always careful."

Ista watched the doors close behind her, hoping she was right. But at least, she thought, at least I have the files. And if I've stirred up Security, well, at least it's a sign I'm onto something.

▪7▪

CORPORATE SECURITY WAS always an odd beast, born of the anomalous position of the extrasolar corporations, which were not only a law unto themselves but government, planet, and society as well. NSMCo was no exception to that rule, though they owned the rights to several planetary claims as well as to the two systems that produced the bulk of their profits. The company existed outside the Federation, or more precisely alongside it; their structures ran parallel and in tandem to the Federation's, and where there was no Federal presence, the corporate presence was presumed to take its place and its rights.

This was, of course, a sore point within the Service caste, particularly among the more conservative entities like the Patrol in its various manifestations and the Infonet librarians: when did a corporate patrolman, for example, rank equal with an agent of the Patrol, and when could a company library technician claim the perqs and status of a certified infonaut? In practice, of course, the two groups did much the same jobs according to very nearly the same sets of rules, and dissipated any fellow feeling in arguments over precedence.

Tarasov was aware of both the rivalry and of its pointlessness—was well aware also of the Traveller theory that said that Management encouraged the hostility, to keep Service subservient, too busy with its feuds to effectively oppose Management, and while he didn't fully agree with the idea, he had to admit that it functioned that way in practice. But even knowing all that, it was hard to keep from sneering at NSMCo's security, comparing it in his mind to the programs and people he had worked with on Bestla. And that, he knew perfectly well, was pointless—conditions were too different to admit of a true comparison—but even so, every time he saw a security shower or a lurking netminder, he could imagine Anjait4's whispered strictures, and had to keep reminding himself that NSMCo couldn't have survived as long as it had without having good security. The empty wildnet still worried him, and it was hard not to attribute that to some horrendous Company miscalculation. There was no evidence of any such error, of course, and there were other, more likely explanations, but he found himself watching the wildnet in his spare time, looking for trouble.

He leaned over the display dome, wishing he'd had time to rig a slave projector in the ship's commons—it was small enough, but larger than the cockpit—and adjusted the focus to bring an icon into closer focus. It was a fossor, a standard floral program and the only one of its kind he'd seen, and he frowned thoughtfully as it went through its stereotyped routine at the edge of a plate of parqueter. A paraclete budded from the fossor's side, its spadelike quasihand shimmering as it matched the size of the parqueter's individual units, and then in a single movement, like a cook flipping a corncake, the quasihand slipped into and under the nearest unit of parqueter and levered it free. The block fluoresced bright green, the halation crawling back up the paraclete's stubby arm, but it paled before it reached the fossor itself. The paraclete, its hand shrunken now beneath the damaged parqueter, retreated toward the fossor, which opened a receptor for it. Normal behavior, Tarasov thought—except that it's the most normal thing I've seen on these nets, which makes it distinctly out of the ordinary. He could see a shower of security in the distance, a familiar flickering like lightning, but couldn't make out what it was hunting.

"Hey, Sein?"

Rangsey's voice crackled from the speakers above the console, and Tarasov reached for the response switch without taking his eyes from the display. "Yeah?"

"The—Ista's here, and she's got the information we wanted. You want to come down?"

"Yes." Tarasov touched controls, triggered the shutdown he'd automated his third day on the Agglomeration. "I'll be right down."

Kelly2/1 Ista was sitting at the narrow table, a carryall balanced between her feet, her elbows resting on the table in front of her. The Traveller bracelets covered her arms like gauntlets, and Tarasov distinctly heard the softer clash of the metal beads in her hair as she looked toward him. There was something in her expression, still and cold and strangely tense behind that mask, that made fear clutch at his stomach.

"What's wrong?"

"Nothing, I think," Ista said, and Rangsey turned away from the samovar, a trio of cups balanced in his hands.

"You hope," he said, and set the glasses on the table. Tarasov reached automatically for the twin jars of sugar and milk powder.

"I have the files you wanted," Ista said. "Like I promised."
I expect you to do the same, her tone implied.

Tarasov said, "Let's see."

The girl opened her cupped hands, slid a datablock across the table toward him. Tarasov caught it, swung in his chair to face the commons' wall-mounted player. The room was small enough that, with a stretch, he could fit the block into the player's slot without getting up.

"Hang on," Rangsey said, and set his cup aside. "Let me get the display dome from the vidiki set."

Tarasov nodded, his attention focussed on the small screen beside the limited playback menu, roused himself enough to say, "And the i-board from the cabin, please?"

Rangsey nodded, and vanished into the main corridor.

"I can give you the gist of it," Ista said.

There was a note of challenge in her voice that startled Tarasov for an instant, and then he swung back to face her. "I'd appreciate your talking me through them. But you understand I'll want to read them over."

He saw her shoulders relax slightly. "Of course."

"So what have you got?"

She counted them off on her fingers, the first gesture he'd seen from her that betrayed her age. "Digest from the news morgue, reports on every incident that could possibly have been an attack. Then a set of five locations from Accounting for the most recent attacks—it looks as though the others were erased in the general course of business. But the main thing is a file from Maintenance that gives details on each one of the destroyed mines."

Tarasov whistled softly, impressed in spite of himself. "And what do they say happened to them?"

Ista gave a quick grin, showing good teeth. "No official comment—attack by person or persons unknown when they absolutely have to say something, otherwise it's just unknown causes all around. But they do give last known locations, and locations where the wrecks were spotted, when they were. I haven't had a chance to run a correlation, though—I don't really have the power for that kind of datachange, unless I buy it, and I didn't really think that would be smart right now."

Tarasov nodded.

"Then let's start there," Rangsey said, from the door. "Right, Sein?" He set the heavy dome down on the table with a thump, and Tarasov plucked the i-board from under his arm, began stringing cables from the wall console to board and dome.

"I think so." He had mapping programs in the ship's library, and called them up, wishing that Anjait4 was here. This kind of job had always been her responsibility, her particular pleasure as well as her talent; still, he knew the basic techniques, and the program would do the rest. He moved automatically through the necessary steps—copy the data to the sorter, wait for that to clear, then set the parameters and start the program running—and heard Rangsey stir behind him.

"You want to talk about the trouble you don't think you have?"

Ista gave him a look Tarasov could read even out of the corner of his eye. "No particular trouble, I said. But the Maintenance file was coded for mid-level access only, and I know I triggered some alarms getting it."

Tarasov turned away from the progress indicators skittering across the i-board's self-screen, saw the same icons flickering in the depths of the display dome. "Security's been tighter than usual the last eight hours all over the invisible world, on the wildnet as well as in the controlled nets and habitats. Was that you?"

Ista started to say something, then stopped, managed a rather rueful smile. "It could be. But if it was important enough to make all this fuss, I don't know why it wasn't coded higher than that. The way I got it—" She stopped abruptly, as though she was on the edge of saying too much. "It just wasn't that hard."

"Hiding in plain sight, maybe," Rangsey said, hopefully. "Which should mean this is important."

"Might mean," Tarasov corrected. "It could just be that NSMCo doesn't want to be embarrassed."

"Still, it's interesting. What could be so important—some kind of pattern to the attacks?" Rangsey went on. He sounded more like his old self, less like the part he'd been playing for the past week, and Tarasov smiled in spite of himself.

"It could be, I suppose, but if it's that, why leave it in the files at all?"

Rangsey grinned. "Like you always said, if people were smart enough to destroy the files, they'd be smart enough to get ahead legally."

Tarasov winced at that, the break in their cover, saw in the same moment Ista's head come up and the flicker of painful embarrassment cross Rangsey's face. He willed the other man to let it go, managed to make his own voice easy as he answered. "But if they did that, how'd we manage to make a living?"

Rangsey forced a laugh that rang false to Tarasov, and he slanted a glance at Ista, was not surprised to see her focussed and aware. At that moment, the display dome beeped, signalling the end of the modelling run, and he reached eagerly for the i-board.

"Let's see what we've got."

He touched controls as he spoke, and watched darkness bleed into the dome, bright points popping into existence against it, first the vivid golds of the planets in their relative positions, and then one after another the red dots that marked the mines' last known positions. Some were surrounded by a haze of light, others were doubled, hard to see except as a slight elongation against the dark background, a few—three, maybe four—were single points, but all of them were spread across a broad wedge of the Outer Reach. The asteroids were visible only as a grey haze barely lighter than the background, and the red shone against it like beacons thrown by the handful against the sky.

"They're all in the same place," Ista said, and Tarasov saw her blush. "Well, the same quadrant, anyway."

"You'd think someone would have picked up on that," Rangsey said, almost to himself, but Tarasov was aware of the other man's eyes on him.

"You would think so," he agreed, and touched the i-board to check the program's categories. "All right. The plain dots—"

He highlighted them with a quick movement. "—are the cases where there was a distress call, or some other definite indication of where the attack happened. These with the halos are projections based on the last known position and the probable or reported course—the dot's the most likely position, and the halo is the margin of error. And then these double dots show last known position plus the position where the wreckage was first sighted."

Rangsey nodded. "What about current locations?"

"I was only able to find a partial file on that," Ista said. "The Union won't go near them if they can help it, so I got a file from one of the nav-chips."

Rangsey looked up at that. "I'd like to read that. Is it in chip form, or just text."

"It's the chip file." Ista looked faintly embarrassed again. "I didn't have time to break it out to text."

"I prefer the chip," Rangsey said. He looked at Tarasov. "Can you work out a rough set of positions until I can read that?"

"Give me a minute," Tarasov answered. He was already feeding data to the modelling program, setting parameters and adjusting the approximations. At last the program signalled its readiness, and a network of blue dots spread across the display. They covered more of the system, perhaps half the span of the asteroid belt, but there was still a distinct shape to the cloud.

"I remember when I was seven," Ista said suddenly, "the Company had to send a tender out into the Outer Reach to blow up a wrecked station because it was drifting into the FTL lanes. I wonder which one of those it was?"

Tarasov skimmed through the files, shook his head. "I don't have that listed."

Ista was still staring at the display, tipped her head to one side with a clattering of beads. "You know, if you just look at the red lights, it looks almost like there's a common center to it. You know, like a central point."

Rangsey lifted his eyebrows at that, surprise rather than

disbelief, and Tarasov gave the girl a second wary look. You ran into that talent now and again, especially among people born and raised in space, and Union folk and Travellers in particular, the ability to see spatial relationships in more than three dimensions almost by intuition. "Have you been tested?" he asked, and Ista made a face, but didn't pretend to misunderstand.

"Yeah. I scored a forty."

Enough to show she had the talent, Tarasov thought, but not high enough to win a Company placement or a Union berth. He nodded, and touched the i-board's controls to set up the query. The program considered for a moment, and flashed the answer: a single point glowed green in the heart of the wedge.

"And what if you adjust for time, run the point year by year?" Ista asked. "Where are the attacks in relation to it?"

Tarasov made the adjustment, watched the pattern change, pulsing into a new design with each year. As best he could tell, the point stayed more or less constant in relation to the attack locations—almost as though, he thought, there was some slowly moving thing out there that attacked mines that drifted into a specific radius. A slowly fluctuating radius, he amended, but the flux was regular, like the beat of a pulsar.

"You know," Ista began, and then stopped again, flushing.

"What?"

"It looks a little bit like the way a dead-lurk hunts." She shrugged. "The way they lie there, go after anything that comes within range."

Tarasov nodded thoughtfully. She was right, it did look like a dead-lurk's pattern, and, while no dead-lurks existed outside the invisible world, the hammals could still provide a useful metaphor.

"So where the center is now is where the attacks might be coming from?" Rangsey asked.

"It's possible," Tarasov said. "I just think it's very interesting that there doesn't seem to have been any follow-up." Of course, he added silently, it was possible that either Company security or the local Patrol had indeed investigated the pattern and found that it was a dead end. Macbeth would know, had had access to NSMCo's records, and he made a mental note to ask her as soon as possible.

"What are the coordinates?" Rangsey asked. He had moved to the wall console, was studying a file from his own records.

Tarasov touched virtual keys to flip him the numbers, and was rewarded with a soft sound of satisfaction.

"I thought that looked familiar," Rangsey said, and favored them both with his smile. "You know what that is? That's real close to where that mine you were found on is, Ista. And I think that's very interesting."

"Mama said that everybody who went looking for the wreck had bad luck," Ista said quietly. "There was a fast wrecker that vanished right afterward, and then a Union crew, and then a salvage ship—no, they didn't get attacked, but they claimed they saw someone and decided not to stick around."

"Very, very interesting," Rangsey said, and looked at Tarasov again. "You know what that means, Sein."

"I know what you want to do," Tarasov answered, and heard his voice go grim. "Bear in mind that going out there means we run the same risk as everybody else."

"But nobody's expecting us," Rangsey said. "We don't have to file a detailed flight plan—we're Travellers, we go where we want. They, whoever they are, won't know we're coming until we're there."

"It's not getting there that worries me," Tarasov muttered, but the idea was tempting. Their STLship was faster than it looked, a Patrol VMU installed along with a standard camouflage package and a pair of light cannon concealed beneath the wing surfaces; they could outrun most commercial STL-ships, and the cannons were military issue, would probably be enough to let them break free from an attacker, particularly since no attacker would expect them to be armed.

"If you're going out there," Ista said, "I want to go with you."

Rangsey looked at her, eyebrows drawing down into a frown, and she met his stare without flinching.

"I have a right to be there. It's where I came from, it's more my business than anybody's, and you wouldn't've found out about this without my file. You owe me that."

"We don't know if we're going ourselves," Tarasov began, and the girl made a hissing noise.

"Don't give me that. You're going. And I want to go."

Rangsey laughed then. "She's right, you know."

Tarasov sighed. "It's going to be dangerous, and maybe pointless."

"If it's pointless, it won't be dangerous, will it?" Ista asked, and Rangsey laughed again.

"You're not helping," Tarasov snapped. "Ista—"

"I want to see where I came from," Ista said. "Where I was found. There won't be anything, I know that, everybody's already looked, but I want to see just the same."

There was no good answer to that, no fair answer, and Tarasov nodded, putting aside his misgivings. "All right. If we go, you can come."

Ista made her way through the gently-curving corridors of the docking ring, keeping as much as possible to the shadows of the cargo paths. Not that it was likely now that anyone would connect her presence with a visit to the unnamed STLship, but if she could avoid having to answer any questions from Kelly2, she would be much happier. At the smaller of the two hubs, she paused, and then climbed the narrow standing-stair that led to the market level. She could lose herself there, get something to eat—not an incidental thing, she realized, abruptly, but rapidly becoming a necessity—and then make her way blamelessly back to *Fancy Kelly*. No one would care if she'd wasted most of a day in the markets.

She turned down the right-hand curve of the broad circle, took the first inward-pointing path, heading for the foodstands that formed a middle band around the central pillar where Orbani had his headquarters. To her surprise, the corridor was unusually empty, just a few Company employees browsing at a stall that sold imported soaps and perfumes, and another pair, further down, pricing vidiki. Beyond them, standing in Orbani's doorway, she could see the reason for the quiet: Company Security, conspicuous in their orange-and-black armor vests. There were maybe a dozen of them, all carrying hotsticks, and as she watched, Orbani appeared, shaking his head at a woman who had to be their leader. Instinctively, she started to turn away, melt out of sight between the nearest stalls, but stopped herself, realizing that at least two of the officers were watching her, and not idly, either. Beneath the half-mask of their dark-lensed display glasses, their mouths were tight and angry, and she made herself keep walking, her whole body stiff and clumsy, until she'd reached the cross corridor where the food stalls were located.

She drew a sigh of relief as she turned down it, out of Security's gaze, stopped at a stall run by a woman who claimed band-kindship with Kelly2. She wasn't there, but the young man tending the box-cooker was someone Ista had known from the Ragged Schools sessions. She leaned on the counter, trying to remember his name—Nalud Ihsan, it was, Nalud, though he was probably 18 and Nalud2 now—and the young man turned toward her with a professionally polite smile that trembled on the edge of recognition.

"Kelly Ista," Ista said, helpfully, and Ihsan's smile became genuine. "We were in school together."

"I remember," Ihsan answered. "You were, what, two years behind me?"

And in most of your classes. Ista smiled and nodded. "It's good to see you again."

"And you." Ihsan glanced to his right, back the way she'd come. "What can I get you?"

"The panne looks good," Ista said, more or less at random, and Ihsan moved to the counter, began stuffing rice and vegetables into the thin bread shell. "What's with all the security?"

Ihsan glanced to his right again, lowered his voice until she could barely hear him over the gentle rumble of machinery. "I don't know for sure, but I heard there's been a break-in upstation, and everybody's pissed."

Ista let her eyes widen, not needing to act her shock. "What kind of a break-in?" she asked, and hoped he would take the quaver in her voice as surprise.

"Computer, I think, so you don't have to worry." Ihsan tucked the last bit of rice into the shell, slid the fat package into the nearest cooker. "I heard somebody's codes got stolen. So I don't know why they're bothering us, but, hey, that's life, isn't it?"

Ista nodded, and bit down hard on her fear. Computer theft, codes stolen from upstation, that could only be her and Stinne—well, it was possible that someone else had chosen just now to steal some other set of codes, but it was hardly likely. She would have to call Stinne, warn her, make sure she was all right— She was staring, she realized suddenly, and forced a smile. "Figures they'd blame us," she said, and was glad that her voice sounded almost normal.

"Mmm." The cooker dinged, and Ihsan turned away to retrieve the panne, set it on the counter in front of her. "Want sozu with that?"

Ista shook her head, and reached into her pocket. "No, thanks. What do I owe you?"

"Two-fifty, three if you've got scrip."

Ista produced the necessary foils—Company plastic, all of them—and took the panne in its box. She needed to call Stinne, that was certain, and as soon as possible, but from where? Not *Fancy Kelly*—not only would Kelly2 want to know what was going on, but it would be too dangerous, too much of a connection to her and the ship. There were public telecon stations in the market, of course, but they were equally unsafe with Security hanging around—and she would need to warn Rangsey and Tarasov, too. Security loomed ahead of her, a tall man frowning at a hand-sized display board, and she held her breath as she slipped past him. It would have been better if she'd managed a smile, but she knew she couldn't pull that off convincingly. She felt as though he was staring after her, but when she reached the top of the nearest stair and could risk looking back, he was nowhere in sight. That was somewhat reassuring, and she turned into the tangle of support corridors, taking the shortcut to the nearest bank of stations.

Luckily, there was only a single figure at the half-dozen machines, a stocky, grey-haired man who hunched his shoulder politely and pretended he didn't see her. Ista took the machine furthest from him, turning her own back, and studied the menued options. She would pay cash for the access, she decided, despite the premium surcharge, and she'd use the more complicated public number rather than the private number Stinne had given her. Both would make it harder for Security to trace her call, if they were monitoring communications with Stinne's family—and they probably would be, if it was her break-in they were investigating. And if I was really good at this, she thought, I'd've remembered to borrow a scrambler from Trindade—but there's no point in worrying about what can't be fixed, especially when there's no time to fix it. She fed the foils into the machine, building up a reserve, then punched in the first of the numbers. The system beeped, flashing a string of icons to inform her that she could get significant savings through a local comm account, but at last the screen cleared except for the setting icons. She set the protocols quickly—the cheapest, crudest repro rate, sound on, video off—and pushed the last button to activate the program. Out of the corner of her eye, she saw the grey-haired man finish his business and move away from his machine, and she braced herself against the narrow ledge of the control panel, willing Stinne—or someone, anyone—to answer. For a long moment, nothing happened, the connect icon pulsing forlornly in the corner of the screen, and then the screen filled with a familiar message. ALL CIRCUITS AT THIS CODE ARE BUSY OR OFF-LINE. PLEASE TRY AGAIN, OR LEAVE A MESSAGE AT THE PROMPT. Ista swore under her breath, and killed the program before the prompt appeared. The machine spat foils at her, the balance remaining on the temporary account, and she collected them automatically, not even bothering to count. She had to find Stinne and warn her—she should warn Rangsey and Tarasov as well, but Stinne came first. The only trouble was how to find her.

She took a deep breath and stepped away from the bank of telecom stations, trying to stay calm, to think what Trindade or Kelly2 would do. I suppose the question is where Stinne would go, she decided, because if she's still at home, then she knows what's going on—always assuming this is us, and not just some weird coincidence. She tipped her head to one side, considering, and then dismissed the thought. There was no way this could be coincidence, and even if it was, she didn't dare treat it that way. So where would Stinne go? Downstation, certainly, to her friends here, and probably—Ista smiled, unable to repress the sudden warmth of the idea—to warn me. Which means the best place to start is the Bubble.

The Bubble was crowded, surprisingly so, at this hour, until she looked again and saw the corner table where a couple of women in Union jerseys sat with a noteboard open and running in front of them. The rest of the people in the bar were mostly Union, and most of them were covertly watching the women, waiting for them to signal. Even as Ista watched, the shorter of the women lifted a hand, and a tall man left his table and came to lean against theirs, nodding in answer to some question from the second woman.

"On your left," a brisk familiar voice said, and Ista shifted automatically to the right to let Lohse Teenie edge past with a full tray. He set the glasses down in front of a group of Union workers, and collected the scrip they held out to him, looking back over his shoulder. "Hang on a second, Ista, I've got something for you."

Ista nodded, waiting for him to make change, then moved away from the tables to the relative privacy of the doorway. "What's going on, hiring?"

"Yeah, they're fitting out a new mine—Chandrasours, they are." Lohse tucked his tray under his arm. "Listen, that girlfriend of yours, the redhead, Merette something? The one who hangs out with you and Fredi."

"Stinne," Ista said, and kept her voice steady only with an effort.

Lohse nodded. "She came by about an hour ago, said she was looking for you. She looked really upset, so I said she could wait in your room. Was that all right?"

Ista took a deep breath, had to swallow hard before she could answer. "Yeah, Teenie, that's fine—that's perfect. I was looking for her."

Lohse lifted an eyebrow. "Are you two in some kind of trouble?"

Ista shook her head. "No, not at all." She could tell she didn't sound particularly convincing, and forced a quick smile. "Thanks, Teenie, I appreciate it, but I got to go now."

She turned away, bumping an empty chair, and nearly tripped over a Union man's outstretched feet. She waved away his apology, knowing her face was scarlet, and was all too aware of Lohse's curious stare that followed her until she ducked through the private door behind the bar. It was very quiet in the back rooms—as well it might be, she thought, given how busy it was in the main room. She caught a quick glimpse of Barabell himself, bent over the input pad of the precooker, and was glad that he was occupied.

She paused at the closed door of her own room, the key already in her hand, but decided to knock instead. There was a moment of silence, and then Stinne's voice came blurred through the door's molded fiber. "Who's there?"

"It's me. Let me in, Stinne."

She heard the soft click of locks releasing, and then Stinne swung the door open. "I am so glad to see you. We're in trouble, Ista."

"I know, I think." Ista shut the door behind her, grateful for the familiar gold-tinged light, the slightly stale smell of cold incense and perfume and her own sweat. She slid her carryall off her shoulder, let it drop to the tiles beside Stinne's own carrier, sat down on the carelessly-made bed. "What happened?"

Stinne sat beside her, drew her knees up to her chin, and wrapped her arms around them. She looked cold, and very young, and Ista started to reach for her, then drew her hand back, embarrassed. Stinne stared at the floortiles, still hugging her knees. "I shouldn't've used Dad's codes, I guess, but I didn't think they were that high class. But Security was down on us like a mine load, first thing this morning."

At least it took them that long to trace it back to you. Ista swallowed the words, recognizing pointless pride, and said, "Did they know it was you?"

Stinne shook her head. "They were asking everybody who

had access to the codes, did Dad leave them in open files, stuff like that. I think I really got him in trouble, Ista."

"It was my fault," Ista said, around the knot of fear in the pit of her stomach. The Company was not likely to be very forgiving of an outsider who stole access codes—worse, who persuaded an employee to steal access codes; all she had wanted was to help find out who was attacking the Company's mines—to help the Company—and instead she'd screwed any chance of Company favor. She pushed that thought down, and looked again at Stinne. "Exactly what happened, Stinne?"

"What happened to you?" Stinne said, in almost the same instant, and Ista made a face.

"I'll tell you in a minute. But first what happened with Security?"

Stinne looked slightly embarrassed again. "I didn't actually talk to them, myself. I was looking out the front windows when I saw them come up off the lift, and ducked out the back when I realized they were coming to the house. I didn't think I wanted to answer questions."

"So how do you know what they wanted?" Ista asked.

"I called Astevan on his line—don't worry, I called from a call station. He said that was what they wanted, and that they were really pissed."

Peyre/1 Astevan was Stinne's younger brother. Ista nodded slowly. "What did he say about you?"

"I don't know," Stinne answered. "I didn't get a chance to ask. He said somebody was coming and hung up."

Ista nodded again, trying to assess the situation. If Security was that interested in Stinne—or in where the access codes had come from—it wouldn't be long before someone mentioned her own name. And that meant they couldn't stay here much longer, and they certainly couldn't go back to *Fancy Kelly*. In any emergency, her teachers from Kelly2 to the Ragged School teachers to Trindade had said, the thing was to stay calm and think things through before you acted—which was, she thought, a lot harder than you would think from that blithe advice. She took another deep breath, trying to pull her thoughts together, and was glad when Stinne spoke.

"So what happened with you?" Stinne asked. "What was in those files?"

"A lot." Ista ran through what she'd found, and then the projection that Tarasov had created. When she'd finished, Stinne shook her head again.

"We are in serious trouble, Ista. If you're right about that file, then somebody in the Company has been covering up what they knew about the mines all these years."

"Somebody who's in a position to keep Security from making a real investigation," Ista interjected, with some bitterness. It didn't surprise her that Security could be bought off, or at best frightened off, but it was hard on the people who'd been killed.

"Which means they're in a position to set Security on us. They run things," Stinne said. Her eyes were wide and frightened as she shifted to face Ista, and Ista knew the expression mirrored her own. "What—how do we fight that?"

"I don't know," Ista said, softly, and something else she had been told, something Kelly2 had told her once, after a particularly difficult trip through the Inner Reach, surfaced in her mind. Sometimes, Kelly2 had said, it doesn't matter what you decide as long as a decision gets made. "But we'll work something out." She looked around the familiar untidy space, clothes piled haphazard on the chair, and empty dinnerpack on the floor beside the trash slot. "Have you got the remote? I think we should start with the newscasts."

Stinne blinked, but fumbled obediently for the boxy controller, touched the keys to light the small media box. The picture focussed, revealed a Company newsreader in the corner, and over his shoulder a set of graphs showing steadily-increasing profits over the last five years. The lines seemed to be levelling off, however, and the newsreader was shaking his head slightly, deploring the trend. "Who cares?" Stinne said, and damped the sound. "Why are we watching this?"

"To see if they say anything about a security alert, or a break-in, or anything," Ista said. They sat in silence for a while, watching as the system spun through three more stories, each less important than the last.

"I think if they were going to mention it, they'd've done it already," Stinne said at last, and Ista nodded. They were running out of time anyway; sooner or later, someone was bound to mention that Merette/1 Stinne was a friend of Kelly2/1 Ista, a hypothecary-in-training, and it wouldn't take long after that for someone to mention that she had rooms at the Bubble. Even taking into account the reluctance of both Union and Travellers to talk to Security, they couldn't expect to stay here much longer.

"I agree," she said, and Stinne flicked off the machine. "So what now?"

"I don't know—" Ista bit off her words, and tried again. "I think—we go back to the ship, not *Fancy Kelly*, Rangsey and Tarasov's, they haven't named it yet. I owe them warning, at least, and they were pretty hot to find out what was going on. And nobody should know to connect us to them."

"You hope," Stinne said, but uncurled from the bed, reaching for her carryall.

"Well, it's the best I can think of." Ista tipped her head to one side. "Unless you think your folks would help us?"

"Not a chance." Something, a scarf or part of a tricoteil pullover, had spilled out of Stinne's carryall, and she concentrated on stuffing it back in. "They're Company to the bone, the Company can't do wrong to them. They'll just tell us to turn ourselves in." She closed the carryall with a vicious twist of her wrist. "Any trouble we're in is our own fault for getting involved in the first place."

Ista sighed, accepting the other girl's judgment. Kelly2 would be willing to help, and defer any questions until after they'd dealt with the Company, but *Fancy Kelly* would be the first place Security would look for her. Better to warn Tarasov and Rangsey, and contact Kelly2 from there. She pulled open the box that held her clothes, pulled out her best drape and tossed it to Stinne, who caught it gracelessly.

"Your turn to dress up," Ista said. "Wind it over your hair, it'll make you a little less conspicuous."

Stinne did as she was told, the bright orange fabric turning her skin sallow, and Ista pulled out underwear and spare shirts, the clothes she usually brought with her on *Fancy Kelly*. She stuffed them into her own carryall, along with the bag of her jewelry—money if she got desperate enough to sell it—and the thin folder of notes from under her mattress. She had missed her last payday from Barabell, and made a face at the thought. Still, this would be enough for a few days at least, and with any luck all she would have to do was warn the two men, and then wait for Kelly2 to come and get her.

"We may be able to get out on Mama's ship," she said aloud, and Stinne looked at her.

"Don't you think they'd be checking that?"

Of course they would. Ista made a face at her own stupidity, but said, "We might be able to get Rangsey and Tarasov to take us to her, rendezvous somewhere in the Middle Reach."

"Maybe," Stinne agreed, "but what then? What can your mother do for us?"

That was the real question, the crux of the matter, and Ista sighed. "I don't know," she said, "but it's better than just handing ourselves over to Security."

Rangsey hung suspended in the blood-dark, body-warmed universe of the borrowed captain-chip, hemmed in by the absence of crew and ship, his reach curtailed by the closed-in system. Steady question and response pulsed through his body, a dulled and distant beat like a sluggish heart, a hibernating heart, a drone at the base of his spine that would be meaningful only by its absence. He reached out in the darkness, found the virtual key and pressed it, triggering the question he had set up before. Light blazed around him, gold and then red, dying toward embers, and the answer formed at the back of his mind. Without the ship to give it words, it was little more than a conviction, a certainty of emotion that was nonetheless absolute: *if you see that thing*—a flash of image, iconic, the shadow of a particular ship-trace—*in this place, run away*. He had expected that, but even so the adrenalin rush took him by surprise, the taut fear that turned the darkness red again and made him tighten all his muscles against the learned responses. He took a slow, deep breath and then another, cooling the hormone flow, and reached for the release.

The light changed around him, became the simple familiar darkness of closed eyes, and he opened them again, reaching into his shirt to unplug the borrowed chip. Its owner looked back at him soberly.

"You see what I mean?"

Rangsey nodded, refastening his shirt with one hand, and held out the chip with the other. "It's very definite."

The chip's owner—he was one of the Blan Varros who had worked NSMCo's mine platforms for most of his adult life— accepted it, slid it back into its case and into his pocket in one smooth movement. "There's a reason for it."

"It seems to me," Rangsey said, "there's reason to take a look round there, too."

The Varro made a face, as though he would have spat if they'd been on-planet. "Yeah, right. And what good would that do? Company still owns the system."

And that was also true, and truest of all that without the Company's cooperation there would be no investigation of anything. Rangsey nodded again, accepting the verdict at least for now. "Thanks for the loan."

The Varro shrugged, deflecting thanks. "You got to be careful out there." He smiled suddenly. "We don't know for sure what it is, but we surely know what it does."

"I will be careful," Rangsey said, and the Varro nodded, stone-faced again.

"I know your cousins. They wouldn't thank me if I didn't tell you."

And that, Rangsey thought, was the way of it, in the Union. Not only did your own kin look after what they thought were your interests, but they enlisted their friends in the cause as well. "I'll tell them," he said, and started back up the sloping tunnel that led to the main corridor.

It wasn't a long walk back to the ship from the disused cargo tube that served as the Union local on the dock level, not nearly long enough to decide what they should do. Tarasov was right, this was an incredibly promising lead—and he was equally right when he pointed out that anything that promising should have been followed up years before. So either the Company itself was somehow implicated, or the lead wasn't as good as it looked but Company Security had never noted down the finding. That didn't seem terribly likely—even Company pride should pale beside the need to prove to the Patrol and the Federal agencies that they'd done everything possible—but it also didn't help them make sense out of what was going on. As far as he could see, there was still no reason to attack mines in the first place, not when you factored in the expense of selling what was taken from them. The ore would have to be at least rough-processed, and then carried to another system by FTL-ship, and even then the seller's price wouldn't be as high as it would have been if the material could be proven to have come from the Grade-A sources in Audumla. Unless the rock was being fed back into the Company books somehow? If one Union faction was double-crossing another? Then a mine could claim to have found the material that had been stolen, and it would go through the Company sales process normally, just like any other cargo. But the problem with that theory was that it was almost as hard to ambush an STLcraft as it was to find a decent core fragment: there just didn't seem to be enough profit in it.

He came through the last broad hatch, stepping automatically over the low combing, and saw the Company Security team standing by the directory kiosk that dominated the lobby. He blinked, suppressing the old rush of wary fear—after four years living with a Patrolman, it galled him that he still twitched every time he saw an enforcement officer—and swung wide to avoid them. They were armed for the station, he saw, nothing more than hot-sticks, though he wouldn't have been surprised to see a projectile weapon at the commander's waist.

"Excuse me, Mian."

The voice was less polite than the words, too certain of obedience to bother with more than token courtesy, but Rangsey stopped anyway, turning to face the speaker. "Yes?"

"Where are you going?" The man's eyes were invisible behind the flat planes of his display lens, but Rangsey could feel them moving over him.

"To my ship."

"Ship?" The corners of the man's mouth curved into a frown. "You're not Union, then."

Rangsey shook his head. "Registered Traveller. I—we're docked down there."

"ID."

Rangsey produced the folder Macbeth had given him and handed it across, feeling a shiver of fear as the man ran a portable reader over the sensor bar. It had to be good enough, it had passed Customs on Bestla and aboard the *Tiger*—hell, for all he knew, it was the real thing, officially issued by the Patrol offices on Bestla—but he couldn't quite shake his own awareness that it was a fake. Or he was a fake, one or the other, and he shoved that thought away as totally useless.

The Security man stared at the words and numbers projected on the inside of his glasses for an interminable moment, then, almost reluctantly, handed the card back to him. "What ship?"

Not for the first time, Rangsey wished he hadn't been so stubborn: even a bad name was better than the constant explanations. "SKW 5122."

To his surprise, however, the Security man made no direct comment, still staring at something on the inside of his glasses. "Go ahead."

"Thanks," Rangsey muttered, and then wished he hadn't. The Security man looked through him, through the images probably still crowding his sight, and Rangsey stepped past him, moving down the tube that led to their docking point. The corridor was empty until the first curve took him out of sight of the Security team; beyond that, a dark woman, a Traveller trapata wrapped around her shoulders, lounged in the open hatch of her docking tube. Her eyes followed him as he approached, but she said nothing, and drew back into the tube as he came closer. Rangsey couldn't help lifting an eyebrow at that, but kept on going toward the ship.

"Mian Rangsey."

The voice came from the hatch opposite the ship, was familiar and unfamiliar at once. Rangsey turned, startled, and saw the hatch open further, letting Kelly2/1 Ista squeeze out into the corridor. He caught his breath at that—there was no ship attached to that point; the inner hatch was supposed to stay firmly sealed while the outer hatch gave onto vacuum— and another girl in a Traveller drape slipped out into the corridor. Not a Traveller, though, Rangsey amended, seeing the bare wrists and neck, and Ista turned to the control box, carefully resecuring the hatch.

"Jesus, girl," Rangsey said, in spite of himself, and Ista gave him an apologetic look.

"I'm sorry, I know the risks. We had the hatch sealed on our side until I heard you coming."

"Heard—?"

"On the intercom," the second girl said. She had a soft, educated voice: an employee, Rangsey guessed, rather than Union.

"Can we come aboard?" Ista went on. "I need to talk to you. It's really important, and I don't want to do it here."

"Do I need to ask if that Security was for you?" Rangsey asked, the persona slipping over him again, and reached for the box that controlled his own ship's tube. "Sein?" There was an indistinct noise in answer. "I'm coming aboard, with Ista Kelly and a—friend of hers?"

Ista nodded.

In the tiny screen, he saw the internal telltale flick from orange to green, and punched in his own code to complete the transaction. The hatch sagged free of its seals, and he tugged it the rest of the way open. "After you."

The fair girl gave him an uncertain look, but Ista nodded, and started briskly toward the ship.

"I hope this is important," Rangsey called after them, no longer sure if it was himself or the persona that was speaking, and carefully resealed the hatch behind them. There was a people-counter on the box, a crude record of the numbers allowed on the ship, and he used the ship's privacy routine to disable it: better to keep Security away until he knew what was going on.

The girls were in the commons ahead of him, seated warily on the bench that ran along one side of the bulkhead. Tarasov had just flicked on the samovar, and met his stare with a speaking look.

"So what's going on?" Rangsey said, and leaned heavily on the back of Tarasov's chair.

The red-haired girl flinched just a little, but Ista answered, "A lot of trouble, I'm afraid." Her voice was absolutely steady, and Rangsey nodded his admiration. "The files I gave you, I had to use Stinne's father's codes to get them—this is Merette/1 Stinne, by the way—"

"Pleased to meet you," Tarasov murmured, and Stinne nodded as politely back at him.

"—and Security has cracked down hard." Ista folded her hands on the tabletop. "I figured I owed you the warning."

"I'll say," Rangsey began, knowing what the persona would do, and Tarasov waved him to silence.

"Hold it, Jus. Let's hear the rest of it."

"How'd you know there was a rest of it?" Ista didn't sound resentful, merely curious.

"There always is," Tarasov answered.

Ista smiled, a fugitive expression that lightened her features for an instant. "Security is treating this as a break-in, a theft of codes—"

"Which I guess it is," Stinne said, with reluctant candor.

"—and they're bound to realize that Stinne's connected to it when they can't find her," Ista went on. "And then they're bound to connect her with me. Which could be a problem for you."

"My mother doesn't approve of Ista," Stinne said.

Tarasov grinned, but Rangsey shook his head. "Not could be, it is a problem for us. We don't need a hassle with Security—" He broke off abruptly, sick of the persona, the person he'd been pretending to be. Besides, Macbeth would fix any problems they had—but she was unlikely to exert herself on the girls' behalf.

"What did you have in mind?" Tarasov asked.

Ista fixed him with her serious stare. "I can't risk going to my mother—Jenna—directly, but I figure, the least you could do is take a message for me. Tell her where I am, and what's going on, and I need her. She'll think of something."

"She's not going to like it," Rangsey said, in spite of himself, and Ista smiled again, ruefully, this time.

"No. She's going to be really pissed, in fact. But I don't know what else to do."

Rangsey looked at Tarasov, seeing his own concern mirrored in the other man's eyes. Kelly2 Jenna might certainly put aside her own anger to protect her adoptive daughter, but just how effective that protection would be, against NSMCo, was another matter entirely. He looked back at Ista, and the girl looked away.

"Well, I don't know what else to do."

"It's not a bad beginning," Tarasov said. "Maybe—well, I think the main thing is to get you off the station for a while."

"I was thinking, if I couldn't get to *Fancy Kelly* on-station, you and Mama both have plans to leave the station," Ista went on. "Maybe we could meet somewhere in the Middle Reach, I—we—could transfer there."

"If they let her leave the station," Tarasov said.

"Then I could just go with you," Ista said. "If you think it's important to get off-station."

"What about me?" Stinne asked, and in the same instant, Rangsey said, "What about Stinne?"

"And go where, anyway?" Stinne went on.

Ista shook her head, looking embarrassed again. "It's not important."

"The hell it isn't—"

Rangsey held up his hand. "Ista was going to come with us to look at the mine platform where she was found." He paused for a moment, but that clearly wasn't going to be enough for the fair girl. "It seems to be the center of the attacks, and that means the center of whatever's behind them."

Stinne sighed. "I'm not sure I want to go along, unless I have to. I guess it's better than talking to Security." She didn't sound very sure at all.

"I'm not sure I'd want to take you," Rangsey said, and looked at Tarasov. "That's just asking for trouble, Sein. Kidnapping, things like that."

"Don't tell me—" Tarasov broke off, scowling, and Rangsey made a sympathetic face, knowing he'd been about to say, *don't tell me my job.*

"Sorry."

Tarasov nodded. "I think Ista's right, Jus, the first thing we do is contact Kelly2." He took Rangsey's arm as he spoke, turning him firmly toward the door. "Help yourselves to tea, the cooker's on."

Rangsey blinked, but let himself be propelled into the corridor. "What?"

"Talk to Kelly2," Tarasov said. "I think Ista's got the germ of a good idea, if Kelly2 can get away—if they'll let her off-station, that is. But I also think we need to tell Macbeth what's going on."

That made sense, and Rangsey nodded, reaching into his pocket where he'd stowed his notebook with the callcodes he'd transferred from the databutton. "All right."

"I'll stay here, start plugging in a course plot for the Outer Reach," Tarasov went on. "The sooner I file that, the better— the less suspicious, anyway."

"Are we still heading for that mine?" Rangsey asked. "That'll give me a rough vector if she wants to set a rendezvous."

"I don't see why not," Tarasov answered. "You have our narrowbeam beacon frequencies, right?"

Rangsey nodded. "I'll see if I can find her."

"But tell Macbeth," Tarasov said again. "She may be able to take the heat off discreetly."

Unless she's created the heat. The thought popped unbidden into Rangsey's mind, and he hesitated, unable to shake it completely. They'd done what Macbeth wanted, made themselves

available, and this was what happened. They had stirred up
the Company, and confirmed the suspicions Macbeth must
have had from the start—but she couldn't have expected Ista,
hadn't known about Ista until they'd told her themselves, and
that did change things. He said, "I don't know if we should
tell her, Sein. I mean, she warned us, this is what she was looking for—"

Tarasov was shaking his head. "That's exactly why we have
to tell her. And she needs to know about that file, too. Hell, Jus,
it just isn't smart to head out without letting someone know
where we're going."

Rangsey sighed, but accepted the logic of that, drawing the
adopted persona around him like a jacket. "I guess nobody's
going to think anything of it if we price retrieval contracts."

"Not given the questions we've been asking," Tarasov said,
and shut the hatch behind him.

Macbeth was not at the wrecker office, but the bored clerk
volunteered that she spent most of her free time at the
company-owned boarding house where she kept a suite of
rooms. Rangsey found the house—it was an interior volume,
really, a six-story hexagonal tower melded to a major bulkhead only a few meters from a power core—with some diffi-
culty, not having realized that the company the clerk referred
to was Guo Fils Repair, the parent of the wrecker operation,
rather than NSMCo. As it was, he nearly missed it, only spotted the tiny Guo Fils logo beside the entrance because of the
carefully trained pinlight that struck sparks from the linked
gold characters. There were no other living volumes in this
plaza, and Rangsey pushed warily through the door into the
lobby.

It was very dark, even by the Agglomeration's standards,
the walls painted the color of old wine, the thick carpet woven
in a pattern of dark blue and black, the furniture made of near-
black plastic. No, not plastic, he amended, as his hand brushed
the back of the nearest chair, not plastic, but wood, or if it was
plastic, it was a very good fake. Four pinlights threw the only
light, two focused on enormous blood-red urns, each heaped
with red and gold flowers, that stood in alcoves to each side

of the room, the others trained together on the slim scroll-carved column of a mechanical concierge. It was probably supplemented by a human worker somewhere in the private spaces, Rangsey thought, had to be, no one would trust a program, however carefully bred, to handle the lobby without some kind of human supervision. The effect was still impressive, and Rangsey held himself stiffly, trying not to stare too obviously. This was Centrality style, a plausible imitation of Centrality wealth—no wonder Macbeth had decided to stay here, no matter how out of character it might be. Though of course, he added silently, it probably only meant that Guo Fils was based somewhere in the Centrality worlds.

It took him a moment to find the viewscreen hidden among the carved scrolls, and another second or two to find the button that activated it, and he was glad that the lobby was empty. The screen lit at last, sounding a muffled chime, and a woman's face looked out at him.

"May I help you, Mian?"

He could see her eyes move, assessing the IPUs and the Union clothes, but to his surprise her expression didn't change. "I'm looking for Devora Macbeth. She's with one of the wreckers, they told me at the office she might be here."

"A moment." The woman's eyes shifted fractionally, then came back to his face. "I'll inform her you're here, Mian—?"

"Rangsey."

"A moment." The screen went blank then, and Rangsey schooled himself to a long wait. To his surprise, however, it lit again within a minute, and Macbeth looked out at him.

"Oh, it's you. I'll be right down." She cut the connection before he could answer, and he turned away from the column, wondering where the doors were hidden in the featureless walls.

It was some minutes before she appeared, and he was looking the wrong way, so that he jumped a little at the sound of her voice.

"Well, let's go, then. Don't want to keep them waiting."

Rangsey nodded, not knowing what she meant, but knowing enough to play along, and fell into step at her side. She led him back out through the main doors, and then across the plaza and up a tunnel ramp, pausing only when they had reached the next half level. It was full of plants in glass cases, each with its own dedicated support systems, and the different shades and intensities of light wove a net of shadows across the volume. It seemed to be a popular meeting place, however, each case surrounded with a wide ledge, and a dozen or more people were sitting there in twos and threes. Macbeth led him toward a slim red-leafed tree whose case rose nearly to the ceiling, and stopped in its shadows, contemplating the ripple of explanatory text projected on the inside of the glass.

"What the hell do you want, coming here like that? This better be important."

Rangsey swallowed instant anger. "I wouldn't do this if it weren't. I—we've found something important."

"It wouldn't have anything to do with this break-in NSMCo Security's all excited about?" Macbeth asked, and gave a sour smile at his frown. "You think I'd miss that? So what have you stirred up?"

"A possible physical source for the attacks." Quickly, Rangsey outlined the discovery, glossing over the theft of the data as much as he dared. "But these two girls—Company Security is too interested in them, and if they get them, they'll find out what we know. I want—you're supposed to be working officially with them in some way, right? I need you to take the heat off them."

Macbeth shook her head. "It can't be done, not without jeopardizing the job."

"It doesn't have to be you," Rangsey said impatiently, "but you said there was an official team here, too. They could do it."

Macbeth shook her head again. "No. Look, I'd rather they were hunting these kids—and you and Tarasov, if necessary—it'll keep them busy while we track down the people who are really in charge of this operation."

"I don't mind them chasing us," Rangsey said. "Or at least that's what we're being paid for. But Ista—these are just kids, they could get really hurt, especially if Security is involved. We need to protect them."

"You should've thought of that before you let them get involved," Macbeth said.

"Ista already was involved," Rangsey answered. "You knew that."

"Look," Macbeth said, "I want the people who are running this operation, not just the mules and the low-grade hired help, and I will do anything to get them. You, these girls—I'm sorry, you're just not worth losing this chance."

Rangsey stared for a moment, recognizing the logic of her words and still furious at it, unable to articulate what was wrong. "Then we're going to have to get the hell off the station," he said, and Macbeth shrugged.

"That might be best. But I can't offer you any backing off-station. Not yet."

"Fine." Rangsey reached into his pocket for the datacard that held their map, but hesitated. Did he want to give this to her, when she'd said she would sacrifice all of them to get her targets? Tarasov's words echoed in his mind—it wasn't smart to head out into the Outer Reach without letting her know their real destination—but what she would do with the information. . . . He shook the thought away. He had to trust her, had no choice but to trust her, if he wanted any hope of a back-up. "Here. That's what we've found. And now we are getting the hell out of here."

He shoved the datacard at her. She caught it instinctively, fumbled it for a second, but he turned away before he saw whether she dropped it.

"Probably a good idea," she called after him, a mocking note in her voice, but he suspected—hoped—it was part of the act.

There was more Security in the core plaza above the Bubble, but none on the crowded level where the bar itself was located. A group of people in Union jerseys were waiting outside the door, and one of them put up her hand as he reached for the door switch.

"If you're hiring, this is the line."

Rangsey shook his head. "Not me." He saw the disbelief in her eyes, and lifted his own hand to show the meager stack of bracelets. "I'm in the Travelling life now."

The woman nodded, her friends relaxing as well, and Rangsey flipped the switch and went on into the cool darkness. The room was crowded, all right, all attention focussed on a pair of women who sat at a corner table. They looked tired, and the smaller woman's voice was hoarse as she called a string of names. The air smelled of spilled beer and too many bodies, despite the ventilation running at full blast. Rangsey moved up to the bar, careful to stay well clear of the Union folk waiting to be called, and was not surprised to see a knot of Travellers clustered at the far end of the bar. Barabell Deen had been a Traveller himself, for a while, and made his former compatriots welcome. By all accounts, he was also fond of Kelly2, and might be willing to get a message to her.

He leaned both elbows against the bar, peering past the ranked bodies to see if he could spot Barabell, and a woman's voice said, "Here, I want to talk to you."

He turned, unable to believe his luck, and Kelly2 scowled at him. "I'm looking for my kid, and you were taking a bit of an interest in her."

"And I was looking for you." Rangsey stopped himself from looking over his shoulder. "Can we talk in private?"

"She's in trouble." The anger didn't quite hide the fear in Kelly2's voice.

Rangsey hesitated, but answered honestly. "Yes, but not of my making. She's OK, though—but can we talk in private?"

Kelly2 took a deep breath, nodded. "Come on back to the back, I've got a key to Ista's room. That's still sort of private— though I had to take Security through it not two hours ago."

"Damn," Rangsey said, and Kelly2 looked sharply at him. "You know what's going on, then."

"Yes," Rangsey said again. "Sort of, anyway. Did they take anything?"

Kelly2 made a sideways motion of her head, and lifted the counter for him. "They downloaded stuff from her media wall. I don't think she keeps much there, though."

Nobody with any sense did—certainly nobody who wanted to be a hypothecary would leave sensitive data on a standard wall system. Rangsey allowed himself a sigh of relief as he followed Kelly2 through the second door. It closed behind him, cutting off the noise of conversation, and Kelly2 swung to face him. "Let's get one thing straight, Rangsey. If you, if anyone's, hurt my girl, you'll pay for it."

"She's not hurt," Rangsey said again. "She asked me to find you for her."

Kelly2 seemed to relax fractionally at that, and laid her key against the lock sensor. The door slid back, the lights coming on in the same instant, and Rangsey caught a quick glimpse of chaos, unmade bed, clothes and datablocks and empty food trays piled haphazardly. The walls were undercoated, painted the same shallow grey as the rest of the station, except for a single flatscreen display of the Audumla system. "I thought you said they didn't take anything."

Kelly2 grinned. "That's not their mess." The smile faded as she looked past him to the media console. "But if you want to talk—business—this might not be the place for it after all."

Rangsey nodded, thinking of bugs and sleepers and the rest of the panoply of Security programming, and stepped back to let the woman close the door again behind him. She led the way to the end of the short corridor, where an arched door led into an open room stacked high with pot-bellied cylinders that Rangsey guessed contained some of the Bubble's beer. More lights came on at their movements, and Kelly2 reached across to touch controls on a wall panel.

"I just want to let Deen know who's been here."

Another set of lights came on as she spoke, reflecting on a boxy desktop machine set up on a corner. Rangsey eyed it warily, and Kelly2 went on as though she hadn't noticed. "He keeps his inventory from here, too." She settled herself on the edge of a crate. "So. Where's my daughter, and what the hell is going on?"

Rangsey took a deep breath. "You know my cousin lost everything on that mine, and I intend to find out what happened."

"And I told you to stay away from my girl."

Rangsey nodded. "She came to us—it doesn't matter if you believe me, but it is true. She said she could get some information for us, locations of the attacks, things like that, and we took her up on it. But when she brought us the file, all this broke loose."

Kelly2 made a face. "They were saying a break-in—she got access codes from that upstation friend of hers, didn't she?"

"I think so," Rangsey said, "but that's what's caused the trouble. She came back to our ship because she didn't think she could get to you without getting you into trouble, asked us to contact you."

"A little after the fact," Kelly2 muttered. She shook her head. "God, I don't know what I can do—I don't have the friends I used to on this station. What the hell is in these files, anyway?"

"It's not any particular file," Rangsey said, "it's what these files together look like. At least, that's what we think it is."

"Think it's what?"

"If you put all the information together—it's from the maintenance files, and some others, places like that—you get a pattern for the attacks. And there's a center to the pattern."

Kelly2 made a soft noise between her teeth. "And if you could figure it out, one wonders why the company hasn't done it a long time ago."

Rangsey nodded. "Which may be why Security's so interested."

Kelly2 swore under her breath, rocking forward a little on the edge of the crate. "And Ista's in the middle of it."

Rangsey didn't answer, silenced by the simplicity of the statement. After a moment, Kelly2 shook herself. "I owe the Company some major money," she said, "but if I have to. . . ." She didn't finish the statement, and Rangsey nodded. Running out on a legitimate debt was all but impossible these days, with the shared dataverse that made it easy to connect each alias, each set of false ID, to the original debtor. "What about the Patrol?"

That was a shock, coming from a Traveller. Rangsey tilted his head to the side, pretended to consider. "I don't know," he said. "They might believe us, they might not—and I'd still want to be out of the system before I tried talking to anyone." *And that includes Macbeth,* he added silently. *Maybe especially Macbeth.* Which wasn't fully fair—the lieutenant was the first SID officer he'd met who'd seemed willing to believe Union folk over their employers, and she seemed genuinely determined to break up whatever was going on in Audumla-system, but after her willingness to sacrifice Ista and Stinne he didn't know how far he dared trust her. It was one thing to use him and Tarasov as bait, they were at least professionals, but the girls were another matter. Maybe warning the Patrol on Mayhew was the right thing to do—except that there was no telling who in this system was involved in this, or how deeply.

Kelly2 nodded morosely. "That's for certain. Look, Rangsey, I want my daughter back."

"She wants you," Rangsey answered, and was startled by the quick, bitter smile that passed across the other's face. "We thought—she suggested it, and Sein and I agree—that we could make the transfer in space, off the station." Kelly2 frowned, and he hurried on, wanting to override her skepticism. "We need to work, and we've got most of the toolkit aboard now anyway; you must be about due for another trade run. So we set roughly the same vector, and rendezvous once we're out of range of the station's sensors."

"That would be well into the Middle Reach," Kelly2 said. "And probably it'd be better to wait until Mayhew takes over traffic control, that's at the edge of the Outer Reach."

"That makes sense," Rangsey said. "How long will it take you to get there?"

Kelly2 shrugged, eyes focussed on distance as she made the calculations. "At my usual speed, with the usual stops—all of which I think I should make—about four days after I leave the station."

"And if we claimed engine trouble," Rangsey said, "there's be a good excuse to make contact."

"It's thin," Kelly2 said.

"Not that bad." Rangsey drew a breath. "Look, the only contact between us is legitimate: we bought tools from you, and not just from you. Hell, Orbani Matteen set it up, even, not any of us. You told us to go to piss off when we asked about Ista that first time, there's no way anybody can claim any different—"

"Except for people who saw her with you," Kelly2 said, but she sounded less skeptical than before.

"And if anybody noticed, which I don't think is that likely, we were asking about her background, and she told us the same thing you did." Rangsey spread his hands. "It's simple. There's nothing to connect us."

Kelly2 shook her head. "I wish I had another choice."

"So do we."

"All right." Kelly2 pushed herself off the crate. "I'll need your beacon numbers, emergency and standard, any private frequencies you use, or encryption—"

Rangsey held out his notebook. "I can copy them to you now."

"You came prepared," Kelly2 said, not without approval, and reached into her own pocket for a slightly bulkier model. They matched cables in silence, and then Rangsey triggered the transfer.

"I didn't think we'd get a second chance," he said, watching the numbers spool down toward the zero of completion.

"Probably not," Kelly2 agreed. They were silent again until the zeros appeared across the board on Rangsey's notebook, and he began tugging the cables from their sockets. Kelly2 did the same, but stopped abruptly, fixing him with her cold stare. "She's my only—only daughter, only kin that matters since I left my band. I will do anything for her. I want you to understand that."

Rangsey nodded, silenced by the quiet ferocity of her words.

"As long as we understand each other," Kelly2 said, slipping notebook and cables into her pocket, and turned away.

■ 8 ■

STLSHIPS ARE BUILT to a pattern, the better to fit the close tolerances of the FTLships' great frames, and it is simpler—cheaper—to keep the interiors as standard as the framing. SKW 5122 was no exception, and any but the rawest newbie, the youngest Traveller or Union child, could come aboard and find their place in the familiar layout. The captain's cabin lay closest to the control room, opposite the narrow cubicle of the computer room, and the floor plates that gave immediate access to the ship's spine, the circuitry backbone that connected the control room to the rest of the systems. Commons lay next to the computer room, the bulkhead that held the cooking machinery always carefully set the compartment's width away, and next to it was the space that served either for back-up engine control or the engineer's cabin. If there was an engineer technician, or even just an engineer chip in the set, the unlucky person who had it was supposed to sleep in the narrow bunk, directly below the access hatch that gave onto the crawlway that ran the length of the ship, in case cargo shifted and made the engines themselves inaccessible. Few ships followed that rule strictly, and those that did generally went out of their way to make the space more livable; the rest stuck the duty engineer in the little space and swapped chips often. The spare cabins—really one largish space that could be cut up into one or two or even three cubicles, depending on crew and cargo—lay opposite the commons, and it was there that Ista set down her carryall, stood staring around the bare white-walled space. It seemed empty, but she could see the shadows of the furniture behind the paneling, ready to be drawn up from the floorplates or out of the bulkheads, and the toilet chamber bulked large in one corner.

"We're sleeping here?" Stinne asked, and set her own bag on the floorplates. "Not that I mind a little discomfort if we're having an adventure, but, honestly. . . ."

Ista grinned, tracing the fittings almost eagerly. Kelly2 never let her rearrange the furniture much on *Fancy Kelly*, but she knew how to operate the systems. "There's a bunk here," she said, tracing its outline, "and more there and there. And we can pull out a partition if you want your own space." She hoped suddenly that Stinne wouldn't take her up on the offer, and was gratified when the other girl shrugged.

"Not really. Look, do you trust these guys?"

Ista stopped, a chair pulled half out of its well. "What do you mean?"

"I mean—" Stinne grimaced. "I just don't know why they wouldn't turn you over to Security."

"We made a deal."

Stinne touched her tongue to the center of her upper lip. "I know, Travellers' word is sacrosanct and all that, but you said yourself they were new. Suppose nobody told them how important it was?"

Ista let the chair slide back into the well, hearing the soft rumble of wheels on well-lubed tracks. "They'd still have to worry what I'd tell about them—it's not a chance I'd want to take." She paused then, infected by Stinne's uncertainty. "But maybe we should go up to control, see what Tarasov's doing. We can tell him we just want to watch a course being set."

Stinne nodded, and Ista followed her out into the main corridor, pausing only to glance at the main hatch panel. The telltales glowed green and orange, a familiar lopsided star: it was still locked, at least, and still set to palmprint-only.

They found Tarasov in the narrow control room, frowning over a navigation set-board. He looked up as they entered, and the frown shifted slightly, changing from concentration to puzzlement. "I thought you were setting up your cabin."

Stinne shrugged, and Ista said quickly, "I wondered if we could watch you set up the course instead. It's something I've never had a chance to practice. And Stinne's never seen it before."

"There's not much to see," Tarasov said. "But suit yourself."

"Thanks," Ista said, and seated herself in the captain's

couch. Stinne leaned gracefully over the back of the chair, and Ista was suddenly very aware of her presence. Tarasov gave her a single distracted glance, and turned his attention back to the board and screens in front of him. Ista looked at the screens, expecting to see the familiar flow of icon and text, the rippling dialogue between chip and user, but instead the symbols moved in a different rhythm, and she looked back at Tarasov, startled to see his hands moving to the same beat.

"Oh," she said, and Tarasov looked up.

"Mm?"

"Nothing." He was still looking at her, vague question, and Ista could feel herself blushing. "I just didn't know you weren't Union, that's all."

"No, I'm not." Tarasov's eyes focussed on her then. "What made you think so?"

Ista shrugged, wishing she'd never spoken. "Union usually sticks to Union, that's all."

Tarasov gave a half-smile. "Yeah, I know." The numbers in the screen were still dancing, but more slowly now as the program came to the end of what it could do without further input, and he turned his attention to the set-board again. The numbers shifted and reformed, and then blossomed briefly into a schematic of the system, provisional courses outlined in green, before Tarasov had banished them, adding in still more variables. It was like watching a juggler, a good one, better even than Fredi's cousin, and Ista wished again that she'd kept her mouth shut.

A light flashed on a secondary console, and she felt Stinne's start through the chair's cushions. Tarasov made a face, and leaned across her to hit the intercom button.

"Yeah?"

"It's me." It was Rangsey's voice, completely casual, but Ista found her hands closing on the arms of the couch. If he'd brought Security back with him, there was nothing they could do, no place they could run—

Tarasov leaned back again, flipped a couple of switches on a breadboarded pull-down panel. "Clear."

Rangsey didn't answer, but a set of lights went from green

to orange, and then back to green again. Ista tipped her head to the side, listening for the sound of booted feet, and saw Stinne's hand close into a fist against the couch's drab padding. Then Rangsey appeared in the hatchway, alone, and Ista let out breath she hadn't known she'd been holding. Rangsey gave her a curious glance, as though he'd guessed her suspicions, but said only, "Good news, at least mostly. I talked to your mother, Ista, and she's agreed to meet us once we clear Agglomeration control."

"That's when we transfer traffic control to Mayhew, right?" Tarasov said, and adjusted something on his board. "The edge of the Outer Reach."

"Right." Rangsey braced his arms against the edges of the hatch, stretching, and looked at Ista. "You'll transfer over then."

"And then what?" Stinne asked. "Look, I don't want to sound ungrateful, but I don't see how this helps either of us."

"For one thing, it keeps you out of Security's reach until there's been time for this to blow over," Rangsey answered. "And that gives Kelly2 time to call in favors, or whatever else she can think of that might buy you off."

It sounded thin, and Ista looked uncertainly at Stinne, seeing the same question reflected in her eyes. But then, delay was always important, especially if you couldn't do anything else—you never knew, Kelly2 always said, what could happen, how your options might change if you just managed to hold off a decision.

"It also gives the Patrol time to make something of all of this," Tarasov said, and swung himself away from the setboard. "And I think one thing we can do—should do, Jus—is pass on these files, one way or another."

"Anonymously, I'd think," Rangsey said. "All right, I can do that."

"Did you get in touch with Macbeth?" Tarasov asked, and Rangsey blinked.

"Um, yeah. Gave her the message, like you said."

Tarasov nodded. "I've got the basic course plugged in, so all that's left is getting clearance."

"Supplies?" Rangsey asked, still braced against the edges of the hatch.

"Somehow I don't think laying in extra stocks would be the smartest thing we ever did," Tarasov answered, not looking up from his boards. "We're in decent shape already, and then there's the year's emergency rations. And water plant's just been resealed, supposed to have three years' supply for two."

Ista made a face at the thought. She had tasted emergency rations once, on a dare rather than necessity, and couldn't imagine eating them except when there was nothing else. She saw Rangsey looking at her, an ironic smile on his lips, and smoothed her own expression hastily. After everything they were doing, it seemed at best ungrateful to balk at less-than-perfect food.

Tarasov went on, "So you two might as well get yourselves settled—make free with the config programs, and Jus'll get you anything else you need."

Ista nodded, and levered herself up out of the chair. "Thanks," she said, softly, and headed down the corridor.

It didn't take long to put the spare cabin into decent shape. Ista worked the mechanisms—stiff at first, as though they hadn't been used in a long time—and with Stinne's help dragged the built-ins out of their wells and locked them into their fixed positions. It was a bigger space than she was used to, and she pulled out a table and two chairs as well as the standard bunks. She was balanced on one of the chairs, Stinne bracing her as she slid one of the cone-lamps along its track, when there was a knock at the door. At her nod, Stinne let go, and worked the hatch controls, while Ista popped the cone into its final position. She stepped down from the chair to see Rangsey standing in the doorway.

"I brought a couple of sleepsacks from the surface gear, and a hex wrench if you want to tighten the locks." He smiled then, the irony directed at himself this time. "And Sein said I was to be sure and tell you, we've got supplies aboard for the two of us for three months. There's no problem feeding the two of you."

"Thanks," Ista said, and was ashamed at her own relief.

"If there's anything else you need," Rangsey went on, "just yell. One of us'll be in control."

"I think we're all set," Ista said, "but we'll let you know."

Rangsey nodded, backing out of the hatchway, and Stinne closed it carefully behind him. There was a palmprint lock on the door, Ista saw, and came to study it.

"You think we ought to program it?" Stinne asked.

Ista shrugged. "I don't think we need to, but I don't think it's a bad idea, either." The captain-chip would contain an override to all the locks on the ship, but she put that thought out of her mind, and touched the button to initiate the programming sequence. She set her palm against the sensor plate, waited while the scanners considered and recorded the patterns, print and IR and metabolic echoes, then stood aside for Stinne to do the same. At last the confirmation lights flashed— no voice on this ship, Ista realized, and frowned.

"Something wrong?" Stinne demanded, and Ista shook her head.

"No, it's just kind of weird, that's all."

"What is?"

"This must have been a Union ship before they bought it. There's no voicelink to the ship-system." She frowned again, working out the ramifications.

"But Tarasov's not Union," Stinne said. "So how does he manage without the IPU?"

"Set-boards, things like that," Ista answered. "It's not that hard, I just—" She broke off, unsure herself now what exactly seemed so odd. "With only the two of them, you'd think a decent voice-link would make it a lot easier on both of them. Though I guess one or two trips wouldn't be that bad. . . ."

"Maybe they were short of money," Stinne said, and dropped the bundle of sleepsacks on the nearer of the two chairs.

That was probably it, Ista thought—it would be expensive to retrofit the system—but still, it didn't feel quite right. Like not naming the ship: neither one, she realized, felt like the decisions of men who were really committed to Travelling.

"Maybe so," she said, but couldn't muster much conviction.

Stinne looked at her, a sleepsack half unfolded in her hands. "You think it's something else."

"I just think it's weird," Ista said. "They don't act like Travellers, Stinne, but I don't know, they could just be new."

"Or maybe they're not Travellers," Stinne said. "Smugglers? Or what if they're part of all this?"

Ista froze, the awful, vidik-familiar scenario unrolling in her mind: the villains, having tricked the heroes into confiding in them in the first place, persuade them to join forces, and use that as a ruse to lure them someplace where they could safely be disposed of— She shook the thought away, shook her head hard. "No. If they were involved in this, if they even knew what was going on, they wouldn't've let me get involved. They'd just let Security deal with us, while they got away."

Stinne considered that for a moment, then unrolled the sleepsack with a brisk gesture, disgorging a pillow and a mesh insect cover. "Yeah, that makes sense. Which bunk do you want?"

"You pick." Ista lifted the second sleepsack, waited until Stinne tossed her lump of bedding onto the bunk that ran along the cabin's rear bulkhead, and unrolled her own onto the other bunk. They would be lying head to head, the bunks forming an L in the cabin's corner, and Ista was suddenly glad they would be that close. She spread the sleepsack out on the narrow mattress, inhaling the faintly antiseptic storage-smell that rose from it, then drew herself up onto the bunk, resting her back against the wall. "So. I guess we're settled."

"I guess." Stinne copied her movement, but drew her knees to her chin, and said nothing more.

Ista eyed her nervously. "Look, Stinne, I'm really sorry I got you into this."

Stinne shrugged, not moving from her knot. "My own fault. I shouldn't've given you the codes."

"I shouldn't've asked."

Stinne was silent for a long moment, and Ista winced, recognizing the unspoken blame. Then Stinne sighed, and shook her head. "No, I mean, if the Company's involved, I'm not sorry, I think—I don't know what I mean."

"I'm sorry," Ista said again. "I'm so sorry, Stinne."

There was another silence, and then Stinne rocked a little, drawing herself into an even tighter ball. "I just don't know what we're going to do. I mean, so we manage to put them off for a while, then what? The Company's still against us, and even if we do find out what's going on, and if they decide to believe us, either Security or the Patrol or anybody, and if it's something they can actually do something about, something real, I mean, what's going to stop the Company from blaming us for bringing it all out into the open?"

Ista shivered, recognizing the truth of what the other girl said—they had both lived on the Agglomeration long enough, and Stinne had been Company all her life, to know that you couldn't depend on the gratitude of any Company. "I know," she said, "and, Stinne, I know I owe you, if they kick you out, you know you've got a place with us, me and Mama, or any-place we can help with—" Stinne didn't say anything, didn't even seem to hear, and Ista broke off, searching for the right words. "But we had to do it," she said at last. "I'm sorry I dragged you into it, but somebody had to do it. There were too many people dead already not to."

For a moment, she thought Stinne hadn't heard her, was too lost in her own thoughts, fears, to respond, but then she saw the other girl's body relax fractionally, and one hand released itself from around her knees, reached blindly across the mattress. Ista took it, not daring to do more, and they sat in silence, fingers twined, until the intercom chimed, and Rangsey's voice announced dinner.

Going STL is almost precisely the opposite of going FTL. Aboard an FTLship, everything builds to the peak of the jump itself, and then begins the long unwinding back to the nor-mality of ordinary space; on an STLship, the trip begins in a flurry, the first-firing and the complex maneuvers away from the docking rings and through the always-crowded space around planet or station, and then tuning the VMU to bring the apparent mass into proper relation to the planned acceleration, and then at last the substantial second burn and the inevitable corrections, course and tuning together, until at last the proper balance is achieved, and the crew can relax for the duration. Then the sensors signal destination-approach, and the process begins all over again. Even in a system as relatively uncrowded as Audumla, where all traffic emerged from two discrete points, the Agglomeration and Mayhew, and the patterns they wove were relatively predictable—relative to, say, N-Harmony, where three inhabited planets, six space stations, and an actively-mined asteroid belt between planets four and five created a snarling knot of traffic that required a special pilot-chip to navigate its complexity—the first thirty hours of any trip were the most active, and the first fifteen were busiest of all. Rangsey, balanced on the knife-edge between the ship-world and the real, held there by the captain-chip that had a little bit of all the other chips' functions incorporated into its structure, felt that urgency coursing through his body, the needs of the ship as real as the beat of his blood. In his screens, the VMU panel blinked steadily, demanding his attention, but he could feel that disharmony already, a virtual itch along the wires under his skin. He reached out, through a crowd of ghost displays that melted away from his touch, adjusted the sliders that had bloomed on his i-board in response to the captain-chip's signal, and felt the worst of the sensation fade, become the faintest touch of bubbles against his skin.

"Coming up on seventh burn now," Tarasov said, from the copilot's couch, and Rangsey nodded. If they had calculated it correctly, they and the ship together, that final adjustment would erase the last of the VMU's fuzzing as the ship and the field that contained it came into alignment with the general shape and flow of spacetime.

"Speed?" It was a meaningless question, really, a misnomer, when they were talking about a combination of acceleration and field strength and the grain of space, but it was Union shorthand, and the chip was Union. Still, he saw Tarasov frown slightly, considering how to answer.

"We're within eighteen hours of our intended ETA," he said at last, touching controls on his i-board to reconfirm the figures. "We should achieve planned ETA after the eighth burn."

The eighth burn was to correct velocity. Rangsey nodded again, seeing the virtual notices dance and bob against the real screens, and the captain-chip pushed a screen to the front. "I show the seventh burn in forty-five seconds."

"Confirmed." Tarasov's hands were already poised over the controls, human backup to the controlling chip, and Rangsey watched the countdown numbers click over, his virtual display not quite centered on the real numbers, an oddly-doubled vision. He saw Tarasov tense as the countdown reached five, and then the engines fired, exactly on the zero. He felt the double kick, steering and mains, a thump and rumble along the length of the ship, and the ship displays reeled as the captain-chip recalculated the course.

Lights glowed green behind his eyes, the bubbles faded from beneath his skin, and a heartbeat later, Tarasov said, "On the money. We're perfectly placed."

"Excellent," Rangsey answered, and saw symbols shift in his virtual displays and on the boards behind them. "I'm showing thirty-two minutes to what should be the final burn."

"That's what I've got," Tarasov answered, and leaned back in his couch.

Rangsey relaxed too, reaching for his own i-board to dim the chip's displays. They would flare bright enough in any emergency, but for the moment it was a relief to see the control room uncluttered by the bright ghosts of the iconic patterns. "Any sign of *Fancy Kelly*?"

Tarasov shook his head, even as he swung the sensor horn aft to scan the departure lanes again. "Not yet. She may be having trouble getting clearance."

"It wouldn't surprise me," Rangsey said.

"Nor me." Tarasov returned the horn to its neutral position, locked it to a general sweep. "What are we going to do if she doesn't make it?"

"Take them with us, I guess," Rangsey answered. He sighed at the expression on Tarasov's face. "Well, have you got a better idea?"

Tarasov grimaced in answer. "Leave them on Mayhew, maybe, there's a Patrol station there. Or get somebody else to check out this convergence point."

"Except we don't know if we can trust the Patrollers on Mayhew," Rangsey said. "I told you what Macbeth said, they're after bigger fish and they're willing to do just about anything to get them. Besides, there's a good chance that Mayhew's working with Company Security, and we've already alerted them that we're onto them."

"Oh, I know," Tarasov said. "I just don't feel right bringing them into danger—it's a cliché, but that's what I joined the Technical Squad to stop."

Rangsey smiled. "That's what I like about you, Sein. You mean it when you say things like that."

Tarasov gave him a startled glance that eased into a sheepish smile. "Thanks."

There was a little silence then, and Rangsey ran his eyes over the displays. Everything was still green, everything optimum for the final burn, and he reached under his shirt to rub the skin around the IPU. It tingled at his touch, warning him that he was approaching his physical limits, and he glanced at the chronometers, confirming the time. He'd only have to stay on the chip for another hour at the most; after that, Tarasov could handle the final set-up.

"You're really enjoying this, aren't you?" Tarasov asked.

Rangsey blinked. It hadn't really occurred to him, or more truly, he'd been avoiding thinking about it, but he was enjoying it, far more than he'd ever expected to. "Yes," he said, "I am."

Tarasov nodded, mouth wry, looked back at his boards.

Rangsey said, "I missed being in space, Sein. Hell, I even missed the chips—it was neat, not having them to rely on, but I missed them, too. You knew that."

"You never said it." Tarasov made a face, his eyes still fixed on unchanging readings. "Yeah, I knew. But that's not what I meant."

Rangsey sighed. I wish it was, he thought, and said, "Yeah, I like the undercover stuff, too. I'm good at it, Sein."

"Social engineering," Tarasov said, and gave a bitter twist to the words.

"At least I'm working for the Patrol," Rangsey said. He shook his head then, answering the unasked question, the question Tarasov didn't dare ask, maybe didn't want answered. "I don't know, I don't think I want to work for SID permanently—"

"They'd take you," Tarasov said. "Like a shot. They can use people who can pass for Union, hell, who are Union."

"Maybe that's why I don't want to do it," Rangsey answered. He frowned, refusing to be deflected. "But, no, I don't want to go back to Bestla."

Tarasov shook his head. "I knew you were going to say that, too."

"Look, we could try somewhere else—"

"I hate this," Tarasov said flatly. "I don't like being closed up, no room at all, no air but what's in the tanks—I can live with it for a while, but I don't like it. But I really hate not having a home, some place permanent, some place that's mine."

"That's social conditioning," Rangsey said.

"It—" Tarasov stopped. "Maybe it is, but it's still real. I won't live vagabond, Jus."

The word was a wall between them, the oldest, most basic insult between citizen and Union. Rangsey took a slow breath, controlling his automatic anger and the fear that fueled it. "Maybe we can work something out," he said, cautiously, not wanting to give more than he got, and saw the other lift one shoulder.

"Maybe."

Rangsey drew breath for an angry answer, the whole feeling of Bestla, living in the Patrol's constant eye, rushing back, and the intercom chimed. He swallowed his words, and Tarasov reached for the response button.

"Yeah?"

The proper answer was "control here," but Rangsey said nothing, too glad of the distraction to continue the argument.

Ista's voice came from the speaker at the center of the display. "Anything from Ma—Jenna yet?"

"Not yet, I'm afraid," Tarasov answered. "But we expected she'd have delays getting clearance."

"I know." In spite of her best efforts, the disappointment was audible.

Rangsey said, "We're keeping the ship's ear out, and we'll let you know the minute we hear anything."

"Thanks," Ista answered, still sounding subdued, and the light went out below the speaker.

Tarasov reached out anyway, made sure the connection was closed before he spoke again. "I am worried about having them with us. The more I think about it, the more likely it seems to me that we're going to run into whatever it is that's attacking the mines."

Rangsey nodded slowly. "I've been thinking that, too. If the attacks happen when a platform gets to close to the center point, which is what it looks like, then we're definitely asking for trouble." The captain-chip pulsed then, expressing a touch of concern, a remote warning singing through his nerves. "The chip agrees, by the way. I've been getting little twinges every time it reviews the course."

"Does it know about the Patrol hardware we've got on board?" Tarasov asked. He touched controls, bringing a new display into the screen, and entered a series of passwords that dissolved that display, resolving it into an unfamiliar military pattern.

"I don't know," Rangsey said. "It ought to, it's supposed to configure itself to the ship's capabilities when I first plug it in, but with all that stuff shielded, I don't know."

"And I'm not a hardware specialist," Tarasov said. "The camouflage suite looks good—it's government issue, ex-military, so you'd think it would be enough to fool whatever's out there."

"I'd say it will have to be." Rangsey looked at the display, picking out the various components: camouflage suite, the wingtip cannons, the override drivers for the VMU and the maneuver engines, the computer package with its carefully pedigreed programs. The chip seemed unaware of them; he felt none of the usual tickling that came when he reviewed the ship's other components. "I don't think the chip can access these. I'm not feeling anything, anyway." And that, he thought, could be dangerous. He relied on the chip's accuracy, on its decisions based on the ship's capacity, its strengths and weaknesses; if it didn't recognize the Patrol systems, then its readings would be seriously at fault.

"I wonder what Ista knows about Union chips," Tarasov said.

"What do you mean?"

"It all depends on where the systems are blocking the chip," Tarasov said, still staring at his displays. "If it's in the computers, I can probably override it myself, but if in the chip—I don't know much about chip structure."

"Typical," Rangsey said, without heat. "Not you, I mean the system. If you ask Ista, you'll have to tell her who we are."

"I know," Tarasov nodded. "It's been in my mind we ought to do that anyway."

"Probably."

"But not, I think, until we've made the rendezvous with Kelly2." Tarasov dismissed the images on the screen. "Or not made it, as the case may be. We can decide then."

Rangsey nodded, watching the displays reform into a different pattern before vanishing completely. The chip was beginning to whisper within him, a wordless murmur that was also a kind of tension, and he reached for his own board, calling up the course plot to start the preparations for the next burn.

It went as scheduled, the maneuver engines firing a final time to shift the ship into the groove of its orbit. The last faint fuzz eased away as the VMU came into perfect alignment along the grain of space/time, and Rangsey allowed himself to relax, popping the chip from its socket for the first time since they'd left the Agglomeration. They'd done everything they could; old-fashioned physics would take the ship the rest of the way to the deceleration point.

It was another thirty-six hours before he put it in again,

thirty-six hours spent partly sleeping, partly running the routine checks that kept the ship in order, and partly—the best
part—spent with the others in the crowded commons, eating
or cooking or reading or playing the dozen games stored in the
ship's systems. Ista admitted, with some shyness, that she
owned a magic book, one of the strange illuminated texts from
Eden in the Territories, and they each in turn spent time scanning it, trying to decipher the strange text and pretty moving
pictures.

"Trindade says they send these out to trap us," Ista said, toward the end of the thirty-fifth hour, and Rangsey looked up
from the scene of dancing bears. She had an oddly serious look
on her face, and Stinne turned away from the samovar where
she had been reinstalling a balky filter. She was good with her
hands, and with the eccentric machinery of the commons'
gallery wall, though she had no reliable sense of what spices
would go well together.

"How do you mean?"

Ista glanced at her friend. "They think that once you've
heard their Word-of-Truth, you have to believe it or be
damned. So they send these out, which counts as telling us,
and if we don't believe, we're damned."

"Nice," Stinne said, and curled her lip.

Rangsey looked down at the now-still picture. The clever an-
imates lost some of their appeal, viewed as a lure or a snare,
and he flicked the tablet off again, handing it back to Ista.
"That doesn't sound like the Territories." Even as he said it,
he doubted his own words: the Territorial government didn't
exert a great deal of control over its member worlds, and the
realities of the situation meant that it couldn't always enforce
the few standards it claimed to keep. That was part of the
temptation as well as the danger, of course, the hope that
somewhere among the worlds would be one that was perfect
for an individual's temperament. It might not be true, but it
was part of the myth, and a stark contrast to the Federation,
where the differences were only of degree—where if you know
the basic culture of one world, Centrality or frontier, you know
them all.

Ista shrugged, and tucked the book back in her pocket. "That's what Trindade told me, anyway."

"I'd believe it," Tarasov said, from the hatchway. "By all accounts, Eden's a strange place even for the Territories. I wanted to ask you a question, Ista, if you don't mind."

The girl shook her head, but her expression was wary.

"I was on the wildnet a bit before we left the Agglomeration and I found a dead long-liner. Nothing had scavenged it. Is that normal for here?"

Ista looked startled. "No, usually things get recycled pretty quickly. And we don't see very many of the greater hammals, either. What was the cycle count?"

Tarasov grimaced. "I don't know for sure—my sync wasn't accurate. So it may not have been as long as I thought it had. But it seemed strange, the rest of the wildnet being, well, empty."

"There have been some bare patches lately on the frontage," Ista said, slowly, "and around the gateways. But that's about it."

Tarasov nodded, his expression still not satisfied, and looked at Rangsey. "I need you in control, Jus. We're coming up on the first deceleration burn."

"Right." Rangsey rose, reaching into his pocket for the captain-chip in its case, and turned his back on them all to slip it into its socket. The first rush of data made him sway slightly, colored lights and symbols filling his vision as the sensation of the ship itself, of the ship's health and strength, ran in the wires beneath his skin. Everything was as he had expected it would be, the fizz of dissonance between the course plan and the ship's position and speed, the list of required actions spread out across his range of sight, partly obscuring the room. He reached blindly for the wall controls to dim those colors, and saw Ista looking at him.

"Can we do anything?" she asked, and Rangsey glanced at Tarasov. There wasn't anything for them, really; the deceleration was already planned and locked into the system, needed only the two, pilot and copilot, to manage the inevitable fine-tuning.

"Stow everything in here," Tarasov said, "and then come on up to control. You may need to handle comm if we hear anything from Kelly2."

"Still nothing?" Stinne asked, and Tarasov shook his head. "Not so far."

The deceleration went smoothly, balancing the increasing apparent mass against the steady pulse of the forward-directed jets that slowed the ship. Rangsey lost himself instantly in the rhythm of it, the pattern dictated by the chip, by the computers, at a level below words, so that he responded to the itch of the detuned fields, the corresponding thick air that could only be cleared by the kick and rumble of the jets. The feelings beat against him like the ocean waves he had seen on Nimue and on Bestla before the freeze rimed the beaches with impassible ice, and like waves they carried him, and he swam with and against them, orchestrating their steady slowing.

At last, the heavy beat died away to a barely perceptible pulse and then to nothing, a steady red glow behind his eyes warning him that the ship was nearly stationary too close to a marked shipping lane. That at least had been planned, and he dismissed it with the blink of an eye, dragging himself back into his ordinary self. Ista and Stinne were there already, he saw, and blinked again, seeing the chronometer reading. He had been linked with the chip, part of the ship and the computers, for nearly nine hours.

"You've got control, Sein," he said, and had to clear his throat twice before he could speak.

"I have it," Tarasov answered.

On a Union ship, the phrase would have been, *I have the chip;* he would have passed it over, and Tarasov would have plugged it in, still body-warm from the nine hours' usage. Rangsey put that thought aside, and glanced toward the communications board. "What's the word?"

"Nothing yet." It was Ista who answered, bent over the improvised console, Stinne beside her.

"We need to warn Mayhew that we're stopped," Tarasov said. "Otherwise we're a traffic hazard."

"Do we have to?" Ista asked. Despite the protest, her hands were already moving, setting up the transmission: Kelly2 had taught her well, Rangsey thought, still vague from the chip, taught her ship discipline. "I mean, is it smart?"

"It's required," Tarasov answered. "And it would look damn odd if we didn't. Tell them—oh, I don't know, tell them we're checking out an impedance fault, that seems to be the all-purpose excuse."

Rangsey grinned, remembering days when Tarasov had come home complaining about incoming Union and Traveller STLships, and Ista said, "All right. I'm transmitting now, with our position."

"Excellent," Tarasov answered, and Rangsey felt the sting of the burst transmitter firing.

"What's the lag?" he asked, and Ista looked down at her board.

"About twenty minutes."

Rangsey leaned back in his couch, trying to relax again, watched as the chronometer counted off twenty, then twenty-one minutes. Tarasov swung the sensor horn steadily, a manual search to supplement the shorter-range automatics, but the approach screen stayed serenely grey-green and empty.

The com console chirped softly, the sound echoing directly in Rangsey's ear, and Ista said, "From Mayhew."

"Put it through," Tarasov said.

"Putting it through," Ista answered, her voice almost perfectly steady, and Rangsey thought again how well Kelly2 had taught her. Out of the corner of his eye, he saw Stinne's hand close on her friend's shoulder, mute comfort, and he looked away.

"Synthesis running," Ista said, and the central speaker crackled softly.

"Acknowledged, SKW 5122," a synthetic-sounding voice said—not really synthetic, Rangsey knew, but imperfectly extrapolated from the radically compressed transmission file. "Your position is noted and a warn-off is posted until further notice. Also, you have mail."

"Mama," Ista said, softly, and her hands moved on the board again. She curbed herself with an effort, and looked at Tarasov. "I assume they should forward it?"

"Yeah, and go ahead and acknowledge the warn-off," Tarasov answered.

"Right."

Glancing back, Rangsey saw Ista frowning over the board, Stinne's hand still closed tight over her shoulder. He leaned back again, trying to ignore the faint demands of the chip—status reports, an insistent pulse of worry from the navigation systems, which knew they were sitting dead still close to a heavily travelled shipping lane—and watched the chronometer tick down the minutes. Finally, he felt the faint click as the communications system sprang to life, and in the same moment, Ista said, "Message received."

"Let's hear it," Tarasov said, and Ista hit a final combination of keys.

"It's text only," she said, a second later. "Shall I read it?"

"Go ahead," Tarasov said.

"SKW 5122 Tarasov/Rangsey," Ista began, "and I'm skipping the rest of the routing codes." She took a breath, resumed her reading-aloud voice. "I'm not able to make delivery as planned because my daughter's gotten into some trouble on the Agglomeration and my movements are being restricted, not that I wouldn't stay anyway. Sorry about the driver, but you should be able to make do with the version you have until you get back. I will of course refund half your prepayment, or all of it if you find a replacement at Mayhew." She looked up again. "And it's signed with her full name."

"Damn," Rangsey said, under his breath, and earned a glare from Stinne.

"You don't think we really want to be here, do you?"

"Well, why would they want us on board?" Ista asked. The words were reasonable enough, but her voice shook fractionally. "We're bound to be in the way."

Tarasov twisted in his couch, looking awkwardly back over his shoulder. "You're right, actually, we'd rather not have you on board, but it's not for the reasons you'd think. Let's go back to commons."

"I'd rather have it out now," Ista said.

Rangsey heard the note of desperation in her voice. Tarasov said, "There are some things we haven't told you."

Stinne giggled at that, a high-pitched nervous sound, quickly cut off: not amusement, he realized, but waiting for the rest of the disaster.

"That we figured," Ista said, and sounded bitter. Rangsey glanced back to see her braced and ready, though he doubted she knew herself for what.

"We're not exactly committed Travellers," Tarasov went on, and Rangsey stilled his own instinctive answer. The girls deserved—needed—to know the truth now, in case something happened; he shoved aside the weird feeling of disappointment, of being forcibly returned to his old self, and concentrated instead on Tarasov's words.

"I'd guessed that much," Ista said, still in that bitter, brittle voice, and Tarasov gave her a rueful smile.

"We're Patrol. We were recruited for this because of Jus. I'm—or I was—a sergeant in the Patrol Technical Squad on Bestla. Jus was with External Affairs, a translator. We—an SID officer, from the Centrality, but attached to our, Bestla's, local SID, was mounting an investigation into the mine attacks here in Audumla-system, and she wanted a team who could pass for Travellers. Though I guess we didn't do it all that well."

"No." Ista's voice was remote, on the edge of anger.

Stinne said, "If you're Patrol, why the hell did you bring us with you?"

"Because—" Tarasov began, and Ista cut him off.

"Because you don't trust Security, which I don't blame you for, but maybe you don't trust your own people, either. Am I right?"

"Not entirely," Rangsey said.

"Our immediate superior has an axe to grind in this," Tarasov said, "and we don't know what it is. Which is the reason we're not comfortable putting you off on Mayhew. Her I trust, mostly because I think I know what she wants, but I don't know how far we can trust the rest of the team."

"This sounds like a bad vidik," Stinne said.

"I wish it was," Rangsey answered, and surprised a smile from both girls.

"So what you're saying," Ista said, "is that you may have the answer to these attacks—hell, we saw that for ourselves—but you don't know if you can trust your own colleagues to stand up against the Company if it's involved."

"I don't know what Macbeth's after," Tarasov answered, "or why she's willing to get involved after all this time."

"What we do know," Rangsey said, "is that we maybe have part of the answer. We owe it to—hell, to ourselves, put the worst face on it, we owe it to ourselves to find out exactly what we have."

Tarasov nodded, pale face sober with agreement. "It's our job—it's what we have to do. I just wish you two weren't part of it."

Ista shook her head. "I'm not sorry—well, except for getting you into it, Stinne."

"I'm not sorry, either," Stinne snapped, and sniffed hard.

Ista reached up and grabbed the hand that was still clutching her shoulder. "Then I'm not sorry, because this is my business as much as—more—than anybody's. I need to know who I am, and if I can't find that out, then I need to know something that I can trade for it, for real ID. So I'm not sorry."

Rangsey nodded, feeling the tension that had filled him dissolve like the icons in front of his eyes. Whatever else happened, at least they would do this, do their best to solve this problem—and Ista was right, she deserved to be in at the finish. She had been there at the beginning, much too young to make a choice; young as she still was, she deserved the chance to change that now.

They let the ship lie idle for another six hours anyway—that was about the average time, Tarasov said, it took to correct an impedance fault, and it let Rangsey grab a few hours' sleep before reinstalling the captain-chip for the acceleration—and then slowly brought the ship back to course and speed. Once that was established, there was nothing to do but wait, and try to fill the eighty-hour trip with maintenance projects. Tarasov buried himself in the ship's computer, trying to bypass the system blocks that kept the captain-chip from reading the ship's added capabilities. Periodically, Rangsey would plug in the chip again to check, and finally reported that he could see the control grids for the camouflage package and the wing-tip cannons. The chip was uneasy about them—nothing in its experience bank gave it clues on how to use these new tools— but he could feel the program running simulations, the responses flashing past too fast for him to perceive more than the echoes of the emotion. Ista and Stinne spent most of their time together, studying the maps of the Outer Reach and the pattern woven by the attack locations. Luckily, the computers were fairly free, the steady course demanding no more than ordinary use; they were able to create file after file, watching the pattern change year by year, spreading like spilled ink across the dark background. Something in its shape was familiar, but Ista couldn't quite place it, and she sat for hours staring at a display dome as the shape grew and vanished and grew again. Stinne watched with her, affirming the familiarity, but couldn't make the connection either.

Ista ran the program yet again, her head tilted to one side as she watched the red dots spread across the starscape, then shook her head as the image froze at the current date.

"It does look like something," Stinne said, for the third time. "I just don't know what."

Ista made a face, and pushed herself away from the display dome. The two men were elsewhere, Rangsey in control, Tarasov either sleeping or with the computers—sleeping, probably, she thought, since they hadn't gotten any break-messages from the main systems—and for once the commons seemed almost spacious. She tugged open the food locker, stared at the neatly boxed remains of the previous night's dinner—Tarasov was a better-than-average cook—without really seeing them, and let the door fall shut again.

"I wonder," Stinne said suddenly, and Ista turned toward her. "This isn't a complete system map, is it?"

Ista shook her head. "It's the standard short-form."

"What happens if you superimpose it on the long-form?"

Ista eyed the image uncertainly. "Why?"

Stinne made a face. "Because I think this runs parallel with something, but I can't think what."

"Wouldn't they have checked it out on the Agglomeration?" Ista asked, dubiously. That simulation would require a larger chunk of the ship's computing power, not to mention time.

"I don't know." Stinne shrugged. "Do we have anything better to do?"

That was true enough, and Ista reached for the intercom panel. "Control?"

"Yeah?" To her surprise, it was Tarasov's voice that answered.

"I was wondering if we could use more of the system to run another sim."

"How much more?"

Ista glanced at the displays ringing the dome. "Five percent," she said, and crossed her fingers that she'd estimated right.

There was a little silence, and then Tarasov answered, his tone the equivalent of a shrug. "Go ahead, I don't have anything big running here."

"Thanks," Ista said, and turned back to the dome. Stinne had already plugged in the i-board, and had selected the files from the ship's archives, fitting them into the expanded algorithm.

"Do I run it?" she asked, and Ista nodded.

"I'll brew some tea."

The samovar had finished its run long before the dome display faded from grey back to the normal black of the map. Ista put aside her third cup of tea untasted, and leaned over the dome. Even reduced to the relevant quadrant of the Outer Reach, the display was much more crowded than it had been, the red of the attack sites almost lost among the multitude of colors. She squinted at the image, trying to make sense of the various icons, and Stinne touched her controls to activate a key display. With its help, Ista could pick out the faint wash of color that indicated actively mined area of the asteroid belts—the area where the attacks had taken place was barely tinted at all, the center completely empty—and then the pale green lines of the standard traffic lanes, converging on the purple square of the jump point. There were a couple of yellow dots as well, both in the asteroid belt and both clear of the area where the attacks had taken place, and she looked at Stinne.

"Mine operations?"

Stinne nodded. "Those are the big finds, the permanent claims."

The ones that would take more than a single mine platform or a single tour to exploit, Ista knew. The ones that every Union miner dreamed of finding, of adding the claim bonus to the plain profit, and then, in the best cases, taking a percentage from every other mine that ever worked that find. It was depressing to see how few there were, only two in a quarter of the richest belt in the Outer Reach, and she looked back at the red dots of the attack sites. At first glance, the patch seemed to have grown, but then she realized that there were two different shades of red. The vivid red of the attacks was now interwoven with a hot pink, and she glanced at the key to find what those dots meant. They were data-relay devices, the ubiquitous house-sized half-intelligent satellites that made network access possible from the Outer Reach, and kept traffic control possible, and she frowned, considering their positions.

"Stinne, can you get rid of everything except the attacks and the DRDs?"

"Sure." Stinne made the corrections to the selection criteria, and leaned back while the dome turned grey again. "What's up?"

"I don't know yet." Ista stared at the empty display, willing it to fill again. After what seemed like an interminable time, the starscape reappeared, the red and pink interlaced. It was easier to tell the colors apart without the other symbols to distract the eye, and Stinne touched her controls again, brightening the pink even further. Ista stared at the image, trying to empty her mind the way Trindade had taught her: there was a pattern there, and an important one, if she could only read it. "Can you show the entire system, still with just those things?"

"All right." Stinne frowned at her board, and made an adjustment. The scene in the dome swam slightly, fuzzed, and then reformed with the sun at the center of the image. The pink dots wove a net across the system, a pattern that looked vaguely hexagonal, each cell defined by half-a-dozen dots; the red dots were a compact blotch across the third quadrant, covering nearly six of the pink dots. A full cell, Ista realized, and the attacks looked as though they had been planned to take in the space defined by the satellites. She squinted, blurring the individual icons, and the pattern resolved itself into an amoeboid shape, with stubby pseudopods reaching out to encompass each of the satellites.

"Hot damn," she said, and Stinne looked at her.

"What?"

"It's the satellites," Ista said. "That's what it's all about. Look at the pattern—squint at it, that makes it clearer, but you can see all the attacks are taking place around the satellites."

"Six of them," Stinne said, her own eyes wide. "A full hex."

"So whatever it is, they have to get control of the DRDs." Ista reached for the intercom again. "Control? I've got something I think you should look at here."

There was a slight pause before Tarasov answered. "I'll be right down."

"Could it be wild programs?" Stinne asked. "Illegal breeders using the DRDs to move their programs into the normal dataverse?"

"It could be," Ista said, slowly, still staring at the screen, "but I don't understand why you'd do it here. I can understand why you wouldn't risk the Agglomeration or Mayhew, Company Security's pretty good—"

"Tell me about it," Stinne muttered.

"—but out here seems, well, a long way from any buyers," Ista finished.

"What's up?" Tarasov said, from the doorway.

"I've found another pattern for you," Ista said. "Take a look."

Tarasov glanced at the dome, frowned, and reached for the i-board. Stinne relinquished it without a word, and Tarasov flicked through her back trail, his frown deepening as he went. "Nice work," he said at last, but his eyes were still on the display.

"Somebody should've spotted it," Ista said, greatly daring, and Tarasov looked at her.

"Not without the attack locations. But I agree, somebody in the Company should have made the connection."

"All Security isn't crooked," Stinne said.

"No." Tarasov gave a bitter smile. "But someone highly placed is either crooked, or completely incompetent."

"We were thinking it might be illegal breeders," Ista said hastily, cutting off whatever protest Stinne might have made.

Tarasov frowned again. "The Company net is strange," he said. "There aren't enough big programs, and the little ones behave oddly—and there was that dead long-liner that hadn't been scavenged."

"And we—Trindade and I—saw a mandaleon outside the WQA gateway," Ista said.

"Which wouldn't fit," Tarasov said, "Unless someone's breeding big fauna. And here would be nicely separate, far enough out to make contact with the Company net difficult, but close enough, with those DRDs, to let whatever you're breeding harden off on the true wildnet. And they're right on the traffic routes to pass on programs to people going out-system. Oh, this makes the most sense of anything I've seen so far."

"Somebody's breeding programs out there," Ista said, slowly, "maybe even using what's left of platforms they destroyed as the shell for the computers, then selling them to people passing in and out of the system—no, first they test them on our wildnet, that would explain the empty patches, and then they sell them."

"It makes a depressing amount of sense," Tarasov said. He

shook his head again. "A good breeding station is worth killing for, and this—well, if we're right, this would be the best I've ever come across."

"The Company has to have known," Stinne said. In the commons' harsh light, her face looked pinched and ill. "In fact, a lot of people have to have known."

"More than just the Company," Tarasov said. He looked at Ista. "I'd say that either Travellers or Union folk have been helping to get the programs out of the system."

"Probably Travellers," Ista said. "We have more freedom than the Union." And how much does Trindade know about all this? she wondered. If there were strange programs loose in the wildnet, she must have recognized them—and her constant watch for the demogorgon might mean she did know something, had noticed the new programs—but would she have recognized them as illegal, and would she have cared? She could feel a cold knot settling in the pit of her stomach. Stinne was right, this would have taken a lot of people, a company within the Company, and plenty of Travellers would have had to have known who her parents were, how they had died—and, most of all, someone had to know who she was. She closed her fists over the frustration, and Tarasov reached past her to trigger the intercom.

"Jus? You want to come in here?"

"What's up?" Rangsey sounded surprisingly awake, and Ista pictured him reaching for the captain-chip.

"No trouble, just some new information," Tarasov answered. "I think the girls have figured out what's going on."

From anyone else, Ista thought, I'd've objected to the 'girls' but from him it sounds right enough. It sounds right enough with the praise attached.

Rangsey appeared almost at once, still settling his shirt on his shoulders, left it loose over his worn karabels. "You figured it out?" he said, and there was no disbelief in his voice, only the simple question. "So what have we got?"

Ista looked instinctively at Tarasov, expecting him to take over the explanations, but the fair man was looking at her instead. "We think it's an illegal breeding station," she said, and pointed to the image in the screen. "The attacks overlap six of the DRDs." She ran through the rest of their discovery as concisely as she could, watching Rangsey's attention sharpen, the fine brows draw down in concentration. When she had finished, he swore under his breath, stood for a moment shaking his head as he looked at the display dome.

"That makes too much sense," he said. "Too much."

Tarasov nodded. "It would explain some of the programs we've been seeing in the invisible—Bestla's wildnet, I mean. We knew there was a nearby source, but we couldn't trace it."

"So they were coming from Audumla," Rangsey finished, "but there was no way to trace them because the attacks weren't being reported."

"The Company knew," Stinne said again. "Somebody high up has to have known—has to be running it."

Tarasov laid a hand lightly on her shoulder, took it away again when she didn't respond. Rangsey said, his voice suddenly gentle, "That's not our concern, at least not directly. What we need to do—" He looked at Tarasov then, and Ista's attention sharpened, recognizing some private message passing beneath the words. "—is get the information to Bestla. Once it's there, this will be too big to cover up."

"You hope," Stinne said, bitterly. "As long as this has been going on—"

"NSMCo controls Audumla," Rangsey said, "but they don't have the same power on Bestla. One thing that place doesn't need is slag."

Tarasov grinned at some memory, but the expression vanished as he looked back at Stinne. "The main thing is to stop the process—stop the attacks and the killing, and then stop the breeders. That we can do. The rest—" He sighed. "When I started out with the Technical Squad—I came late to it, I was born to Transport, worked FTL for a few years before I figured out I really hated the work—the first thing I had to learn was that you had to rely on your colleagues in the other Squads, and the second thing was how far you could rely on them. I think we can trust Macbeth to finish the job right—no, I'm sure, I'm betting on it."

Betting our lives, Ista thought, finishing the cliché, and then wished she hadn't. But she was already committed to this—and anyway Tarasov was right, this was the only thing to do. She glanced at Stinne then, and saw the other girl nod, as though she'd read the thought.

"What do we do now?" Rangsey asked. He was still staring at the display. "If they've corrupted the DRD relays, then they've got entirely too good a reading on our course-and-speed."

"I agree." Tarasov chewed at his lower lip for a moment, then looked at Rangsey. "You said the captain-chip gives a warn-off when you're getting too close to the danger areas, right? I think we should wait until that point, and then switch on the camouflage program. We can set it to show us turning away, use it to fox the DRDs—hell, we can use the DRDs against them, for once."

Rangsey nodded.

"Why wait?" Ista began, then shook her head. "Never mind, I see."

"So it doesn't look suspicious, right?" Stinne asked, and Tarasov nodded.

"The last thing we want is to attract any more attention than we must already have done. Jus, how long before the captain-chip kicks in?"

"I've no idea," Rangsey answered, and gave a wry smile. "I think the best bet is to set up the program first, and run it when we get the warning."

·9·

THE STL CHIPS were the standard variety, a complex, near-life decision matrix compiled from interviews taken from the few unmechanized STL crews still working, plus the compounded programming of a dozen previous chips, blended by careful programming to eliminate personality and leave only the correct responses to any conceivable situation. Or so the makers claimed: in all the years Rangsey had worked with chips, he had never yet found one that did not have, somewhere in its makeup, some hint of the dominant personality among its mix. SKW 5122's captain-chip, strictly speaking, didn't belong to the ship, having been transcribed for use in Audumla, and Rangsey could guess its descent almost as well as Tarasov could name the pedigrees of the programs he watched on the wildnet. Compared to others of its lineage, it was cautious, given to quick alerts and flurries of scanning, inclined to the strongest reaction to any situation—but given the problems in Audumla-system, Rangsey thought, that was hardly surprising. In fact, it was only to be expected, and indeed the chip he'd tried on back on the Agglomeration had felt even more nervous.

He closed his eyes against the flicker of the control room displays and leaned back in his couch, letting the steady murmur of the chip's activity sweep over him. Still nothing, nothing more than the constant pulse of the status monitors, the environmental controls linked to his own body, so that he heard his breath and heartbeat doubled, reflecting the health of the ship against his own skin. He could feel the chip's attention cycling outward then, flicking over the navigation systems, a wordless focussing, and felt the first tremor of concern in the pit of his stomach. It was small, hard to read, just enough to catch his attention over the general noise of the ship and the chip's routine activity, and he found himself reaching for the nearest i-board. The chip had already shifted the controls, and a navigation schematic bloomed under his hand. It was the twenty-four hour projection, the close-range, and the chip prodded him again, the controls changing to display the longer-range course projection. This time, the spike of alarm was much stronger, a definite surge of adrenalin that made him grin and reach for the intercom.

"Sein? The chip's panicking."

"Great," Tarasov answered. "What's it suggesting?"

Already, a set of revised coordinates were flashing into the display: a hard burn that would send the ship well clear of the danger zone, or a set of smaller burns that adjusted course to

skim the edge of the attack area. Rangsey leaned across
Tarasov's couch to retrieve the bookboard that lay discarded
against the cushions, pressing the button to recall the course
change Tarasov had sketched. It was nearly identical to the second of the chip's two courses, and Rangsey's grin widened.

"Looks like you called it," he said, to the intercom, and
Tarasov answered from the hatchway.

"Excellent. Let me get the camo on line."

Rangsey nodded, feeling the chip's unease, its rising insis-
tence, one course or the other. He did his best to ignore it, the
pressure rapidly becoming physical, a hard knot at the base
of his stomach, while Tarasov bent over his console. A moment
later, he felt the pressure ease, replaced by the floating feeling
that was the chip's interpretation of the camouflage unit.

"Tell it you'll take the second option," Tarasov said, and
Rangsey obediently pressed the proper icons. The pressure
eased still further, was replaced by an odd, not entirely pleasant watchfulness. The chip seemed to be accepting the camouflage unit's effectiveness, but maintained the ghost of its
earlier watchfulness, and the unease that went with it. He
could feel the steady beat of the sensor sweep, a flicker across
his skin as the chip ordered increased surveillance, and the tips
of his fingers tingled strangely.

"The chip's primed the cannons," Tarasov said.

Rangsey glanced at his own monitors, saw the icon glowing red. "Shall I override?"

"No, leave it." Tarasov touched a final series of controls. "So
far, so good. The deflection routine is telling the DRDs that
we're firing rockets, and shifting our sensor image to match.
In another two hours, we'll be able to see the ghost on our
screens."

"Then how much longer to the platform?" Rangsey asked.

"Assuming it is the platform, and it is where we're calculating—" Tarasov's smile pointed the uncertainties. "—then
we should reach it in another eighteen hours."

The sense of weightlessness, an odd not-quite emptiness
just below the breastbone, grew worse as the division between the actual course and the one projected to the DRDs

widened. Rangsey turned the sensation as low as he dared, over the chip's protests, and finally unplugged himself altogether. The engineer-chip—a warmer, calmer chip, friendlier than the captain-chip without losing the core of competence—was an easier monitor, though it offered no opinion on anything outside the hull. It could confirm that the camouflage system was working, however, and that was all he asked. Tarasov and the two girls took turns watching the sensor display, making up for the captain-chip's absence, and Rangsey drowsed in the pilot's couch, waiting for the signal to reinstall the captain-chip.

"Something on the long-range sensors," Stinne said, and Rangsey struggled to full wakefulness, aware of her wary glance.

"I'm awake." He stretched hard, trying to make it true, and brought the couch to an upright position. "Can you put it on my screen?"

"Uh-huh." Stinne worked her board, fingers moving smoothly on the invisible keys, and the sensor readouts popped one by one into Rangsey's screen.

He studied the patterns, the engineer-chip throbbing gently under his skin, confirming the accuracy of each of the systems that produced the composite images. They were well into the belt now, following the usual path just above the band of highest density, relying on deflection fields to shunt aside the smaller rocks that still crowded the volume around them; the blip on the sensor was below them, relative to the ship's course, a strong metallic image perhaps eight hours further on. Definitely a human-made object: nothing in the belt, not even the biggest core fragments, had ever contained that much pure metal.

"Looks like we've got it," he said, and saw Stinne smile.

"Shall I tell Sein?"

Rangsey glanced at the readings again, calculating the times in his head. "Let him sleep a little longer. Anything interesting about the blip—is it a platform, do you think?"

"You've got what I've got," Stinne answered. She took a deep breath, sounding faintly defensive. "I can't really put it together."

"It's probably shielded," Rangsey answered, and looked at the EM graph for confirmation. There was less than he'd expected, not much more than the generally active background hum of the belt, and he frowned.

"If it is," Stinne said, "It's really low power."

She sounded doubtful, and Rangsey didn't really blame her. He reached under his shirt, disengaged the engineer-chip—a cascade of quick sensation down his nerves, and then the odd blankness of an inactive chip—and freed it from his chest. Out of the corner of his eye, he saw Stinne wince, and then the color rising in her cheeks.

"I'm sorry," she began, and Rangsey shook his head.

"Don't worry, doesn't bother me." He slipped it into its case, and leaned across to retrieve the captain-chip from the ranked cases in the holder above his station. "You haven't dealt much with the Union, have you?"

Stinne shook her head, still pink. "Can—there's a question I always wanted to ask."

"So ask," Rangsey said, and did his best to make the words encouraging.

"Doesn't it hurt?"

Tarasov had asked that, too, lying skin to skin in the sticky heat of Bestla's summer, one finger tracing the scar ridge around the main input box, then sliding down his arm, following invisible molecular wires to the tattoos that circled his wrist and framed the gold jack nestled between the bones. Rangsey blinked away that memory, heat and sweat and sex he could taste, and answered honestly, "Not any more. It hurts like hell the first week after installation, and you walk around like you're drunk until you get used to the extra input. But just pulling the chips in and out—" He shrugged, as always stopped by the inability to find the right words for the feeling. "It's like a pop, a little snap. It doesn't hurt, you just know you've done it."

Stinne nodded. "Fredi—Shannin5/2 Fredi, he's a friend of mine, and Ista's—he doesn't have his implants yet. So I couldn't really ask."

Rangsey nodded, trying to keep it ordinary, not reveal that

he'd had this conversation a hundred times before—any Union member who had citizen friends had had this conversation more than once, the shy questions, reaching out from unbridgeable privilege—and said, "Some families make a bigger thing of it than others. My people were Colored, it's not a huge event, just a party after you've acclimated, but some of the Afram families make an adulthood ritual of it."

Stinne nodded again. "Don't tell Ista I asked, would you?"

Rangsey looked at her in some surprise. "All right," he said. "But you know she's Traveller. They don't have the implants, either."

"Oh, I know that," Stinne said, sounding at once impatient and embarrassed. "But they know more than me. At least about this."

And that was unarguable truth. "I won't say anything," Rangsey said, and slipped the captain-chip from its case. He fitted it into the socket, held his breath at the rush of sensation, the emptiness that filled the center of his body, a not-quite-queasiness, hollowing the heart instead of the guts. He swallowed hard, fighting back a sympathetic nausea, and realized that Stinne was watching him.

"Are you all right?"

"Yeah." Rangsey nodded for emphasis, hoping he could convince himself. She was still looking at him, and he swallowed again. "The chip's not optimized for some of the equipment we've got aboard—the camouflage unit in particular. That's all."

"Oh."

She didn't sound precisely convinced, but Rangsey turned his attention to the new displays floating in front of his eyes. The chip didn't like the sighting, wanted urgently to change course away from it. He could feel the navigation controls emerging under his fingertips as the burn calculations appeared on the screen beneath a graphic of the proposed new course, and he took his hands off the board while he scanned the secondary readouts. To his disappointment, however, the chip hadn't added to the analysis on the screen, was content to recommend flight on that basis alone. He made a face, barely aware he was doing it, and flicked the state-change button at the corner of the board until the sensor controls appeared. The chip seemed reluctant to focus on the information that reappeared, but after a moment the analysis shimmered into the space in front of his eyes. The patterns were consistent with a mine platform; however, power emissions were unacceptably low, well into the danger zone, and the chip recommended pinging the platform with a warning and an offer of assistance. Rangsey refused that with the touch of a finger—and heard a sharp intake of breath from behind him. He glanced back, and found Ista looking over his shoulder.

"I came to relieve Stinne," she said, by way of explanation, but her eyes were fixed on the screen. "We've found it?"

"Yeah." Rangsey shook himself back to business, typed in his signature and codes, and saw the form fade from both the screen and his line of sight. "It looks that way, anyway." He paused then, considering the readings that danced in front of his eyes. "And that's really interesting. If this was a dead station, we shouldn't be getting any emission signature—not unacceptably low, none at all."

"Core storage," Ista said. "It's only been sixteen years, those things last fifty, easy."

Rangsey shook his head, watching the icons tremble as they matched his viewline. "That would be really minimal power. This is more than that."

Ista stared for a moment longer, then looked at Stinne. "Your time's up—there's rice in the kitchen, if you want some."

Stinne nodded, unfolding herself from the couch, and Ista took her place. She ran her hands over the i-board, and then flicked the displays back to the sensor readouts.

"So that's the platform," she said, and Rangsey jumped slightly.

"Yeah."

"How soon will we be in visual range?" Her voice sounded tight, emotion leashed but not banished, and Rangsey remembered, with a sudden and painful clarity, that this was where she had been found—where she had nearly died, along with her parents, though he hoped she hadn't yet thought of it that way. She was young for that glimpse of her own mortality.

He shook that thought away, and touched his own controls. "Not for another seven hours, at least, probably more. Not without using active video."

"And we can't do that," Ista said. "I know."

She was silent then, and Rangsey risked a glance at her. She sat very still, her face in profile at once closed and vulnerable, her brown eyes fixed on the images in the screen. He watched her for a minute, wanting to say something, offer comfort or at least company, but there was something in her expression that silenced him. Probably the only person who could have said anything to her then was Kelly2, he thought, not just her mother—maybe not by birth, but the closest thing she'd known, and genuinely maternal in that fierce defensive love—but the woman who'd been there first, who'd found the ship and the bodies and the living child. He had rarely felt so inadequate, and was glad he had the chip to focus on.

Tarasov returned to the control room two hours later, and Rangsey retreated to their shared cabin to try to get some sleep before he had to ride the captain-chip through the thickest part of the belt and to the derelict platform itself. And probably onto it, he thought, one arm thrown across his eyes to deepen the darkness. That would be interesting, certainly—he'd never docked to a mine platform before, there had always been more experienced people on the STLships he'd crewed, and they'd been given the pilot- or captain-chip for the job—and he considered the captain-chip, tuned to its lowest possible level, but still a tangible presence, shifting sensations at the back of his mind. He was used to the feeling, but not to the hollow feeling that came with the camouflage unit. It was unsettling, weirdly like drunkenness, and he turned his attention firmly away from it, putting it as much as possible to the back of his mind.

He managed a few hours of sleep in spite of the chip's strangeness, work to an insistent pressure beneath his skin and Tarasov's voice sounding in his ears.

"The nav-system's saying it's about time to start down into the belt. You ready to take over?"

Rangsey stretched, hearing the muscles of his back crack against his spine, and swung himself off the bunk. "Give me ten minutes."

He made it to the control room in a little more than ten, but refreshed with a shower and a change of clothes. Ista slipped out of the pilot's couch for him, and he settled himself in front of the controls, bringing the captain-chip up to its full input strength with a single movement of his fingers. The strength of the sensations—and their complexity, the way impulses within the chip warred with each other, the adrenalin-sharp fear that urged him to run, the conflicting urge to ping the platform, to see if anyone was still aboard, and to help them if they were—made him close his eyes for a moment, to sort everything into its proper place.

When he opened them again, a new image was centered on his screen, a false-color, jagged-edged shape with the flat-bell scoop and dumbbell main section of a standard mine platform. "Long-range scan?" he asked, and saw Tarasov's nod out of the corner of his eye.

"Passive scan only, heavily enhanced. No life-signs, but you wouldn't expect any at this distance. No change on the emissions, either."

"So they're not scanning."

"No sign of it," Tarasov answered. "And I've had the tolerances at the maximum. If there are scanners running, they're purely passive."

"Which means we should be in good shape, right?" Ista said, from behind the couches, and Rangsey jumped. Though I should have expected her to stay, he added silently. In her place, I wouldn't go back to the commons, either. He glanced back, and was no longer surprised to see Stinne with her, pale face solemn and intent on the displays.

"At least until we get into visual range," Tarasov answered, and Rangsey reached for his board, drew up the course projection.

"That's here, right?" he asked, and touched the board to draw a red x across the course line.

"Assuming they're using military hardware, yeah," Tarasov said.

"I think we should assume."

Tarasov nodded. "We're still about an hour out at that point, but I'm not picking up any signs of weapons on the platform."

Rangsey eyed the misshapen image. "So far."

Tarasov gave a fleeting smile. "That's the way I'd do it—also the way I've seen it done."

Rangsey banished the platform's picture to a corner of the screen, searched for and found a wide-band scan of the belt around the ship. There was nothing on the screen, no suspicious concentrations of metal or emissions trails, not even the ghost of a recent course correction, nothing but stones and the distant glow of a DRD.

"I'm not picking up anything out of the ordinary, but if this operation follows the usual pattern, there'll be a ship stationed somewhere along this line." Tarasov sketched a circle on his own screen that was repeated instantly on Rangsey's diagram. "I'd expect them to stay inside the belt, but that doesn't limit it much."

"Not really," Rangsey answered, and considered the diagram. Perhaps a ten-degree arc of the circle Tarasov had sketched lay outside the confines of the belt. The chip seemed equally uneasy with the remaining segments of the circle, nothing in its programming to warn them away from any one sector, and he switched to the navigation console, running time-distance calculations. "So if we assume that this operation follows the usual pattern—I assume they keep the protecting ships at a distance to keep from attracting attention?"

"And so that they can salvage something if the Patrol raids in force," Tarasov said, nodding.

"And if the platform signals them when we come into visual range, then we can count on, what, five hours to search the platform before we have to abandon it."

"I make it closer to six," Tarasov answered, "but, yeah, that's about it."

"Will that be enough time?" Ista asked.

"I don't know," Tarasov said. "But I guess we'll have to make it enough."

"Easier said than done," Rangsey muttered, still staring at his own display. Just like timing their departure to get and stay ahead of any incoming STLships, coming from some mysterious point along a hypothetical line in space. But then, Tarasov did know how breeding operations generally worked; he would have to trust that the other man was right, he told himself, and turned his attention to the course the chip had chosen to take them into the belt. Luckily, this was not one of the areas that swarmed with tiny fragments—the chip produced the word *dusty*, and a fleeting image of a sky glittering with scraps and motes of stone—but instead had a relatively few large rocks that moved with Newtonian precision along their predictable orbits. It was classic mining territory—the scanners had already noted the presence of seven respectable metallic sources within an eight-hour radius of their current position— and it was no wonder, Rangsey thought, that the platform had come this far into the belt.

The chip had laid out a fairly conservative course, giving the nearer asteroids a wide berth, and making well over a dozen minor course corrections to bring the ship into its final alignment with the platform's docking ring. It was a sane and sensible course, and one that was guaranteed to attract attention at the maximum distance. He reached for a stylus and began sketching a modified version of the same line, eliminating all but two of the minor burns. The resulting course swung much closer to one of the stones, but that same stone would, he thought, help hide the ship from any observation programs on the platform. The chip considered, its own calculations a brief fizz under his skin, and then spat back a revision. This required longer burn times, but kept the ship out of the cloud of miniparticles that surrounded the largest stone. The masking effect was reduced, but all in all, Rangsey thought, it was a good compromise.

"First burn in ten minutes," he announced, and called up a recheck to run the calculations a final time.

"Ten minutes," Tarasov confirmed, and behind him Rangsey heard Ista make a soft, excited sound.

"Sorry," she said then, and Rangsey didn't have to look back to see that she was blushing.

"Don't worry about it," Tarasov said. "This is big."

Bigger than I'd like, Rangsey thought, watching the numbers flicker past on the screen and in the air in front of him. This is hare-brained, Sein, and you know it; we should've abandoned this and headed back to the station to tell Macbeth what was going on just as soon as we knew that Kelly2 couldn't get off the Agglomeration. But if they had done that, they would have lost any chance of catching the breeders: warning Macbeth would inevitably have warned the breeders, if not through direct contacts then through the necessary preparations for sending a Patrol fleet. And this needs to be stopped—I just wish we hadn't had to bring the girls along.

The air in front of him turned red, and his hands tensed over the firing controls as the last seconds clicked past. At zero, he reached for the switch, but the chip was there ahead of him, as always, and he heard the short rumble of the jets above him, tilting the ship down into the thickest part of the belt. The red light faded, was replaced by a success icon, and then the revised course estimate: everything, so far, was according to plan.

Another set of controls swam into existence beneath the i-board's smooth surface, new sliders and the hot red dot of the panic button filling the lower third of the board. The other controls had shifted toward the top edge, and he reached for them, keying in his inquiry. The chip answered instantly, displaying the current panic course, a hard burn and a compensating VMU shift that would point the ship back up out of the belt. Even as he watched, the course swam and reformed, taking into account an approaching asteroid's orbit.

"Looking good," he said aloud, and Tarasov grunted. "I'm putting the visuals on the middle screen."

The course plot, a duplicate of the one in Rangsey's screen, faded as he spoke, was replaced with a false-color image, black and grey and silver touched here and there with the darkest of blues. Rangsey frowned at it for a moment, trying to match shapes and shadows to the brighter points of light in the navigation displays. Then, slowly, the pieces began to fall into place, and he could make out the closest of the asteroids, a massive blue-black boulder, a flying mountain, the scarred high edges of the impact craters tipped with grey and silver. It was bigger than he'd expected, or they were closer—or both—and he stared at it as though mesmerized as its image swelled in the screen. The light behind his eyes turned orange, warning him of the upcoming burn, and he shifted his hands back to the jet controls. The countdown numbers flared, the light turned red, and then the jets fired, precisely on time. The ship tilted, the asteroid swinging ponderously in apparent counter-rotation, and the red light faded, to be replaced with the bright line of the revised course.

"Good burn," he said aloud, and saw Tarasov nod. "Anything more on the platform?"

"Nothing," Tarasov answered. "We're still at long range unless I want to use active scan, and that rock will obscure our view for a while longer anyway."

"Just as well," Rangsey said.

"Probably."

They sat in silence for a while then. The burn had been accurate as calculated; there was no need to do anything more until the next course correction, almost an hour away. Rangsey felt the chip busy with the ship's routine, paid only cursory attention to its constant fiddling, letting his mind drift.

"We're coming out of the asteroid's shadow," Tarasov said.

Rangsey let his hand hover over the panic button. If there was going to be trouble—if they'd guessed wrong, if the breeders were on the station, if there was active defense there, hidden by electronic camouflage better than their own—this was the time for it, when the STLship emerged from behind the eclipsing asteroid. He realized he was holding his breath, all senses at full stretch while the chip puttered on about its business beneath his skin, and made himself take a slow breath, and then another.

"We're getting a better picture now," Tarasov said, and

sounded, to Rangsey unreasonably smug. "No sign of any response." He leaned back in his couch. "I don't think there's anyone there."

"Good," Rangsey said, in spite of himself, and Tarasov grinned.

"We're in long visual range now from the platform. That starts the clock."

A new stopwatch appeared in a corner of Rangsey's vision, not quite in the line of sight, and he frowned, and dragged it to a more comfortable position.

"I've put six hours on it," Tarasov went on, "but I'd be more comfortable with four."

"One hour—no, more like forty minutes—to dock, and then three on the platform to see what you can find." Rangsey nodded, watching the numbers, blue this time, bob slightly as the program tuned itself to his movements.

"My God," Ista said. "Look at it."

Rangsey looked up, startled, blinked twice to clear the displays from his vision. In the middle screen, the platform hung off-center, almost dwarfed by an asteroid that loomed blue-black and silver-touched behind it. All the familiar features were in place, the massive scoop and the double cluster of grappling arms to either side, above that the wasp-waist of the control pod, and then the smaller bulge of the living quarters, all drawn in a false-color charcoal grey touched here and there with a dark, dark red that looked almost black against the grey. Hot spots, Rangsey thought, groping for normality, or relatively hot, the maneuvering jets and the congealing core of the engines and any wire systems that still have a spark of life. Usually, the mines were festooned in lights, sight-navigation beacons echoing the more sophisticated electronics, the pinpoints that marked safe-approach ranges or warned off unwary Travellers competing with the spotlights that watched the payloads into the bays or the arms' tearing grip. Now everything was dark, and the grapples, the multiple shapes of the various toolheads, hung slack and empty, bent at odd and uncertain angles around the scoop opening.

"You came from that?" Stinne said, and Rangsey glanced

back, to see Ista's face closed tight over her emotions.

"That's where Mama found me," she answered, and Rangsey saw Stinne's hand lift to her shoulder, and falter, then seize the other girl's hand in a tight and silent clasp.

"Still nothing," Tarasov said. "Can you make the dock?"

"I'm not sure I've found it," Rangsey answered, fighting to keep his tone normal, to keep from being overawed by the silent platform. The chip obligingly presented him with an overlay of pale green lines, sketching the main features, and he squinted dubiously at the screen. Apparently, a patch of flatter grey just above the taper of the control room was the docking ring, though at this distance the visual scan couldn't give more than gross details. "All right, I've got the ring—one of them, anyway. I can't tell if it's operational, of course."

"It ought to be," Ista said. "All the platforms are set to allow manual operation in an emergency."

Rangsey nodded, looked at Tarasov. "Any sign of other damage?"

"Not yet," the other man answered. "Looks like there's some dust scarring, but nothing more."

"That's odd," Rangsey said, and Ista gave a little yelp.

"That proves it, somebody's looking out for this place. If it was really derelict, there's be a lot more damage."

Rangsey didn't answer, made himself relax despite the constant seething of chip activity, watching as the image of the platform swelled on the screen. He could make out the docking collar without the schematic enhancement now, a paler circle against the darkness, the locking sensor tinged faintly, barely red against the black. He touched the upper bank of controls, calculating the course change that would bring them in at the proper angle to engage the collar's automatics, and said, "It looks like the lock is partly live, at least."

"I saw that," Tarasov said.

Something in his voice made Rangsey look curiously at him. "You think there's a problem?"

Tarasov shrugged. "I was thinking of booby traps, actually. But I don't want to try to find a second lock, or cut our way in."

"Then we'll have to risk the collar," Rangsey answered, with some annoyance, but the chip was already offering an alternative. "We could disable the automatic locking. As long as it's not a contact device, that should give us a chance to at least look for traps."

Tarasov nodded. "I doubt it would be contact triggered—suppose a rock hit it?"

Rangsey nodded, studying the numbers on his screen, spelling out the final course corrections. One thirty-second burn now, to swing the ship to a better angle, and then half a dozen one- and two-second adjustments on the final approach to mate the ship's dock to the waiting collar. The chip nudged him as he started to reach for the keys that would disable the automatic locking mechanism, suggesting that he leave it engaged for the approach and corrections—use its readouts until the last minute, and disable it only after the last corrections had been cleared. "Stand by for burn," he said, and watched the chip count off the last seconds. The jets fired precisely, sending the stars rolling in the viewscreen, and cut off as neatly, leaving only the green confirmation icons flashing in his eyes. "Looks good."

"Thirty minutes to docking," Tarasov answered, and the first of the flurry of checklists flashed onto the screen.

Rangsey flicked the icons impatiently away, responding only to the most important, and saw, out of the corner of his eye, Tarasov retrieve the others, begin working through the list. He scowled, and Tarasov gave him an apologetic glance. "I need something to do, Jus."

Rangsey nodded, mollified, and turned his attention to the course projection and the murmur of the chip in his ears. It had been years since he'd piloted an STLship—his jobs had been mostly in information and manufacture, not space—but he shoved those thoughts away. There was no time left for doubts; he would simply have to manage.

"Twenty minutes," Tarasov said, and Rangsey shoved him the next set of checklists as the air turned orange and then red.

"Stand by for burn," he said again, and the chip corrected

him, prompted him with the right words. "Stand by for final series."

He felt his couch shift, as one of the girls grabbed its back. Properly speaking, they should be in their cabin, or even back with the lifepods, but he couldn't bring himself to suggest it. Ista had been waiting too long for this; no safety regulation could compete with that need—and besides, if something did go wrong, if they'd guessed wrong about a contact device, then being in the cabin would do no good at all.

The countdown numbers clicked to zero, and the jets fired in staggered sequence, brief squirts of propellant that tipped the ship over onto its back and into position for the final approach. The confirmation icons flared for an instant, just long enough to be noticed and acknowledged, and then the ship replaced them with the familiar targeting grid that would bring them the last few hundred meters into the docking collar. A second set of lights clicked on as well, informing him that the automatic locking system was operational, and wasn't getting a confirmation from the platform. He silenced it with the push of an invisible button, touched a further set of keys to disable the system. The platform loomed huge in the screen, filling the visual window; a few sparks of silver showed over the shoulder of the crew module, not stars but the nearer asteroids. The docking collar was visible, but still shadowed, even with enhancement, and he glanced at Tarasov.

"Lights?"

"I think we can risk it," Tarasov answered, and a moment later beams of light shot from the triple searchlights, their circles roving across the mine's dulled paint before they centered on the collar. Under the harsh glare, the enhancement was too strong, and Rangsey adjusted his view, watching the false colors fade to the true industrial greys of the platform's standard paint job. A logo was still visible at the center of the hatch, a spot of bright color, and he heard Ista draw breath, and then settle back in disappointment as she recognized the marks.

"At least now you know where they came from," Stinne

said, tentatively, and Rangsey felt the couch tremble under him as Ista shook her head hard.

"Diviasa's the second biggest department in the whole Company."

Rangsey shoved their conversation from his mind, concentrating instead on the screen and the target ring that hung just outside the perfect center of the docking circle. Numbers flashed, suggesting corrections, and he touched the switch before he could think too hard about it. "Switching to manual," he said, and felt the controls come alive under his hands. The target ring seemed to tremble at his touch, though that was an illusion, and he frowned at the calculations that flickered past. The chip nudged his hands, and he punched buttons, felt the microjets fire, their ignition shuddering through the fabric of the ship. In the screen, the ring moved, and the chip signalled for the counterjets to fire. The movement slowed, came to rest again just beyond the target. Rangsey swallowed a curse, punched in more commands. The platform filled the screen now, even at the lowest magnification, the docking collar for the first time looking as massive as it actually was. The chip gave its approval, and Rangsey touched the keys, felt the microjets fire a third time, little more than a shiver, a dull murmur of propellant from under his feet. In the screen, the ring shifted, and was met by another countering burn. It slowed even further, slid to a stop centered perfectly on the collar. The chip flashed confirmation, a string of icons slipping past, then suggested that the automatic locking be turned on again. Rangsey dismissed the recommendation with a touch of a finger, and looked at Tarasov.

"So far, so good," he said, and couldn't quite keep the nervousness from his voice.

Tarasov nodded, his eyes fixed on the screen. "No sign of anything that shouldn't be there."

The searchlights' brilliance threw harsh overlapping shadows from the locking points, turned the shallow connectors into deep wells in the platform's surface, but the central disk of the hatch remained grey and featureless except for the long pale streak of a dust scar. "I don't suppose there's much point in not using active sensors now," Rangsey said, and surprised a tight grin from the other man.

"Already scanning. Still nothing."

A light flashed in front of Rangsey's screen, and he said aloud, "One minute to contact."

He heard Stinne murmur something, felt his couch tremble again as one of the girls jostled it, getting closer to the other.

"Still clear," Tarasov said.

"Thirty seconds." Rangsey held his breath, repressing the sudden desire to grab Tarasov's arm, and poised his hand over the panic button. "Now."

Even as he spoke, the ship thumped gently against the platform's side. He could feel the beginning of the rebound, and then the second solid thump as the collar caught and held their lock. A new constellation of lights appeared on his screen, a steady rosette of orange. "We're in and secure," he said, "but there's no response from the platform."

"Which is probably just as well," Stinne said, her voice a little too loud. "Sorry."

"No problem," Tarasov said, absently, his hands busy on the his i-board. "No life-sign aboard even on active scan, but I might be getting a power reading—shielded core, maybe."

"So now what?" Ista asked.

"Now—" Tarasov looked back with a wry smile. "I want to go aboard. I figure we've got at least four hours, and probably five, before we're likely to see any response, and I want to use that time to look around."

"I want to come with you," Ista said, and he nodded.

"I wouldn't dream of stopping you."

"And what do you expect me and Stinne to do?" Rangsey asked, but his tone was more accepting than the words.

"Stay here," Tarasov answered. "Put the scans up to full gain, active and passive both. There's no point in hiding anymore—if anyone's monitoring, they already know about us. Just yell the minute you see anything odd."

Rangsey nodded, suppressing the desire to go himself, knowing Tarasov was the right and logical choice. "Be careful," he said, and added, tardily, "Both of you."

"We will," Tarasov answered, and levered himself out of the couch. Ista followed him out of the control room, and Rangsey took a deep breath, reaching for the i-board to start the active sensors. It was too late to worry, he told himself, knowing perfectly well it wasn't true, too late to do anything but go through with what they'd planned. And that was true, but not much consolation: he shoved the thought aside, and dragged the chip closer to the surface of his thoughts, hoping that would help still the fear.

There were emergency suits in the wall lockers beside the main airlock, not the armor-suits Tarasov would have preferred, but serviceable enough. Ista seemed to know what she was doing, squirming into the tight over-skin and then checking tanks and environmental pack—no surprise there, Tarasov thought, most Travellers learned that at their mothers' knees, and Ista was no exception. He sealed his suit, locked helmet and pack into place, feeling the first soft thread of air against his cheek, and said, "Ista?" The word fell into the closed dead air of the helmet, and he touched the chest pad to open the short-range com. "Ista?"

An icon glowed against the inside of the faceplate, warning him that both channels were live, and in the same moment, Ista said, "I hear you. Are we ready?"

"Almost." Tarasov turned to the airlock's display panel, red and green symbols displayed in parallel across the board: everything live and functional on their side of the lock, the platform's systems dead and closed. The ship's sensors should have spotted anything in the lock's chambers; he touched keys, trying to wake the platform's emergency-response circuits, tapping into the faded remnants of power left in the core. A light flickered to orange, and then faded back to red. If there was a device, he thought, it wasn't wired into the system. "All right," he said, and took a deep breath. "I want you to go back to the main corridor and seal both hatches behind you as you go."

He saw Ista's head lift in protest, though the helmet hid her expression. "I'm coming with you."

"I know," Tarasov said. "But if there is a device, I'd rather you didn't go with me."

There was a brief pause, the helmet tipped to one side, and then she nodded once, and retreated back through the first hatch. He heard the first set of seals thud home, and then, nearly a minute later, Ista's voice sounded again in his ears.

"Both hatches are sealed."

"I confirm that," Rangsey said, from the control room, and Tarasov took a deep breath. He didn't really expect that the lock was booby-trapped, but the possibility was there, tightening the muscles across his back and shoulders. He shrugged hard, shaking himself, and keyed in the lock sequence. The inner door slid back, and he stepped through into the main chamber, waited while the door closed and sealed again behind him.

"I'm in the chamber," he said, and Rangsey answered instantly.

"Confirmed."

On the bulkhead in front of him, a second panel of telltales shone red, and Tarasov reached for the manual controls. They were stiff, not often used; he had to throw his weight against the breaker bar to start the wheel, and then it took his full strength to keep it turning. The outer lock slid back, terribly slow and completely silent, and the light from his own ship spilled out to reveal an empty chamber the twin of his own. The padding was scarred, the familiar thick tiles gone brittle in the near-vacuum, and a few flakes, disturbed by the opening hatch, drifted toward him, drawn by the ship's VMU field. There was no sign of anything like a device, just the empty grey space, and he took another breath and stepped cautiously across into the platform's chamber. He expected weightlessness, the soft pop as the suit sealed itself fully, but his foot came down into matching gravity, his own mass holding him to the chamber floor.

"Damn," he said aloud, "we've got live systems."

"Live how?" Rangsey answered instantly, and Tarasov could almost see him leaning forward over the blind displays.

"I've got gravity." Tarasov touched his chest pad again.

"And air. It's cold but breathable, I think."

"And I'm getting live readings, too," Rangsey said. "Core's up, you've got VMU and lights and full environmental—there must have been one hell of an ECM package going, Sein."

"Body count?" Tarasov asked, and wished he had the full panoply of his Technical Squad gear. Even if he rarely went armed, most of his tools could double as effective weapons.

"Nothing," Rangsey answered. "I think I'm getting a true reading, but I can't be sure."

"All right." Tarasov looked at the platform's inner hatch, studying the familiar fittings. "I'm opening the hatch, then."

"Be careful," Rangsey said, and then there was silence.

There was no point in waiting. Tarasov touched the automatic controls, and to his surprise the lights went from red to green. The floor under his feet shivered, and the hatch slid back in its socket. Light spilled out to meet him, the common Sol-spectrum light of human spacecraft, revealing an empty corridor. Like the airlock, it looked worn, the floor tiles and the wall padding scuffed and peeling in places, but more than that it looked startlingly normal.

"You there?" Rangsey asked, and Tarasov shook himself.

"Yeah. The hatch is open, and you're right, the platform's live again. No sign of people."

"No body count here, either," Rangsey answered.

"All right." Tarasov examined the corridor a final time, the plain, yellowing pads and the darker tiles. "Ista, come on back. We're going over."

"On my way," Ista answered, and a minute later the lock lights flickered a warning. Tarasov checked the seals, then touched the confirmation sequence. The hatch slid back, and Ista stepped cautiously into the lock chambers.

"My God," she said, and reached up to unfasten her helmet. "It really is live."

Tarasov nodded, and released his own faceplate. He slipped off his gloves as well, and left them dangling from their catch. "Platform control, it's down that way?"

He pointed, and Ista nodded. "There should be a cross-corridor. We go, um, left there, and then we should see the well."

The main vertica[1] corridor, she meant. "Right," Tarasov said, and there was a click of static in their ears.

"I'm getting primary power readings from the processing station," Rangsey said. "Not control."

"Control's on our way there," Tarasov said. "We'll check it out first."

"Confirmed," Rangsey answered, and the faint static vanished.

There was a cross-corridor, all right, but more than one, four identical tunnels radiating out from the end of the lock corridor. Tarasov checked, confused, and Ista said, "This way."

She was pointing not down the leftmost opening, but the one next to it. "You're sure?" Tarasov asked, and she nodded impatiently.

"It's the red line."

On second glance, he saw the darker line, more orange than red against the yellowing walls. "Nice going."

Ista shrugged, her shoulders barely denting the heavy fabric of her suit. "Where are the people, anyway? I'd expect them to keep an eye on their programs."

Tarasov made a face. "Breeding's a dangerous process. If something gets loose, you don't want to be around when it crashes something important." Unbidden, the memory of a training vidik rose in his mind: the corridors of an STLship, weightless, liquid drifting in dark globes, a hand floating in the overlapping circles of a helmet light brushed angrily away while the Technical Squad team fought to stabilize the environmental systems so that they could attack the programs that had overrun the ship's computers. They had failed, that time, and the vidik had recorded the Patrol mothership blasting the freighter into incandescent fragments, dead crew and ship together.

The girl nodded, and they came out together into the platform's central volume. The lights seemed brighter here, or maybe it was just the contrast between the unlit corridors that led back into the lowest level of the crew section. "The lifepods should be along there," Ista said, pointing into one of the dark openings, and Tarasov looked blankly at her before he remembered. She had been found near there, abandoned in a carrier while her parent or parents struggled to—what? Stabilize the ship, fight off attackers, protect the child?

"I think so," he said, trying to remember what he knew of both her story and platform construction. "We don't have a lot of time."

"I know," Ista said, but she was still looking down the corridor.

"We need to find the breeding station," Tarasov said.

Ista stared for a second longer, than made herself look away. "All right."

A pressure hatch led into the well, the main vertical corridor. All the telltales showed green, but Tarasov made himself check the failsafes first before he worked the controls. The hatch opened smoothly, with none of the stiffness he'd expected, and he stepped into the narrow lock. Ista followed, sealing the hatch behind them, and Tarasov worked the second set of controls to let them out onto the narrow landing. A set of stairs spiralled around the inside of the tube like the threads on a screw, the smooth progression broken only by the landings at each level and the strips of the tube lights that made a dashed line up the sides of the well. Tilting his head back cautiously, Tarasov could just make out the end of the well, a dark green hatch that, if he remembered correctly, would lead to the secondary sensor dome. He swallowed hard, suppressing vertigo, and decided not to look directly down. Everything still seemed in perfect repair, and that triggered a memory.

"I thought your mother said the platform was stripped."

"That's what she said," Ista answered. "They must have rebuilt it—they would have had to, wouldn't they?"

Tarasov nodded. "Let's go." He started down the long spiral without waiting for an answer, was surprised to find it easy going. The treads were well placed, the pitch not too precipitous, the whole thing planned to accommodate human vision, so that someone on the stair had to make an effort to see too far either up or down. Of course, it might well be harder going up again, he thought, but at least this part wasn't too bad.

The wall surface changed as they passed into the platform's waist, and Tarasov glanced back at Ista. "How many entrances are there to the control level?"

"Just one, I think."

"Then this must be it." Tarasov stopped on the next landing, checked the failsafes again. The indicators all showed green, and he worked the door controls. These were stiffer than the first had been, and he touched the suit's chest pad. "Jus, we're heading into the control area. Anything happening?"

"Nothing," Rangsey answered, with reassuring promptness. "But, like I said, the power readings are below you."

"Thanks." Tarasov gave the lock wheel a final turn, and the hatch slid back at last. The corridor beyond was dark, and he touched his chest pad again, switching on the helmet-mounted lamp. A second circle appeared as Ista matched him, and he flinched at the unintended echo of the vidik. Ista stumbled, avoiding him, and the circles of light bounced for a moment across the pale grey walls. The air was suddenly very cold.

"I don't think anyone's been here in a while," Ista said, and her voice echoed oddly in the darkness.

"Still no life signs," Rangsey said, from the ship, and Ista made a smothered sound somewhere between laughter and a curse.

"We're not seeing any either, Jus," Tarasov said, and looked at Ista. She seemed to have herself under control again, but her face was very still in the sudden harsh light. "You don't have to come," he began, but she shook her head, hard, making her own light dance and weave across the far wall.

"I want to see."

There was no denying that, though maybe, Tarasov thought, I ought to. God only knew what would be waiting in the control room. He said, "This way, then?"

Ista nodded, and they started together down the corridor.

It ended in a closed hatch, and Tarasov tilted his head to light the telltales. They all showed green, pressure and gravity the same on both sides of the barrier, but he touched his chest pad anyway. "Jus? Can you see what conditions are like inside the control pod?"

To his surprise, it was Stinne who answered. "Justin says, can you hold on a minute?"

"Trouble?" Ista said, sharply, and beat Tarasov by half a breath.

Stinne stifled a giggle. "He doesn't think so, just something he wanted to check—"

"Sensor bleep," Rangsey said. He sounded faintly breathless. "I wanted to run the check for myself."

"Well?" Tarasov demanded.

"I'm ninety percent sure it's a rock," Rangsey answered. "Hell, if we were a mine, we'd've made a nice profit from it, there's plenty of metal in it."

"What does the chip say?" Tarasov asked.

"The chip says we shouldn't be here in the first place." Tarasov could almost see the other man's smile. "Besides, Sein, if it's trouble, it's probably already too late."

"How long?"

"Two hours, maybe less. But I don't think it's a ship."

Tarasov took a breath, tasting the cold in the back of his throat. If there was a ship two hours out, then Rangsey was right, even leaving the platform now probably wouldn't buy them enough time to get away. But Rangsey said he thought it was a rock, and they would have to trust him. "All right," he said. "We're going to check out control, and then head for the power source you spotted."

"We're keeping an eye on the blip," Rangsey answered. "We'll let you know the minute anything changes."

"You do that," Tarasov said, and looked back at the telltales. "Can you tell what it's like on the other side of this hatch?"

"I'm not showing any change," Rangsey answered. "The hull looks sound in that area."

"Thanks." Tarasov took another deep breath, and reached for the manual controls. They were as stiff as the ones that had admitted them to the control level, and he was sweating by the time the hatch rolled back in its closure. The air inside was even colder, and carried an odd unpleasant smell, dry and very old. He saw Ista wrinkle her nose as the scent reached her, and hoped she hadn't thought too much about what it could be.

"Anything?" Rangsey asked, his voice tinny in their ears.

"Not yet," Tarasov answered, and stepped cautiously over the high combing, turning his head to swing the light across the widest possible range. The familiar fittings of an STL craft seemed to leap out at him—navigation console, couches, multiscreen monitors, a half-empty rack of chips and an i-board dangling from its input cord—but none of the humped shapes that might be bodies. The smell was fading fast—and besides, he told himself, the people who'd taken over the platform would have disposed of the bodies, for their own sake, if nothing else. He took a step toward the unlit consoles, and his foot struck something that clattered loudly away. He caught his breath, training his light on it by reflex, and a dented drink tin appeared from the shadows. The floor underfoot was stained, too, as though the contents had dried there long ago.

"Everything here's been stripped," Ista said, and Tarasov dragged himself back to the matter at hand, annoyed that he'd let the darkness and the cold get to him. He was supposed to be the professional; she was doing a better job of it than he was so far.

She was right, he saw, as he moved to join her by the consoles. The surface components were intact, but the complex inner boards that had been hidden from his view by the backs of the control couches were completely missing, leaving only gaping holes in the front panels. He freed his light from the helmet clip and wormed his way between the pilots' couches, crouching in front of the console that had controlled main sensors. Its front panel was as open as the others; when he bent to peer inside, the flooring cold under his bare palm, he found nothing but empty clips and a few dangling wires. That was what he'd expected, and he scrambled sideways, stretching out in front of the copilot's couch to investigate navigation. It, too, was gutted, and he hitched forward further, reaching for his pocket recorder to scan the interior.

"What have you found?" Ista asked, and he left the scan run while he answered.

"You're right, this was gutted. It looks like somebody took everything that could be reused in a computer-intensive system. It's the same with the data analysis."

He pushed himself backward, awkward on the cold floor, turned the scan on the sensor console as well, carefully recording the missing pieces. Then he dragged himself to his feet and returned the helmet light to its bracket, using both hands to do a general scan of the room, switching from visual light to the all-purpose multitrack and back again. As he finished the sweep, the helmet's light fell on Ista, standing now by the foot of the pilot's couch, her face very still.

"Are you all right?" he asked, and she forced a smile that barely moved the stiff muscles of her face.

"Yeah, it's just—" She shook her head, hard. "I'm fine."

"I'm sorry," Tarasov said, softly, and wished there were more. He could guess what she'd been hoping, that there would be something left intact that might give some clue, however small, to her parents' names, to her own identity. No matter how often Kelly2 had told her that there was nothing, that the mine's database was long gone, she must have hoped, at least until she saw the control room. I wish I could find the words that would make this better, he thought, I wish there were words for it, I wish I was your mother who might know them, since she's been dealing with this since she found you, I wish we didn't have to move on, wish I didn't want so much to find the real core of all this. . . . She seemed to read his thoughts, and her smile tilted a fraction further.

"I'm really all right," she said again. "Jus said there was power in the mine?"

"That's right."

"Then let's go," she said, and started toward the hatch.

Tarasov followed, careful of the suit fabric as he edged out from between the couches. She was tougher than he'd realized—tougher than I was at her age, he thought, maybe tougher than I am now. But I wish we'd found an answer for her.

Ista followed the long spiral down toward the mine itself, the sound of her feet and Tarasov's dulled only a little by the enclosing helmet. The empty control room hung in her memory, the gutted consoles gaping where she'd hoped, unreasonably, and knowing better, to find some semblance of a name, some hint of an identity. Kelly2 had told her as much, had said from the beginning, from as early as she could remember that there had been and would be nothing on the mine that offered any clues. For an instant, she was angry, screamingly, irrationally furious that Kelly2 had told the truth, that she was right and there was nothing there at all, but then that anger vanished, swallowed in the numb reaction. That was familiar, at least, the same dull absence she'd felt when she'd first understood completely that Kelly2 was not her mother, and cautiously she welcomed it, at least for now. She could rage, mourn, later, when she could afford it, when Kelly2 was there, maybe, target or comforter, but the one sure presence in her life—the thing, she realized suddenly, she had hoped to find here, and should have known was actually at home. She smiled at the irony, and had to catch herself to keep from stumbling on the stairs. They weren't far from the bottom now, and she wasn't surprised to hear Tarasov's voice in her ears again.

"Jus, where exactly are you getting the readings?"

Rangsey's voice was only slightly distorted in answer. "The highest readings seem to be coming from the processing chamber."

"Right," Tarasov said.

Ista kept walking. She knew the mines by hearsay rather than experience, conversations in the Bubble and on *Fancy Kelly*, but so far that knowledge had been good enough. The closest hatch to the chamber was not the one she was passing, but the last one, the one at the very bottom of the well. She stopped there, stepping gingerly on the metal lattice just a few centimeters above the solid meters-thick slab of the hull, and looked back. The well, and the spiral stairs running up its sides, vanished into distance and yellow light, though she knew perfectly well that it ended in an identical cap and landing at the far end of the crew bubble. On a working mine, she remembered vaguely, there was some sort of car that ran the length of the well, for getting from one part of the structure to another in a hurry, but she couldn't remember precisely how Fredi had said it was rigged. She looked at the hull beneath her feet, and found no fittings to mar the smooth metal.

"Everything all right?" Tarasov asked, his voice sharp, and she looked back at him.

"Just waiting for you." He smiled at that, and she was glad she'd managed to pull it off. It was too strange, being here on the mine—being back on the mine, she corrected herself, but the thought didn't seem quite real. There was sorrow at the core of this knot of feelings, an aching grief more frightening than her anger, and she shoved it hard away.

Tarasov leaned over the telltales, habitual caution, then hauled on the manual controls. This hatch peeled back easily, and he glanced over his shoulder. "Looks like this is the main entrance."

"So what are you expecting to find?" It was a question she should have asked before, but until now she hadn't quite been able to admit her ignorance. Travellers were supposed to know all about all the illegal businesses, all the odd dodges people used to cheat the authorities' notice—hell, the Travellers were popularly supposed to have invented most of them—and on top of that she was a hypothecary, and should know how illegal breeding was done. Except that Trindade kept more secrets than she'd realized.

Tarasov stooped through the narrow hatch. "Computers. Some kind of storage, and then processing units for the environment. All of it tied in to the mine's main power source." He glanced over his shoulder, a wry smile on his pale face. "At least that was the set-up on the other one I've seen. They told me that one was typical."

So he didn't know much more than she did. Ista absorbed the thought, trying to decide if she found it comforting, and ducked through the hatch after him. The wall padding here was darker, with thick bumpers mounted at waist height and thicker padding below them that still showed the scars and gouges of heavy traffic. She laid her hand on the nearest wall, and felt the whisper of power beneath the pads.

"Definitely live," Tarasov said, and she realized he was talking again to Rangsey. "There's a chamber ahead."

"That should be it," Rangsey said, but sounded doubtful.

"The hatch is locked," Tarasov answered, and Ista stood on tiptoe to peer over his shoulder. Sure enough, the row of locklights glowed bright red, and the familiar blank plate of a palm-reader was spot-welded to the hatch frame beside them. "Anything I should know about?"

"Nothing on my screens," Rangsey answered, and Ista saw the other man sigh.

"Right," he said, and reached for the toolkit hanging at his belt. Ista watched as he produced a thin box a little smaller than his hand, and held it just above the surface of the plate. There was a little silence, and Ista shivered in the cool air. Then she saw a scattering of lights pass across its back, and Tarasov set the box firmly against the reader. There was a brief pause, and then the locklights went from red to green and the hatch slid back a few centimeters in its socket.

"Not so good," Rangsey's voice said in their ears. "There's been a burst transmission from the mine. It's encrypted, but I'd say you didn't pass inspection."

"The hatch is open," Tarasov said, and pushed it the rest of the way open, stepped through without waiting for an answer.

"If this was the first warning," Rangsey went on, "you've still got six hours."

"We're not going to count on that," Tarasov said firmly, and Ista stepped through the hatch after him.

The chamber was brightly lit, a whiter light than had filled the well and the other corridors. Ista blinked, startled by the brilliance, and then again by the size of the machines. The processing chamber had been huge to begin with, but the machines—old-fashioned faceless blocks linked at top and sides by bridger bars—nearly filled it, stretching back to the far bulkhead where the scoop emptied into the chamber. The light was dimmer there, but it looked as though the scoop door had been sealed shut, the bright metal beads of the welds reinforced with thick yellow ribbons of superseal. A single console, fixed i-board and screens and oracle, sat in front of the machines, dwarfed by their blue-walled bulk. The screens were mostly blank, except for a simple tracer running in the lower corner of the smallest display, and she heard Tarasov sigh.

"I wonder what kind of password set-up they've got?"

He seated himself at the console without waiting for an answer, but to her relief, didn't touch any of the controls. She moved up to look over his shoulder, and saw icons stirring sluggishly below the surface of the oracle.

"I think that's live," she said, and he looked sharply from her to it.

"Now why would they leave it active?" he asked, and shook his head. "That doesn't make sense, unless it's a breeding cycle. . . . Or else when they pick up the programs, they want to make a quick getaway."

Ista considered the position of the ring-mounted controls, repressed the desire to lay her hands against them to confirm the pattern. "It's locked, too," she said, "but ready to power up at signal."

Tarasov nodded, still studying the i-board and its controls. "Anything interesting in the oracle?"

"Nothing I don't recognize," Ista said. "And I don't think they're illegals."

Tarasov spared the display a quick glance. "No, but they're not pedigreed, either. All right, we've got two choices. We can just sit here and watch, record what shows up in the oracle, or I can try to break the locks and get us control of the viewers."

Ista stared at the oracle, watching the icons slide past. She recognized a centaury among the flock of chogsets, and the slow-moving disk of a hug-me-tight. Even as she watched, it extended a loop toward a scurrying vant, but the smaller program evaded it with ease. "I'm seeing a lot of programs right here," she said, and Tarasov looked at the oracle again.

"And I'd hate to risk destroying things before I know what

they are." He reached for his recorder, handed it across. "All right, you monitor the oracle—here's an extra datablock, you've got about three hours left on this one. I want to take a look at the hardware."

Ista nodded, absently adjusting the recorder for the close focus of the oracle's display. Twin lights glowed reassuringly bright under her thumb: a full charge, and plenty of room still left in the datablock. She started to slip the spare into her pocket, remembered what she was wearing, and tucked it into the suit's toolbelt instead. In the display, the hug-me-tight had changed direction, pulling into a fat disk to move more efficiently across the dark landscape, and in the distance, Ista thought she saw a godwit moving away from her vantage point. Or maybe it was something else: there were several programs just in the oracle's view that she didn't recognize, though Trindade had taught her to read the basic forms. The notched bubble that wove a crooked path among the chogsets had to be some kind of cunner, but she had never seen the routine that rode its rounded back like a sail of lace. Equally, the flattened pyramid that moved slowly across the view had all the indicia of an ossifrage—the slowly pulsing lights that framed its edges, the thickened smaller pyramids that sprouted like paws from each of its intersections—but it didn't look or behave like any she had seen in the Agglomeration's nets. Unless it was a hodad? she thought. The Company's wildnets were largely free of deceptor programs, but Trindade had told her that she would see more of them in most other parts of the invisible world. She leaned closer over the display, fixing its image in the recorder's memory, and felt a sudden pulse of heat against her thigh.

Startled, she stepped back, and saw the controls flicker to life around the oracle's edge, bright lights beckoning her to explore. She hesitated, tempted, but made herself step back again. "Sein? The oracle's unlocked, and I don't know how I did it. If I did it."

Tarasov was beside her in minutes, breathing hard, scanned the oracle's controls with an expert eye. "What'd you do?"

"I was trying to get a record of a program I didn't recognize," Ista answered. "It's gone now. I guess I leaned against the lock, triggered it somehow."

Tarasov shook his head, still staring at the controls. "I don't see how," he began, and Ista nodded.

"I don't either. But it is unlocked. Did you do anything?"

Tarasov shook his head. "No. I suppose it could be something actually in the system itself, maybe, but that doesn't seem all that likely." His voice trailed off, but then he shook himself. "You're the hypothecary, does it look viable to you?"

"Yes," Ista answered, and qualified it instantly. "As far as I can tell."

Tarasov looked at the oracle. "So far, I haven't seen anything that would justify all this—" He gestured widely, the movement taking in the computers, the gutted mine, even the deaths. "—and we don't have a lot of time. Let's risk it."

"Then let me do it." Ista held out the recorder, and Tarasov took it automatically. "Like you said, I'm the hypothecary."

For a moment, she thought he would protest, but then he nodded, and adjusted the recorder for his grip. She took a deep breath, and reached for the oracle's control ring, sliding her fingers over the surface, alternately warm and cold, until she found the current configuration. Trindade had taught her well: she shifted her hands automatically, looking for the stable where the lens hosts were kept, and conjured those shapes into the center of the display. They were very different from the beetles Trindade used, square, stocky shapes that seemed to have been bred for defensive strength, and she heard Tarasov make a satisfied noise behind her.

"That's more like it. Those are definitely breeders' hammals."

She didn't bother answering, and indeed Tarasov didn't seem to expect an answer, just leaned a little closer as she selected the sturdiest-looking hammal from among the pack and sent the commands that linked the lens to its perspective. It felt rough under her touch, the familiar directionals suddenly stiff, and she had to struggle for a moment before she could turn it away from a tempting chogset. A stand of joint grass loomed on the horizon, knobby tubes that seemed in the lens's view as thick as her own wrist, and she nudged the host in its direction.

This wildnet was crowded, far more crowded than the Agglomeration's nets had ever been, wild or controlled, but the programs seemed at once fragile and hyperactive. The joint grass, on closer inspection, didn't have the usual thick walls, but instead was thin and delicate-looking. Even as she watched, a cubical program—some kind of diabrotica—extruded a pair of bright-toothed claws and shattered one of the strands at its base. The entire structure collapsed in a rain of glittering fragments, and the diabrotica exchanged its claws for a feeding structure and began to graze.

"This is really weird," she said aloud, and felt rather than saw Tarasov's nod.

"It looks like hothouse growth, doesn't it? Forced growth, and apparently they don't care about quality. I wonder if they're feeding something big?"

"What do you mean?" Ista tugged the host away from the shards of joint grass, forcing it on toward the virtual horizon.

"Well, you can't sell this lot," Tarasov answered. "So the only reason to keep it is for it to be absorbed into a more complex program."

That made sense, Ista thought. And it might explain why she hadn't seen any of the usual plates of parqueter or wallaroo: both those programs needed time to achieve a viable mass, and if this volume was heavy in the larger fauna, those programs would hardly have the chance to grow. "So let's see if we can find some of those hammals," she said, and swung the host in a complete circle to study its surroundings.

Despite the mandaleon, or maybe because of it, Ista hadn't seen many large faunal programs in the Agglomeration's sparsely inhabited wildnet. Trindade had made her memorize the indicia, but even so she nearly missed the signature among the teeming low-grade flora. The fragments that the chogsets were feeding on didn't look very different from the rest of the debris until she recognized a datahook among the remains. The fragment was still squirming a little, still trying to bond with another program—like so many programs, it had begun its existence as an independent, parasitic subroutine—and the chogsets gave it a wide berth, not wanting to be taken over. She took a closer look at the rest of the fragments, and guessed they had come from a devilet. There was a thicker concentration of chogsets in the distance, a whole swarm of them gathered in the lee of a stand of glossate pseudo-lilies—out of reach of the lilies' tongues, but close enough to pick up the scraps that lay just out of their reach. She turned the lens toward it, swinging wide to avoid the chogsets, but they were too intent on the scraps of code to pay much attention to the lens. Even the lilies didn't bother to snap at it, and she frowned.

"They must have fed really well, and recently, too."

"I agree," Tarasov said. She could feel his presence close at her shoulder, but didn't take her eyes off the display. "Ah, look at that."

He didn't have to point; the shattered program was all too visible as she came around the lilies. The basic body had been a goaty or a fossor, that much was obvious, but there were stumps and broken protrusions that had held parasites or modifications that Ista could no longer recognize, and the remains of its routines had been scattered across virtual meters. "It has to have been a vortext that did that," she said.

"Looks likely," Tarasov agreed, and Ista fumbled under the collar of her suit for her monocle. Tarasov caught her wrist before she could shake loose the connecting cables. "Don't, we don't know what's out there."

Ista froze, as appalled by her own carelessness—worse, inexperience—as she was startled by his grip. "You're right," she said, and swallowed her own embarrassment. "Let me see what I can get visually."

Tarasov released her without a word, and she trained the monocle on the oracle's display. For a moment, she got only a hash of color, but then the little machine acclimated itself to the oracle's vision, and began sorting out the various components. Parts moved, shifted, and reattached themselves with blinding speed, and then at last the monocle presented her with a sketchy image. It was only a vector outline, but it was still unmistakable: not a goaty, or a fossor, but a fully developed firedrake, hood up and ready to defend itself. "It's a firedrake," she said, involuntarily, and heard Tarasov's intake of breath.

"It can't be, there's no way a vortext could dismantle one of those."

"I know." Ista stared at the outline, then looked back at the fragments, tracing their shapes in the monocle's drawing. "Maybe it was sick, out of time?"

"I still don't think a vortext could take it down. Let me see?"

Ista handed the monocle over her shoulder, glanced back to see Tarasov shaking his head. After a moment, he handed it back, still shaking his head.

"Maybe they're selecting for cooperation? I don't know."

"I don't see why," Ista answered. Most faunal programs were all too eager to join, to merge with another program to form something larger and stronger than itself. Trindade had said that the real trick to breeding was to keep the usable, or potentially usable, programs from merging with totally unsuitable programs, while at the same time allowing them the freedom to rewrite their own structure and to join the right sets of programs. She shook the thought away, and steered the lens around the remains of the firedrake. A fragmentary subroutine—part of the phlogistic complex, the segment that created the storm of useless code that overwrote the firedrake's victims—lay in her path, and she steered the lens away. The chogsets were avoiding it, too, but she could see a smallish fairweather easing toward the crumpled-looking cube. That was not a merger she wanted to see consummated at too close range, and she nudged the lens to greater speed.

The plane ahead was surprisingly empty, after the teeming programs of the earlier sections. Underfoot—beneath the lens's feet, at any rate—the surface shaded from grey to white, and that whiteness merged with a matching pallor, as though they'd reached the edge of the station's wildnet. She sighed in disappointment, ready to turn the lens around, and something moved in the distant white. No, she realized in the next instant, not in the white, but the whiteness itself was moving, roiling up, gaining the faintest of shadows, ivory and palest oyster, creating a shape that was all smooth edges, like a ball of steam or a handful of polydown. Shapes emerged at its base, like vortexts, like spinning paws, slid toward the lens, and dragged the mass of the icon with it.

"Jesus, Mary, and Joseph," Tarasov said. "Break off now."

"What—?" Ista glanced back at him, and he put his hands on hers as though he could find the controls that way.

"Break off," he said again, and she hit the emergency disengage.

"What is it, what's the matter?"

"That," Tarasov said, "is a demogorgon. Or what one is theorized to look like, anyway."

The program no one wanted to see, the potentiality that the Lifers had used to argue that the nets should be abandoned, the program that could mean the end of everything. Once it had appeared, it could only grow, or so theory inexorably predicted, expanding and absorbing everything in its path until there was no wildnet, no invisible world, only the single massive and useless program that was the demogorgon. The oracle was frozen on the view from the abandoned lens, the white shape filling more than half its dome, and Ista checked again to be sure that the connection to the oracle, and thus to the station's systems, had been severed. She could see the vortextpaws swirling still, more rounded shapes boiling up behind them to frame, to cradle a single pearly sphere. The vortexts shot out, budded, spun off two, four, more lesser copies of themselves, so that the lens was completely surrounded by the whirling shapes. And then they pounced, the concerted blow ripping the lens into shreds of code. The display dome filled with white, shadowless, and Ista looked again at the telltale lights. They were all red, and she cleared her throat.

"It's like it knows we're here."

"That's not possible," Tarasov began, but he didn't sound as certain as she would have liked.

"Sein? What's the problem?"

That was Rangsey's voice, suddenly so close that it made her jump, and Tarasov slapped his chest plate to answer. "Nothing you need to worry about. Why, what's happened?"

"Didn't you send that signal?"

"What signal?"

Rangsey's voice sharpened. "We just got an emergency transmission, our emergency frequency, I mean, but the system couldn't translate it. What's wrong, Sein?"

"Did the ship accept it?" Tarasov asked, and Ista felt the station's cold strike to the bone.

"What—?" Rangsey stopped himself, answered. "Yes. But the system reads a garbled file."

"Trash it," Tarasov said, "trash it now. Erase it and isolate that part of the system. We—I think we've found a demogorgon."

"Damnation." Rangsey's voice cut out for a minute, leaving only dead air, and Ista looked at the other man.

"Do you think it tried to get on board?"

"I don't know," Tarasov answered.

Rangsey said, "All right. The system says the file's gone, but I've told it to firewall the emergency circuits anyway. It wasn't that big a file, Sein, I think we're OK."

"How big?" Tarasov, Ista realized suddenly, was holding his breath.

"Three, four gigs. Not big enough to do damage."

Unless it was a reproductive packet. Ista saw Tarasov sigh explosively, realized he was thinking the same thing. "Let's hope not," he said. "All right, send a transmission to the Agglomeration, tell Macbeth what's going on—use the nearest relays, and send in clear, it's too late—this is too important—to do anything else. Copy it to the Patrol station on Mayhew and to any nearby ships. Tell them what we've got out here. We're coming back on board."

"I'll send when you're here," Rangsey said. "Not before."

Tarasov sighed, but he was already moving toward the hatch. "Right. Come on, Ista, let's get out of here."

• 10 •

N O ONE REALLY believed in demogorgons. They were
theoretically possible, a logical culmination of virev-
olutionary trends, but they were hard to imagine, and
too dangerous to bear thinking about for too long. They—or
it; the prevailing theory said there would only ever be one of
them, a single program that grew and choked its native wildnet until it overran the cultured nets as well—were simply too
threatening, and, the theoreticians said, too possible, to risk
discussing the details of how it might form, and how it might
proceed, for fear someone would try to create one. If one
ever did appear, the theories said, it was the beginning of the
end.

Rangsey knew all this, had learned it both from the Ragged
Schools and from the dozens of gruesome rumors that circulated among the Union's adolescent and pre-adolescent
populations. Those said that the demogorgon, which was also
artificial intelligence, or its first, best precursor, was also
malevolent, genuinely and irremediably hostile to human life.
Some of that was Lifer propaganda, he knew, but some of it
was genuine theory, the experts' best guess as to where the
programs' virtual evolution was currently heading. He leaned
forward to check the sensor display again—still nothing, mercifully—and Stinne said, "Do you think it's really a demogorgon over there?"

"I don't know," Rangsey began, then shook his head. "Sein
knows what he's doing, and so does Ista, I'd say."

"She does."

Then it's really a demogorgon. Rangsey said instead, "Do me
a favor, go keep an eye on the hatch, just in case. Don't open
it without a manual signal."

"Right," Stinne answered, and swung herself out of the copilot's couch. Rangsey caught a glimpse of her pointed face,

pale under her red-gold hair, and then she was gone, leaving
the control room hatch open behind her. He turned his attention to the displays—everything green, after that one transmission from the mine, the sensor boxes still blandly empty,
only the two life signatures on the mine, and the glow that represented the transponders in the suits—and saw lights flicker
on the hull console as Stinne operated the manual controls. He
waited until he saw them flash green again, and touched the
virtual key that released the prepared transmission. Tarasov
was right there, they had nothing more to gain by hiding, and
their warning might give Macbeth the chance to wind up her
operation before the people behind the breeding program simply disappeared. Besides, he added silently, they owed the
people who worked the belt fair warning, and themselves the
chance of protection. The chip poured a stream of data across
his vision, confirming the transmission, and he felt a matching tickle in the skin surrounding the input box. He sighed,
and reached under his shirt to rub at the scars without easing
the tingling.

"We're sealed," Tarasov said, and dropped into the copilot's
couch without waiting for an answer. He pulled his i-board to
him and began running the disengagement check; the chip
spat its protest, and Rangsey hastily touched his own board
to transfer those controls to the other man. "And just about
ready to disengage."

Rangsey heard a faint noise from the hatchway, glanced
back to see the two girls peering in, still wary of their welcome.
"Come on in," he said, and Tarasov spoke without looking up.

"Or you can strap yourselves in if you want."

"We'll watch," Stinne said firmly, and Ista nodded her
agreement. Rangsey had to admit he sympathized: the cabin's
media console, while accurate, just didn't feel the same as
being there.

"Suit yourself." Tarasov's voice was remote, his attention on
the controls. "Jus, can you free me a reading on the cannons?"

"That's on your board," Rangsey answered, and saw
Tarasov frown.

"Are—oh." Tarasov's frown deepened, but he moved his hands over the controls, conjuring a response. "I wanted to see if we could destroy the platform."

Rangsey blinked, startled. "Are you sure?"

"That it's a demogorgon?" Tarasov asked. "Yes. And that means it has to be stopped, now."

"Destroy the host," Ista said softly.

Rangsey knew the phrase, had learned it with the other words for ultimate disaster: the real nightmare behind the fears of the demogorgon, that to destroy it the Federation would have to destroy the networks it had struggled so hard to maintain, sever its connection to the invisible world. And yet there was no other way to be sure that the program had been destroyed, once it had formed, except to destroy its habitat as well. It made sense to blast the platform, but even as he worked to phrase the question, the chip had rejected it. "I doubt we can," he said. "These mines are pretty well built."

"This is supposed to be Navy equipment," Tarasov said through clenched teeth, and Rangsey shook his head.

"Small arms, really. It'll take time, Sein."

Tarasov made a disgusted noise, and adjusted his board again. Rangsey glanced back at Ista, still hovering behind his couch. "You agree with Sein, then? That it's a demogorgon, I mean."

"I think so." The girl nodded, looking past him to whatever she'd seen on the mine. "Yes."

"What are you doing with Navy equipment?" Stinne asked.

It was the last question Rangsey had expected, but he forced a grin. "You pick things up," he began, groping for an answer, an excuse, and Tarasov stiffened beside him.

"I'm getting a sensor reading." His hands worked the board, and Rangsey touched his own controls to copy the results to his own displays.

"Very faint and far off," Tarasov went on, "but I'm reading a VMU shift."

Sparks of red appeared in both screens, too vivid against the black-and-silver asteroids. At first glance, there seemed to be almost the width of the belt between them, but the schematics could be deceiving, and Rangsey touched controls to attract the chip's attention. Instantly, his vision swam with red, the adrenalin rush making him gasp, and he reached under his shirt to manually lower the input levels. The red faded to bearable levels, and he took a deep breath, fighting the panic back to useful levels. "So we've got company. How far out?"

"Six hours."

"Nice call." The chip was flashing icons in front of his eyes, and he obeyed, touching the heated buttons. The ship shuddered gently, and he looked at Tarasov. "Ready to disengage."

"Lock's clear," Tarasov answered.

The controls shifted again under Rangsey's hands, and he adjusted the VMU fields under the chip's directions to push the ship gently away from the platform. A new schematic appeared in his main screen, the ship and the mine, relative distance increasing between them. At the chip's prompting, he called up the manual jet controls and fired three short bursts, flipping the ship end over end. A new course appeared on his screen, and he glanced again at Tarasov. "Are they in the belt? And what's their pitch?"

"As best I can tell, their VMU's at seven," Tarasov answered. "And it looks like they're riding a little bit above the main band, more or less the way we came in."

Rangsey nodded, considering his own display. The belt itself was too dense for speed; diving through it might slow the pursuing ships, but it would certainly slow them. He touched his controls, bringing the VMU to its lowest level, and the firing pattern that would bring the ship up out of the belt appeared under his fingers. He touched the start button, saw the countdown begin—a quick one, this time—and felt the jets fire. He adjusted the VMU as the first acceleration began, shifting it as far as he dared to boost the acceleration, and the gravity seemed to stagger for an instant, the couch wavering beneath him. Tarasov swore under his breath, and then glanced back at the girls.

"You may want to strap down after all."

"We're all right," Ista said.

She sounded steady enough, and Rangsey couldn't take his attention off the controls to see for himself. He said, "I'm trying to get us to speed as fast as I can, so there's going to be more of that."

"We'll be fine," Ista said again.

Rangsey nodded—there was nothing he could do but believe them—and frowned at his screen. The chip had given him a panic course out of the belt, a simple curve up and over the only large rock presently in the vicinity, levelling out to an acceleration course as soon as the density dropped to acceptable levels. "How's it look to you?" he said, to Tarasov, and the other man grunted.

"Good enough, I think." He touched invisible keys. "At current speeds, we'll have a six-hour lead."

Unless the pursuers increased their speed as well. Rangsey touched his own board, converting a corner to a simple query pad, and punched in his request. The numbers bounced back almost instantly: their highest pitch was 7.8, eight if you were willing to run at the red line. At present acceleration, they would slowly pull away from the pursuing ships, but there was no reason to think they were coming in at their true top speed. I'll bring us to 7.3, Rangsey decided, chording the commands to the chip, and see what they do then. The chip seemed to consider for a moment, and then absorbed the information, flashing back the icons that warned of the next course correction. The controls shifted under his hands, and he leaned back to wait out the countdown.

"Did you get out the transmission for Macbeth?" Tarasov asked.

"It went just after you came aboard," Rangsey answered. "Isn't it on your schedule?"

"I'm not finding it."

Rangsey frowned, but the numbers in his vision were getting too close to the burn point. "Hang on a minute, I'll find it for you." The red haze filled his vision, and the numbers clicked down the last three to zero. Nothing happened, no pulse of jets, and he slammed his hands down on the controls.

The jets fired then, two, no, three seconds late, and he swore, watching the course line shift on the screen as the chip adjusted to reality.

"What the hell—?" Tarasov said, but Rangsey ignored him, concentrating on the screen and the layer of icons between it and his vision. To return to the optimum course, they would need to make a corrective burn, and maybe a second, and the sooner the better. He fed the last of his numbers to the chip, and instead of the usual instant response, got nothing, as though the chip's attention was focussed elsewhere. And then it was back, a familiar presence in his mind, and the lines flickered and shifted as the chip reran his calculations. A confirmation icon appeared, and the air around him turned red again as though countdown began. It reached zero, and this time Rangsey hit the manual controls without waiting to see if the chip would fire the jets correctly. The jets rumbled, kept firing for the full three seconds, and the line in the screen shifted again, came to rest on the projection again. Rangsey allowed himself a sigh of relief, the red fading from his sight, and called up a secondary control to access the diagnostic subsystems. There was a pause, an odd hollowness in his chest, and then the controls and the screen appeared. He touched keys to start a basic check on the engineering systems, and looked across at Tarasov.

"Sorry. We had a late burn, I had to correct it."

"System failure?" Tarasov asked, and Rangsey shrugged.

"I'm running a check now. So far everything looks all right."

"When you get a minute," Tarasov said, "can you find me the transmission record?"

"When I get a minute," Rangsey answered. Checklights were already appearing in his screen, almost filling the narrow display space he'd allocated to that program. Most were green, but a handful—maybe a dozen, out of the nearly a hundred— were orange, shaping an unfamiliar pattern. He queried the chip, and got an equally unfamiliar answer: data overload, system patched to compensate. The chip didn't seem worried, or at least there was no adrenalin spike from it, demanding instant action. He frowned, and touched more keys to transfer the readings to Tarasov's board. "Sein, you ever seen this before?"

"What else was running?" Tarasov asked, and Rangsey grimaced.

"Whatever you had—have—and then I had nav and sensors over here, plus whatever the chip was accessing."

Tarasov frowned over his own board, fingers moving on invisible controls. Rangsey saw him shift state once, then again, then shake his head and return to the original configuration. "It looks as though the chip might have been working with the nav system—we might just have been unlucky, everything spiking at once and the chip was too busy to set priorities."

"Or?" Rangsey could think of one particularly nasty alternative, couldn't quite bring himself to ask aloud.

"Or that was a breeding packet that came in with the emergency call," Tarasov said grimly. "And if it was—well, we've got real problems."

Rangsey made a face. That was an understatement if he'd every heard one—a demogorgon could easily contaminate, take over, their computer system, and without it, there was no way two, even four, people could control an STLship.

"Should we go looking for it?" Ista asked. "If it's there, we might be able to contain it before it causes any more damage."

"I'm already doing that. And I'm not finding any more sign of it," Tarasov said. Rangsey glanced sideways through air that suddenly looked orange again—first notice of the upcoming VMU pitch shift—and saw Tarasov working a VALMUL lens, skimming through the ship's various virtual volumes. "You said you firewalled it, right, Jus?"

"As best I could, yes." Rangsey adjusted his own controls, setting up manual controls to handle the VMU shift if the main system failed. "And it wasn't a big packet, Sein."

Tarasov glanced over his shoulder. Rangsey, following his gaze, saw through the haze of deepening red Ista still frowning at Tarasov's screen, and looked there himself. In the circular vision of the lens, icons shifted and circled around a central narrow cone, and then that vision was replaced by yet another set of angular, vaguely insect-like shapes, then a third. The numbers at the corner of his eye passed five minutes, and he turned back to his board.

Ista said, "What about the basic checks, machine-level memory?"

"All those say everything's normal," Tarasov answered. "Nothing showing that shouldn't be there."

"What good does that do?" Stinne asked. "I mean, couldn't the demogorgon change those numbers, too?"

"Hammals, all AL programs, are supposed to be restricted from affecting machine-level coding," Ista said. She looked at Tarasov. "Like fish can't manipulate the water they swim in, right?"

The words sounded alien on her tongue. Rangsey hid a grin, but Tarasov's tone was matter-of-fact as he answered. "That's the theory, anyway." He looked at Rangsey. "I suppose it could just be coincidence, but I think we'd better keep a close eye on things."

Rangsey nodded, his attention on his own display. The light was very red now, the numbers clicking past twenty at last, and he felt the controls solidify under his fingers. He held his breath as the countdown reached zero, and hit the firing button without waiting for the computer's response. At the same moment, he slid the VMU levers forward to raise the pitch another three points. For an instant, they seemed to resist his touch, and he felt a second of panic, not quite overridden by the chip, but then the levers moved, and the ship seemed to revolve around him before the fields stabilized again. The pitch read five, and the course display showed them rising out of the belt, stable on a course that would lead them back toward Mayhew and the Patrol outpost there. Another acceleration burn, two at most, would let him raise the pitch to 7.3, which would leave them with slightly under a six-hour lead. He touched keys, reworking the calculations, and the chip bounced the answer back almost instantly: a five-hour-and-forty-three-minute gap separated the ships, and would remain constant—assuming, of course, that the pursuing ships maintained their speed. Rangsey made a face at the thought. They almost certainly wouldn't, but he, his ship, had some power to spare. It would all come down to who had the better VMU. Or, he added silently, whether or not the demogorgon had gotten aboard after all. He closed his eyes, listening to the beat of his blood and the busy hum of the chip. Everything seemed normal there; he could only hope it remained that way.

"I'm surprised we haven't gotten some response from Mayhew," Tarasov said. "Or Macbeth, for that matter."

Rangsey opened his eyes, fingers groping automatically for the status board. The chip read his gesture, provided the necessary controls, and he touched keys to set up the question. The answer that bounced back was the one he'd expected, and he looked at Tarasov curiously. "There hasn't been enough time, not even with the DRDs at full stretch. We've got another, oh, I'd say four or five hours before we can expect anything— after all, Macbeth's going to have to decide what to do about it all now."

Tarasov gave a soft snort of laughter. "True enough. I guess—I don't know what I was thinking."

"You were thinking we were closer in," Rangsey said, and the other man's smile died.

"True enough."

Ista cleared her throat, said in the voice Rangsey had come to recognize as her most adult, "This Macbeth you've mentioned, twice now. Who is she, or he?"

Rangsey blinked, startled, and a light flashed, demanding his attention. He touched his board and the icons shifted in front of his eyes, then returned to their normal state. Tarasov said, "Our contact on the Agglomeration. The person in charge of our part of the investigation."

"Are you sure you can trust her?" Ista asked. She sounded bitter, and Rangsey glanced back to see her braced and ready, though he doubted she knew herself what she feared.

"Yes," Tarasov answered, more patient than Rangsey had expected, and Ista shook her head.

"You said you couldn't trust your colleagues. You said that, and I believe you, and that's more than just what Mama'd say, or Trindade, just staying away from the Patrol when they can. But you meant it when you said you couldn't trust them, because you knew a good reason not to. So can you call them for help now?"

We've been over this before. Rangsey could almost see Tarasov swallow the words, try again. "I believe we can trust Macbeth. She started this up when she didn't have to—I'm not saying she's altruistic, she's after something, but whatever it is, it isn't what the breeders are after."

Ista looked at Rangsey. "You're Union, do you believe him?"

Rangsey caught his breath at the naked classism of the words, the same naive assumptions that had so infuriated him coming from Tarasov's partners. She met his eyes without apology, not quite able to hide her fear, and Rangsey bit back his own anger. She had a right to ask, not just because she was a Traveller and he was Union, but because that meant they spoke the same language of trust and anger and trust betrayed when it came to the authorities—and most of all, she had a right to ask because she was in the middle of this, and they hadn't told her all the truth they knew until it was past the point at which she could have refused to be a part of it. "Yes," he said. "I don't like Macbeth, but her agenda, whatever it is, includes stopping the attacks. Whatever it takes."

Ista nodded slowly, the anger draining from her face, but she said nothing.

"I guess it's a good thing you have cannon," Stinne said, after a moment, and Tarasov looked at her as though he was grateful to her for changing the subject. "What else have you got?"

"Not much that's out of the ordinary—the cannons and the camouflage package. And the VMU will go to 7.8."

Stinne nodded, looking thoughtful, but Ista said, "Does this make any difference with the demogorgon? If it's aboard, I mean."

"I don't know," Tarasov said. "I just don't know."

They locked eyes for a moment longer, hypothecary and technician meeting head to head, and Rangsey cleared his throat, putting aside a twinge of unexpected jealousy. "I think we should send the message again once we're clear of this DRD hex. That's only another three hours, it won't make that much difference."

"You hope," Tarasov said, but nodded. "I agree."

"We've got one more burn to bring us to 7.3," Rangsey said. "And then, like you said, in three hours we'll be into the next hex." He glanced at the sparks on the screen, still too distant for even their expanded sensor suite to resolve into definite images. Their pitch was the same—no surprise, they were overtaking, slowly but steadily, would catch up with them well outside the sphere of Mayhew's direct observation if the Traveller ship continued at its present rate. He touched his controls, setting up a series of hypothetical courses and pitch variations, added in the time it would take a Patrol craft to get from Mayhew to the various intercept points, and from the Agglomeration to Mayhew. They should make it, he decided. As long as the pursuers couldn't go higher than 7.9, they should be able to rendezvous with Patrol rescuers some hours before the pursuers came within firing range. *And if the Patrol doesn't come?* a voice whispered in the back of his mind, and he shoved the thought away. They would come, Macbeth would force their hand, she wanted this as badly as anyone. "We'll repeat the message then."

Ista settled herself on her bunk in the cabin she shared with Stinne, cradling a cup of coffee in her hands. It was still a novelty to her, thick and sweet with the soyacreme Tarasov mixed from powder, and she sipped cautiously at the cooling liquid, enjoying the hint of the bitterness under the sugar. It was a good break, a pleasant respite from the control room and the red dots that hovered at the edge of the sensor screen, but the memory curdled some of the pleasure, and she was glad when the door slid back and Stinne came into the cabin.

"How's it going?"

Stinne shrugged. She looked tired, shadows showing under

her pale eyes. "So far, so good, I guess. The VMU's at 7.3 now, and so far there's no sign from the pursuit ships."

There was a rote quality to the words, and Ista wondered if the other girl had any real sense of what that meant. She could see the chase laid out in her own mind, like the game she'd played with Fredi before Stinne came to the Agglomeration. In the game, you started with a handful of counters, generated a starscape at random in the board, and then paid out your counters one by one to set your course, acceleration and course correction, and finally the deceleration that brought you safely into the goal-dock. The loser paid four or five counters to the winner, so everything depended on paying exactly the right number for each increment of pitch. And, of course, saving something for the goal-dock: that had been her biggest problem, learning to keep enough counters to slow for docking—until she'd learned to shape her courses to take advantage of the game system's gravities and orbits. Once she'd figured that out—and she could still feel the thrill of it, the understanding that was deeper than thought, juggling courses and planets and ships and the handful of counters to make everything come out even—Fredi had lost interest, and she hadn't known anyone else who wanted to play.

"We're still almost three days away from the Agglomeration," Stinne said. She shook her head. "At least those ships haven't speeded up—yet."

"Yet," Ista echoed, and crossed her fingers against the warm plastic of the mug. She knew the Audumla system pretty well, could guess the relative positions of planets and stations, could place their own ship and the pursuit ships against that backdrop. They would be less than eighty hours from the most likely rendezvous, assuming that this Macbeth sent someone—or, ideally, more than one—to meet them within, say, ten hours of getting the message. That was a reasonable time, she thought, would give them enough time to prep an armed ship and get underway. She tried to imagine Macbeth—an SID lieutenant, Tarasov had said—but her experience failed her, threw up instead images of vidiki heroines, slim fair-skinned women who managed to juggle love and adventure and sometimes children. From what Tarasov had said, Macbeth was nothing like that, but she couldn't form a clearer picture. It was easier to imagine the planets and ships in their inevitable courses.

A light flashed on the media console, drawing her attention, and Tarasov's voice said, "The pursuit ships have gone to 7.5. Stand by for acceleration."

"Damn," Stinne said, under her breath, and her skin was suddenly paler than ever.

Ista set her cup hastily on the floorplates, and scrambled for the media console's controls, but the jets and the VMU fired together, a sustained burst that made her stagger as the floorplates seemed to shimmer under her feet. She caught herself on the edge of the nearest built-in chair, and heard Stinne swear again. The sensation faded after what seemed to be minutes, and she reached for the intercom buttons.

"What's our speed?"

"We've gone to 7.8," Rangsey answered. "I'll let you know when they respond."

The connection clicked off. Ista stared at the boards for a moment longer, watching the status displays reflecting the activity in the control room, and wished she could be there. She shook the thought away, angry at her own impracticality—there was nothing she could do, except be in the way—and saw that her coffee had slopped over the rim of the mug when the gravity shifted. She reached into the supplies cabinet for a cloth, wiped it up mechanically, and wiped the bottom of the mug for good measure.

"Ista."

She looked up to see Stinne staring at her from the depths of the further chair, her face still very pale.

"Do you think they can match this speed?"

Ista hesitated, not wanting to think about it herself, and realized she was still rubbing the bottom of the mug. She put it down as though it was twice as hot, and stuffed the cloth into the cleaning slot. "I don't know."

"You can make a guess. Better than I can."

Ista sighed. "Probably. Most Traveller STLships are rated for 7.5, which means 7.7 would be their emergency speed, and they'd want to be faster than them."

Stated so bluntly, the odds sounded worse even than they were. She winced, and Stinne said, sourly, "You're a comfort."

"Well, you asked."

"I wish I hadn't." Stinne sank still further into the chair, drawing her knees up as a barrier against the world. Against me, Ista thought, with a pang, and scowled to hide the hurt.

"If you can't handle it, you shouldn't have."

"Oh, what's the use?"

Ista took a deep breath, trying to think what Trindade, what her mother would do. Not get angry back, at least not until later—though now was probably as good a time to argue as any, since there was nothing else they could do. Except, she thought, I don't want to argue. Not with Stinne, not now. She said nothing, still groping for the right words, and Stinne slowly straightened.

"I'm sorry," she said, her voice muffled. "I just—" She broke off then, forced a wobbling smile. "This isn't my idea of an adventure, that's all."

"Mine neither." Ista picked up her coffee, only lukewarm now, came to perch on the arm of Stinne's chair. For a moment, she thought the other girl would order her away, but then Stinne grabbed her free hand, held it tightly. They sat like that for a minute, two, and then Ista said, "I thought we'd at least find out what was going on, I could claim a reward, go with you to University or at least to Constantine if they wouldn't let me in. When they told us they were cops, I thought, great, they're not eligible for rewards, so it's all for me, because they'll have to tell how they found out. In my wildest dreams, I thought maybe I'd even find something on the mine that everybody else had missed, something that'd tell me who I really was, and then—well, who knows, I could've been anybody. And most of all I thought it was so great to have you along because then you'd see what I could do. But now I wish I'd never done any of this. I wish you weren't here."

Stinne leaned against her shoulder, not a firm touch, but tentative, as though she weren't sure either of her welcome or her own desire. "I wanted to find out, too. Partly for the Company, because I know they, people like my parents, they wouldn't put up with this if they knew, but mostly because of you. And you didn't make me do anything, it was my idea to use Papa's password." She pulled back then, glaring as though Ista had contradicted her. "My idea more than yours."

Ista nodded, admitting that, but said, "You didn't have to come—"

"What, I should've stayed on the Agglomeration, with Security asking all kinds of questions?" Stinne forced a smile. "I don't know, I might be safer here."

"I still wish I hadn't gotten you into any of this," Ista said.

"You didn't."

"It's my problem, I should've handled it myself." Ista sighed, suspecting she was lying just as much as Stinne was. She was glad Stinne was there, guiltily glad to have the company even if it meant they were both in danger. She tried to imagine being there alone, in the white-walled cabin, and couldn't bring herself to complete the thought. "But I'm glad you're here, Stinne."

Stinne smiled, the expression wry but genuine. "If you have to be here—I'm glad I'm with you."

The coffee was cold now, and Ista looked into her mug, grateful for an excuse to get away from something she didn't want to deal with, not now. A part of her was laughing—she had wondered for months, back on the Agglomeration, if someday she might get Stinne into just this position, hear something very like that declaration, and now she was the one to shy away—but she suppressed that knowledge. This was not the time, or if it was, it was for something she wasn't sure she wanted after all. "Do you want some more coffee?" she asked, and pushed herself off the arm of the chair.

Stinne nodded, and Ista thought she saw the same relief in the other's eyes. "Might as well."

Ista nodded back, and they headed for the commons.

* * *

Tarasov stared at the sensor display as it expanded to fill his primary screen. The pale blue wedge that marked the STL-ship's position was just passing the edge of the asteroid belt, and the scattering of silver that simulated the rocks and debris filled half the screen. At the screen's lower edge, the sensors' limit, five red dots glowed among the silver. Tarasov made a face, seeing them still in position, and touched his board to display the DRD stations. To his relief, they were leaving the contaminated hex—probably contaminated, he corrected himself, automatically cautious, and then made a face at an ingrained and useless habit. But he was still glad to see that they were finally in range of a station outside the area where the attacks had taken place. He selected the station, then touched his board to call up its address. The system offered a token protest, shot back the addresses of two closer DRDs, but Tarasov overrode it with a gesture, and the address appeared in the transmission screen.

"I'm sending again to Macbeth," he said, and Rangsey nodded, preoccupied with something on his own screens—or under his skin, Tarasov thought, and shoved the image away. The communications console reminded him again that there were closer DRDs, a more efficient use of power, but he ignored it, and triggered the transmission. A string of lights flared across the screen, icons travelling too fast for him to follow, but then they steadied into confirmation: the DRD had received the message, and would relay it to Mayhew and the Agglomeration. He allowed himself a sigh of relief, and a secondary program chimed for his attention. He frowned, called it forward even before it registered that this was the program he'd set to watch the pursuing ships, and his frown deepened as he saw the numbers spilling across the screen. "Jus."

"The chip told me." Rangsey reached under his shirt again, rubbing his chest, the box implanted into the muscles there. "What are you reading?"

Tarasov reread the string of icons, hoping he'd misunderstood, but they remained the same. "They've raised pitch again—no, I'm sorry, it's not all of them, just the three lead ships. But they're at 7.9."

"At least we've lost two of them," Rangsey muttered.

It didn't seem worth an answer, and Tarasov didn't bother, fixing his attention on the screen again.

Rangsey made a face, then closed his eyes, listening to the chip for a long moment before he spoke again. "We can make eight, at least in theory, but the chip says not for very long."

"What does it consider very long?"

"Fifteen hours, maybe a little more."

Tarasov sighed, staring at the numbers on his screen. At these relative pitches, the pursuers would slowly overtake them, would come into attack range—drone range, he amended, assuming they had Rovers on board—in about sixty-five hours; in sixty-eight hours, they would be in cannon range.

"There's another problem," Rangsey said. "The chip—the ship's not feeling right."

"What do you mean?" Tarasov thought he could guess, but hoped he was wrong, didn't want to say it aloud.

Rangsey managed a lopsided smile, as though he'd read the thought. "Response isn't what it should be, not by a long shot. I think something's clogging the system, Sein. Maybe your demogorgon."

"Damn," Tarasov said, hands already moving to summon a different set of controls. The machine coding was still routine, nothing out of the ordinary except the increased VMU use, and he shook his head. "I'm still not showing any of the usual signs of infection."

Rangsey lifted an eyebrow, but said only, "It doesn't feel right. I'm having trouble getting responses through—everything's slow, preoccupied, really. It's like the chip's attention is elsewhere."

That sounded bad, Tarasov admitted silently. And while lesser hammals couldn't manipulate the machine codes, the demogorgon just might be able to make that transition. In fact, if it really was precursor-AI, not merely AI, it would almost have to develop that ability in order to evolve further. He glanced at the codes again, and realized that they hadn't changed in the last minute—and that, he thought, was wrong. Maybe not very wrong, but at the least unusual, and under the circumstances not something he dared ignore.

Rangsey said, "So I was thinking maybe we should go to eight now, while I've still got full control of the ship, and set a deadman to break us back to 7.8 after fifteen hours."

Tarasov considered the idea, still staring at his screen. As he watched, the numbers finally shifted, but not in the usual cascade, the changes rippling like water across the ranked characters, but in chunks, blocks replacing each other along the rows and columns. It could be natural, he thought, without conviction, the ordinary response of a system stretched to the limit, and then dragged himself back to Rangsey's idea. "If they can make eight, or better, then they'll just match us, and then we'll be worse off when we have to cut back to 7.8. And the demogorgon can probably override any deadman we set up."

"But it won't," Rangsey said. "Not if it wants to stay intact. If the ship breaks up, it goes with it."

"I suppose," Tarasov said, then shook his head. "I don't know, Jus, I don't like the idea much. Let's save it until we have to risk it."

"If we wait too long, I may not be able to compel the shift," Rangsey said. He shook his head in turn, as though he couldn't find the words. "I've never felt anything like this—it's like the ship's, well, not fighting back, but isn't really paying attention to me. And it resents my asking it to do things."

You're anthropomorphizing, Tarasov started to say, but swallowed the words unspoken. Of course he was, there was no other way to deal with this program, and that was what made it so frightening. It crossed the line, or threatened to cross it, the fragile line between human and hammal, man and machine—in its own way, it was as alien and as much kin as the mechanized. It's a good thing it feels hostile, or we'd both feel very strange about this. "I think we can risk that," he said, slowly. "At least for now. As you said, it's got to think of its own survival."

"All right," Rangsey said, and rubbed his chest again. "So what do we do?"

I wish I knew. Tarasov swallowed that as well, knowing it was unhelpful, and said, "I suppose we start by finding out if it's on board."

"Something is," Rangsey said.

"Or what it is," Tarasov agreed. He stared at the viewer, wishing it had the specialized controls of the tools he had taken for granted back on Bestla, then pulled the i-board to him, touching controls to shift modes again. "Then—" He broke off, not knowing what to say. He had no idea what to do when—*if*, he told himself fiercely, as though denying it might keep it from actually being true—if the demogorgon was in their system. The program he and Ista had seen in the mine's oracle was a true monstrosity; even with all the tools he'd had on Bestla, he wasn't sure he could exorcise it from the ship's systems. Of course, it wouldn't have had time to grow to that size and strength, but it would still be formidable.

The pseudo-oracle formed in his board, the ring of controls circling emptiness, while a new display opened on his screen. He called his lens into existence, and considered for a moment before sending it trundling through the maze of subsystems toward the communications volume. The demogorgon had come on board through that vulnerable point; even if it was no longer there, there would be traces of its entry. The system stopped him at the edge of the volume, the firewall like a pale haze in the air in front of the lens, and rerouted him to a single port-of-entry, a pi-gate blazing with security. It recognized the lens' codes, however, and let him pass; he slipped through into a plane that looked surprisingly ordinary after all.

He invoked a chameleon routine anyway, let the lens take its outward shape from the other hammals that frequented this volume—evangels, mostly, all pedigreed, and a few paracletes and ortolans—and saw an evangel's flat wedge-shape surround the lens's icon, a half-transparent overlay. The chameleon was a good one: the false evangel's wings—extensions, really, a thinning of the wedge to gossamer—rippled convincingly, searching and changing the datastream around it. Compilers spiked the horizon, the fat round tubes of DRD transmitters and other external connectors, the medusa-head of the in-ship systems, which, as he watched, sprouted another dozen snaky locks that wound around each other before spitting out an ovoid shape like a bright pink egg that bobbed uncertainly above the crumpled-looking surface of the plane. An evangel swept close, thin pseudopod shooting out to test the bright surface, and then it swung away again. The beat of its wings sent the egg tumbling further, and Tarasov turned to follow. He avoided the compilers, not wanting to test the lens's camouflage too closely, and sent the lens in cautious pursuit.

A little beyond the cluster of compilers, the volume's floor-plane dipped suddenly downward. The lens skidded a little distance, its evangel-shell lagging for a moment until the program caught up with its host, and then recovered itself. Tarasov blinked, as startled as the program. There were almost never hills in the wildnet, and certainly never this steep or this abrupt. Then the texture of the plane registered: no longer shades of grey like crumpled paper, but spiked with jagged lines, as though it had been shattered and reformed. At the bottom of the hill, a cluster of fragile-looking chogsets were busy around the remains of what looked like an evangel, and beyond them a chattermark was dragging a wing fragment out of the debris, ignoring the chogsets that clutched at it. Tarasov knew that it was all but impossible to eliminate all the smaller programs from even the most vital volumes, but it was still a little disconcerting to see quite so many chogsets in the communications system. They looked young, too, barely formed—not the hothouse growth he'd seen on the mine, at least, but there was a fragility to their structure, a suggestion of crystalline rigidity, that was alarming.

The pink egg—some sort of system messenger, though it was impossible to tell precisely what it was from the external details—had almost reached the bottom of the hill—no,

Tarasov corrected, not a hill, but a shallow crater, like a miniature meteor strike, or the explosion of a small bomb. A second
slope rose out of the crater on the opposite side, and he caught
a flash of green as a small paraclete teetered on the edge and
then swung safely away. He turned his attention back to the
egg, and saw it bobbing above the level of the chogsets, unable to find a way back up the slopes. He made a face, not liking to risk the lens's overlay among the hungry chogsets, but
he had no other option, if he wanted to return the egg to its
proper function. He turned the lens down the slope, careful to
stay well within the shell of the chameleon program, and
headed into the swarm of chogsets. Most of them moved aside
as the lens approached—an evangel was no competition, and
there was no point in risking its defenses when there were
code fragments ready for the taking—and for the first time he
saw the shards of pink that littered the cracked plane beneath
the ruins of the dead evangel. At least one, and probably more,
of the pink eggs had fallen into the pit and been destroyed, and
their information had vanished with them. Already this one
was sinking a little, no longer buoyed by an active datastream,
and Tarasov frowned. He edged the lens closer still, and was
relieved when the chameleon shell copied the other evangels'
response. A pseudotongue appeared, licked the egg, sending
it higher, and then the beat of its wings pushed the egg
halfway up the further slope.

Tarasov pursued it, turning the lens to get the most out of
the shell's weaker effect on the datastream, and was relieved
when the egg finally bobbed over the rim of the crater. Tarasov
turned the lens to survey the depression and the swarming
chogsets a final time, but saw nothing else useful. Something,
something large and powerful, had penetrated the communications volume, damaged it and at least some of the resident
programs, and then had—what? He swung the lens again, a
full circle, scanning from the crater and the compilers behind
it across the empty plane where the the haze of the firewall was
the only movement. Gone elsewhere, it looked like, and he
scowled at the image on the screen. The communications volume was small enough that if the demogorgon were still in-

side the firewall he would definitely be seeing other signs of its presence.

Still scowling, he directed the lens back around the edge of the crater, set it to retrace its course to the pi-gate, and then leaned back in his couch, wondering what to do next. Standard procedure required that he compartmentalize the ship's systems as much as possible, and he keyed in those commands without really thinking, looking up only to warn Rangsey. The other man replied with a noncommittal murmur, his attention obviously elsewhere, and Tarasov returned to his problem. It was unlikely that compartmentalization would do more than slow the demogorgon down a little, if at all; the main thing now, he thought, is to find where it's seeded itself, and see if we can still root it out without losing too much ship function.

The lens had reached the pi-gate again, shed its chameleon icon and slipped out through the firewall. Tarasov stopped it before it could go any further, and touched keys again to adjust its state. In his screen, the image shimmered, seemed to diminish, as though the lens risen from the main plane of the ship's internal net and floated now a dozen virtual meters above the surface. From that perspective, system-height, Tarasov could see the communications space and its neighbors on three sides, divided by the walls of the now enforced compartmentalization into isolated demigardens. Icons bloomed and scurried in each, all familiar even from this perspective, nothing out of the ordinary, and he touched the oracle's controls to survey the next section of net.

Everything seemed ordinary here, too, except for the way the colors seemed to fade a little in the main system volume. One segment of that volume, a long rectangle that normally served as hub and mainspace for the ship's hammals, looked oddly bleached, as though the colors had been left too long in a strong sun. Tarasov frowned at that, and brought the POV lens a little closer, until he could make out the details on individual icons. They were still there, still had their normal shapes and signs—bendies and anserates, a few evangels trapped outside their home domain when the firewall went into effect—but weaving around and through and over them was a cloudy web, a net like a half-spun cocoon, ravelled silk. At the edge of the web, a boshvark struggled to free itself from the tangle, twisting against the grain of the plane and of the net. Boshvarks were useless programs, heavy breeders and feeders, the sort of hammal Tarasov spent most of his life trying to clean out of people's networks, but he found himself leaning forward a little, urging it on. As he watched, the boshvark broke away from the main body of the web, but it was still trailing a thin line of white. Tarasov swore under his breath, seeing that, and in the screen the boshvark froze, its color fading. The white line seemed to thicken, and tendrils curled from its sides, filling in the space between it and the main body of the web. It wasn't fast, but it was inexorable, and Tarasov swore again.

"I take it you found it," Rangsey said.

"Main system," Tarasov said. He swung the pov again, found the compartment barrier enclosing the main system on the demogorgon's edge, and scanned beyond it. That domain—engineering, he thought, or one of the other low-density volumes, where the machines ran straight calculations and few hammals were in use—seemed normal, but a closer look revealed a few white tendrils protruding beyond the wall. It was hard to tell if they'd been cut off by the compartmentalization, or if they'd managed to penetrate the coding, but at least they didn't seem to be spreading as rapidly as they were in the main system.

"Of course," Rangsey said. "Where else would it go?"

Tarasov heard the irony in the other's voice, and allowed himself a rather bitter smile in answer. "Navigation might be worse, ultimately."

"Or at least at the moment."

Tarasov nodded, touching buttons to leave this level of the oracle's controls. Under his hand, the ring changed shape again, became a warm oval surrounded by sharply contoured touchpoints. A faint flush of color appeared in the i-board at the same time, delineating the arrangement, but he ignored it, focussing on the image in the screen. "If I set up another hard compartment here—" He drew his finger lightly across the screen, not quite touching its surface. "—how would that affect ship's function?"

Rangsey leaned close to look, and Tarasov saw his eyes flicker closed as he consulted the chip. "Badly," he said, after a moment, and Tarasov redrew the line closer to the demogorgon.

"What about there?"

"We could manage," Rangsey answered, after a moment. "Is there any chance of making it a firewall?"

"It got past the one in communications," Tarasov said, and Rangsey nodded.

"We'll lose some response time, and one of us will have to monitor the control room pretty constantly. But we can function."

"Right," Tarasov said, and touched controls to set up the strongest wall the system could provide. It wasn't perfectly solid, of course, no codewall ever was, but with luck it would contain the demogorgon, keep it from growing any larger as well as from spreading into the rest of the main system. He slaved the construction kit to his screen, and drew his finger carefully across the screen, the receptive surface faintly sticky to the touch. For an instant, the icon refused to follow his gesture, formed but stayed clumped as the demogorgon fought its introduction, but then the resistance vanished, and he drew the wall fully across the image. He touched controls to seal it, and then looked at Rangsey. "That's the best I can do for now. Now I've got to figure out what to do about it."

Rangsey nodded, his attention momentarily focussed inward, reading the chip's reaction, but then he opened his eyes. "Do you have something in mind?"

"Not yet," Tarasov answered frankly, "but I'm hoping maybe Ista and I together can come up with something."

"That's a lot to put on a sixteen-year-old," Rangsey said.

"You're the one who's always telling me you were working a full line job when you were fifteen."

"That's not hunting demogorgons, is it?" Rangsey said. "Besides, I was thinking. Maybe we should put them, both the girls, off in a lifepod once we're in decent range of Mayhew."

"Do you think it would do any good?" Tarasov asked. "Come on, Jus, if it was just the demogorgon, I might say risk it, they could tell whoever picked them up to destroy the pod, but with these guys on our tail—" He adjusted his board again, brought back the image of the ships and the asteroid belt, now fading astern. "They'd be used for target practice."

"And if we don't get this demogorgon under control, they're likely to end up frozen or suffocated or whatever it decides to use to clean house." Rangsey smiled suddenly. "Of course, so are we, but at least we're getting paid for it. Almost eight hundred a week, and travel."

Tarasov laughed in spite of himself. "Makes you feel rich, doesn't it?"

"I figure we'll be millionaires in another two lifetimes." Rangsey sobered slowly. "All right, they stay on board. But I think we should offer them the option, once we're closer in."

"Agreed." Tarasov sighed, and reached for the intercom controls. "In the meantime, let's get started."

The call came on the intercom as they were waking from a restless and unsatisfying sleep. Ista dragged herself awake, the muscles along the sides of her shins burning—they had stiffened while she slept, after the long climb up the mine's central well—and bent over to massage them back to life. Behind her, she heard Stinne's voice, querulous and muffled, answering the summons, and then Tarasov's voice suddenly distinct.

"Can you two come to commons? There are some things we need to—discuss."

Stinne darted a glance behind her, eyes wide, but her voice when she answered was steady enough. "We'll be there in—in twenty minutes all right?"

"Fine," Tarasov answered, and broke the connection.

So it wasn't an emergency, Ista thought, still rubbing her legs, or at least not an instant one. She swung herself out of the bunk, wincing again as a calf muscle tightened toward a cramp, and carefully straightened her legs, easing it out.

"They found the demogorgon on board," Stinne said, and reached into the wall compartment for her one clean shirt. The tricoteil was limp and a little faded, after the nearly daily trips through the ship's washers, but the color was still bright against her pale skin.

"Well, we were expecting it," Ista said, and stepped into the narrow shower. The hiss of the cleaning mist drowned any answer Stinne might have made, but she wasn't surprised to find the other girl still waiting when she emerged from the compartment.

"I said, you might have been. If they were expecting it, why didn't they start looking sooner?" Stinne scowled as she wound her hair into a ragged knot. It collapsed before she could get the pins into it, and she flung them away, leaving her hair loose over her shoulders.

Do you really want an answer, or do you just want to fight? Ista suppressed that response, pulled on shirt and karabels, and said, carefully, "You don't want to mess around with the ship's computer systems. They're not like the wildnets, there's not a lot of room for mistakes."

Stinne muttered something, then shook herself. "Sorry. I'm a little on edge. I wonder where those ships are?"

"Still gaining," Ista said, sourly, and headed for the commons.

Tarasov was waiting by the big samovar, mixing a jar of soyacreme. There was coffee as well, and Ista poured herself a cup, cut it half and half with the soyacreme Tarasov handed to her. Stinne drew herself a cup of tea, and came back to stand beside the display dome that once again filled the little table. Tarasov gave them both a nod, and reached across to trigger the intercom. The wallscreen lit, and Rangsey's face looked out of it, the two-way icon at the base of the screen glowing green to indicate a live connection. Seeing that, Ista felt a chill of fear. If they could no longer risk leaving the control room unmonitored, then the demogorgon had taken solid hold somewhere, and they were in real trouble. *Not that we weren't before,* she added silently, but this is on board, and right now, not fifty hours away. She realized that Stinne was looking at her, and composed herself hastily, came to sit beside the dome's controls.

It was showing the starscape again, and the pursuing ships, and the asteroid belt now fading in the distance, as well as the DRD stations picked out in vivid yellow. There were only three ships behind them now, and she looked up in genuine excitement, only to be silenced by the look on Tarasov's face.

"We have a problem," he said, and in the screen, Rangsey made a sound that might have been laughter.

Stinne said, "The demogorgon?"

Tarasov nodded. "It's taken up residence in our main system space. I've compartmentalized the entire system—that's why Jus's still in control, we can't run that way without a human assist—but I don't know how long that will hold it. That's why I want your help, Ista. Even if we can't get rid of it, if we can figure out how to contain it until we can rendezvous with Macbeth, then we'll be all right."

"You still haven't heard from her," Stinne said, flatly, and Tarasov shook his head.

Rangsey said, "There really hasn't been enough time for a response—even with the relays, it's a good ten-hour trip."

"You're sure she'll come?" Stinne asked.

"We're sure," Tarasov said, but Ista, watching the screen, thought that Rangsey was less certain. Not that it matters, she thought. We have to assume she's coming because otherwise there wouldn't be any point.

"Right now," Tarasov went on, "we should reach a rendezvous point here." He touched something on his input board and a new set of lines and dots sprang to life in the dome. "That's the green cross. The red crosses show where the pursuing ships will be at that point, assuming they hold course and speed."

"So we get there, what, three or four hours ahead of them?" Ista asked.

"Right." Tarasov touched controls again. "We'll be in drone range for about an hour before that, but my guess is that they'll pull out once they see Macbeth's ships on their screen. And of course we don't know if they actually have drones aboard."

Or if Macbeth is actually coming, or a whole lot of other things, Ista thought. She stared at the image in the dome, knowing how fragile its relationship to reality really was.

"Now," Tarasov said, and touched his i-board again. The starscape vanished, was replaced a moment later by an image from system-height. Solid-looking walls, mock brick white as the demogorgon, defined each subsystem, and within those compartments hammals slid and scurried. There were no gates anywhere in the walls, Ista realized; if information had to be translated from one subsystem to another, that transfer would have to be confirmed in the control room. She glanced at the wallscreen, and was surprised to see how relaxed Rangsey looked. It was not a job she would have envied.

"The demogorgon's taken up residence in the main system volume," Tarasov went on, and Ista leaned close over the dome as the image changed. Sure enough, one section of the volume had been walled off, the mock bricks a checkerboard of yellow and red this time, a temporary compartment, and within that wall a lumpy white carpet spread across the virtual floor. It ran thick and thin, so thin in places as to be almost translucent, but it covered every virtual millimeter of the compartment and was beginning to climb up the confining walls. There were no signs of the cloud-form it had taken on the mine, or of the vortexts it had used there—unless, she thought, some of the thicker patches were going to develop into them? It was hard to tell; they could be developing subforms, or disintegrating ones, hammals in the process of being absorbed by the larger program.

In the wallscreen, Rangsey cleared his throat. "While you two are looking at that, I could use some help up here."

"I'll go," Stinne said at once, but Ista barely looked up from the dome.

"We have to kill it or contain it," Tarasov said, to Ista, as the hatch closed again behind the other girl, "but I'm damned if I have any clever ideas. What do you know about demogorgons?"

"It looks like it's contained at the moment," Ista said, but even as she spoke she doubted her own words. The way those tendrils were climbing the compartment walls, Tarasov would either have to build them higher, or redraw them further away. And if he did that, they would lose still more of the ship's automatic functions. "What do I know about the demogorgon?" she said aloud. "Trindade talked about it, she was very Orthodox—" She stopped abruptly then, trying to remember. Trindade had said, the day she, Ista, had harvested the black medusa, that the demogorgon was vulnerable. She closed her eyes, trying to pull the precise words back into memory. *They're vulnerable*, Trindade had said, *because they cannot be invulnerable. Programs, hammals and flora, and people, they all die, and there's a death gene that lies in all of us to cause it.* "Trindade said," she said again, "Trindade said there was a bit of code, like a death gene, at the heart of the demogorgon. If you could trigger that, you could get rid of it."

"Death gene," Tarasov said. "Like a kill switch?"

"I guess."

Tarasov lifted an eyebrow. "That's something breeders put in, to keep hammals from getting out of control. Which would make this deliberate, not a natural evolution—" He shook his head, looked back at the dome. "I suppose they might have bred this, and put in the kill switch either at the beginning or spliced it in later, but why would you want one?"

"Well, would you want it loose?" Ista asked, and Tarasov shook his head.

"I wonder what form it would take." He bent close to the dome, and Ista reached under her shirt for her monocle.

"Trindade said that the proper remedy was to breed a crabbit with a kebbick or a fairweather, making sure the neumes were cataletic." Ista faltered, aware of how silly she sounded, a child spouting nursery remedies. Trindade was Orthodox, half of what she did was based on image magic, laws of similarity and difference, not the structural laws that truly ruled the invisible world.

"Go on," Tarasov said.

He sounded genuinely curious, and Ista looked back at the

image in the dome. "Then you feed it to the demogorgon. The crabbit burrows toward the code center, that's what they do, and then the neumes kill it. That's what she said, anyway."

"I can't fault the delivery method," Tarasov said, and Ista nodded. Crabbits were tough, hard-shelled, fast-breeding hammals that were mostly useless on their own, but formed a solid core in the lineage of a number of useful programs. "But cataletic neumes?"

Ista shrugged. "That's what she said." She could understand his disbelief: there was no reason for a cataletic string to trigger a death gene, it was no more than a lopsided neume set, and only the most fragile programs were susceptible to that sort of arrhythmia. Unless, of course, they were programmed to respond to it, and if they were, how would Trindade know? She shoved the thought aside, and Tarasov spoke slowly, echoing her thought.

"You'd almost have to code that in, with a program this size—this complexity, sheer size doesn't mean anything. . . ."

His voice trailed off as he examined the dome, and Ista said, "If it started with a simple program, a flawed program, if that was at the core, then it would work."

"Yeah, it's possible, would make sense, even, if breeders are involved—but how would she know it?"

"Travellers know a lot of things," Ista said, "and not all of it gets reported, to the Patrol or to anybody. Someone might have solved the problem before this, and passed it on to other hypothecaries." It was weak, she knew it as she spoke—for one thing, if anyone had encountered a demogorgon, even among Travellers, it would have been almost impossible to keep the secret—but Tarasov didn't answer, still staring into the dome.

"Well, if it works, it doesn't matter how she knew," he said at last, and Ista knew he didn't believe his own words. "The main thing is, will it work?"

Ista adjusted her monocle, shaking loose the connecting cords. She hesitated for a moment, then plugged them into the jacks. Tarasov closed his mouth over a warning that had come too late, said only, "If we don't kill it, you'll lose that. Maybe even then."

"I know." It hurt to think about it, losing the first adult present her mother had given her, but she knew she had no choice. Without it, she'd never be able to read the structures at the center of the demogorgon. She set her fingers into the shallow controls, feeling her way into the compartmentalized systems, and found her way blocked. She looked up, startled, and Tarasov reached for his board.

"Where are you?"

Ista read the code string from the monocle's central display, and Tarasov nodded. "All right, go."

She squeezed the controls again, and found herself abruptly in the main systems volume. The image flickered, and then steadied as the monocle found a new source line. In its circle, the demogorgon looked more frightening than ever, patches of pale web connecting larger areas where the weave was almost solid. Automatically, she adjusted the controls to see the structure, and the web was suddenly interlaced with brighter, multicolored lines. Toward the center, a larger lump rose from the surface; she turned the monocle toward it, and was rewarded by a sudden glimpse into the inner structure.

"I've got it," she said, and then corrected herself. "Or I've got something."

"Let me see." To her surprise, Tarasov didn't take the monocle from her, but leaned over her shoulder, squinting into its circle. "Damn, that does look promising. I think you've found the nerve center."

Ista nodded, staring at the tangle of lines, trying to relate them to the cloud-and-pearl structure she had seen on the mine. She recognized some of them, but not all, and trying to trace the interrelationships made her dizzy. "So what do we do now?"

"Try to parse it," Tarasov said, and leaned back, sighing. "See if there really is a kill switch somewhere in there. And then we figure out how to trigger it."

Ista shook her head, thinking of the work, the time it would take to tease out each of the structures. "Do we have the time? Couldn't we just find a crabbit and work from there?"

"I want to tailor the neumes to the internal structure," Tarasov answered. He shrugged. "We've got forty-nine hours. After that, it's not going to matter."

He was right about that, and Ista turned her attention to the shapes in the monocle's circle. She selected a strand, isolating it, and began the slow process of untangling it from the rest of the structure to determine its function. At his i-board, Tarasov was doing the same thing, but she ignored him, concentrating on her own work.

Rangsey drowsed in the pilot's couch, the captain-chip for the moment set back in its case. He was vaguely aware of Stinne in the copilot's couch, i-board balanced on her lap, a kludged checklist program running to test data before she allowed the transfer from one compartment to another. So far, it had caught and blocked half a dozen attempts by the demogorgon to port bits of its code past the compartment walls, but it was only a matter of time before something slipped past. Rangsey put that thought aside with practiced ease. That was Tarasov's problem, not his; his only problem was to keep the ship flying, on course and in control. If—when—the pursuing ships caught up with them, he would be the one to handle them, too—not a demogorgon, he thought, with a half smile, but bad enough. The thought triggered another memory, and he sat up, stretching, rubbing away the sleep from his eyes. Stinne gave him a wary glance, and he made himself smile again.

"Something just occurred to me. If you're going to play copilot, you'll want to take a look at the cannon system." He reached for his i-board, unlocked the hidden controls and transferred access to the copilot's boards. "There's a simulation, you might want to familiarize yourself with it."

"You want me to handle ship's cannons?" Stinne asked.

"There's only four of us," Rangsey answered. "If Ista was free, I'd make her work through it, too."

Stinne nodded, thoughtfully, and turned her attention to the board. Rangsey sank back into his couch, and a few minutes later heard the soft sound of effects as Stinne began working her way through the tutorials. The first level ended with a cascade of cheerful beeps, a decent score by the sound of it, and she looked at him.

"It's just like a game," she said, and Rangsey couldn't tell if she were indignant or delighted.

"Everybody's played the games," he said. "They try to make it easy for the recruits."

Stinne looked at her screen, and Rangsey leaned forward to read the score. As he'd thought, she'd scored well into the five hundreds, a better-than-respectable first attempt.

"I expected it would be different," she said. "Or feel different. Or something. Does it feel different when it's not practice?"

"I don't know," Rangsey said. "I've never fired cannon, except in sim. And that was when we got this job."

"Oh."

He couldn't read her tone, regret or disappointment or, oddly, approval, and glanced sideways, but her face was as closed as her voice. He looked away, not knowing what to say, and she bent over her board again, touching virtual keys to summon up the next stage of the sim. Before it could load, however, a chime sounded, and Rangsey reached for the captain-chip, freeing it from its case and snapping it into his chest in a single movement. He was instantly submerged in the chaos of its data, a waterfall of lights and icons across his vision, a rush of information in his ears, and over it all, Stinne said, as coolly as an experienced pilot, "Incoming communication. Repeated from DRD 82737."

The data tide was ebbing already, just a few icons nagging for his attention, and Rangsey said, "Play it."

One of the icons faded from his sight, and a mechanical voice said, "From Macbeth. Your message received. Ships despatched from Agglomeration timecheck 20198.892. Confirm time and course for rendezvous."

Rangsey suppressed a whoop of joy, and heard a soft yip from Stinne. "Can you run that for me?" he said aloud, and she answered instantly.

"Already running."

An instant later, the chip presented him with the same information, and then the screen filled behind it. The cross where they would meet Macbeth's ship—*ships*, he corrected himself, *the transmission definitely said more than one*—glowed green at the end of their course-line, forty-five hours away. He grinned, and reached for the intercom button. "Sein? We've had word from Macbeth."

"Yeah?" Tarasov sounded tired, but that was no surprise. Rangsey hurried on.

"Good news. They're on their way. We intersect in a little under forty-five hours."

"Forty-four hours and fifty-one minutes," Stinne said, and Rangsey repeated the numbers. When Tarasov spoke again, he sounded more alert.

"That is good news. What about the pursuit ships?"

"Still steady, still on course," Rangsey answered. The chip was prodding for his attention, half a dozen housekeeping chores that had to receive his approval, and he began working his way down the list as he spoke. "At this pitch, we'll still be in drone range for a little under an hour before we make the rendezvous, but we'll have Rover protection from Macbeth's ships for about half that. If we go to eight now, we can cut those times by about a third—less depending on their acceleration."

"Not bad. I say do it."

"The chip agrees," Rangsey said, and reached for his board to begin setting up the change.

"How's it going down there?"

Tarasov sighed. "We're getting there, I think. Ista's teacher has a way to beat the demogorgon, maybe, and we're checking the command structure to see if it'll work." He paused. "Ista's put some dinners in the box, do you want anything?"

Rangsey heard his stomach rumble in answer, but before he could say anything, orange warning lights exploded across his vision. Moving under the chip's urgent prompting, he called up the screens it demanded, and the navigation and sensor displays filled his screen. In the same moment, Stinne said, "The pursuit ships have changed pitch. They're at eight now."

The revised rendezvous course gleamed against the starfield, the cross now flashing red: the pursuit ships would be in cannon range almost three hours before the first of Macbeth's drones could reach them. Rangsey swore under his breath, querying the chip with one hand, and a set of possible revisions flashed across his screen. None of them did much good, and he swore again. Stinne gave him a frightened glance, but he ignored her, touched the intercom again.

"Bad news, Sein. They've gone to eight."

"Fuck."

In spite of himself, Rangsey smiled. "Not a practical solution." Tarasov muttered something uncomplimentary, and Rangsey went on. "The chip says we should hold at eight as long as we can. They're not likely to be able to do more than 8.1, if that, and that leaves us in drone range for more like an hour and forty minutes. Less if we can stay at eight for more than the fifteen hours."

"Can we trust the chip?" Tarasov asked.

Rangsey hesitated, a new and unpleasant series of possibilities dancing through his brain, but then he firmly rejected them. "We have to," he said. "I can't fly this thing without it."

"Then do it," Tarasov said. Rangsey heard him sigh. "We'll keep at the program down here."

"Good luck," Rangsey said, but softly, not wanting to attract ill intention, and broke the connection. In his chest, the chip was pounding for attention, the course and the change of pitch already laid out on his board, but he resisted its pull for a moment longer, scanning the calculations. They looked accurate, and besides, he told himself, the demogorgon had every reason to keep them, or more precisely the ship that hosted it, alive for as long as possible. He touched the invisible keys, feeling them change state, melting to reform for the next sequence, chasing the pattern of warmth across the shifting board. The jets fired, and with them the VMU, the pitch shuddering upward, a lurch that he felt in the pit of his stomach, and when it steadied, he could feel a new vibration in the hull that echoed the faint warning hum beneath his skin. The orange lights faded, and the course line shifted again, confirming the change. They had done the best they could, but it still wasn't going to be enough. They would have to fight, and against three ships, there was no way they could win.

"Send another message to Macbeth," he said, to Stinne. "Give her our new course and speed and tell her—"

"No more signals," Tarasov's voice said, from the intercom. "Remember how the damn thing came aboard? We can't risk it getting into the DRDs."

"We're setting up the message manually," Rangsey said, "and running it through a scrub routine. We have to risk it, Sein." He didn't have to add, *or we're all dead.*

There was a little silence, and then Tarasov said, "You're right, of course. But no repeats."

"Agreed," Rangsey said, and looked at Stinne.

"Set up and ready to send," she said, before he could ask, and he nodded.

"Go."

The girl jabbed stiff-fingered at the controls in her i-board, and icons bloomed and faded like fireworks in Rangsey's eyes. "Message is cleared," she said, after a moment, and Rangsey nodded again.

"Thanks."

"You said you were hungry," Stinne said, tentatively. "Do you want me to bring something?"

Rangsey considered, but the adrenalin rush, the chip's demands and the hum of the stressed VMU, had killed what appetite he had. "Maybe later," he said, and added. "But thanks." They'd done everything they could, he told himself again, and tried to ignore the certainty that, unless Macbeth could raise her ships' pitch by at least five, it would not be enough.

Ista looked up from the half emptied box of her dinner as Tarasov turned away from the intercom, and looked hastily away again as she saw the despair in his face. She pushed the food aside, no longer hungry herself, and came to look into the dome again. The demogorgon had grown even since her last look, the center thickened into solidity, rising now into a triple hump that was now sprouting smaller lumps—incipient vortexts? she wondered—at what could become its leading edge. The tendrils were more than halfway up the compartment's walls, and higher in places, and she lifted her monocle, which Tarasov had left on the edge of the board.

"I think we've got it parsed," Tarasov said, and Ista risked another glance in his direction. The despair was gone, and she allowed herself a sigh, hoping she'd imagined it. Just because she couldn't see a way out, even if they did mange to kill the demogorgon, was no reason to think the others didn't. They were Patrol, after all, trained for this sort of thing—except that Tarasov was Technical Squad, not SID or Border Guard, and Rangsey was only a civilian employee, a translator, not someone who knew how to handle a space-borne attack. Or a demogorgon, for that matter—but they were trained, she told herself firmly, and they were Patrol. And she was a hypothecary, at least in training; all of it had to count for something.

"So how does it look?" she asked, and was proud to hear herself as cool and steady as either of the men. She leaned over Tarasov's secondary display. The structure seemed to leap out at her, a maze of colored lines, interwoven like a toy she'd once had, a pliable wire form that she had been able to shape into what had seemed an infinite number of shapes, and she trained the monocle on the image, squeezing the control points to flip from one view to the next. Broken apart that way, sorted by color and function, the structure came clear at last: fiendishly complex, multiply redundant, but with a weakness, a flaw, at its heart, where a single touch would cause all the rest to fly apart. She looked up, unable to stop the grin that spread across her face. "But that's it. We've got it."

Tarasov smiled back, though, she thought, with restraint. "Yeah. But you heard Jus."

Ista shoved the words, the fear away. "But we've got it. You said yourself, that was the main thing, stop this."

Tarasov seemed to shake himself. "Yeah. So, a crabbit, your teacher said, bred with a kebbick?"

"Or a fairweather." Ista closed her eyes, bringing back the

memory. "Just as long as the neumes are cataletic."

"Right," Tarasov said, and adjusted his board, selecting a neighboring compartment.

"Let me," Ista said. "I'm good at finding hammals."

"All right." Tarasov moved aside, leaving her with the familiar ring of controls, and the tiny round display of a virtual oracle. Ista frowned into it, recalling her lessons, and worked the controls to conjure a list of the various compartments. The main system volume would be her last choice, just in case the demogorgon had succeeded in contaminating the fauna before the compartmentalization went into effect; that left communications, engineering, and the linked all-purpose volumes that changed state according to demand. Communications would have been better, but Tarasov had said the demogorgon had damaged it and its hammals fairly seriously. Better to start with the all-purpose volumes, she decided, and hope that at least one of them had developed a base population.

She turned the controls, conjuring a VALMUL lens into the largest of the volumes. Immediately, the display turned black, and then the familiar rich brown of a populated volume, and she reached for her monocle, linking its collection function to the virtual oracle. In the lens's viewpoint, a small stand of joint grass wavered in the datastream, and she heard Tarasov sigh.

"I thought we'd cleaned that out of here."

She smiled—joint grass was prolific, almost impossible to eradicate once it was established, but, more than that, it was a common fodder flora, easily absorbed by most of the lower fauna. She swung the lens past it, touching controls to boost its speed, and expanded its viewpoint to the maximum. At that range, the images were small, and not perfectly certain, but she could make out the important indicia. She passed a chevrotain, not the type she was used to, but a brighter, pedigreed variety with a long red echo-mark along the inside of its vee, and then a quartet of vants, in typical formation, scurrying away from a scattering of chogsets. The compartmentalizing wall loomed on the virtual horizon, and she bit back her disappointment. There were four more all-purpose volumes to investigate, and then the rest of the dedicated compartments; she had no reason to be worried yet.

She swung the lens back toward her entry point, and saw a tiny stand of fairweather, half crushed under the compartment wall. She swung the lens closer, shifting the magnification, and winced at the damage to the main part of the program. A large chunk of it had been crushed by the closing, and lay in tatters, its colors, pale green and a once-brighter gold, bleeding away into the dark plane. One segment seemed unharmed, however, the tiny spot of red at the disk's center still dark and solid, and she held her breath, adjusting the monocle's controls. Her first pass was too close to the wall, and she flinched as the feedback jolted through her fingertips. She shook her hand, hard, not daring to look at Tarasov, and tried again. This time, the collecting edge sliced cleanly through the budding join, and the catcher scooped it neatly up before any of the lurking scavengers had time to react.

There were no crabbits in this volume, or in the next one, and she leaned back, stretching, before she tried the next. She was tired, she realized suddenly, and afraid, a dull deep fear that left her drained. And this was no time to think about it, she told herself angrily, there was no time for fear, and she touched the controls again to drop her lens into the next volume. This one was more crowded than the others had been, almost clogged with centauries and chogsets and even the tall multilimbed spire of a hug-me-tight. Its arms were full, all four feeding sets of them, and even as she watched a chogset was pushed toward it, and the hug-me-tight seized it in a manipulator pair.

"Why is this one so busy?" she asked, and Tarasov leaned over her shoulder.

"I don't know," he said. "Either they were avoiding the demogorgon—aren't those comm evangels over there?—or maybe they were just trapped when the walls went up."

His voice trailed off, uncertain, and Ista adjusted her point of view, pulling back almost to system height to survey the mass of programs. The flora were suffering badly, even the borderline pseudo-corals being tugged apart by quarreling devilets, and she realized she'd have to hurry if she wanted to find any program undamaged. She spun the lens in a quick circle, avoiding an evangel that leaped out of the mass, trailing a damaged wing, and saw at last a crabbit by another stand of joint grass. It had pulled in on itself, the solid dome of its code-shell almost completely closed, and even as she watched, a jagged bullcomber dove at it, the triple set of serrated jaws closing on the rounded surface. They slid off, leaving shiny silver streaks across the crabbit's mottled shell, and Ista swung the lens toward the bullcomber, deliberately dropping it between the bullcomber and the crabbit. For an instant, she thought she'd made a mistake, that the bullcomber would simply accept the lens as its new target, but then it sheered away, clashing its jaws in apparent frustration. Ista touched the monocle's controls again, swinging the lens in the same moment, and saw the virtual net spin out from her point of view, neatly trapping the crabbit. It sprang away, a single convulsive leap propelled by its tough underlegs, but the net held firm.

"Got it," Ista said, and touched the controls to return to the main volume.

"Nice work," Tarasov said, and adjusted his own i-board. "I've got a holding volume ready."

Ista adjusted the oracle's ring, and felt the controls shift under her fingers as the programs were released again. "Are they all right?"

"They look all right so far," Tarasov said. His hands were busy on his controls, and it was Ista's turn to look over his shoulder. In the screen, hammal and flora lay bound in webs of pale pink light, and Tarasov frowned over the structures that shone ghostly beneath their surfaces. "The neume count is right, anyway."

Ista nodded, aware of a sudden relief, a release of tension she hadn't known she was holding. "Then we can do it."

"If your teacher was right," Tarasov said, then shook his head. "And my guess is she was, so that doesn't count. I think we've got to graft these, I don't think we've got time to wait for normal uptake."

It wasn't a statement, Ista realized, he was genuinely waiting for her opinion. She trained the monocle on the icons, squeezing its controls to study the subsurface, structural indicia, and nodded. "I agree."

Tarasov nodded, and adjusted his board again. In the screen, a tiny silver wedge appeared, and he touched controls to maneuver it toward the crabbit. Squinting at the screen, he excised a triangle from the top of the codeshell, revealing the bright pink interior structures. He was good, Ista thought, wincing, but it was at times like these that the hammals seemed entirely too alive for comfort. Tarasov released the fairweather from its holder then, and switched to another tool, carefully pruning the codes that protruded from the budding edge until they approximated the structures visible through the gap in the crabbit's codeshell. Then he set the fairweather carefully into the gap and released the holding field. The crabbit bucked and struggled, but the fairweather had already sunk temporary roots into its structure; the disk bobbed wildly, but remained attached.

"You did it," Ista said, and felt herself blushing. "I'm sorry, I didn't mean to sound surprised—"

"Wait and see," Tarasov said. There was something in his tone that made Ista look up, to see him displaying fingers crossed for luck. "If it takes, the shell will start growing back—"

"I think—yeah, it is." Ista pointed to the image in the dome, then reached for the controls to adjust the point of view. In the extreme close-up, they could see the individual hexagons of the codeshell, and even as Ista watched, a new hex budded from its neighbor and locked into place, creeping a little bit further up the side of the fairweather. "But won't it cover the eye?"

"It shouldn't." Tarasov was consulting his board again, and his answer was preoccupied. "The structures are compatible. They ought to hybridize, and the shell should form a collar just below the eyestalk."

Ista watched another plate flick into existence, another fragment covering the fairweather's vulnerable side. "How long will that take?"

"I'm running the numbers now." Tarasov leaned back in his chair. "Six hours."

"Six hours?" That was almost a fifth of the time they had left—more than that, now, Ista thought. "And how long will it take to reach the demogorgon's core?"

"I don't know," Tarasov answered. "I'm getting estimates from three hours to never, and just about everything in between."

"But—" Ista broke off, not wanting to say what she was thinking. There might not be enough time, after all, and she couldn't bring herself to say it.

Tarasov was looking at her, an odd expression on his face. "We were talking, Jus and I. He suggested that once we get into decent range of Mayhew that we could put you two into lifepods, release you toward the station. If we disable the transponders, there's a chance that the pursuit ships won't see you."

"Then how will anybody know to find us?" Ista demanded.

"We can rig a switch, let you signal manually when Macbeth's ships are in range," Tarasov said. "It may be your only chance."

Ista shook her head hard. "No. There's too much chance they'd see us, and then there'd be no chance at all. We've got cannon, maybe we can hold them off until Macbeth gets here."

"There's not much likelihood of that," Tarasov said, gently. "There are three of them to one of us, plus we're a standard STLship. We're not very maneuverable."

"But—" Ista stopped again, not knowing what to say.

"I'm serious, Ista," Tarasov said. "I think—I don't know if you'll survive otherwise."

Ista clamped down hard on the panic that threatened to overwhelm her, heard her voice shrill and frightened anyway. "If that's how you feel, why are you even bothering about the demogorgon?

Tarasov shrugged. "I don't really know," he said, after a moment. "It can't hurt, it's something to do, and, I don't know, the pig may sing. The miracle might happen."

Physics outlawed miracles: it was one of Kelly2's favorite sayings, and Ista felt a surge of irrational anger toward her for ever having quoted it—and for not being there, for not having taken better care of her. And that was unreasonable enough that it shocked her back to a kind of sanity. There was still one variable in the equation, not a big one, but there. Macbeth's ships might be fast enough to reach them in time—they were Patrol ships, after all. The idea was thin, and Ista knew it, but she clung to it anyway. She said, "Then I think we should stay aboard."

"Talk to Stinne. You may want to reconsider," Tarasov said, and Ista nodded.

"We've got time for that."

▪ 11 ▪

THE NEXT THIRTY hours passed like a nightmare, worse indeed than any nightmare because not even sleep brought full relief. Ista spent her time alternately in the control room and in the commons, watching the hybrid crabbit regenerate its shell. That was proceeding normally, at least, but in the control room screens the pursuit ships maintained their inexorable approach, steadily overhauling. There was still no response from Macbeth via the DRDs, and they were still too far away to pick up anything on even the very long range sensors. Five hours in, the first tendrils of the demogorgon topped the compartment walls, and Tarasov swore loudly. Ista stared past him into the display dome, unable quite to believe that that lacy strand of white was the beginning of a breach, and Rangsey's voice spoke from the intercom.

"Problem?"

"The demogorgon's over the first wall." Tarasov touched his board, running more calculations, his eyes darting now and then to the crabbit in its protected volume. "I can't put up another wall without seriously affecting ship's function."

"Then don't." Rangsey's voice was reassuring, almost relaxed, a strange undercurrent of amusement in it that Ista found obscurely comforting. "I'm on the hop enough as it is. When's your little program going to be ready to go?"

"Another hour, according to the first projections," Tarasov answered. "Maybe a little less."

"Everything's still status quo up here." Rangsey paused. "Not that that was all that great to start with."

Tarasov smiled then. "At least it's not worse."

"Yet," Rangsey said, almost happily, and Tarasov laughed. "Nothing new on sensors?"

"Nothing. They're still overhauling, but at the same rate. The projection's the same." Rangsey paused. "I'm going to have to shift down to 7.8 soon, though. It doesn't affect the ultimate projection, but it will upset the chip."

"Do you need to take it out?" Tarasov asked.

"I'll let you know when it happens," Rangsey said. "I'll keep us at eight for as long as I can."

"Thanks, Jus," Tarasov said, and Ista looked away, half embarrassed by the affection in his voice.

The crabbit was ready fifty-four minutes later, and all four of them gathered in the commons to watch its release. Even Rangsey was there, rubbing hard at his chest and the chip implanted there—the engineer-chip now, Ista knew, because the captain-chip couldn't cope with the constant adjustments to the VMU that had kept them at eight for almost two hours past the limit. Even Ista could feel the tension in the hull, and guessed that it wouldn't be much longer before they finally had to gear down. Rangsey stood close to the intercom controls, an i-board plugged into the systems there in case he had to adjust something, but his attention was on the dome. In its hemisphere, the demogorgon had grown enormously, almost all solid now, with only a few bits of webbing remaining at the fringes. In the center, the mounds were starting to show dimples, the first signs, Ista guessed, of the cloud-like texture she had seen on the mine.

"We're ready," Tarasov said, and Ista felt cold fingers seize her hand. She drew Stinne up beside her, and nodded to Tarasov.

"Ready here, too, I guess."

"Everything's ready in the system," Rangsey said.

"All right." Tarasov looked down at the image, touched the dome gently. "That looks like the best place to me."

The webbing looked thinnest there, a faint hint of the underlying plane still showing through the cloudy surface. Ista nodded. "I agree."

"Then I'm releasing it now." Tarasov touched controls, frowning, in concentration, and a moment later the crabbit appeared, falling gently from system height to the plane. It landed on the thin patch of web and seemed to sink into it. Strands rose to surround it, to bind it into the fabric, but they slid and scrabbled across the crabbit's back. A thicker strand landed, and then another; they slid on the codeshell, but clung to each other, and more strands followed, weaving a blanket to smother the crabbit. The fairweather's eye contracted to a ruby pinpoint, bright as a laser, and the strands that touched it seemed to wither and fall away. The rest of the crabbit was invisible, buried under the white blanket, and Ista felt a sudden surge of panic. It couldn't end like this, not after all their efforts—

And then the crabbit moved. Still more than half covered by the smothering strands, it lurched forward, toward the center of the demogorgon. It rose a little as it moved, freeing a few virtual centimeters of the shell, and then vanished again under the folds of code. This time, the eye was covered, too, and Ista held her breath, biting her lip to keep from urging it on aloud. The lump that had been the crabbit stayed motionless, and then Ista saw a tiny hole, like a pinhole, or the eye of a cyclone, appear in the demogorgon's fabric. It widened, and then the lump moved, slow and jerky, but toward the center. The hole widened as it went, a tiny but growing tear in the monster's body.

Ista let out a sigh of relief, and realized that her fingers were hurting. Stinne released her in the same instant, and Tarasov said, "So far, it works." His voice was shaking a little, and Rangsey reached out to touch his shoulder.

"How long before we know if it's going to work?"

"If it keeps on at this rate, and it'll probably slow toward the center, which I'm programming in. . . ." Tarasov fell silent again, his fingers moving on his input-board. "It should reach the center in another twelve hours."

"The pursuit ships will be in range in about fourteen," Rangsey said. "Maybe a little less."

"So what do we do now?" Ista asked.

Tarasov looked at her. "We wait."

Two hours later, Rangsey dropped the VMU to 7.8, no longer able to keep the wobbling systems at the emergency pitch. Ista saw the warning flash across the cabin screen and touched the remote to mute the audio warning. She clung to the edge of the bunk as the jets fired—a different set this time, decelerating—and the ship seemed to waver around her as the pitch restabilized. When the floorplates steadied again, she reached for the remote, calling up the relay slaved to the control room systems, and saw the success icons glowing on the screen. Beneath them, the course display showed a different image. The cross icon that marked the projected rendezvous glowed a hotter red than ever, warning that they would still be in attack range for more than three hours before they could possibly come under the protection of Rovers from Macbeth's ships. If Macbeth's ships were coming, she added silently, and touched the intercom button. To her relief, it was Stinne's voice that answered.

"Control."

"Any sign of Macbeth?" Ista asked, even though she already knew the answer, and she could almost hear the shake of Stinne's head.

"Nothing yet. But Justin says we won't be in range to see them for another four or five hours."

I knew that, Ista thought. *Why did I even bother asking?* She said, "Thanks," and Stinne cleared her throat.

"I'm coming back. Can I bring you anything from commons?"

"A cup of coffee?" There were three unfinished cups on the floor by the bunk, and Ista moved hastily to empty them down the bathroom drain.

"Sure," Stinne said, and closed the connection. Ista stacked the cups on the table, and settled herself on the bunk again. There was a hard knot of fear in her belly, a weight between lungs and guts, and she took a deep breath, trying to loosen it. Fear was exhausting, and yet she couldn't seem to sleep, had managed only to doze for an hour or two at a time since they'd found the demogorgon.

"I'm tired of being tired, and I'm tired of being scared," she said aloud, and her voice sounded too loud in the empty cabin. She'd been frightened before, on *Fancy Kelly* more than once, especially the last two tours, when she'd had enough experience to recognize the risks Kelly2 took routinely and not enough to know how good a pilot Kelly2 really was, but those had been quick fears, minutes, maybe half an hour, an hour at most, of intense anxiety, and then there had been the flurry of action and it was all over, resolved with Kelly2's unflashy competence. There had never been anything like this, the hours of waiting, with nothing at all to do—worse, with everything already done, and only the result to be worked out twelve hours from now.

The cabin door slid back, and she looked up gratefully, to see Stinne balancing another mug of coffee and her own cup of tea as she worked the door controls. "I brought your coffee," she said, and Ista took the mug, feeling Stinne's fingers briefly warm against her own.

"Thanks." The coffee was hot, but not as sweet as she liked; even so, she took a careful swallow, and then another, wishing it could burn away the fear.

Stinne sat cross-legged on her own bunk, and folded her hands around her cup of tea. "I wish I was back on the Agglomeration."

"So do I," Ista said. *And I still wish I hadn't gotten you into this.* The words trembled on her lips, and with them came unexpected anger. *I also wish you wouldn't keep reminding me—* She killed the thought, said instead, "How does it look?"

She had asked the question barely five minutes before, and cringed, but Stinne merely shrugged. "About the same. Sein's asleep, Justin's still in the control room—he said would we spell him in a couple hours—and I checked the demogorgon when I got the coffee. Your hammal's still moving, and it looks like the spreading's slowed down while the demogorgon tries to deal with it."

"Well, that's good," Ista said.

Stinne nodded. "Jus says it isn't affecting his controls much yet—the spread, I mean."

"Also good." They sat in silence then, and Ista caught herself watching the other girl out of the corner of her eye. She knew what the vidiki told her she should be doing now, what all the heroes did in mortal danger, but she didn't feel like even thinking about making love. The idea made her feel a little queasy, an emotional overload on top of the fear, and the thought of even proposing it to Stinne—*well*, she thought, *what would I say? This is maybe our only chance, so let's do it?* It wasn't the most flattering proposal, one she herself would reject out of hand, and she laughed in spite of herself.

"What?" Stinne said.

"Nothing." Ista shook her head. "When does Justin want us up there?"

"A couple of hours," he said."

"That's fine." Ista took another sip of her cooling coffee, bitter on her tongue, and hoped she wasn't blushing. "God, I wish I could get some sleep."

"Me, too," Stinne said. She sighed. "I wish a lot of things."

"Oh?" For a moment, Ista felt a rush of panic—if Stinne brought up the question, what would she do, how could she react?—and Stinne sighed again.

"Do you think Macbeth will get here in time?"

It was funny, Ista thought, remotely, how they'd both started talking about Macbeth as though she were someone they actually knew. "It's possible," she said, and suppressed her own fears. "It's certainly possible."

The next hours passed with excruciating slowness. They took Rangsey's place as he'd requested, freeing him to snatch a few hours' sleep, and then Ista returned to the cabin, pacing between it and the commons and control room until she couldn't stand it any more, finally falling asleep from sheer exhaustion. She woke four hours later, still tired, her mind buzzing with dreams she couldn't quite remember—something about her mother, and *Fancy Kelly*, and Trindade. She was too tense to sleep again, the now-familiar lump of fear massive beneath her heart, and she dragged herself out of her bunk and headed for the shower. The tank indicator showed the edge of the orange, but it hardly seemed to matter: if they survived, they would be too relieved to worry about living dirty, and it wouldn't matter to their corpses—not that there would be enough left, probably, to make that an issue. That sounded like something Rangsey would say, and she allowed herself a smile, punching the cycle button to rinse away the soap. It was a short cycle, automatically cut off, and she considered punching for a second, but couldn't overcome a lifetime's habit. Besides, there was still a chance; she stepped out of the compartment, dressed, and headed for the commons.

Stinne was there ahead of her, sitting in front of a half-finished dinner box, and staring at the image in the display dome. Ista checked it herself—the crabbit was still moving, slower now, the hole left by the fairweather's eye harder to find at the end of the track. It was close to the center, well inside the reach of the paws that were clearly vortexts now, but ahead of it, the demogorgon's fabric had thickened, looked stiff and slightly greyed, compared to the rolling clouds around it. Ista caught her breath at that, and Tarasov said, from behind her, "I don't think it's as bad as it looks."

"It's trying to develop a defense," Ista said.

Tarasov nodded. "I don't think it's going to work. It may slow it down, but it won't stop it."

The intercom crackled then, and Rangsey's voice said, "I've got a sensor reading from ahead of us."

"Finally," Tarasov said, and relief and fear were equally

blended in his voice. "We're on our way."

Ista scrambled behind him into the control room, Stinne at her heels, and stopped abruptly at the look on Rangsey's face. For the first time since they had started this run, he looked completely exhausted, all shadow of humor gone from his dark face. "I said a reading," he said softly. "I can't make out what it is. If it's Macbeth, she's too far off."

Tarasov lowered himself into the copilot's couch, frowning at the screen—not despair, Ista thought, with a sudden lurch that might almost have been hope, but concentration. His hands danced across his input board, adjusting a set of controls Ista didn't recognize, and produced a static-hazed window at the bottom of his main display. He glanced at that, still frowning, and adjusted his controls again.

A new window opened in the navigation display, and a set of chimes sounded, icons spilling in the same instant across the screen. Ista caught her breath, unable for a split second to understand what she was seeing. Then she recognized the formation, familiar from a hundred vidiki—the shape of rescue, of at least fictional salvation—and heard Stinne smother a sound that might have been delight or fear. She saw Rangsey reach into his shirt, adjusting the chip in its socket, closing his eyes over something too big for mere relief. Tarasov's voice cracked, and he cleared his throat, started over.

"Gods, I've been an idiot."

"They came in shielded, sensor-blind," Rangsey said. "No wonder we didn't see them."

In the screen, the intersect point blinked from green to red and then back again, and a handful of gold dots—five of them, Ista realized, and a sixth, the source of the first reading, some way behind the others—appeared on the starfield ahead of them. The four dots were still holding the attack diamond, and she said, before she could stop herself, "This means we're all right, doesn't it? We're going to make it after all."

"Maybe," Tarasov said. "We come into range of both of them within minutes of each other. So it depends on how badly these guys want us."

"They won't," Rangsey said, and reached across to catch Tarasov's shoulder in a bruising grip. "They—look, they're already sheering off."

In the screen, numbers flashed, and the red icons changed shape, the tips of the wedges no longer pointing toward the sun, but back toward the asteroid belt.

"They must have gotten the same signal, made the same decoding we did," Tarasov said. His hands danced over his board, apparently oblivious to the other man's touch. "But I don't think—they shouldn't get away, not if the Patrol ships can keep up their pitch."

"That's what they're built for," Rangsey said.

Ista stared at the screen, the icons that had been their future, unable quite to believe in what she was seeing. Their probable deaths had been weirdly unreal; it was taking time for their escape to catch up with her. Then she took a deep breath, and felt the fear ease a little, the knot loosening in her chest. Now there was only the demogorgon to worry about, and they had contained it, could keep it controlled until they were able to transfer to the rescue ships.

"I'm getting a transmission from the leading ship," Tarasov said.

"And not before time," Rangsey said.

Tarasov touched a control, grinning, and the ship's mechanical voice broke from the speakers. "SKW 5122, this is Macbeth. Report your status." There was a pause, and the voice repeated its message.

"Well, that's typical," Rangsey said.

"It's a loop," Tarasov said. He adjusted his board, frowning, and Stinne leaned forward.

"Aren't you going to answer?"

"Not until we're in LR range," Tarasov said. "I don't want to go through the commset—I want to be sure we don't transfer any part of the demogorgon's programming."

That made perfect sense, but Ista wished they could send their answer now, confirm their survival. It didn't seem fair that they had to wait, that they were still trapped by the slow time of STL travel, but she curbed her impatience, made herself take another slow deep breath. They were almost safe, almost home; they couldn't afford to take chances now.

"We should be in range in, what, twenty minutes?" Rangsey asked, and Ista thought she heard the same eagerness in his voice.

Tarasov nodded. "I'm putting it on the screen, and putting the message together now."

Ista glued her eyes to the countdown numbers at the bottom of the screen, watching them tick off the seconds and then the interminable minutes. She was very aware of Stinne beside her, of Rangsey in his couch, rubbing at the chip slot in his chest, and Tarasov bent over his board, composing the message that would resolve their journey. It still didn't quite seem real that they had survived, that the pursuit ships—and they had never really seen them, had never seen more than a blip on the screen and a silent transponder—had turned away, were running back for their base. She glanced at Stinne, and the other girl gave her a lopsided smile in return.

"Seems strange," she said, quietly, and Ista nodded.

And then the countdown had reached zero at last, and Tarasov touched invisible keys to send the message on its way. There was a long silence, a second set of numbers counting off the minutes until the Patrol ships could receive it, and then an icon appeared on the screen.

"Message received," Tarasov said, and Rangsey leaned all the way back in his couch.

"Thank God. We really may get out of this after all."

There was a silence then, everyone watching the communications console, until at last the chime sounded, and Tarasov touched the controls to play the incoming transmission. The ship's voice came from the speakers, clear and accentless and just a little stilted from the compression routines.

"Our trailing ship will match velocities and take you on board via your lifepods. Do not, I repeat, do not bring any computer systems or anything that has had contact with your computer systems when you leave SKW 5122. Eject pods when you reach coordinates *X261A8390U17." The ship's voice paused. "Message repeats—"

Tarasov hit the controls to silence it, and looked at his boards, frowning. In the same instant, Rangsey said, "That doesn't give us much time."

"About an hour," Tarasov said, grimly. "Let's go, people—can you trust the autos, Jus?"

"For that, yes," Rangsey answered, but didn't move. "I assume they're going to destroy the ship, then."

Tarasov nodded, and Stinne made a small noise of protest. Ista looked at her, and saw the color rising under her skin.

"I know they have to do it," Stinne said. "I'm just—sorry, that's all."

"Me, too," Rangsey said, and Ista felt a sudden rush of relief.

And then it was all fast time again, scrambling to collect belongings that suddenly seemed to have spread throughout the ship. Ista jammed the last of her shirts into her carryall, saw Stinne methodically tucking her spare slippers into a corner of her bulging bag, and held up a notebook.

"Do you want this?" she asked. "It's read-only—never interfaced with the ship."

Stinne held up her hands and caught it when Ista tossed it to her. "Did you get your magic book?"

Ista nodded. "In my carryall."

The intercom sounded then, and Stinne stretched to answer it. "Yes?"

"Are you ready? We're half an hour from the drop." It was Tarasov, this time, and Stinne looked at the other girl.

"I'm ready," Ista said, and reached reluctantly under her shirt, drawing out her monocle on its cord.

"We'll meet you at the pods," Stinne said, and cut the connection. "I wish you could bring that, it's not fair."

"I know." Ista weighed the squat cylinder in her hand, wondering if she couldn't bring it with her after all, couldn't smuggle it on board under her clothes. Kelly2 had given it to her, the tangible confirmation that she might make a hypothecary after all—and that, she told herself, is why you have to leave it. You know the risks—you, of all people, can't do it. She set it carefully on the mattress, and looked at Stinne. "But I used it here. There's a chance it's contaminated."

"I'm sorry," Stinne said. "I—" She broke off, shaking her head. "Let's go."

The men were waiting beside the pod bays, one door already open, the strap of one of their carryalls dangling over the edge of the knee-high hatch. Rangsey saw it as they approached, and flipped it inside. Tarasov said, too briskly, "You're ready?"

Ista nodded.

"We thought you could share a pod," Rangsey said, and touched controls to open the heavy hatch.

"Thanks." Ista stooped to look into the pod as the lights flickered on, emergency power whining up to power. A control panel lit, displaying environmentals—all green, she saw, with relief—and then a second, showing navigation and VMU settings.

"I've already plugged in the coordinates," Tarasov said. "Manually. All you have to do is stow your gear and strap in."

Ista nodded again, not able to find the words, and ducked through the hatch. Stinne followed, and they knocked elbows and knees for a minute until Stinne found the storage area and they wrestled both bags into its shallow interior. The couches were narrow, but well padded, and the security webbing as Ista drew it out of its well was stronger than she'd ever seen. Stinne fastened her web beside her, and Tarasov said, "Ready?"

"As we'll ever be," Ista answered, and he gave them what was meant to be an encouraging smile.

"I'm sealing you in. You'll launch in five minutes." He closed the hatch, and Ista heard the seals grind shut.

"Where's the manual switch?" Stinne asked abruptly, and Ista felt a moment of panic before she found it on the board beside her couch. She could recognize most of the fittings, had trained on simulators that matched this model, and realized suddenly that she was no longer afraid.

"I've got it," she said, and saw Stinne relax.

The numbers clicked down, and Ista cupped her hand over the switch. Then the launch rockets fired, kicking them hard against the webbing as the pod's smaller VMU struggled to match vectors and velocities. Ista swallowed hard as the gravity lurched again, flinging them back and then sideways, and saw Stinne close her eyes. Then the field steadied, and a beep sounded from the control panel.

"They've locked onto our field for pickup," Stinne said.

Ista nodded, remembering the icons at last, and the field lurched again, spawning a new clutch of icons. "Fields matched," she said, and Stinne read off the next symbols.

"Bringing us aboard." She worked one arm free of the web, and reached across to tap Ista lightly on the shoulder. "Remind me not to play with my father's codes any more, will you?"

She had meant to be funny, but the reminder was a sudden weight on Ista's heart. "I—" she began, but the pod shook again, a hollow bang that shivered through the hull, and the hatch lights turned green again. She reached for the webbing release, and the hatch opened onto a bright corridor and two tall men in Patrol grey. A woman stood behind them, dark and stocky in karabels and a loose jersey, and Ista had to look twice before she saw the SID insignia at her throat.

"This way, please," the nearer Patrolman said, and his partner jerked open the storage compartment, hoisting their bags over his shoulder.

"Hey—" Ista began, and the woman shook her head.

"They have to be inspected and decontaminated. You'll get your stuff back later."

She had to be Macbeth, Ista realized, and the first Patrolman said again, "This way."

The next twenty-four hours remained a blur in her memory. They—she and Stinne and the two men, who appeared at some point she wasn't sure of—were pushed through a series of scans, their baggage torn apart to make sure none of them were carrying anything that could carry any code from the demogorgon, and then the lifepods were released for what Macbeth called "target practice." Ista heard the distant thump of the cannon, and minutes later the wallscreen showed a series of silent explosions, two small and then one much larger. Rangsey winced at that, and Macbeth gave him a curious glance.

"Decided you liked Travelling, Rangsey?"

"I liked the ship. And it had a good set of chips."

Macbeth grunted. "Tell me about this demogorgon."

Ista did her best to contribute when asked, aware of Macbeth's sardonic stare every time she opened her mouth, but the long hours of sleeplessness finally overtook her. She knew the conversation wasn't making any sense, that something she herself had said was completely incoherent, that Stinne was soundly asleep, a warm weight on her shoulder, but couldn't open her eyes to protest.

When she woke again, she was in a narrow cabin that she recognized from a hundred vidiki as military issue. She eased herself out of the cubby-bunk, little more than a recessed shelf in the wall, and saw her carryall sitting in the open storage niche above it. The toilet/shower cubicle was open as well, and she used it gratefully, returning to find a light flashing on the intercom console. She touched the button, and a mechanical voice—not at all like SKW 5122's voice, she thought, with a pang—said, "Lieutenant Macbeth's compliments and she would like to see you in Commons 2 when you're awake."

There was no setting for a response. Ista dressed, scanned the intercom panel for a locator code, and couldn't find that either. There were people in the corridors, though, and a heavy-set woman in engineering fatigues walked her to the door of the proper compartment. The others were there before her, Tarasov and Rangsey sitting at the round table, Stinne leaning warily on the back of a chair, and Macbeth just turning away from a control console, hanging a privacy set back on its hook.

"Good, you're here," she said. "Have a seat."

Ista did as she was told, shook her head at Rangsey's silent offer of coffee, and Stinne subsided reluctantly into the chair beside her.

"You'll be pleased to know," Macbeth went on, "that our people managed to take one of the ships intact—mostly so, anyway."

"What about the other two?" Ista asked, and then wished she hadn't.

"Destroyed," Macbeth answered, and looked at the two men. "Well, you certainly managed to stir things up."

"I thought that was what you wanted," Rangsey said.

Macbeth smiled. "Up to a point, yes. At least there was enough confusion once the breeders realized where you were headed that we were able to sort out most of the middlemen through the net and DRD traffic."

Tarasov swore under his breath, and Macbeth nodded.

"Oh, yes, the people behind it got away. I've an idea who they are, mind you, but I couldn't prove it in this lifetime." For an instant, Ista caught a glimpse of something, a white-hot rage and something else, a deeper frustration, maybe, behind the lieutenant's ironic mask, but then the shutters closed again, and Macbeth went on smoothly. "Still, we've busted enough of the middling sort to set them back five years. It'll take them longer than that to get a set-up like this again."

"What about the demogorgon on the mine?" Tarasov asked.

"A demolition team's on its way to deal with it, and Decontamination's checking out the DRDs. Plus you—or Trindade, rather—were right about the kill switch, so there shouldn't be any problem even if it did manage to plant offspring in the DRDs, or anywhere else." She smiled unpleasantly. "They're supposed to be virus-proof, but it looks like at least that one hex is tainted, and maybe most of its neighbors. I don't envy NSMCo the cost of replacements."

"So that's it?" Ista said, in spite of herself, and Macbeth looked at her, the smile fading.

"Not entirely. I have some bad news for you. Trindade Ramary was one of the people we arrested."

"Trindade?" Ista blinked, unable for a moment to believe it. But it made sense as she considered it, explained how Trindade had known about the kill switch, maybe, certainly explained why Trindade had reacted so strangely when she'd asked her to let her retrieve her mail—why she hadn't wanted to know what was going on, why she'd refused to be involved. At least she liked me that much, Ista thought, she didn't want to get me into trouble even if she couldn't help me. "So that's how she knew how to destroy it," she said, and Macbeth nodded.

"As far as we can tell, she helped set up the original breeding system—that's why they took that mine, to get a physical location for the equipment and their connection to the invisible world—and then helped design the basic parameters, which included the kill switch. We're not fully sure why they wanted a demogorgon, mind you, the rank and file weren't sure themselves, but it might have been for blackmail. In any case, Trindade seems to have been genuinely worried about what would happen if it got loose, which seems to be why she told you about the switch."

"And a damn good thing she did, too," Tarasov said.

Macbeth went on, her voice almost gentle. "She's been involved for a long time, from the beginning. She was the one who set up the mine crew in the first place, the one you came from."

No—Ista bit back the word, fixed the console in a fierce stare. If she didn't blink, she wouldn't cry, and she didn't need to cry, couldn't afford to cry, not until she'd heard it all. There was no reason for Macbeth to lie, no reason for her to be hurtful, and she swallowed hard. "Does she know who I am?" she asked, and was remotely pleased that her voice was steady. Under the table, she felt Stinne's knee touch her leg, and she returned the pressure gratefully.

"She wouldn't say," Macbeth answered. "Under interrogation, we got enough tangential information to think you were probably born Deljanin Esther, daughter of Deljanin Immarie who was a corporate gypsy worker, but I can't prove it. Not well enough for Records."

Not even Union, or honest Traveller. Ista swallowed again, the tears burning her eyes, but refused to blink, refused to give in to them. She took a deep breath, and then another, fought her voice under control. "Thank you for asking. Is there any chance I could see her?"

"I wouldn't," Macbeth said, bluntly. "She blames you for a lot of this."

"Sounds to me like she should be blaming herself," Rangsey said. Ista gave him a grateful glance, but had to look away again from the sympathy on his face.

Macbeth gave a brief, wintery smile. "So she should. As for the rest of you—there's a standard reward offered, and split four ways it's substantial, almost five thousand each, and I'm going to give you some advice with it." Her smile vanished. "Take the money and run. Light out for the Territories, and stay there. These people don't enjoy losing, and they're likely to start up a new operation by getting rid of you, just in case you know something. I'm authorized to issue the vouchers, and will be glad to do so. I'd suggest you cash them and leave as soon as possible."

Tarasov and Rangsey exchanged glances, and then Rangsey laughed softly. "What do you say, Sein, you ready to quit the Squad?"

Tarasov smiled, but shook his head. "I don't know about the Territories," he began, and Macbeth held up her hand.

"Make your own decision, I've said my piece." She looked at Ista. "Your mother insisted on following us, and will rendezvous with this ship in less than two hours. I suggest that at least the two of you go with her."

"I'd be glad to," Ista said, and looked at Stinne.

"My folks aren't going to be happy with me," she said, bitterly. The she shrugged. "But the scholarship they got me, it's mine, in my name only, and it's supposed to be transferrable. So if it doesn't work out at home, well, can I come with you, Ista?"

Ista nodded, and looked back at Macbeth. "With our vouchers, please."

Macbeth looked vaguely pleased. "I'll have them ready."

Tarasov said, softly, talking to Rangsey as though there was no one else in the room, "I'll go with you—I want to go with you. If you want me."

Rangsey nodded. "Yes."

Tarasov took a deep breath. "Then if there's room on your mother's ship, Ista—Esther—it fits, doesn't it?"

He stopped in surprise, and Ista tilted her head to one side. The name didn't sound familiar, but she could see how a baby's voice could twist the one into the other. "Ista," she said, and Tarasov nodded.

"Ista, then."

"At least for now," Ista amended, but guessed it would stay the same.

"If there's room, we'll come with you."

"*Fancy Kelly*'s built to carry six," Ista answered, and heard the quiet pride in her own voice. "There's room."

Kelly2 brought *Fancy Kelly* alongside exactly as scheduled, matching fields and velocities with a negligent skill that made Ista giggle, thinking of the expressions on the faces of the Patrolship's bridge crew. Macbeth had warned Kelly2 what to expect, and she was waiting at the end of the docking tunnel to welcome them aboard. She gave the two men a curt nod, pointing them toward the commons, and tapped Stinne gruffly on the shoulder. "Glad you're back safe. Your folks would never have forgiven us."

"Glad to be aboard," Stinne said, in a subdued voice, and Ista braced herself for the inevitable reprimand. Kelly2 caught her by the shoulders, and pulled her into a tight embrace.

"Thank the gods you're all right." She loosened her grip for an instant, and then tightened it again. "I couldn't lose you."

Ista felt tears stinging her eyes again, and could no longer hold them back, buried her face against her mother's shoulder. She felt Kelly2's arm move under her, releasing her for an instant to work the hatch controls, and then the hatch slid shut behind them. "It's all right," Kelly2 said. "It's all right. You did well, all through, you did well. I'm proud of you."

They stood like that for a moment longer, and then Ista pushed herself away, sniffling hard, and Kelly2 rummaged in her pockets for a cloth. Ista accepted it with a nod of thanks, and Kelly2 said, "Right, then. This lieutenant said we should head for the Territories, and for once I agree with the Patrol. We're heading into the Agglomeration to pick up supplies, and then we're out of here. Does that suit you?"

Ista nodded, grateful for the familiar brisk tones, and Kelly2 smiled. "I am proud of you," she said, and turned away, heading down the corridor toward the commons. Ista stood for a moment longer, letting the words roll over her—not that Kelly2 had ever stinted her praise, but this was different, on a different scale altogether—and then shook herself. She could—would—savor this later, but right now, there was work to be done.